OF AURAS
AND SHADOWS

By the Author

The Witch Queen's Mate

Of Auras and Shadows

Visit us at www.boldstrokesbooks.com

OF AURAS AND SHADOWS

by

Jennifer Karter

2024

OF AURAS AND SHADOWS

ISBN 13: 978-1-63679-541-6

This Trade Paperback Original Is Published By
Bold Strokes Books, Inc.
P.O. Box 249
Valley Falls, NY 12185

First Edition: January 2024

CREDITS
Editor: Cindy Cresap
Production Design: Stacia Seaman
Cover Design by Tammy Seidick

Acknowledgments

I want to start by thanking my spouse and my dad, who have made this book not only possible but a joy. They remain my worldbuilding copilots, navigators, passengers, and backseat drivers. Thank you for your ideas, inspiration, and love.

The next thank yous go to my family, biological and chosen family, who have made me a strong, creative, proud-to-be-me woman. Sharing my stories has been an avenue for sharing parts of me with the people I love, and I have never been more proud and felt more blessed to have all of you in my life's story.

Innumerable thanks to my early readers who loved me enough to give me their honest feedback and priceless recommendations. This book would not be the same without their generosity and brilliance: Lanna, Roslyn, Barb, and Sunaina.

A huge thank you to Bold Strokes Books and my fabulous editor, Cindy Cresap, for making me a better writer, a better storyteller, and for helping craft the stories I love. I owe you majorly.

And a huge thank you to my readers. I like to think that I write for me, to let the characters in my head live out their life and love on the page, but I publish for you, to share that love and adventure with you. Thank you for joining me on this journey through the Dark Lands, and I cannot wait to dance with you again.

To Ashley

Alba is not Ashley, but Ashley is my Alba

CHAPTER ONE

Ichor and Omen

The air was especially crisp that morning, as it always was on Choosing Day. Eryn cast her gaze up to the golden-blue shimmer of the dome far above and sent a silent thank you to the Goddess for all that was her life, the thriving Community, and its resilient system. Today marked the next step on her journey to being the woman the Community needed — choosing her guardian.

The other heroes of Eryn's cohort streamed around her, joking and bragging about what they wanted in a guardian. To them, this moment was one of celebration, not reverence as Eryn saw it. She supposed some of them were simply masking their restlessness and uncertainty with jests and lighthearted banter.

After finishing her prayer, Eryn surveyed the worn training grounds. If the other members of her cohort trained as often and as vigorously as Eryn, the hero training arena would be just as frayed as this field. It was a positive sign for the diligence of the guardian she would choose.

Spread throughout the field at militantly even intervals were pairs and groups of three guardians—a mentor and their one or two protégées—standing like obedient statues in perfectly ironed, purple uniforms. Eryn scanned the area, finding her target easily.

Guardians were rarely honored with signs of their achievement— to serve the Community was the greatest honor—but the woman standing near the center of the field was decorated with regalia. Though her broad, muscled body held perfectly still, her eyes flashed around the field, taking in everything around her with clear acuity. Even her shoulder-length, chestnut hair remained stationary despite the gentle breeze.

This was Claine, head guardian, whose name was known more than any other guardian, though Eryn supposed very few guardians were spoken of by name. Most were simply referred to by whose guardian they were. Claine had earned respect as well as notoriety beyond her role as Ardon's guardian for her dedication to the Community and her skill in both fighting and training. Even more impressively, she had gained this reputation years before becoming head guardian, even before the foresight that she would be a commander.

Approaching Claine and her mentee, Eryn could tell Claine did not squander time and did not endure those who did. "Eryn, may the light of the Goddess be in you this day," Claine said.

Eryn smiled inwardly. Everyone knew Eryn's name, even if she was less than half Claine's age and all her greatest accomplishments were ahead of her. "And you, head guardian," Eryn said. Pleasantries done, Eryn turned to the task at hand. "Who is the best guardian of this cohort?"

Claine's red-haired mentee looked up, her purple-irised eyes flashing in interest. She looked like the kind of young woman who saw a challenge in everything, not because things were naturally difficult for her, but because she had something to prove. She had the kind of broad shoulders and stout, V-shaped body Eryn associated with strength and dependability. Perhaps this would be her guardian. It stood to reason that the best guardian would train the best junior rank guardian.

Claine pointed off to her left. "Syrana, the guardian with the dark brown hair and the mentor with the graying beard." Claine's answer left no room for doubt. Eryn didn't need to ask about Syrana's swordsmanship, her intelligence, or her skills. Syrana had outperformed her cohort in a score that had been tallied since the age of six, just as Eryn had. Eryn inclined her head in thanks, then strode confidently toward the woman who would become her protector, attendant, and partner.

Around Eryn, conversation touched at the edges of her concentration. "What are his weapon specializations?" a hero asked a mentor and after the brief answer turned to the younger guardian, "And how are your *sword* skills?" He drew out the word to emphasize the euphemism.

The guardian nodded and stated, "Very good," a small smile touching his lips. On Eryn's other side, a hero questioned her target about his favorite positions for pleasuring.

Heroes were told from the age of two, when their eyes first took on their characteristic gold iris coloring, that they carried the fate of the Community on their shoulders. Eryn couldn't understand how anyone could hear that for seventeen years and prioritize their guardian's performance in the tent over their ability to protect them from monsters and shadows. With the dome shrinking more every generation and the swelling tide of shadows, Eryn wondered how anyone could be thinking about sex.

One phrase had carried Eryn through her training: "I am uniquely positioned to help the Community." It was her way of understanding her separation from her peers as a good thing. It had taken years for her peers to understand that Eryn wasn't rubbing her superior skills in their faces; she simply couldn't sit still, couldn't relax and have fun, couldn't do anything without giving it her best. It had taken as many years for Eryn to accept that her peers weren't on her level, and that was okay. That was normal. She was the one who wasn't normal, and that was okay.

Her peers would contribute to the Community as all heroes did. Eryn would do so much more.

Around the field, heroes of different ranks dropped tokens matching their rank into the bowls of junior guardians that sparked their interest. By checking the tokens in the bowls, heroes could assess the level of interest from higher-ranked heroes. If a guardian's bowl had tokens from higher ranks, it indicated they were likely chosen. Based on the clatter of metal on fired clay, the strategy of the day was to spread wide, rather than to search for depth.

Eryn palmed her singular token with a "1" on it. She didn't need multiple tokens. Whoever she picked would be hers. She had no interest in asking as many lewd questions of as many guardians as she could in one hour. Instead, she would use the time to get to know the woman who would be her defender until death.

As she approached Syrana, Eryn admired her powerful physique. She stood larger and more muscular than her peers, radiating strength but also grace. Her profile revealed a proud, attentive smile, as if today nothing could go wrong. She stood gazing into the distance, seemingly envisioning her future playing out exactly as she imagined it.

Syrana gave an almost imperceptible nod as Eryn approached. "Hero, may the light of the Goddess be in you this day."

"And you, guardian," Eryn said, acknowledging Syrana's mentor with a respectful nod. Turning her attention back to Syrana, Eryn said confidently, "I am the best junior rank hero the Community has ever trained. I am going to do more for the Community than any hero before me. I'm going to bring back enough ichor to expand the dome to a size we haven't seen in generations, and I'm going to make sure we have the resources to keep it that way." Eryn raised one eyebrow, her lips pursed in challenge. What did the best junior guardian have to say about that?

Syrana accepted Eryn's challenge with a prideful smile. "I am the best guardian of my cohort. You have a grand vision and I'm going to get you there."

"We'll get along nicely," Eryn said, dropping her token into Syrana's bowl.

As Eryn, Syrana, and Syrana's mentor, Keddeth, got to know each other more, discussing everything from fighting techniques to Community philosophy, Eryn couldn't help liking Syrana more and more. She had finally found someone who not only shared her way of thinking, training, and living but also complemented her perfectly in combat. While Eryn excelled in ranged fighting, Syrana thrived in close combat, displaying a blend of strategy, tactics, philosophy, and practicality. Above all, Syrana embodied dedication. She didn't just strive to be the best, she strived to be her best, which put her leaps and bounds above the rest. That was the kind of person Eryn needed by her side.

An hour later, the chapel bell tolled, summoning the young heroes to make their choices. As the heroes gathered in rank order, Eryn didn't bother joining them. She was uninterested in watching the overacted drama of choosing play out. Instead, she took Syrana's hand and led her toward the chapel. She preferred to spend the remaining time basking in the light of the Goddess's fountain, praying with Syrana by her side.

The dirt road at the edge of the guardian quarter served as one of eight spokes radiating from the chapel to the edges of the dome like a wagon wheel. The road was lined with people from every caste, gathered to watch the pairs that would venture outside the dome in search of ichor, the Goddess's lifeblood that fueled the dome. Applause and excited cheers erupted from the crowd as Eryn and Syrana passed by. Eryn recognized familiar faces beaming at her and nodded back in appreciation. For years, she had celebrated their achievements, and now they were here to celebrate hers.

The chapel stood in the center of the Community, a beacon as much as a place of worship. From its tall steeple rose the column of ichor, the Goddess's blood, which formed the protective dome encircling the Community. The dome resembled a giant fountain, cascading down like honey on Frost Night, creating a shell. To Eryn and heroes like her, it was golden in color with a fake sky superimposed on it. The blue-sky image extended to the ground where the ichor gradually melted into the soil. A light at the peak brightened throughout the day and faded to darkness at night.

The thick wooden doors to the chapel stood open, welcoming the next generation of hero-guardian pairs. Carved deeply into the ancient wood was the story of the Community.

The door on the left depicted the banishment of the Goddess to the Dark Lands and Her creation of a safe haven for Her people, shielding them not only from monsters, but also other gods. Around the edges, people from all nine original castes toiled joyously in service to the Goddess and the Community.

While the left door was a celebration of creation, growth and life bursting from the darkness, Eryn had been captivated from a very young age by the door on the right. The jealous gods, casting malevolent glares upon the Goddess and Her creation, made Eryn's peers hurriedly avert their gazes.

Eryn paused before the doors, bowing her head and silently reciting one of her favorite prayers of thanksgiving and devotion. She was pleased to feel Syrana do the same beside her.

"I have seen adults brought to tears by the depiction of the death of the Goddess," Eryn said to Syrana.

"I have always seen the Goddess's transformation into a mountain to protect Her body and life force and preserve it for us as an act deserving reverence, not sadness. I feel honored, not weepy." The last word Syrana said with dissatisfaction, as if this wasn't a new annoyance for her either.

Eryn wasn't sure how Syrana could be more perfect for her. "The Goddess sacrificed Herself for love of Her people. I always view this door as a reminder to repay that debt every day."

The Goddess's final act created the last three castes, which stood with solemn expressions etched on their faces at the door's base, aware of the sacrifice the Goddess made, and the responsibility bestowed upon them. With reverence, the mountain folk excavated the living corpse of the Goddess, extracting the resources she once freely provided. Guardians vigilantly stood beside heroes outside the Community's glow, protecting them as they sought the Goddess's ichor to fuel the dome. Today, that mantle felt all the heavier and more important.

They proceeded into the chapel hand in hand and knelt on the front-most cushions of the spacious nave. Eryn watched the golden liquid churn languidly in the base of the fountain before being swept up into the column in the center and launched out of the ceiling where it would reach its peak and cascade down into the dome.

For several minutes, Eryn lost herself in the swirl of ichor, praying. Her focus was not lost as the other hero and guardian pairs filed into the room.

"May the light of the Goddess be in us this day," the head priest said from her platform next to the fountain. The phrase reverberated around the room as every person took up the mantra. "The Goddess so loved Her people and they Her as to draw the ire of the dark gods. If they could not be happy in their banishment, neither could She. But the Goddess refused to leave us and, in Her death, transformed into the living corpse of the mountains that surround and protect us. It is Her body upon which you will venture, Her lifeblood that you will seek, Her promise to us that you will fulfill."

The priest swept her unseeing white eyes across the crowd. "Heroes, will you accept this burden? Will you face the horrors beyond the dome with valor? Will you put reverence of duty before pride? Will you put the needs of the Community before your own?"

"I will," Eryn said in time with the rest of her cohort.

"Guardians, will you accept this burden? Will you protect your hero against the evil that will seek to destroy them? Will you lay your life before your hero and their mission? Will you dedicate every day to the needs of your hero and the Community?"

"I will," the guardians replied.

"Everyone serves the Community," the priest said.

"Everyone serves the Community," the entire room repeated.

From the recesses of the chapel, priests emerged, some with white eyes and others still with their foresight ahead of them, their eyes black-irised. Each priest took a length of glowing golden thread, picked a hero-guardian pair, and began to wrap their hands together. As Syrana held their intertwined hands toward the approaching priest, one of the black-eyed priests veered in front of his companion as if pulled by invisible strings. He grabbed their hands, his grip cold and fierce.

The black of his eyes began to swirl with white as if a drop of milk were being stirred into the pupil. As he spoke, the white expanded until it was the blackness that was eddying into the white depths. "You and your guardian will reverse the degradation that has afflicted the Community. You will dispel the shadows that plague us and reclaim what was lost. Our hope, our future rests with you."

The whole room fell silent. It was a great honor to hear a priest channel the Goddess and speak Her truth.

Occasionally, a priest's foresight did not come true. However, such instances were rare and usually caused by forces outside the Community's control. Eryn felt this foresight was about as guaranteed as any she'd ever heard. Everyone had known Eryn would accomplish great things, but she couldn't imagine better proof of her obvious potential. She and Syrana were going to save the Community, collect ichor, expand the dome, and banish the shadows.

The priest wrapped their hands with his golden thread, fumbling only slightly with his new blindness. He would have learned to navigate the chapel and surrounding buildings wearing a blindfold since early childhood to prepare him for this eventuality—when he received his foresight and lost his sight.

Around them, other priests began to move again, wrapping hero-guardian pairs. Eryn felt a pleasant burn as the thread around her hand began to melt into her skin. Her and Syrana's fates were now bound together—a fate even the Goddess had promised.

Eryn looked from her hand to her guardian, taking in Syrana's beaming expression. She looked like a woman who had just been told that the Goddess was planning to come to dinner in her honor.

Syrana was the most beautiful woman Eryn had ever seen. She wasn't sure if it was simply the fact that in this moment Syrana was the physical representation of Eryn's dream for her future. She was sure that Syrana was everything she'd ever wanted.

Sex with her guardian had always been the least of Eryn's concerns. For a moment, Eryn found herself lost in the fantasy—Syrana between her legs, masterfully bringing her to an explosive orgasm. She gave Syrana what she knew must have been an entirely silly grin. Tonight was going to be glorious.

With a look of pure bliss, Syrana brought their intertwined hands to her lips to place a gentle kiss on the back of Eryn's hand. Eryn guessed that very little invoked an emotional response from Syrana, which made the small gleam of tears in Syrana's eyes all the more powerful.

"It is time." The head priest raised her arms above her head, the ichor fountain framed between her arms. "Go forth and serve the Community."

"Everyone serves the Community," everyone responded.

Eryn returned her attention to Syrana. Her guardian seemed just as overtaken with emotion and yet Syrana seemed somehow lesser than a moment before. Eryn's fantasies had been replaced with visions of a successful mission. Any other frivolities would be fine if they didn't distract from the mission, nothing more. "I'll meet you at the dome," she said.

Determination ruled Syrana's expression, as if she understood that doing their job was the best way to show Eryn how she felt. "Let's make the Community proud." Syrana gave Eryn's hand one last squeeze before following the rest of her peers back to the guardian quarter to retrieve her gear.

Eryn retrieved her own gear and reported to her designated spot at the edge of the dome to wait with the other four heroes assigned to that spot. Syrana was distinctly behind her peers when they came into view, but was soon trotting ahead of the group. Eryn suppressed a chuckle as the five guardians arrived. Syrana's pack looked small compared to the others until the whole group gathered closely enough for her to see that Syrana's pack was the exact same size as the others, she was simply large enough to mask the comically large, person-sized load. Unlike all future trips, their first outing into the Dark Lands would only last five days. Eryn could only imagine how large Syrana's pack would be when it was loaded for a ten-day trip.

The heroes and guardians shared a moment of prayer, reciting the Community's covenant.

"Ready?" Syrana asked, her smirk saying she'd been born ready. She held a bardiche, an intersection between an axe and a spear, in one hand and wore a sizable gauntlet on the other. The pack on her back held enough rations for a week, camp materials, and their ichor lantern. She wore a bandolier of alchemical weapons, and a silk net hung from her belt. She did indeed look ready for just about anything.

Eryn drew her bow and nodded. It was time. She stepped through the dome with Syrana, the flow of ichor splitting to allow them passage.

Eryn had been six the first time she left the dome. It was her first day as a junior hero and she scored many points that day toward her newly minted rank for her courage and unflappable approach to the twisted and corrupted landscape. Now, after many such trips into the wilds immediately around the dome, the landscape felt less like a death trap and more like a familiar obstacle course.

She and her fellow heroes had never been able to venture deeper than the outside edge of the dome. Mountain folk were the only caste that could exist in the Dark Lands in numbers greater than two without drawing the attention of the dark gods who would still revel in destroying the Goddess's creation.

Eryn paused to take in her environment. It was what a good warrior did. Her true motivation, she knew, was also to mark this moment in her memory. She wanted to remember exactly what it felt like her first time.

The golden glow of the dome began to fade immediately, giving way to the appearance of constant late dusk. There was no light source above them like in the dome. Instead, the dim light seemed to come from everywhere and nowhere, giving everything a surreal and uniform, muted grayness. The undersides of things were equally as light as the top sides. The Dark Lands were a place of emotional and moral darkness filled with monsters and dark gods. The appearance itself was one in which there was neither light nor darkness, but a constant state in between.

Leafless trees were scattered across the terrain with branches that looked like roots, gnarled and reaching out rather than up. There was no sun to provide them with nourishment. Instead, their twisted trunks expanded and contracted to breathe the air and capture small insects.

To grow, the trees needed larger sustenance. When opportunity struck, a tree's branches would whip out, snag a passing creature, shove it into its untwisting trunk, and consume the creature. Trees were even known to cease breathing for long periods of time to convince small creatures that they were dead and available for habitation, thus luring their prey close enough to ensnare.

Death by carnivorous tree was almost as common as death by monsters and certainly more so for mountain folk tasked with collecting lumber from dead trees. Luckily for Eryn and her compatriots, trees didn't like competition and grew far enough apart to allow humans to avoid their areas of threat.

As Eryn looked across the landscape, a flat land of mixed flora providing precarious lowlands before the rise of the mountains, she was struck once again by the disconcerting dissonance before her. All the flora moved as if touched by a gentle breeze. However, all shifted in conflicting directions. There was no wind within the Dark Lands. Instead, every living thing moved of its own accord, reaching for its next prey.

Heroes were taught how to identify and avoid corrosive moss that could eat through even a guardian's ichor-infused metal boots and how to pass through the tufts of razor-sharp bladed grass without losing a foot.

It was out farther, where the mountains began, that the true danger lay. Eryn and Syrana observed their surroundings for only a moment before setting off toward that danger, leaving the others behind to choose their own trails. As they did, Syrana turned to her, holding something out in a closed hand. "I made you something."

Eryn tipped her head in surprise. Guardians didn't give their heroes gifts on Choosing Day as far as she knew.

Syrana dropped a small chain necklace into Eryn's palm. Eryn smiled as she turned over the pendant to reveal her choosing token with the number one on it. Syrana spoke matter-of-factly as if this moment could be emotional, but she didn't feel the need for it to be so. "I only got one token during Choosing, but it was the only one I needed, the only one I wanted. I thought you might like to wear it as a symbol of all we will achieve together. I'm proud to be your guardian."

It must have been the reason Syrana had been hurrying to catch up with the group. Eryn clasped the chain around her neck and smiled at the pendant before slipping it under her gambeson, the padded wool armor all heroes and guardians wore. Eryn couldn't imagine a more perfect guardian.

Eryn had anticipated a quiet first day. It took time to get to the deeper reaches of the mountains where the risk and reward were higher. She'd been looking forward to a chance to discuss Furin's postulate on fate and the Goddess's role in it: did the Goddess foresee fate or shape it? As they reached the base of the mountains, Eryn prepared to ask Syrana for her opinions before launching into her planned diatribe, but Syrana froze in that moment. She was staring directly ahead of them, her eyes focused on something Eryn couldn't see.

"What?" Eryn whispered. "A shadow?"

For a long moment, Syrana was silent. She gripped her bardiche and Eryn could see the slightest tremble of her gauntleted hand. Eryn gripped her own sword hilt, wishing she could see what Syrana did, but only guardians could see shadows. All she could do was wait and hope that Syrana would tell her where to swing when the time came.

"Already," Syrana said.

Eryn wasn't sure if it was a statement or a question. If it was a question, it must have been to the Goddess because Eryn didn't have anywhere near enough context to answer. She had to assume it was a yes to there being a shadow. She waited in another tense silence.

"Shadows always lie." Syrana said it to the spot she was looking at. Eryn gaped at her. Guardians didn't listen to shadows, let alone talk to them.

"I don't listen to shadows. Shadows always lie."

The ludicrous idea occurred to Eryn that perhaps Syrana could read her mind. Tell me how to help you, Eryn thought before rationality pushed the idea away. Was it appropriate to ask what the shadow was saying? If Syrana didn't listen to shadows, it didn't make much sense to ask, but Eryn needed something.

"You leave her out of this!"

Eryn couldn't just stand there. "Tell me what's happening so I can help you. Don't leave me out of this."

"She won't. I won't. Never."

"Syrana, tell me what's happening," Eryn said, trying to keep her volume low. Syrana was already loud enough to call any nearby monsters down on them. If it was a shadow or multiple shadows, why wasn't Syrana attacking? Why wasn't she directing Eryn as she had been trained to do?

Finally, with immense grace, Syrana flourished her bardiche with a look of intense determination. Eryn drew her own sword and took a step toward Syrana to fight at her side. She had been trained to fight an invisible enemy based on the movements and directions of another. Now, she would get to try those exemplary practice skills on a real enemy. She couldn't help a shiver of excitement, even if this was a very awkward prelude to her first true fight. She'd have to talk to Syrana about their communication. A good talking to seemed appropriate.

Eryn looked to Syrana's eyes to tell her where the enemy was, but Syrana's eyes were flickering around the slope rather than locking on a single spot.

"Goddess," Syrana breathed.

"How many are there?" Eryn asked. Shadows hardly ever attacked in groups, at least not until the hero found ichor. Shadows just didn't work together.

"Many," Syrana said. Her tone was different. She was clearly talking to Eryn this time, and there was an apology in her tone as if she had failed Eryn and would never forgive herself for it.

"Tell me where and we'll fight them together."

Syrana's gaze left the battlefield for a single, quick look at Eryn. It only took that second to convey more care, dedication, and authority than Eryn had ever seen. "No," Syrana said. "Eryn, you need to run. Get back to the Community. I need you to warn—" But then they were on her, an enemy Eryn could neither count nor counter.

A sound like claws scraping on metal emanated from Syrana as she moved. She looked more like she was performing a sensuous dance than fighting. Her bardiche was a blur, but a single weapon was insufficient to cover all sides. Syrana growled in pain and spun around, her weapon striking before she swiveled back to face whatever was now trying to flank her. Blood ran down from a gash in the back of her arm through her gambeson and Eryn watched in horror as a new, deep scrape formed at the back of her knee.

What in the Goddess's name am I doing? Eryn launched herself toward Syrana. She didn't need directions. More enemies just meant a higher chance that her blind swings would connect with something. Eryn sliced the air to Syrana's left side, smiling at the feeling of her blade slowly passing through something. It felt like running a spoon through honey. It took four more swings before her sword connected with another and dissipated it. She did her best to provide an area of threat around Syrana in which the shadows couldn't become corporal in order to attack without being struck and dissipated.

"Go." Syrana growled as she was struck again. Then her tone turned to pleading. "Please, Eryn, go."

Eryn doubted Syrana ever pleaded. It made her even more resolute to stay. She couldn't abandon her guardian. She sped up. Accuracy didn't matter, only frequency of swings. Emotion was useless, only logic and action mattered.

Eryn struck shadow after shadow, but Syrana kept swinging. How many could there possibly be?

Something hit Syrana in the back and she went sprawling onto her face. Syrana scrambled to get her feet under her for a moment before she collapsed into the dirt once more.

That was when the screaming began. Muffled at first by moist ground, until Syrana lifted her head and pierced the gloom with a sound like every infant in the Community's nursery wailing at the top of their lungs all at once.

Eryn had never heard a sound so wretched or filled with pain. The cries were joined by convulsions that only seemed to intensify the sound.

Eryn swung at shoulder height furiously and stumbled to Syrana's side. The gashes had stopped forming, but she had no idea if this was because the enemy had stopped attacking or just that their strikes were no longer superficial.

"Syrana!" Eryn yelled, but she couldn't even hear herself over Syrana's screams. Eventually she'll run out of air, Eryn thought, letting the logical side of her mind keep at bay the side that wanted to run away and do some screaming of her own. Instead, she swung her sword again and again, connecting with nothing.

Finally, after Eryn was sure she would have run out of lung capacity three times over, Syrana's screams stopped as abruptly as they'd begun. The convulsions did not.

"Syrana, please." Eryn cut the pack straps and shoved the bundle aside, then tried to get a hold on Syrana's shoulder and failed several times. Finally, she got Syrana flipped over. Syrana's face was bloodied and swollen from smashing it into the ground repeatedly and her limbs flailed as if she were still trying to fight off shadows with her bare hands. If there were any remaining shadows, they weren't becoming corporeal because Eryn's sword swept empty air every time.

"No one told me what to do." She sounded pitiful to her own ears. "I'm the best. I'll improvise." So she hadn't been prepared for this exact situation, she would start the way she always did, with the facts. Eryn did not know what was wrong with Syrana and could do nothing to help her here. Syrana's screams would have alerted all the monsters nearby, so they weren't safe here anyway. Syrana was clearly not planning to get up and walk back, so Eryn would have to carry her.

One look at Syrana's large flailing form dismissed that plan. "I'll have to drag her." Eryn grabbed Syrana's pauldron with one hand and shoulder of her gambeson with the other and pulled.

Syrana slid a couple of inches before the back of her flailing hand slammed into the side of Eryn's head, sending her toppling sideways. Eryn clambered up, grabbed on again, and pulled, earning another several inches.

Eryn dragged, trying to time her pulls with Syrana's convulsions to turn inches into feet. She was just getting the hang of it when a tweeting sound broke her concentration. Eryn could just make out a small brown creature perched in the presumably dead tree off to her right. "Chick-a-dead-dead-dead."

It was joined by a companion whose movement separated it from the dense brambles of the branches. "Chick-a-dead-dead-dead." Then another and another. The cacophony grew until they were at the center of a discordant maelstrom screeching "dead, dead, dead" with an almost sickly sweetness of chickas underneath. There was a smell of rot in the air as if the sweetness of their call had gone rancid within the creatures and was escaping with each screech.

Eryn had no idea how long they'd been watching her or how many had amassed while she was attempting to drag Syrana. All she knew was they were about to become a swarm.

"Chick-a-dreads." Eryn swore. Individually, they posed almost no threat besides a few fetid cuts, but Syrana's screams had drawn so many in addition to other monsters that might be waiting in the underbrush to see how the fight went and pick off the winner for scraps of the loser.

Eryn pulled harder and faster. There was no use in waiting for them to attack. It was inevitable, so she might as well get Syrana as far as she could before the swarm descended.

The movement started with a single chick-a-dread, a wing flap that gave the whole tree the appearance of a second life. As if one creature, the chick-a-dreads swooped down on Eryn and Syrana, still screeching, "Dead! Dead! Dead!"

Eryn waited until the last moment to drop Syrana, draw her sword, and slice up through a chick-a-dread. She cut another in two as three clipped her face, leaving shallow, stinging cuts in their wake. She pushed down the bile that rose at the smell engulfing her head with putrescence. A dozen tore her gambeson while a half dozen more struck Syrana, leaving yet more gashes. Twice as many as struck simply shot by unable to find a gap for attack. Eryn cut three more from the sky before the swarm was above them, swirling as it turned for another run.

Eryn grabbed Syrana and dragged her another several yards before the birds returned. She repeated the process three more times and still had neither cut the swarm in half nor made significant progress. Her face and neck felt as if they were on fire and smelled like days-old infection. Syrana was coated with blood and still convulsing wildly. If the continuing screech of the chick-a-dreads wasn't enough to call additional monsters, the smell of blood certainly would. She wasn't moving fast enough.

After a fifth pass, Eryn couldn't wait any longer. She sheathed her sword, took hold of Syrana, and put every ounce of her strength into running backward. Now that their prey was no longer fighting back, the remaining chick-a-dread swarm became a tornado around Eryn. She could barely breathe, could barely see enough around her to pick up the subtle movements of other monsters drawing near and waiting for their moment.

"I'm going to save the Community," Eryn yelled. She couldn't imagine there was any purpose to trying to be quiet anymore. "This is not how I die!" She blocked the pain, the smell, the fear, the knowledge that her face was actively rotting. All that existed was the strength to survive, to get herself and Syrana to safety.

Eryn felt rather than saw the glow of the dome. The fear she was denying shrank like darkness from a candle. She pushed all the harder, stumbling through the barrier of the dome and leaving the birds and unknown monsters behind.

Eryn collapsed onto the soft pastureland grass of the Community, screaming for help. Tears poured down her face, a mixture of relief, pain, fear, and embarrassment. Her mind couldn't grasp exactly what had happened. All she knew was that everything had gone wrong, and she was lucky to be alive. Syrana might not be so lucky.

"Help!" She continued to yell with all her might long after help arrived. Pastorals, tending to their herds, were the first to find her and immediately sent for healers and priests. Eryn couldn't follow their words. They were all a blur of people, voices, and questions she couldn't understand let alone answer. She was holding on to consciousness just enough to keep pointing them to Syrana. "Help her."

She was being carried. Syrana was in other arms, held tightly as her body thrashed, almost close enough to reach if Eryn had the strength to try.

Consciousness came and went as Eryn was carried to healers' hall. She tried to push off the healers who tended to her infected wounds and redirect them to Syrana. Finally, she heard a healer announce to the room as a whole, "We've done all we can. She'll pull through tonight or she won't. We'll know in the morning."

Eryn let go, sinking into the darkness that had been crashing over her for hours. "Tomorrow" was her last conscious thought.

CHAPTER TWO

Pride and Regret

Rina made two jabbing thrusts with her spear to push her opponent back. She knew neither would strike a blow, but it put her opponent on the defensive and gave her the space to maneuver. The sweat dripping down her neck inside her cowl made her long for the cold drinks her fellow junior guardians were enjoying on the practice field. The night before Choosing Day was always pleasant long past when the dome faded from day to night. Inside the sparring room, the air was musty and pungent with the smell of exertion.

Rina thrust again, this time at the mask protecting Claine's face. Claine blocked the strike as if swatting a fly. Rina smiled at the predicable move. She slashed down, forcing Claine's blade low, and thrust for the chest. Claine dodged. Their practice weapons swirled in a dance they both knew well, neither finding nor providing an opening.

Claine had pulled Rina aside from the merriment of the evening for one final lesson in tactics before Rina's potential trip outside the dome. But once Claine began to speak, her true intentions became quite clear. She began with a simple question. "Have any shadows spoken to you today?"

Rina slashed, catching nothing but air. "Yes." There was no point in lying, certainly not on the first question. Plus, she couldn't be expected to control whether shadows spoke to her or not.

"And what did they say?" Claine easily parried Rina's blow and attempted one of her own.

Rina considered saying she hadn't listened and didn't know what they said, but Claine would know she was lying. "They say I won't be chosen tomorrow."

Claine scoffed, knocking Rina's spear up with a two-handed swing as if to make physical her opinion of Rina's answer. "So, shadows are making my arguments for me these days. Do you believe them?"

Again, the correct answer was obvious. She was supposed to say shadows always lie. But how could she when it was so obviously false? She wasn't going to be chosen tomorrow, so what was the point in saying otherwise? Rina sidestepped Claine and her question, letting the upward momentum of her spear carry her through to face the opposite direction. She was at Claine's back and a quick jab to Claine's armor would score her a point if this were a match.

"Bear claw," Claine said before Rina could strike.

Rina didn't try to hide her annoyance as she dropped to one knee and thrust her spear up at an imaginary dire bear's paw. In the Dark Lands, she would have to be able to think on her feet to survive monsters—dire creatures that were bigger, tougher, and more aggressive than normal animals.

"Do you believe them?" Claine asked again as she tried to strike Rina before she could stand.

"I will not be chosen tomorrow." Rina parried and slid her training spear's rounded tip down Claine's sword, striking the cross-guard. Had she been fighting a shadow rather than her mentor, she would have dissipated it with that blow. Of course, Claine would never provide blatant recognition for a strike unless it brought her to her knees.

Claine struck Rina's spear with an anger that did not show in her voice. "If you are not chosen tomorrow, it will be because you made it happen. I am docking you two hundred points. Shadows always lie."

"Two hundred points!" Rina planted her feet and struck over and over again at the mask blocking Claine's presumably smug expression. Claine's extra thirty years of age could only keep up blocking for so long. "There are twenty guardians, Claine. There are nineteen heroes. I already have the lowest rank. I won't be chosen. Taking two hundred points is just…embarrassing…insulting! What do you want from me?" She sputtered the words with each jab, anger driving her on.

"Swarm of rats," Claine said as her sword swipes began to slow.

Rina strongly considered ignoring the command, but instinct took over before frustration could. She reached to the empty bandolier across her front, opened the pocket that would normally contain gunk oil, pretended to pour it in a circle around her with one hand and drew a match with her spear hand. She acted out striking the match on the pretend bottle as she struck forward at Claine with her spear, then dropped the unlit match onto the ground in front of her.

"Say shadows always lie, Rina. Say it and mean it and I'll give you enough points to be tied for lowest. Nothing is set until I record the change." If Rina's assault had tired her at all, Claine wasn't showing any signs of it. "This is your last chance. Be a guardian. Serve the Community. Say it and mean it."

Claine sprang forward, clearly trying to put Rina on the defensive physically as much as in the conversation.

"It's not that simple and you know it." She swiped Claine's blade aside again and again, getting nowhere but back to the center to swipe again.

"You're being childish and you're being stubborn," Claine said. Her stance shifted subtly, her attacks becoming more fluid and targeted. She was no longer trying to emulate the attacks of a shadow or a monster but attempting to win. These were the moves that made her a master swordswoman and head guardian. "There is no argument you can make that you have not already made a hundred times. Tomorrow you will be a woman in the eyes of the Community, so act like it. Admit you are wrong. Take responsibility for the harm you have caused, and for the Goddess's sake, stop doing more harm. Is this really who you want to be to the Community?"

Rina was tired of this. Tired of Claine cheating her out of every well-earned strike with another pretend dire animal. Tired of Claine dismissing her valid points with a heavy helping of guilt and demoralizing shame. Tired of Claine constantly changing the rules of engagement or simply not following them at all. Tired of Claine.

She waited for Claine's next strike and barely parried, letting the dulled blade slide down her sleeve until it was at armpit height, then brought her arm down around the blade. In a single, smooth motion, she brought the shaft of her spear to Claine's forearm and pressed while twisting away with the sword under her arm. Against a shadow or a monster, she would have been sliced in the side, but against a swordswoman, Claine had two choices: let go of her sword or have her wrist broken.

Claine released, jumping back from Rina's immediate attack at her face. "You always have to be right, don't you?"

"This isn't about being right!" Rina struck out. This time she had Claine. She wanted to serve the Community. It was all she'd ever wanted to do besides make Claine proud. But shadows didn't always lie, at least not to Rina. They always told her bad things, as they did to everyone, but sometimes the bad things they said came true without her doing anything. If she could use that knowledge, if she could listen and react, she could keep those bad things from happening.

Claine turned from Rina's attack, grabbing the end of her spear just below the flexible tip, and broke the wooden shaft over her thigh. Before Rina could react, Claine kicked her in the chest, knocking her backward.

"You've based your entire self-worth on a lie." Claine tore off her facemask and closed the space between them. "And you've invested more." Claine dodged Rina's right hook. "And more." She punched Rina in the stomach, forcing her back again. "Until you feel you can't go back."

Rina tried for a roundhouse kick, but Claine blocked it easily, grabbed her shoulders, and shoved. Rina stumbled backward until her shoulders hit the training room wall.

"You believe that if you can just prove you're right, it will wash away all your sins." Claine advanced on her once again.

Rina's hand went to the knife that always rested in a sheath at her back. It was wrong to do so during a sparring match and she knew it, but at this point she didn't care. Before she could do more than draw the knife from its sheath, Claine was on her, her own knife pressed to Rina's throat.

"Don't even think about it. I could slit your throat before you could ever get it around." The anger in Claine's eyes was real even if the threat was not. Claine always knew the line between beating her and hurting her, at least physically. "You can't wash your sins away, Rina. You can only choose to admit you are wrong and atone or keep committing them. This is your last chance. Admit shadows always lie. Mean it and I'll give you the points to be a guardian or at least to have a chance at it. Say it."

The cold of the steel at her throat was no more convincing than any of Claine's previous attempts to guilt, cajole, threaten, or debate her for fourteen years since becoming Rina's mentor when she was six years old. There was so much more riding on that simple sentence than Claine could ever truly understand.

Rina closed her eyes for a moment, hoping she looked contemplative of Claine's words rather than scheming. She wasn't willing to lose. This wasn't just a sparring match. Their knives seemed the least of the escalation to Rina. She adjusted her stance and felt a cord press into her shoulder. She shifted again and hid a smile as three taut cords rubbed against her back.

Rina bit her lip, as if in indecision, then opened her eyes and looked toward the ceiling. It would look like she was looking toward the dome, an action associated with seeking the Goddess's wisdom. Rina located her target in an instant—the training dummy on the left was directly over Claine's left shoulder. She began to saw at the cord behind her back while moving as little as possible.

"Rina?" She was expected to have an answer.

The snap of the cord provided it for her. The dummy landed hard on Claine's left side and she toppled to the ground under it, her knife skittering across the floor. Rina looked down at her with pride. She had to be proud of herself, because Claine certainly wouldn't be. Thinking outside the box had earned her points when she was young, but now it was all too often conflated with her refusal to simply accept what she was told as fact.

"Shadows don't always lie to *me*."

From the floor, Claine's ever-present stoic countenance slipped, and true emotion took its place. Rina had only seen such momentary vulnerability from Claine a few times in her life and she was fairly sure she was the only person, besides perhaps Keddeth, who ever had. Claine was on the verge of tears, a level Rina hadn't seen before. Surely, she hadn't injured her. But the look was only there for half a second before Claine hid it behind her expressionless mask. "You have won the battle but lost the war. It's three hundred points you lose tonight."

Rina didn't have a response, at least not one that wouldn't simply be a string of curse words and blasphemes. Instead, she turned and stormed away, slamming the training room door.

She wanted to go home, throw herself on her bed, and have a full-on tantrum. If tomorrow would mark her becoming a woman, she felt deserving of one last childish show of emotion. But Syrana was there in their living room, repacking her gear for tomorrow's outing rather than celebrating. "Hey, come to join me in a final pre-check?" She looked up and her smile slipped away. "What happened?"

"Nothing. I don't want to talk about it." Rina could still have her fit; she would just have to keep the screaming into her pillow more toned down than planned.

"Is this about tomorrow? Rina, go talk to Claine. She knows you are the second-best fighter, the second-best archer, the second-best, well, everything. You're less than thirty points behind Grena, maybe you can earn some last-minute points."

"Three hundred and twenty-seven," Rina bit out.

"What?"

"That's how many points I'm behind Grena. Claine took three hundred points because I wouldn't say shadows always lie." Rina's face felt like it was on fire, though she couldn't tell if it was driven more by rage or embarrassment.

"Dark gods damn it, Rina! Why wouldn't you just say it?"

"How many times do I have to explain? How many?" She turned on her heels and stalked to her room. She didn't care anymore if Syrana heard her, she needed to let go of the knot in her throat and the roiling in her stomach. She'd be just as likely to puke as to hit something if she didn't.

Syrana caught her by the shoulders before she reached the door. Damn you and your speediness, Rina thought, refusing to turn around. "I'm sorry," Syrana said. "This is our last night as juniors. Let's not fight." She rested her chin on top of Rina's head and dug her thumbs into the knots of Rina's shoulders in the way that was always both relieving and painful. "Tomorrow, no matter what happens, I want you to remember that I love you. You are an amazing guardian and an amazing person."

Rina felt her anger seep back into the bottle she kept deep inside. She and Syrana were aways arguing, trying to outdo each other and prove the other wrong, but those were debates, not fights. Syrana tended to push too far when she was winning, to drive her point home until it hurt. But she always knew how to make up for it, to show Rina that even as important as winning was to her, Rina was more important. She was Rina's healing salve, whether those cuts had come from Syrana or others. Rina loved her.

Syrana tipped her head to place a kiss on Rina's head before moving to her neck. "Come on, one last pleasure contest?"

Rina rolled her eyes. "Don't think I missed that comment about second-best."

"Since your score is otherwise encumbered, I guess we'll never know," Syrana said as she unclasped the front of Rina's training gambeson from behind. "But tonight, in your bed, I plan to show you who's number one."

"I'm not in the mood," Rina said, trying to pull away. "You're packing and I'm angry."

"Tell me you don't need a distraction right now," Syrana said, her voice full of challenge before softening. "Tell me that what you need right now isn't to feel loved."

Syrana waited a beat, allowing the silence to prove her point. She gave Rina's neck another kiss that raised goose bumps all up and down Rina's legs, then sidestepped her to make a show of stripping on her way to Rina's bed. Rina sighed, trying to release her frustration but knowing that displaying it didn't lessen it. Perhaps some good sex with someone she loved would do her well. Plus, an orgasm seemed a far better release than a long, muffled scream. Syrana's body could do wonders, but it was the heartache she really wanted Syrana to fix. It didn't have to be passionate sex to be compassionate sex.

Tomorrow, she'll have a hero and you won't. She'll have a hero and you will have no one. She'll have a hero and she won't love you anymore.

The incorporeal voice was like carving stone with a sword. She felt a grating unease just from the presence, and the hissing delivery made the hairs on the back of her neck stand on end. Rina tried to block out the shadow whispering at her ear, but she'd listened far too many times to be able to block them with the techniques that came so easily to other guardians.

A second shadow joined when Rina's childhood nursery rhyme did nothing to diminish the first shadow. *Tomorrow, you will lose her. You better take advantage of this pity sex.*

Pity sex! the first shadow repeated, clearly savoring the term.

Pity sex! Pity sex! Pity sex! Pity sex! More and more shadows joined when Rina failed to ignore them and reacted instead, until Rina felt she'd shoved her head into a hive of bees. She was always amazed that Syrana had learned to block them so thoroughly that even when they were chanting at Rina, Syrana didn't hear them. Rina fled into her bedroom, throwing off her clothing and diving into Syrana's welcoming arms, hoping bodily pleasure could drown out what logic could not.

The jeering, doomsaying voices were back in the morning, ready to greet her on an otherwise beautiful day. Choosing Day was always bright, crisp, and clear. She pulled away from Syrana's flirtatious touch, wishing last night had done more for her growing feeling of worthlessness. Instead, she tried to lose herself in the tasks of the morning, ironing her uniform which the shadows pointed out she looked fat in, checking the pack the shadows informed her she wouldn't need, and getting ready for a day that the shadows assured her would go disastrously wrong.

For an hour, Rina stood in the middle of the training field, trying to maintain a stoic expression while Claine informed any hero who came within ten feet of Rina that her mentee was the lowest ranked by over three hundred points. Only two people paused to address Claine: Eryn, the top ranked hero asking for directions to Syrana, no surprise there, and the hero Rina had to assume was the lowest rank hero, who moved on once he established for certain that there was one more guardian than hero in this cohort.

Demoralized and humiliated, Rina stood at the back of the chapel, watching her peers be bound to their heroes, and then wandered back home after Syrana bounded off without her. At home, Syrana barely seemed to notice her come in. She was tinkering with something that she shoved in her pocket before grabbing her pack and running out the door with a simple "wish me luck."

Rina stood in the empty house, staring at the door, and for the first time in her life had no idea what she was supposed to do. There was no assignment to fulfill, no training to undertake, not even any friends to hang out with. She could go to the garrison to get her new schedule for training junior guardians. Surely Claine had already tasked someone with putting it together. She'd been as certain that Rina would not be chosen as Rina had been and done everything she could to ensure it. But going to the garrison felt like admitting defeat.

You're going to walk into the Dark Lands and never come back, a shadow whispered. That ridiculous mental image got Rina moving.

A few laps around the obstacle course would do her mood some good. Then she could get her schedule and let the rest of her life begin.

Rina was still on the obstacle course, trying ad nauseam to overcome one of the challenges that required a level of focus she was not capable of at that moment, when the red-eyed healer boy found her. "There's been an accident," he said, out of breath. "Claine sent me to find you."

Rina ran to healers' hall, leaving the boy behind. Her endurance and speed were far greater than his. She'd been concerned for Claine's health, running the last twenty-four hours of bad blood through her mind with each footfall. But when she arrived, "Eryn's guardian" were the words on everyone's lips. She tried to push past the groups of healers bustling in and out of the commotion, but every time she made it to the door, she was carried back by the surge of people— heroes trying to check on Eryn, priests trying to understand what had happened, guardians trying to direct the chaos, and healers shoving through when their calls to be let by couldn't get over the din.

In the end, it was Claine who threw everyone out besides the healers, Rina, Keddeth, a couple of senior heroes, and a childrearer who had managed to stay out of everyone's way long enough to go unnoticed. They sat in chairs set out in pairs along the hallway, sharing the tidbits they'd each managed to glean until there was simply nothing else to share or speculate about.

Claine sat next to Keddeth, her hand resting on his knee as he wrung his hands in his lap. Rina sat alone, staring at the door, wishing she knew what was going on inside. She gave up praying about an hour in. She barely got a line in before her mind ran off to yet another horrible conclusion, while the whispers at her ear told her over and over again that all her darkest predictions would come true.

She'd known that the day would not go well for her, but she hadn't expected it to go this badly. Syrana was on death's door, and all Rina could do was sit there and feel sorry for herself. As if this was just one more thing in a long line of injustices being done to her. She kept mentally slapping herself and reminding herself that this wasn't about her. Syrana was dying, and she should be praying. Instead, her mind was filled with her own failures and regrets.

Rina wished she hadn't let Syrana win the pleasure contest the night before so handily. She'd made Syrana orgasm twice, but her heart hadn't truly been in it. "Please, Goddess, let her live, let me pay her back, let me show her how much I love her. Please don't take her from me."

Another pang of guilt struck her. Even her prayers were about herself as much as Syrana. She should be asking Syrana not to be taken from the Community.

I wish I'd kissed her this morning instead of pulling away. I wish I'd been appreciative instead of sullen. I wish I'd wished her luck. I wish I'd told her I loved her. I wish…

Rina looked up as a healer emerged from the room into which Syrana had been taken. "Eryn is recovering. There should be no long-term damage. As for her guardian, we've done all we can. She'll pull through tonight or she won't. We'll know in the morning."

The others gathered in the hall nodded as if this were sufficient. Rina could feel her anger rising for an uncountable time that day. How could waiting possibly be the answer? She wanted to get her practice spear and beat the healer with it until he fixed Syrana. Why wasn't he doing more? The Goddess had given him superior ability to treat, so what in the Dark Lands was he doing here giving up?

"If it's good enough for everyone else, it's good enough for you." The Claine in Rina's brain repeated her mantra. Down the hall, the real Claine stood and addressed the small group. "Who will sit vigil?"

"I will sit vigil for Eryn," the blue-eyed childrearer said.

"I will sit for Syrana," Rina said, nearly jumping out of her chair. It should have been Keddeth's right as Syrana's mentor, but Rina didn't care. She couldn't go home without Syrana. She just couldn't.

Keddeth gave Rina a soft smile as if to acknowledge her pain, as if he could possibly understand the depths of her pain.

Tears sprang to Rina's eyes as she entered the healing chamber. The mixture of air thick with decay and sterilizing fluid fumes felt like a physical bite to her senses. The sight of Syrana was far worse. Her skin was gray as a corpse where it wasn't wrapped in bandages. The wounds were no longer bleeding thanks to the work of the healers, but Syrana had clearly lost a great deal of blood. She looked like a dire leech had been sucking on her for weeks, leaving her body as saggy and deflated as a withered turnip. Where was the stalwart warrior who'd bounded out of their home hours ago?

"I'm Alba," the childrearer said as she and Rina took their seats next to their charges for the night. She didn't elaborate on her reason for sitting vigil, giving Rina permission to do the same.

Rina didn't particularly want to try to justify her presence or wrap who Syrana was to her into a single word, if one existed. "I'm Rina."

Alba filled the next few hours with singing, everything from hymns to lullabies, while Rina repeated over and over again under her breath that she was sorry, that she loved Syrana, and that she was going to be okay. All the while, shadows hissed in the background. *She'll be dead tomorrow.* With each iteration, Rina held Syrana's hand and whispered with all the conviction she could muster, "Shadows always lie."

As the hours ticked by, she found it harder and harder to keep her eyes open. She sat with one booted heel digging into the top of her other foot, but neither the pain in her foot nor the one in her chest was doing much to pierce the veil of exhaustion, both emotional and mental, that engulfed her. Syrana would open her eyes and smile at Rina and Rina would smile, her hope rising just long enough to realize she was dreaming and pop her eyes back open before digging her heel deeper into her foot.

"The healers say your loved ones can hear you when they are unconscious," Alba said, pausing her singing. "I can pause if you'd like to talk to her."

"I am talking to her," Rina shot back, immediately regretting it. "I'm sorry, I'm just tired."

"It's okay to be angry with her," Alba said, "to be angry with either or both of them."

"I'm not angry with them. I'm angry at me." She tried to say more, to diminish the power of her last sentence, but nothing came out. I'm not going to cry on vigil, Rina told herself, giving her foot a small stomp to remind her body that she was in charge.

"That's okay too. As are tears."

"Not on vigil," Rina said, keeping her eyes averted. It didn't matter if this childrearer wouldn't judge her for breaking the Community's taboo, she'd broken enough already.

"My husband is a farmer and he's very, well, down-to-earth," Alba said, a smile in her voice. "He once told me that if I ever sit vigil for him, he hopes I will cry. He said it wouldn't tell him that he had no hope of living. It would tell him he had something worth living for. He would fight to live to stop my tears."

"Then why aren't you crying for Eryn?" Rina sounded petty to her own ears.

"Eryn doesn't see tears as a sign of love. She sees dedication as love. What does your loved one see as love?"

Rina smiled despite herself. "Being right," she said before she could stop herself. It didn't sound very kind that way.

Alba just smiled. "It seems like you can get two dire birds with one stone, then. I heard you say that you're angry with yourself. Sometimes the best way to get through it is to let it out. You could tell her why you're angry with yourself, especially if it means she was right."

Rina sighed. Giving a litany of her mistakes didn't feel very inspiring, but she supposed she was berating herself for them anyway, so why not let Syrana be part of her inner dialogue. If Syrana could hear her, it would likely be a more interesting one-sided conversation than "I'm sorry, I love you, you're going to be okay" for the five hundredth time. "Thanks," she mumbled, too tired to show more gratitude or enthusiasm.

Rina took a deep breath and began just below a whisper, "You used to tell me, 'Rina, I get that shadows lying or not is important to you, but it's one aspect of so many other parts of you.' You were right. You have to live so I can share those other parts with you." The list went on from "You told me that I shouldn't carry my frustration like the only friend who really understands me" to "You said cutting my hair that short would make it look like I had a dire fox on my head," always ending in "you were right" and how Rina would do better when Syrana was well.

Dawn brought with it the healers and the crowd that apparently had nothing better to do than chatter loudly despite Claine's constant stern looks. Rina and Alba were shepherded back into the hall to wait.

Commotion within the room brought silence outside it. The door jerked open. "Bring the head priest quickly," a healer yelled from within before slamming the door shut again.

"What's happening?" the crowd demanded before devolving into a cacophony of speculations.

When the head priest arrived, she, Claine, and the head hero were allowed entry while Keddeth made a great effort to send everyone else home or to work. Rina supposed there hadn't been this much excitement and mystery in the Community for a while, but it still made her want to yell at them that this was her friend's life, not some extra-large, Goddess-touched pumpkin.

The debate within Syrana and Eryn's room grew steadily from an indecipherable mumble to the exchange of shouts. The door flew open once more and the head hero emerged, red-faced and indignant. "Where is the extra guardian?" he demanded.

It took a moment for Rina to realize he was talking about her—the extra guardian who had not been chosen. Before Rina could stand, Claine burst into the hall as well. "She was not chosen. She cannot have a hero."

"What happened?" Keddeth said, trying to push his way into the room to see his mentee.

"Eryn's guardian is dead," the healer said from inside the room. The doorway was too jammed for him to try to do more than call over their heads. "And Eryn is quickly following."

"This isn't supposed to happen," the head hero said. "Guardians die with their heroes, not the other way around."

"The binding was too fresh," the head priest said. "This is why the first journey is short, when the danger is highest. Eryn must be bound to a new guardian, or she will die."

The attention of the room turned to Rina, who had failed to stand, failed to breathe, failed to comprehend, failed her friend. Syrana was dead?

"There are other guardians," Claine said.

"She must be bound to an unbound guardian," the head priest said.

"There are unbound guardians." Claine sounded desperate. "Henna!"

"The cripple from last Choosing Day?" the head hero asked.

"She is an amazing archer, a brilliant trainer, and a devout guardian," Claine said, her tone making it clear she found his word choice offensive and dismissive. "She will be the next head guardian." Rina had thought of Henna a great deal during the choosing, wondering how her pain had been different watching heroes pass her by when before her accident she would have been one of the first guardians chosen. Had she accepted that the Goddess gave the Community one extra guardian in that cohort for a reason and that training the next generation was her way of serving the Community or had she felt slighted too?

"But she will never leave the Community," the head priest said.

"Then neither will Eryn," Claine said.

The head hero looked about ready to throttle Claine. He clearly was not used to people stating opinions that differed from his own. "Eryn is the hero we have been waiting generations for. That is unacceptable!"

"We don't have time for this argument. Eryn must be bound now," the head priest said.

Claine's color was rising along with her tone. "Rina cannot leave the Community. She was not meant to be chosen. The Goddess gave us an extra guardian because Rina is not fit to have a hero."

"Do you claim to know the Goddess's intentions?" the head priest asked, raising one eyebrow.

Keddeth stepped in before Claine could answer. He placed his hand on Claine's shoulder and said in the voice he only used when it really mattered, "Claine, Eryn needs a guardian, and Rina is that guardian. It is the Goddess's will."

Claine didn't say anything. For a long moment, she looked at Rina as if this were the pinnacle of her disappointment, then she stepped aside, unwilling to give her acceptance, but simply willing to not stand in their way.

The head hero didn't wait another moment. He swept forward, grabbed Rina's elbow, and all but dragged her into the room. He plopped her down into the chair Alba had used to sit vigil and gave the head priest a look that was disrespectfully impatient, despite the fact that she couldn't see him. The head priest pulled a binding thread from her pocket. As she did so, she said, "Guardian, will you accept this burden? Will you protect your hero against the evil that will seek to destroy her? Will you lay your life before your hero and her mission? Will you dedicate every day to the needs of your hero and the Community?"

Rina looked from the priest to the pale, unconscious young woman on the bed next to her, to the motionless body of her best friend on the opposite side of the chamber. How had everything changed so quickly? Couldn't they give her a moment to mourn, a moment to wrap her head around the idea of pledging her life to the hero who had survived where Syrana did not?

"Will you?" the priest asked again, and the head hero gave her elbow a jostle as if she could be shaken out of this as easily as a daydream.

I'm going to be a guardian, Rina thought. She gave Syrana another lingering look, silently telling her that she had been right yet again. "I will."

The head priest directed Rina to take Eryn's clammy hand and wrapped the thread around their entwined hands. Rina watched the thread melt into her hand, with the stinging heat of dripping melted wax onto her skin. The heat washed over her like sinking into a hot bath. She released a sigh as if all the anger, frustration, and guilt she'd bottled up for two decades were whooshing out in one fell swoop.

Rina brushed her thumb over the delicate hand in her own and looked at Eryn, her hero, taking in all the details that had somehow escaped her before. In the few times Rina had seen Eryn, she'd never truly noticed her beauty. Even ill, she seemed to glow with the Goddess's light. Rina wondered if this was what auras looked like. Her long blond hair was pulled back from her perfect, angular face with its high cheekbones. If only Rina could kiss away the tiny, medicated cuts and breathe color back into her silken skin. Rina found her peaceful, even vulnerable, look deeply endearing.

Eryn was the purpose she had been longing for all her life, the hole she'd been trying to fill with the pride and love of people like Syrana and Claine. The best word she could come up with for how Eryn made her feel was awe.

A light touch on her shoulder drew Rina out of her enamored daze. The head priest and hero were gone and Claine stood with a hand resting on Rina's shoulder. Behind her, a healer was waiting with an expectant look.

"It's time to leave," Claine said. "She needs healing and sleep. We will return tomorrow morning."

Rina realized she had no idea how long she had been sitting there staring at Eryn, but she wished she could stay. She leaned down to place a gentle kiss on Eryn's brow before following Claine out of the room.

"Congratulations, Rina," Claine said, and she seemed sincere. Rina had never known a less passive-aggressive person. Manipulative, sure, but she never gave false praise or expressed a feeling she didn't feel. "No feeling in the lands can compare to what it feels like to have a hero."

Something you tried your hardest to deny me, Rina thought. Her newfound sense of calm and purpose wasn't broken, but it didn't keep her from recognizing how close she'd come to missing this.

Claine's expression softened. "I know that you're angry with me, and you know that I was angry with you. But that's not what is important right now. Right now, all that matters, all that should ever matter to you is Eryn and the Community."

Rina nodded. Eryn and the Community were everything. She could feel that fact as if it were the truth at the core of her being, like it was pumping through her very blood.

"This is your chance to start anew. You no longer need to base who you are on who you were. Our old fights about shadows don't matter anymore. Now you have a new fight that is infinitely more important. But this is what I need you to hear, what I probably should have been saying for a while now. In the Dark Lands, you don't have time or space to listen to shadows. You have to be able to ignore them and act on instinct and training. Eryn's life depends on your ability to drown them out. If you don't, shadows will drown you instead. The past is in the past, let it go and move forward. Eryn is the greatest hero the Community has ever trained. Serve her, and you will be a great guardian."

Rina felt the last knot inside her loosen. Claine hadn't asked her to deny what she knew to be true, only to focus on what mattered more.

A small voice in the back of her mind that she knew to be her own told Rina that none of this was right. Syrana was gone and all she could think about was Eryn. Claine had just cast off almost fifteen years of arguing, guilting, and haranguing by saying it didn't matter and Rina was agreeing with her. Her entire body ached for a woman she barely knew and before this morning didn't particularly like. Rina shook her head, silencing the voice as she had never been able to do with a shadow. None of that mattered now. She was a guardian, she had Eryn, and those two facts were everything.

CHAPTER THREE

Conviction and Climax

Consciousness seeped into Eryn from the outside in. Her body lay on a firm bed and the scent of sterilizing liquid enveloped her, a familiar odor from her years helping healers clean bandages and instruments. The voice of the woman holding her hand was not familiar, but her words were. She was reading from the Book of Prayer, her voice low and melodic and her grip warm and firm.

Finally, with excruciating slowness, Eryn pulled her eyelids open to look at the woman reading to her. It took her a moment to recognize the guardian she had seen on Choosing Day, Claine's mentee.

"My guardian?" Her voice croaked. The healers' herbs were wearing off slower than she would like. What she wanted was to be out of bed and tracking down Syrana.

The guardian holding her hand gave her a somber look that left no question as to her answer. She opened her mouth, but nothing came out.

"But she can't…" Eryn's voice trailed off. She and Syrana were bound by a priest's foresight, destined to save the Community, fight back the shadows, return the dome to its former glory. Foresights weren't guaranteed, but she'd been so certain. How could Syrana be dead?

Shame washed over her. She'd been a full hero for all of a few hours and she had already failed. Would she ever leave the dome again, ever bring back any ichor, ever truly be a hero at all, let alone the hero she'd dreamed of being? Her hand went to the pendant still hanging from the chain around her neck. Everyone had believed in her, and now what? Her entire identity was based on the idea, no the fact, that she was going to save the Community.

Eryn took her hand back to get out of bed. She was stiff from inactivity and her cuts stung as her movements stretched them, but the pain helped her focus. I failed her, I should hurt, I should hurt more, Eryn thought. She stretched, trying to let the pain clear the tears welling in her eyes and the sharp ache in her chest that had nothing to do with injuries.

"I need to..." Eryn said, having no idea where the rest of the sentence was going, but she had to do something. She felt like she was still in the Dark Lands, lost, alone, confused. "Why are you here?"

Claine's mentee looked taken aback. "I'm your new guardian. I'm Rina."

"My new guardian," Eryn said. The phrase was like a spark in Eryn's otherwise darkened, scrambling mind. She had a guardian. Everything had gone wrong, but everything wasn't over. The spark grew as she latched onto it, forcing away everything but the myopic desire to move forward. She could still be a hero, still save the Community, still fulfill her foresight.

"We need to go see Holden, get this all sorted," she said, rising from the bed and shakily leading the way out. She had better things to do than wait around for her body to catch up with her mind.

Eryn breezed through the hero quarter, through the training fields, past the houses and dormitories and into the haven, making a beeline for the head hero's office, Rina constantly at her heels. At Holden's door, she knocked and waited for his call. The head priest was there, so Eryn announced her arrival for the blind priest's benefit.

"I'm glad to hear you up and around," the head priest said and indicated for Eryn to take the other seat in front of Holden's desk. It was a seat Eryn was quite accustomed to. She had received both accolades and reprimands in it many times. Her drive and skills earned her praise but were also often more than she, her peers, or her trainers knew how to handle. The head priest nodded at Rina to confirm she knew Rina was there as well, as Rina took up position behind Eryn's seat.

"I'm feeling well and ready to go on my first mission. It seems judicious to not waste any more time. My new guardian is here and ready." Eryn said, glancing at Rina, who nodded in agreement. This was what she needed, what the Community needed, what Syrana would surely have wanted. There was no way she could stand to wait three weeks until her cohort went out again, sitting around twiddling her thumbs and listening to the stories of other heroes—real heroes. Holden's look of pride only further cemented her confidence.

"With your permission," Holden said to the head priest. "I believe it is indeed judicious." At the priest's nod, Holden continued. "You will have three days, including today. I want you back at the same time as the rest of your cohort who left two days ago."

Eryn's confidence wavered. "We'll accomplish in three days what others do in five," Eryn said firmly.

The head priest raised a hand. "Do not let dedication become folly. Acclimation is the goal of this mission. Learn the Dark Lands, yourself, and your guardian."

Holden nodded. "No one finds ichor on their first outing."

But I always wanted to be the first, Eryn thought. No one says I can't, Eryn insisted silently, pasting a smile she hoped was reassuring onto her face. "Three days."

Holden dismissed Rina with a shooing motion. "Go prepare your pack and meet Eryn at the dome."

"My pack is prepared," Rina said, her attention on Eryn rather than Holden. "I'll meet you there."

Eryn smiled at her again. She wasn't Syrana, but Eryn felt she could get along well with her. Everything really was going to be okay.

Once Rina left, Holden rose from his desk and went to the wide cabinet that held equal parts gold-spined reference books, artifacts from his ventures into the Dark Lands, and small bottles of fruit liqueur. He retrieved one of the bottles, sniffed it with satisfaction, and poured a splash into two small glasses before handing one to Eryn. "You gave us quite a scare, Eryn. I know that this is quite a setback for you, though I imagine you don't know just how much. I must inform you that unlike your original guardian, your new guardian was the lowest ranked in the cohort by over three hundred points."

Eryn could almost hear the crack running up the wall she was desperately trying to construct to block out her feelings and insecurities. Three hundred points? She wasn't even three hundred points ahead of the next hero, though at a certain point her trainers had stopped focusing on giving her more points. Rina had seemed so competent, though she supposed first impressions could be deceiving. "I'll be fine," Eryn said as much to herself as Holden.

"I know you will. If anyone can get her up to speed, it's you. Just cut yourself some slack when things seem harder than they should be. You're the one carrying the weight of this team, and it's not your fault there's more weight to bear." He finished his drink with a final satisfied sip.

The head priest rose to show herself out. Holden turned to her as if he had almost forgotten she was there. "She's not at risk anymore if her new guardian, well, fails to survive, right?"

"She has fully metabolized. She will be fine," she said as if she thought the question was neither appropriate nor surprising. With that, she left, providing no further clarity on what she meant by "metabolized."

"Right," Holden said. "Be safe out there and make us proud. I know you will." He took her untouched glass and ushered her out as if the matter had been successfully managed. The fact that she was not at risk if her guardian failed to survive didn't feel very managed to Eryn.

"I've got this," Eryn said silently. She could compensate for her guardian, do five days in three, and prove that nothing had truly changed. "If anyone can, it's me."

With that, she marched to her home, donned her gambeson, equipment, and weapons, and set off toward the dome.

Rina was waiting for her when she arrived. Compared to Syrana's, Rina's pack looked ready to topple over and crush her. On Rina's stouter figure, accentuated by her thick gambeson and large gauntlet, the ensemble gave the impression that Rina had been a normally proportioned person until her pack had squished her. She beamed at Eryn as if her arrival was the moment she'd been waiting for all day.

"Let's go," Eryn said. She wished she could go back to seeing Rina's smile as dedicated rather than foolish. She wished she could see Rina's calm observation of their surroundings as adroit rather than lackadaisical.

As they traversed the flatland around the dome, Rina turned to Eryn. "I wanted to tell you—"

"You're the lowest ranked guardian in your cohort by a significant margin. I know," Eryn interrupted her.

After a beat, Rina said, "I was going to say it's an honor to be your guardian."

Eryn cursed under her breath. Well, things certainly weren't off to a great start. She skirted sentient trees that were surely tasting her on the air and bushes filled with watchful eyes. A part of her longed to take in the flora and fauna she'd spent fifteen years learning about, but she didn't have time. If an exploding thistle was underripe or creeping ivy was too far away, there was no reason to give it a second glance.

Eryn hiked and climbed, pushing her body well beyond hunger, thirst, and fatigue. She wouldn't accomplish five days of travel by taking breaks. She was relieved when Rina managed to keep up, though she supposed even inferior guardians possessed Goddess-given endurance and strength.

Every couple of hours, Rina contorted her arms to retrieve water or food from her pack without halting their progress. The first few times, she offered them to Eryn, who refused. She didn't need them; she was fine. Rina stopped offering and took a few sips or bites before handing the rest to Eryn. If it wasn't slowing their progress, Eryn supposed there wasn't a problem with her also eating and drinking when Rina needed it.

Without a sun to mark the passing of the day, the time to set up camp was whenever Eryn decided to call it a day. She had no intention of doing so until they'd ventured the equivalent of two days' distance from the dome. The problem was, she had no sense of how far that was or if that would even be sufficiently far to find ichor. There was no standard distance or location for ichor. She would just have to keep going until she couldn't.

As they traveled on, the rocks became more plentiful, shifting under her feet and trying to trip her. Her legs felt as if she were carrying toddlers clinging to each limb. She pressed on.

As Eryn took another step, her boot struck a rock in front of her. She sighed, lifting her gaze from the uneven ground to the rock face before them. She hadn't noticed the cliff until she'd literally run into it. She looked to the left and right at the unending wall of rock that wrapped back the way they'd come. She'd been too tired to look up and walked them into a box canyon. Eryn suppressed a groan. They would lose so much time doubling back.

"An excellent place for a campsite indeed," Rina said, as if Eryn had intended this blunder. It was the first time they had spoken in hours. "Our lantern can go all the way to the wall, so we won't be able to be surrounded while we sleep." Rina smiled at Eryn as if proud of herself for figuring out Eryn's master plan.

The thought of waking up only to backtrack at least an hour's worth of walking sounded less than appealing, even though her fatigued body pleaded for a bedroll.

Rina ran her fingers over the rock face. "I have the equipment to scale this in the, well, it's not really morning, I suppose. I'll make sure to unpack it so it's ready when we break camp."

"We'll scale it." Eryn almost laughed. Of course. Certainly, she would have thought of that if she weren't so exhausted. Perhaps a little sleep would do her well after all.

"I want this to be a condensed stop," Eryn said, pouring a vial of ichor into the small lantern Rina handed her. The twenty-foot-wide shimmering golden dome that sprouted from it would protect them while they slept, eliminating the need to sleep in shifts. Rina nodded, passing Eryn the equipment to set up their tent while she prepared their dinner. "Let's make dinner the abbreviated version as well. Maybe just some more dried fruits and meat."

Rina nodded. "I'll get as far as I can while you set up and we'll eat what's ready."

Setting up the tent took Eryn longer than she would have liked. The stakes refused to find purchase in the rocks, and the poles kept slipping out of place.

"Sorry, I should have given you the twine to start with," Rina said, coming up behind Eryn and looping the lengths of twine through the stake holes before anchoring them to rocks. "Let me fix my mistake, please. The stew is ready."

Eryn's stomach gave an audible growl as she paused long enough to allow her senses any of her brain space. The air within the little domed campsite smelled like rosemary and roasted meat. Eryn tried not to scoff. What a waste of space and weight to have brought rosemary. She filled a bowl from the pot and all but inhaled the contents. She was pretty sure her fatigue improved the quality tenfold because it tasted like the best stew she'd ever had.

Rina ate the remaining stew and cleaned the pot, while Eryn

unrolled her bedroll and removed her gambeson. Efficient, she thought, ready to pass out as much as fall asleep.

Rina's warm hands brushed over Eryn's shoulders, and she sighed as her muscles relaxed. Relief followed Rina's fingers as they trailed down her back. Rina's fingers were both delicate and strong as they worked their way to the hem of her shirt and began to lift.

"What are you doing?" Eryn asked, swatting Rina's hands off the bottom of her shirt.

"I thought you might want some…comfort," Rina said.

Is that what the kids are calling it these days? Eryn could feel the warmth where Rina had touched her threatening to ignite desire. Eryn imagined her peers were happily accepting everything their guardians offered, but they did not have five days to do in three. They would not find ichor. She kicked the feeling out to live with the other emotions that would not serve her on her mission. "No, thank you."

"Oh," was all Rina said.

Eryn climbed into her bedroll and gave Rina a smile to let her know that she was being sincere. She didn't want Rina to think that she had done anything wrong in offering. There were just more important things. "Sleep well. We have an early morning if we can call it that."

Eryn awoke to the smell of eggs and wood smoke. Rina's side of the tent was already packed and empty. Her appreciation and relief were immediately eclipsed by a shot of inadequacy. She was always the first one awake, always the first one training. How was her substandard guardian that much ahead of her?

Once dressed, she found Rina arranging climbing gear by the remnants of the morning fire. "Where did you get eggs?" Her mental image of Rina plucking monster eggs from an oversized nest was both comical and disturbing.

Rina pulled a jar from her pack, half-filled with egg innards.

"You won't be able to do that on our ten-day trips. They won't last, and you won't have room." Eryn wasn't sure why the statement made her feel better. The thought of waking up to eggs every day in the Dark Lands seemed like a miracle.

Rina just smiled. That glint of a challenge was in her eyes that Eryn had seen on Choosing Day. "We can for the first few days. You'd be amazed how much I can pack into this thing." Was this one of the reasons Rina was so low ranked? Did she do frivolous things just to show she could?

Rina handed a bowl of scrambled eggs to Eryn before going about cleaning and packing the cooking materials. "In the Dark Lands, mental fortitude is as crucial as physical fortitude, especially after five days away from the Community, with five more to go. Closing your eyes, inhaling the aroma of a cooking fire, and savoring a hearty bite of eggs can feel like just enough of home to keep pressing on."

Eryn hid her scoff in a bite of egg. Others might require motivation to persevere, but home was Eryn's driving force, not a crutch.

Eryn and Rina packed their bags, donned their climbing equipment, and closed the lantern, taking up a defensive position in case of lurking monsters outside the opaque dome.

It was disconcerting to look at the cliff as the lantern dome came down. The crags and protrusions cast no shadows, making the entire scene look flat and two-dimensional. Everything appeared exactly as far away as everything else, and only size implied distance. Eryn wanted to look down just to avoid the feeling of vertigo.

Eryn turned to Rina and was struck by the sight of her in completely equal lighting. The glow from the dome and the fire had accentuated the contours of Rina's face, but the flat light gave her skin an immaculate radiance. Her lips appeared soft and inviting, and her eyes piercing. Eryn suppressed a shiver, unsure if it stemmed from discomfort or desire.

Eryn turned away, shoving more feelings away. She had places to go, ichor to find.

Rina proved to be an adept and attentive belay partner and they were soon trudging forward, avoiding trees and large thickets of bloodberry bushes that thrived on the remains of deceased creatures, repurposing the blood to entice animals into consuming their berries and spreading their seeds. They walked in silence for hours aside from Rina pausing to point out a dire beehive and recommend an alternate path.

Behind her, Rina stopped. Alarmed, Eryn turned to see Rina looking at an empty patch of air. "A shadow?" Without realizing it, she put her hand to the pendent Syrana had given her.

"Just one," Rina said, looking away and smiling at Eryn as if she'd just seen a nice trinket in the market.

"Shouldn't we…?" Eryn's grip on the small pendant tightened enough to turn the tips of her fingers white.

"No, some guardians attack any shadow they encounter, but I ascribe to the philosophy that shadows are like monsters, if they aren't attacking you, no need to attack them. It just distracts from the mission."

"But what if they start to gather? Many shadows can be dangerous. What if they attack us en masse?" How was Eryn the only one freaked out about this? Was Rina just that lazy or incompetent?

"Shadows don't form groups. Even when they frenzy after a hero drinks ichor for the trip home, they still aren't working together. They're just all attacking the same target. Frenzied shadows are very dangerous, but not before then." Rina sounded so certain.

You don't know! Eryn wanted to yell at her. She hadn't been there. She hadn't heard the way Syrana screamed. She hadn't felt the terror, fought uselessly, and failed.

"Don't worry. I'll stay vigilant and protect you," Rina said, giving Eryn what she could only describe as the smile version of puppy dog eyes. Eryn didn't find it especially comforting.

Instead, she walked slower, constantly glancing back to see where Rina was looking. Eventually, she unclipped her necklace so she could still clutch it but stop putting an indent into her neck from the chain. They didn't get too far before Eryn looked back at the wrong moment and stepped on a living vine.

The snakelike root, the width of a scaley green arm, looked as if it had come down with a nasty brownish rash. It looped around Eryn's offending foot and sent her sprawling to the ground before lifting her into the air and shaking her upside down as if rifling her pockets. Her pendant fell to the ground along with the contents of her quiver, followed by her bow. Without hesitating, Eryn drew her blade and severed the root, tucking her head to brace for a hard landing. Instead, she landed softly in Rina's arms.

Eryn got her feet under her and pulled away. She'd looked foolish because she was having to try to do the job of her guardian as well as herself.

Eryn let Rina worry about the arrows, as she looked for her necklace. A streak of brown shot across Eryn's vision. She watched as a greasy-looking brown squirrel snagged her necklace off the ground and disappeared up a nearby dead tree. "No!" She raced after it, drawing her sword. "Give that back!" Goddess, she couldn't even keep the symbol of what she was supposed to achieve with Syrana.

From above her, the dire squirrel stuck its misshapen head out of the tree and yelled down at her, revealing a mouth full of uneven, razor-sharp teeth. The top half of one ear was missing and Eryn could just make out patches of missing fur where giant boils were coming to a head.

"What did it take?" Rina asked. When Eryn didn't answer, she said, "Just leave it. It's not worth a fight."

"It's important." Eryn didn't need to explain why. She could do it on her own.

The squirrel's eyes flashed, and for a moment, Eryn could have sworn it smiled before beginning to chirp in a boisterous, bleating fashion like a donkey giving birth. Eryn brought her hands to her ears trying to block the sound. She could feel her heart rate rising. It was the chick-a-dreads all over again.

Sure enough, like a tiny army called into battle, deformed squirrels popped out of the hallowed branches of the tree. They stared down with gleeful, beady eyes before they all began to chuck pieces of dead tree at her, cackling as much as yelling at her. The pieces of wood weren't so bad, it was the gooey, stringy, smelly bits that splattered and stuck to her gambeson and smelled all too similar to the rancid mouths of the chick-a-dreads.

She'd killed the birds; she could kill the squirrels. Eryn kicked the tree, which gave a satisfying crunch. They were destabilizing their home and she was more than happy to bring it down around their disintegrating little ears.

The squirrels' tone shifted from angry to scared. Yeah, I'll show you, Eryn thought, giving the tree another kick. She glanced down for half a second to see her progress before looking back up to see an entire sheet of dire squirrels falling at her. She squealed and retreated, but not in time to avoid the deluge of squirrels. They were all around her, biting and scratching, trying to get through her gambeson and cowl.

Eryn writhed, a moment of panic clouding her brain before instinct kicked in. She began to slice, feeling more than seeing the success of her blows. She could hear the twang of a bow being fired in rapid succession in the background and vaguely wondered if the stinging cuts reaching her flesh were from the squirrels or Rina's bad aim.

Eryn knew she was killing dire squirrels by the handful, but they just kept coming, raining down from the tree like she was harvesting hairy, moldy olives. She swung, cutting them out of the air when she could and trying to impale the ones that landed on her.

A hand grabbed the back of her gambeson, and Eryn was hauled back from the tree still swinging. Rina lunged past her, a lit torch in one hand and her spear in the other. The squirrel rain ceased as quickly as it had begun. Eryn saw a glint as the squirrel with one and a half ears scurried farther up the tree with her pendant. "It's getting away."

Rina's spear skewered the squirrel and the necklace in place. She grabbed the cord strung to the end of her spear and yanked, pulling the spearhead out of the tree and catching both it and the necklace as they fell. Rina turned the pendant over in her hand, examining it before giving it back silently. Eryn could almost hear her judgment. You're so full of yourself, you risked attracting real monsters to get your "I'm number one" coin, Eryn provided the words for Rina inside her head. Rina didn't say it, but Eryn couldn't help feeling she deserved it.

Eryn clipped the necklace back around her neck trying to get her head to clear. Her chest ached like her lungs and heart were trying to run loops around the Community. She couldn't make the world, nor the tips of her fingers, hold still. I'm fine, she repeated to herself over and over as she helped Rina retrieve her arrows, each one a perfect headshot.

Rina held up her torch. "We should move a bit away and make camp."

"No." Eryn's voice had an annoying shake. "We need to keep going. I'm fine."

"You're covered in blood, your gambeson is ripped, and we've been traveling for over a day and a half. If we're going to get back after three days, we need to be heading back anyway. We can take a shorter rest and have a long day tomorrow." Rina sounded obnoxiously calm and logical.

Eryn looked over her shoulder at the tree that still rippled and chirped with the fury of its hidden denizens. "We can't stop here."

"Good idea. We can move a bit away and make camp," Rina said, clearly coddling her.

Eryn sighed. She needed to admit she was in no state to keep going if she was going to get anywhere. The point was to find ichor, not to wander around haplessly, waiting for more to go wrong, while she tried to pull herself back together. "Yes," she said.

Rina took the lead in setting up the campsite. She got Eryn situated on her bedroll and all but told her to stay like a dog. This is her job, Eryn thought, trying to rationalize sitting and letting someone else take care of her.

By the time Eryn had stripped out of her gambeson and outer clothing, Rina was back with lukewarm, semi-reconstituted rations. She pulled ointment from her pack and set to medicating the tiny, stinging bite marks on Eryn's arms that were already swelling with pus. Rina had Eryn's arms wrapped and feeling almost normal by the time Eryn finished her meal. She was no longer shaking, but while her physical state had improved dramatically, her mental state was faring worse and worse.

Rina's silent work spoke depths of judgment to Eryn that echoed her own feelings of inadequacy. "Say something," she finally blurted.

"What would you like me to say?" Rina sounded like she sincerely just wanted to be told. She stopped repacking the medical supplies into her bag and took a seat on the bedroll in front of Eryn.

Eryn couldn't meet her eyes. Instead, she looked at her bandaged hands resting in her lap. "You think I am vapid, selfish, and a fraud." Eryn tried to keep the tears from her voice as much as her eyes.

Rina placed a finger on Eryn's trembling lips. "No. I think you're passionate and driven. I think that whatever happened to you on your first trip outside the dome is still with you, making you think you have something to prove."

"I'm through it, not over it." Eryn used Alba's words.

"Claine would laugh that I'm the one saying this, but sometimes being so focused on proving that you can do something is exactly what's keeping you from doing that thing. Eryn, you have nothing to prove, and you are not alone. I'm right here and I always will be. Just let me in."

Eryn lifted her gaze and stared into depthless purple eyes. For the first time in days, she let herself feel something. What rushed in wasn't the tears, the guilt, or the grief she had expected, but the desire and the longing she had been ignoring just as strongly.

Comfort, Rina had called it. She couldn't think of a better word for what she needed. What she wanted most right now, what she truly needed, was to see herself as worthy in the eyes of someone else. In Rina's eyes, she saw endless adoration.

Eryn leaned forward, capturing Rina's lips with her own, and felt Rina melt into the kiss.

"I want you so badly," Rina said as she made short work of removing Eryn's tunic and pants, her movements urgent, but careful. "You're so beautiful." She kissed each uncovered bit of skin, warming it as if fighting off a crippling chill Eryn hadn't realized she had.

Rina laid Eryn back on her bedroll, looking deeply into her eyes as if seeing her in a way no one else ever would. "I want to pleasure you," she said.

"Yes." Eryn groaned. She'd been propositioned many times in the last couple of years, but those had been about mutual enjoyment or because that's what one did at a party. She felt her body react to Rina's touch, begging for more. She wasn't sure how Rina knew exactly what to say, but every word did to her chest what Rina's touch was doing to her groin.

Eryn had expected her consent to send Rina straight between her legs. It was certainly how everyone else had done it. But Rina continued to kiss and stroke her stomach, her inner thighs, her breasts. She continued until Eryn ached for release so badly it was almost painful. She tipped Rina's face up toward her, her hand buried in Rina's short red hair, and saw the same need in Rina's eyes as she felt in every part of her body.

Rina nodded her understanding of Eryn's need. "Goddess, I don't think I've ever been this wet," Rina whispered as if the thought were both exhilarating and a little scary to her as well. She moved deftly between Eryn's legs, turning what had been the sensation of sharp aching into waves of pleasure.

Eryn lost herself in the feeling. For the first time in her life, let alone during sex, she wasn't thinking about what she still needed to do that day or the next. She was surprised she even had the brainpower to breathe and keep her heart beating.

Orgasms in the past had always been distinct events with a beginning and near immediate end, marking the end to a successful romp. Eryn wasn't sure the exact moment she started; all she knew was that it kept going. Between her legs, Rina groaned her own climax, pushing Eryn longer and harder.

"Goddess," Eryn said when she could take no more, pushing Rina away feebly. Rina smiled blissfully at her. She gave Eryn a soft kiss, more good night than postcoital, and tucked Eryn into her bedroll before undressing and climbing into her own bedroll.

She orgasmed with her clothes on, Eryn realized, exhaustion dragging her toward sleep. Had Rina even touched herself? The look on Rina's face left no question as to whether she had found release, but Eryn couldn't imagine how. She was just glad Rina had. She certainly deserved it after a performance like that.

Eryn slipped into sleep, her mind welcomely quiet.

❖

For several minutes, Rina lay on her bedroll staring at Eryn's peaceful, sleeping face, trying to reconcile the explosion of conflicting emotions that were wreaking havoc on her whole body.

The loudest part of her mind was running through her body screaming at the top of its lungs that Rina had just made her hero orgasm, that it had been a truly amazing orgasm, and that this was the greatest day of her life. It was making a list of everyone and everything it was thankful for because they had led her to this moment and prepared her to blow Eryn's mind.

Her body was fairly sure it agreed. She felt truly and deeply sated.

The problem was that the rest of her mind, the quieter and more rational part that typically ran her life hand in hand with frustration and ambition, wasn't so sure. She was a strong, independent woman, so why in the Dark Lands was her happiness and sense of self-worth so deeply tied to whether Eryn's mind was blown? A woman she had met only three days ago.

It had been easy to justify putting Eryn and her needs before Rina's own hunger, exhaustion, and pride. If Eryn didn't eat, drink, and sleep, she would die out here. The whispers of the shadows she encountered were very clear on the matter. The best way, possibly the only way, to get Eryn what she needed was to let Eryn think Rina was the one who needed food and water, even though her guardian body could go far longer than Eryn's without sustenance. She had to let Eryn think every choice was her own. After years living with Syrana, it wasn't too hard to understand how to work with someone who was driven, stubborn, and perhaps a little too smart for her own good.

Sacrificing her pride, Rina understood. What Rina didn't understand was the crushing feeling of inadequacy and worthlessness that engulfed her the night before when Eryn rejected her advances nor her elation at her success tonight. She'd literally orgasmed simply from bringing Eryn to climax.

And Syrana? Why in the Dark Lands wasn't she thinking about Syrana? Her name was near the top of the list of people to thank for teaching her what to do in bed, but that was it. Every time she tried to wonder what Syrana would think or if she would be mad that Rina had moved on so quickly, especially to the woman who hadn't saved Syrana, the loud part of her mind would remind her that this was what she and Syrana had been training each other for, to pleasure their hero.

I thought we did it because we loved each other, the quiet part of her mind objected.

Sure, sure, the loud part said, that's why you picked each other for practicing, but it was all to get to this moment.

Rina sank uncomfortably into sleep, the loud part of her mind reminding everyone that tomorrow was another day, another chance to prove her worth to her hero.

Rina woke a few hours later. She would sleep longer and nap in the weeks between missions and thus didn't need as much during the time outside the dome. She could manage with even less sleep with the knowledge that they would only be out here another day. She packed, built a fire, and made the last of the eggs in silence, still trying to understand why even the thought of Eryn made her heart flutter.

The sight of Eryn coming out of their tent, her formerly sex-tousled blond hair pulled back into a braid, made Rina's breath catch. She held out the eggs. Last night had been great, now she just needed to follow it up with a productive day that would make Eryn feel accomplished, and they could go back home having achieved everything the head priest had said, "acclimation, learning the Dark Lands, learning themselves and each other."

The look of unsatisfied frustration on Eryn's face was like a physical pain to Rina. She wanted to wipe it away the way she would a tear or smudge of dirt. Eryn didn't want to return to the Community empty-handed. If only Rina could do something to help, but where Eryn could see ichor and auras, Rina could only see shadows. Within the Community, shadows couldn't take a corporeal form, so yesterday was Rina's first time experiencing shadows as dark, jagged humanoid shapes watching and whispering to her rather than simply a hissing voice at her ear.

An idea blossomed in Rina. She paused in packing and turned to Eryn, trying not to let the excitement of the loud voice in her head direct her tone. "If an aura finds ichor, it heads toward the dome to find a hero to lead to that ichor, right?"

"Yeah, what's your point?" Eryn said around a mouthful of egg.

"So, if you ever see an aura heading toward the dome, not leading a hero back home, you intercept it so it can guide you to the ichor, right?"

"Yes."

"So hypothetically, even though ichor isn't usually found this close to the dome, an aura could be."

Rina watched the seed take root in Eryn's mind. "I've been looking for the wrong thing." Egg fell from her open mouth and the loud voice in Rina's head made sure to aww at how cute it was. "I just need to find the most likely path to see an aura."

"I've seen several jutting peaks. I could belay you to the top and you could probably see for miles."

"If I see an aura, we could follow it and, imbued with ichor, we'd be able to get home before Holden's deadline. And if I don't, we can feel confident that we wouldn't have found ichor if we had pushed on. Brilliant!" Rina couldn't tell if Eryn's last word had been meant about Rina or herself, but the excitement on her face was what Rina had been aiming for, not credit. Credit, Rina had learned, was a rather frivolous battle around people like Syrana and Claine. She didn't imagine that Eryn would be much different.

It took less than an hour to find a suitable peak, a curving jut of dense, white stone that looked more like a crooked finger than a cliff.

Eryn scaled the rock with ease. The loud part of Rina thrilled at the confidence Eryn placed in the fact that Rina would not let her fall. The quieter part simply enjoyed watching muscle, bone, and equipment work in perfect harmony. Even without the part of her mind that reveled in Eryn's body no matter what it was doing, Rina still found herself appreciating it as she would a work of art.

The past two days, Eryn had been strong and capable, but she had been a cart without wheels, driving her axle into the dirt and leaving a trench in her wake. Her achievements were perhaps even more impressive for the fact that she had accomplished them having come out of an induced coma after narrowly avoiding death. How much better could they have done if Eryn had been willing to stop long enough for Rina to put wheels on her metaphorical cart?

Looking at Eryn surveying their surroundings from above, all parts of Rina's mind agreed: Eryn had her wheels back.

Eryn looked displeased but not defeated as she rappelled. "I guess it's time. I didn't see any auras, but I could see a couple of hero-guardian pairs and they are several hours' walk closer to returning than us. We should keep a good clip to try to catch up."

Rina nodded. She kept it to herself that her body was designed to try to keep up with Eryn when she was suffused with ichor and was not the limiting factor in their pair. It was not a helpful statement. "I will match your pace."

Craggy, uneven terrain gave way to a sprawling field of purple flowers. Rina and Eryn wrapped their mouths and noses in moist scarves, moving quickly through the clusters of purple bell-shaped, noxious fumegloves that seemed to glow in the dim lighting. It was safer to step on them than any of the other flora. Thistles reached for their gambesons hoping to leave seeds that would burrow through their clothing and into their skin. Fire moss threatened to combust with the slightest of pressure.

As they moved deeper into sparce forest once more, Rina felt a prickle of awareness wash over her. It wasn't the immediate, hair standing on end sensation of an imminent threat, but a slow rise in Rina's internal alarm. She moved forward from being at Eryn's heel to in line with her and gave her a questioning look.

"They've been stalking us since before the flower field," Eryn said without Rina saying a thing. Rina couldn't help but be impressed. She felt the familiar thrill of a challenge. If she wanted to keep up with Eryn, she was going to have to be more observant, something she'd never thought was a problem. Eryn spoke casually as if addressing what they should have for dinner. "They're slowly gaining in number, so we might as well deal with them now." She pointed off to the right. "Go over there, like you're relieving yourself. They won't come near while we are together until there are enough of them to be a true threat."

Rina pushed down the loud voice that told her Eryn needed her close and followed directions. She gripped her spear, ready to throw it at the first monster to show itself. Stationed in a bloodberry bush, she crouched and waited. Much as the loud voice told her Eryn needed protection, the logical side was confident what Eryn actually needed was Rina to trust her and to have her back, not run in and try to be her front, side, and back all at the same time.

Five creatures slunk from the underbrush, but Rina could see far more beady eyes staring hungrily from the bushes. The five dire dogs advanced slowly toward Eryn's turned back, brown-tinged saliva dripping from the hooked teeth that jutted up into their ragged lips and down from their lower jaws beneath their wiry chins. Their ribs were sharp and defined and with each exhale, their chests contracted until Rina could see the outline of their organs throbbing inside the cage of their ribs, like a macabre accordion.

Eryn took five more steps as if oblivious to the approaching dogs. They were getting so close, the loud voice in her head yelled for Rina to just throw her spear already and run to Eryn's rescue. She couldn't possibly know how many there were or how close.

Just as Rina's logical voice was losing the argument, Eryn spun on her heel, drawing her bow, and sent three successive shots into the lead dire dog, not killing it, but pinning to it the ground. She walked directly over to its yelping body amidst the other four dire dogs as if they weren't all within biting distance and sliced its head off with a single, clean blow. The dogs ran.

Rina rejoined Eryn as she wiped her blade and returned it to its sheath. She looked proud, and Rina saw no reason she shouldn't be. With as many dogs as had gathered, she and Eryn would have won, but probably not unscathed. Eryn looked over at Rina's face and chuckled. "Nothing in the Dark Lands wants to die. Sometimes they just need to be reminded of that fact."

"Or promised the alternative," Rina said. Eryn's confidence and swagger washed over Rina like a warm breeze. It was so familiar.

Memories of Syrana rose, smirking at her own success and saying, "beat that," like she actually wanted Rina to beat it so the game wouldn't end. Emotion boiled up from the bottles Rina buried deep inside until she felt she would explode. The hardest part was not knowing if the explosion would lead to passionate kisses promising so much more or to blubbering sobs of guilt, regret, and loneliness. She buried the feelings once more. There would be time for grieving when they weren't in the Dark Lands, surrounded by monsters.

The sight of the dome as they crested a final hill, like an opaque blue shell, nearly brought tears to Rina's eyes. Home. She didn't think she'd ever wanted to collapse into bed so badly. She imagined blowing out her unsettling and contradictory thoughts like the flame of a candle and finally having a few hours of peace.

Your home will be cold and empty. A shadow spoke from against the tree Rina and Eryn were skirting. In place of feet, its body came to a single ragged point that floated a few inches above the ground. Its head was the shape of a black flame that shifted in the Dark Lands' false wind. *There is no peace for you.* Rina ignored it, wishing she could ignore the hollowness its words brought.

Passing through the dome felt like a religious experience. Rina hadn't noticed the chill of the Dark Lands until her skin was bathed in the warmth of the Community. The flower field had felt garish and out of place outside the dome, but inside, Rina felt like she was experiencing color for the first time. It was alive and it didn't want to kill her. How had she always taken that for granted?

Rina and Eryn reported to healers' hall to be checked for parasites and treated for any lasting injuries. Rina was glad to see the squirrel bite marks had almost healed on Eryn's arms and shoulders and took full advantage of the chance to watch Eryn strip for her checkup.

Eryn left the hall with a simple "see you in three weeks." Rina stuffed down the ache in her heart at the flippant words to join so many other roiling thoughts and emotions. The only thing she wanted to feel was her bone-deep, physical, mental, and emotional exhaustion.

Rina almost missed the woman waiting in her sitting room. The shadow had been wrong on that one, Rina thought blandly. Her home wasn't empty. She turned to Claine. If she asked her to train, Rina was sure she'd laugh in Claine's face.

"How was your first mission?" Claine asked.

Rina shrugged. She needed a lot more time to process before she was ready to answer that question.

"Did any shadows speak to you?" There was something different in Claine's tone. In the past, she'd always asked this question with a tone that scowled so that her face didn't have to. For the first time, it sounded like Claine truly wanted to know, as if she would decide her next move based on Rina's answer rather than just waiting for confirmation of her preconceived notions.

A lantern flickered on in Rina's mind, pushing the tiredness back with vicious insistence. She'll take Eryn away from you, Rina's mind screamed. Lie!

Rina had not only listened to shadows but had made decisions based on what they said. She'd pushed for breaks, eating, drinking, and stopping based on the whispers. She'd avoided a hive of dire bees by listening to a shadow inform her that Eryn would be stung to death. She'd used a well-timed bathroom break to redirect them away from a rockfall. Sure, shadows had told her bad things that had been lies as well as things that had come true, everything from *she'll reject you* to *your dinner is going to suck*. They'd also insisted many times what Rina couldn't deny—*she thinks you are an incompetent twit*. But listening had saved her and Eryn when it mattered.

All that matters is Eryn and the Community, Rina thought. There was only one correct answer. Only one that protected what mattered.

Rina took a deep breath and let the memory of Eryn drifting off to sleep post-orgasm fill her mind. She smiled with all the pride of that moment and said, "I didn't listen."

For a moment, Claine stood silently as if waiting for the other shoe to drop. She doesn't believe me, Rina thought with a sinking heart.

Claine's stony expression shattered. Her smile created creases in her skin that were entirely foreign. Pride warmed her cheeks and relief seemed to lift her entire body. She flung her arms out, making Rina jump, before pulling her into a full body embrace. "I'm so proud of you, Rina."

Rina sank into the hug. It brought back memories of childhood, before Rina's belief in shadows had created a yawning chasm between herself and her mentor, back when Claine still believed she could mold Rina into her vision of a perfect guardian. She could remember being small and scared, hurt, or angry. She'd fallen during training, or had a fight with Syrana, or been scared by the words of a shadow. Claine had taken her into her arms and told her that everything would be okay, and Rina had believed her.

In this moment she didn't care that it was all based on a lie. She needed someone to hold her and tell her that she had done something right and that everything would be okay.

"You must be exhausted," Claine said.

Rina nodded and mumbled agreement into Claine's shoulder. She could hear Claine's smile in her voice as she petted Rina's hair. "Let's get you to bed." Claine led Rina to bed, half hugging, half guiding her. In a whisper, she sang one of the lullabies she had abandoned over a decade ago when it only served to spark their arguments about whether the glory of the Community should really be used as a distraction from listening to shadows. Claine tucked Rina into bed. She was asleep before Claine left.

JENNIFER KARTER

CHAPTER FOUR

Guilt and Closure

All the other heroes in Eryn's cohort were asleep by the time she and Rina finished with the healers. She felt oddly lonely going home on her own even though she'd been doing it for the last three years since her cohort moved out of the dorms. She could feel exhaustion lapping at her heels, but it was far from reaching her brain.

In bed, her thoughts turned unbidden to Rina. She probably should have said more to her than "see you in three weeks." She could have at least said thank you. She supposed Rina had just been doing her job, but Eryn thanked the laborers who did maintenance on her home and even the mountain folk if she passed them on their return from outside the dome to the muckworks. They were just doing their job, but it felt like part of who she was to thank them for the ways they gave to the Community, so why not Rina? Why not all guardians?

Then again, how well had Rina done her job? It wasn't like she'd actually defended her from anything. She hadn't fought any of the shadows or the monsters, except the squirrels.

"I'm right here and I always will be. Just let me in." Rina's words played again in Eryn's head.

"She defended me from myself," Eryn said to the empty room. And wasn't that what she'd done with food, water, and rest? "I was the biggest threat we faced." Eryn laughed at her own mix of ego and humility. She needed to let the realization humble her. She could have caused them both to die out there if Rina hadn't helped her get her head on straight and taken care of her until she did.

"I'll thank her." She would get another chance in three weeks and again every month after that for the next ten years. She fell asleep to the thought of how good Rina had looked between her legs. She would definitely have to thank Rina for orgasms like that.

Eryn woke long after dawn, still feeling drained. She pushed through her morning exercise routine regardless, missing breakfast. After securing a muffin from the hero cafeteria, she wandered over to her cohort's common room.

The heroes inside were strewn across the couches, cushions, and floor like discarded pieces of clothing, chatting. Two were playing a half-hearted game of Ichor and Shadows, rolling their marbles to try to knock the golden marbles into the center circle and the black marbles out of the ring. One swore as his marble sailed past the golden marble he'd been aiming at and under a couch. He looked up as he did so and bit back whatever he'd been about to say, instead saying somewhere between a statement and a question, "Eryn."

The chatting ceased as Eryn stepped the rest of the way into the room. She rarely graced them with her presence, but they always took her arrival as if they understood that she did so to be part of the team. They seemed to realize that the duration of holding still and the languid socialization that the common room required grated on her, so being there was a strong statement of her desire to be with them.

"We were just talking about our first times outside the dome," Kalia said before grimacing. "Our first missions."

The room was silent again for a long moment. They know I failed on my first trip outside, Eryn thought. She could see a couple of unhealed scrapes and bruises around the room, but everyone else had come back alive with a living guardian. Each of them would remember this as their first real experience. She would remember and have to live with her failure forever.

Henk broke the silence. He gave Eryn his patent charming smile laced with sympathy. "We heard what happened. I'm sorry, Eryn."

Eryn waved her hand the way she did when she fell and someone offered her assistance. She hadn't come here for sympathy; she'd come here for distraction and to not be alone. "Whose turn was it? I didn't mean to interrupt."

The heroes looked around at each other for a moment, clearly trying to come up with an answer. Eryn had a strong feeling they hadn't been doing anything so structured as taking turns.

"Mine," Kalia said and launched into a story about dire rabbits, sparing no gory detail. A couple of people made room for Eryn on the long wraparound couch, and Eryn sank into it gratefully. Normally, she claimed the cushy chair by the door, so she could slip out when the need to do something put her nerves on end. For the first time in a long time, the disconcerting nag in her gut didn't feel like the need to do something, which only made her more confused. Nothing drove her up the wall more than an emotion she didn't have an explanation for.

Storytelling passed around the circle as they had done so many times in lessons. When it was Eryn's turn, she recounted the interaction with the dire dogs and her peers were suitably impressed. Memories of her first trip pressed at her, demanding recognition and release. Even the healers and Holden hadn't asked her for details. To recount it would be to relive it, and Eryn was far from ready for that. She remembered the way she'd shaken after the squirrels, the way she couldn't stop shaking until Rina chased away the chill with kisses.

"It's unfortunate you only got three days," Nim said. He continued despite the looks his peers flashed him. "If anyone was going to find ichor on the first mission, it was you."

"Well, I…" Eryn tried to think of something to say that might deflect her feelings as much as his statement. Pointing out that no one had found ichor on their first mission didn't feel helpful, it felt like an excuse. "I got as far as I could, climbed to get the best vantage point available, and then looked for auras. It gave me the best chance of finding ichor even with only three days."

For a moment her peers stared at her in awe. After a beat, they nodded like they were filing this away for later. "Brilliant," Kalia said.

Except it was Rina's idea. In the moment, it had felt like her epiphany, but it had been like the food, water, and rest. It had been the same as stopping to camp a short distance from the squirrels. Rina had come up with it and let Eryn think it was her decision. She was the worst guardian and yet she'd out-thought Eryn numerous times.

The hero to Eryn's left didn't let the silence hang long before launching into his own series of anecdotes. "It was nice to get out there and finally use what we've been learning. Oh, and have some of that guardian sex the heroes all talk about. Pretty good, am I right?"

Around the room, heroes pursed their lips and nodded, each lost for a moment in reliving their nights outside the dome. The stories began to flow, their previous order and structure falling by the wayside as each story escalated in a lewd competition of retelling. After several minutes, the group turned to the only quiet person in their midst. "How about you, Eryn?"

Eryn hadn't planned to share, not from any prudishness but the time she spent with Rina between her legs, her kisses and caresses, felt personal and intimate. "Um, yeah, my guardian and I didn't do anything the first night and the second she went down on me. It was really good." Really good did nothing to capture what it had felt like. The other heroes had said things like explosive, mind blowing, and grip-the-bedroll good. It had been all that but so much more. Those were physical, the sensations of sex, but what had made it "really good" had been the mental and emotional. Her head, heart, and groin seemed to be on the same page for perhaps the first time in her life, each fulfilled without having to ignore the other two.

Her peers gave her a look like they'd just watched her bite into an apple and come away with half a worm dangling from the bite hole. "That sucks," Nim said. "I suppose your guardian is the worst guardian, but you deserve better."

"You need to demand better," Henk said. He looked ready to go hunt down Eryn's guardian and give her a lecture himself. All Eryn need do was ask and it would be done.

"Yeah, I'd be pissed if sex with my guardian wasn't some of the best I've ever had," Nim said.

"But your guardian is a woman," Lairdin objected. He and Nim were as close to a couple as active heroes got. They couldn't get married until they retired from ichor missions in ten years, but that didn't do anything to stop either promiscuity or jealousy. Eryn wouldn't be surprised if they broke up long before retiring. Heroes hardly ever married each other. Their personalities simply weren't compatible for settling down together.

"So? Gender doesn't affect how good someone is at a blow job." Nim shrugged. The spark in his eyes told Eryn exactly what he was angling for.

Lairdin huffed, annoyed, but not truly put off. Like any hero, he knew a challenge when he heard one. "Seems like I'm going to have to show you what good really feels like."

Eryn watched as heroes around the room began giving each other what she thought of as the look of impending debauchery. She supposed the stories were an obvious preamble, but all she could think about was whether she'd been wrong to turn Rina down that first night. Not wrong because she'd missed the fun. Wrong because how could Rina have taken that as anything but a rejection of what everyone thought was her duty and therefore a rejection of her personally? When she added it to the list of other things she'd done wrong, debauchery was the last thing on her mind.

Eryn rose from the couch, gave her peers a nod, and slipped out. It was far from her first graceful exit as things started to tip toward prurience. She imagined they had all come to expect it.

Her time in the common room had done nothing for the nagging feeling in her gut, so she fell back on what she supposed had often been as much an act of escapism as duty and love: training.

Once in a training room, Eryn wound the thrower, drew a wooden sword from the rack, and took up position on the other side of the room. As the first rubber ball was lobbed at her, Eryn tried to clear her head and sink into the rhythm, letting her reflexes guide her. She smashed ball after ball until sweat streamed down her face and her arms ached, but it wasn't enough. She'd thought each ball would feel less like a chick-a-dread, but instead, every miss felt like an immutable defeat. With each, she berated herself for all the ways she should have hit it, which only decreased her focus on the next ball.

A soft knock at the door drew Eryn's attention away from her most recent round of self-criticism. Holden stood in the open doorway watching her. "First day back and already training. I would expect nothing less." He smiled at her in the way she'd always considered fatherly. She didn't have parents like kids from other castes, not even a mentor like guardians. Many of her trainers through the years had attempted to take her under their wing and claim her as their own. But Holden was the closest, mainly from his own persistence.

He pointed to the thresher setup at the other end of the room. "Care for a round?"

Eryn smiled, not particularly for joy or excitement, but the comfort of reliability. At this point, their games of thresher were as much a ritual as a method of training. She traded in her wooden sword for two small bats, each vaguely dagger-sized while he grabbed his preferred single scimitar-shaped bat. They took up positions on either side of the thresher column and rotated the pegs and rods, each on their own barring, so they alternated between Eryn's side and Holden's. The winner was the one who could outlast their opponent before becoming overwhelmed with pegs on their side. Holden counted down, their bats becoming a blur as he reached zero.

Thresher was a game of strength and speed, but most players leaned into one or the other. Holden was a strength player. He would wear out his opponent with jarring blows deflected by their bat or their body. Eryn relied on speed. If she could dodge a peg rather than hit it, she could spend her swing sending a shorter, hard-to-reach peg at Holden.

For the past ten years, Holden had used thresher as an opportunity to train Eryn, keep himself in shape, and attempt to direct Eryn onto his path for her future. He'd tell her about his council meetings and the politics of the Community, seeking her advice in a poorly veiled attempt to test her diplomacy. He'd say, "When you're head hero, you'll need to know how to understand what people want and show them that your plan gives it to them." He often asked her about her impressions of what the other castes wanted and needed based on her time with them.

Personally, Eryn thought being head hero sounded like the most boring job imaginable. She had no interest in drinking liqueurs, arguing with people in stuffy meetings, and training a protégé rather than spending her retirement training the entire next generation of heroes and going out with mountain folk caravans as often as possible. Eryn enjoyed spending time with the other castes, but she didn't do it to learn how to manipulate them. She just enjoyed serving the Community in their way, side by side with them.

"So, what happened on your first trip outside the dome?" Holden said as he smacked a peg with the full power of his swing.

Eryn was forced to step back and give Holden the benefit of a moment with an absent opponent. Instead of launching into a series of moves, Holden embraced the pause.

Eryn's breath came in gasps and her heart was racing faster than her exertion could account for. She gripped her bats to try to keep her hands from shaking. *What is wrong with me?*

Um, perhaps that you had a traumatic experience that led to someone's death and thus far you've pretended it didn't happen. The voice in Eryn's head was half Alba's and half her own sarcastic voice.

I can't keep pretending it didn't happen, Eryn thought. Holden's patient look said maybe he agreed. He had provided her with a place to go over it without being overwhelmed by it. The bats in her hands would hide the shaking and avoiding Holden's strikes would force her to focus on him rather than her story.

Eryn launched herself back into the game and into her story. With each smack of her bat, Eryn felt the strain slip from her body. The words tumbled out as fast as the blur of her bats.

When Eryn had finished her story, Holden stepped back and dropped his bat, conceding the game. His breathing was ragged, and his face was flushed. Nearly all the pegs were on his side. Eryn realized without much satisfaction that she had probably just played her best game of thresher. She hadn't cared about the game; she'd just wanted it all to be over.

"You never cease to impress me, Eryn," Holden said, bending over to rest his hands on his knees. "You fought shadows you couldn't see, rescued your guardian, and then dragged her back here all while fighting monsters by yourself. Most heroes would have left when their guardian warned them to run. You are truly one of a kind. It really is an injustice that your reward is to have the worst guardian in the cohort, with her score, perhaps the worst guardian period."

He sidestepped the thresher column and placed a hand on Eryn's shoulder. "You should be proud of yourself. You will do great things even if they aren't all the things you envisioned for yourself." He gave her shoulder one last squeeze before leaving her to her training.

Eryn stood for a long moment trying to rally her thoughts and emotions onto the same team. She should be relieved to have it off her chest, to be told to be proud of herself, but she wasn't.

Holden, who had always tried so hard to be her mentor, had helped, but who she really needed was the woman who had never tried to be her mentor but had always been her guide.

Eryn had been seven the first time she was sent to the farmer caste to help in the fields. It was the third time she'd lost herself so thoroughly in the excitement and power of a sparring match as to send her opponent to the healers. Her instructors said she needed a place to get out her energy, but Eryn knew what it was—punishment. She was a hero. To dig in the dirt was humiliating.

For hours, she'd stabbed her mattock into the ground, anger guiding each blow. Even after the dome had turned to dusk and the farmers called it a day, Eryn continued to smash the dirt beneath her feet. If she couldn't do this task better than the farmers, she would do it longer.

It wasn't a farmer who eventually took the mattock from Eryn's exhausted hands, but a farmer's wife, a childrearer by the name of Alba. She sat Eryn down on a stump at the edge of the field and bandaged her hands while Eryn mumbled about the stupid tool and the stupid fields and the stupid dirt.

"You think pretty highly of yourself, don't you? You think you are above this work?" Alba said. She'd been the first person to truly call Eryn out on her ego.

"I'm a hero." It was the only answer Eryn thought she needed.

"So?"

"So, I'm going to bring ichor back to the Community. Without heroes there wouldn't be a Community, and I'm the best hero in my cohort. My instructors say I'm the best they've ever seen." She'd only been tallying points for a year and a half and already outshone all her peers by leaps and bounds.

"I see," Alba said, her expression barely hiding her amusement.

Eryn didn't see anything in her statement that was funny. "What?"

"And who will grow the food you eat so that you can search for ichor?"

"Farmers." Everyone knew farming was important, just not as important.

"And from whose breasts did you get the food you needed before you could eat?" Alba ran a hand across her chest.

"You?"

Alba laughed. "Yes, probably me and many other childrearers. Who excavates the materials for your weapons? Who crafts them?

Who will heal your wounds when you return with or without ichor? Who will bind you to your guardian? And who will protect you every moment of their life to make sure you achieve your high potential?"

Eryn remembered sitting on that stump for several minutes, sullenness and pride warring with the beginnings of a deeper understanding and humility. Alba allowed the silence to stretch between them as she had done during many similar conversations over the last decade.

"Everyone serves the Community," Eryn eventually said. It was a mantra in the Community, but Eryn had always viewed it from the perspective that the Community was the most important thing, and everyone should dedicate themselves to it. She'd never thought of it from the other side. Everyone had an essential role in the success and survival of the Community. She wasn't quite ready to accept the idea that everyone served the Community equally, but she was willing to accept that without them, she couldn't serve.

"Yes, but, Eryn, that's only part of it. Everyone *is* the Community. The Community isn't a thing. The Community is the people. One day when you're fighting monsters and searching for ichor, you won't be doing it for the dome, you'll be doing it for the people who live inside the dome. You'll be serving them."

Eryn and Alba sat in silence for another minute before Eryn said the only thing she could think of: "Thank you."

Over the next twelve years, Eryn went back to the farmers and the other castes while her peers worked on skills she had already mastered or goofed off in their free time. She fixed houses with the laborers, learned to pull calves with the pastorals, and hauled machine parts for the tinkerers. She served the Community, and everyone was the Community.

Eryn strolled down the main road of the housing district, smiling and waving at the people who greeted her. She always enjoyed the walk to Alba's home, taking in the houses with their unique artwork. Along the side of each home were vertical strips of artwork created by generations of inhabitants joining the household. With each marriage and adoption, the oldest painted strip was painted over and provided as a canvas for the newest member of the household. The best strips, in Eryn's opinion, were the ones that started with toddler handprints and finger paintings at the bottom and progressed through the imaginings of childhood, the trials and triumphs of adulthood, and the final years of being an elder. Each house held hundreds of years of history. The hero quarter had its own charms and traditions, but Eryn's simple home paled in comparison.

Eryn climbed the steps onto Alba's porch with its two full-sized and two child-sized rocking chairs. She knocked, anxiety bubbling within her. Visits with Alba were always transformative, a refuge where Eryn could drop her facade and confront her deepest emotions. Today was no different, and tears threatened to spill before Alba even opened the door.

"Peyna, stop pestering your brother. If you need something to do, you can set the table," Alba called into the house, as the door swung open.

Alba's eyes widened momentarily at the sight of Eryn before she enveloped her in a warm hug. "I'm so happy to see you, so happy you are okay. I went back to healers' hall, and they said you'd already left."

The tears that had been pricking at Eryn's eyes turned into an uncontrollable flow as relief cascaded from Alba to her. Eryn buried her face in Alba's shoulder, hoping her vulnerability would remain unseen by others. This wasn't the composed image she usually projected.

Alba ushered her in, sending Peyna to prepare tea for them both. They sat in silence on Alba's couch, Eryn wavering between wishing she could just turn off her childish tears and longing to find solace once more in the comforting embrace of Alba's shoulder until the emptiness caved in on itself. Instead, they sat there, Eryn wiping her nose on the back of her hand, struggling to find a starting point. Alba didn't offer her a handkerchief. She'd once told Eryn that they stopped tears and tears were a good thing.

When the tea arrived, giving Eryn something in her lap to look at besides her snotty hands, Alba gently suggested, "Why don't you start at the beginning."

Eryn managed a mirthless chuckle, amazed at how well Alba understood her thoughts. So, Eryn began at the beginning, how great Choosing Day had felt, like Syrana was her destiny incarnate. The foresight and Syrana's gift of the necklace. She told her about the fight with the shadows, but this time she didn't hold back her fear, confusion, and desperation. Each emotion surged within her, but alongside them, she found clarity to understand them, to give them a voice, and to give them a reason.

"I feel like I failed. This was supposed to be the culmination. Everything was right until it all went so, so wrong. And then I carried it with me on the second trip and I don't know how I'm ever going to stop. And thank the Goddess for my guardian, my second guardian or I might have made everything go wrong again. I just…what did I do wrong?" Eryn's voice cracked, her tears flowing anew.

Alba's voice had its ever calm, reflective tone. "What would you have done differently?"

"So, you're saying this is my fault. That I could have done something differently and I don't know, I have to learn from it?" Eryn understood Alba's question as an invitation to be vulnerable, but all she felt was defensive.

"Who said anything about fault?" Alba sounded almost frustratingly calm.

"I'm supposed to say there's nothing I could have done? I fought shadows I couldn't see, and monsters by myself, and tried to save my guardian and it wasn't enough and that's not my fault. You're saying it's not my fault."

"Who said anything about fault?"

Eryn's voice cracked as she said, "I did! I want to know if this is my fault. I want to know how I should feel. I want to know if I ruined my entire future and I want to know if I'm a terrible person because a woman is dead and I'm grieving my lost potential!" A new bout of tears flowed down Eryn's cheeks.

Alba set their tea aside and took Eryn into her arms once more, letting her cry until the sobs turned to soft, ragged inhales. "You are not a terrible person. You are grieving, and unfortunately that means there isn't a way you *should* feel. You are allowed to feel many things and to grieve many things without one invalidating any others. Your responsibility lies in acknowledging and embracing your emotions, not denying them." She gave Eryn a look that told her Alba knew this was exactly what she'd been trying to do.

Eryn searched Alba's eyes, seeing the unwavering calmness and acceptance that had always characterized their connection. It was a look that conveyed both pride and recognition, affirming that Eryn neither needed nor lacked Alba's approval. It invited Eryn to continue the conversation or conclude it as she saw fit.

"What do I do?"

"You've told me what felt wrong. Carrying it with you, not grieving your first guardian's death, and being so focused on the future instead of the past or the present. What feels right?"

Eryn released a long breath. She wanted to pretend none of this had happened at all. But wishing that didn't feel right. It wasn't just ignoring reality; it was rewriting it in a way that overwrote her first guardian's life and death. "What feels right is honoring my first guardian's sacrifice, her lost potential, not mine."

"Then it sounds like you know exactly what to do." Alba gave Eryn one of her signature smiles.

"Thank you." Eryn ended their conversation. She did indeed know what she needed to do next.

"Stay for dinner?" Alba said, handing her a handkerchief.

"That would be lovely. Thanks."

❖

"Smoke?" Rina woke to the smell of stove fire and breakfast. A rush of affection washed over her before she remembered that it wasn't Syrana in the kitchen making them breakfast. It would never be Syrana making them breakfast.

Your house is burning down.

A physical, sucking feeling in her gut barely left her with enough brain power to register the shadow's lie. Her mouth watered at the aroma of food, and it didn't matter who had cooked what, she needed to eat now! She threw on clothing, whatever she could reach, and followed the scent of food as if it had physically latched onto her nose and was reeling her in.

In her kitchen, she found Claine filling two plates with her famous veggie scramble. It wasn't famous for its deliciousness but for its reliability. If Claine was cooking, they were eating a veggie scramble. As a child, Rina had always groaned at the repetition, glad that most of her meals were prepared in the garrison cafeteria or by Keddeth. Now, her stomach did the groaning. It didn't care if Claine was serving gruel.

One of the plates was the correct size for a meal. The other looked like Claine had smashed the contents of a stockpot down hard enough that she could flip it upside down and leave behind a perfect tower of steaming food. Claine laid the tower of food in front of Rina. The amused smile on Claine's face was the same one Rina received the first time she tried to hide a hangover from Claine. Yes, she was amused at Rina's pain, but because she could remember being in Rina's exact same place thirty years before.

"You'll learn to stop by the cafeteria after each mission and set food to slow cook before going to bed. Or butter up your mentor." Claine's smile twisted upward and grew as Rina mumbled her thanks through mouthfuls of food.

"I expected to be hungry," she garbled, "but I didn't expect to be *this* hungry."

"You slept through an entire day," Claine said matter-of-factly.

"What?" She'd been tired, but surely not that tired.

"You'll get used to it." Claine paused, picking at her food with uncharacteristic hesitance. "There's a lot about being a guardian I didn't teach you. The practical stuff. By the time it would have been useful, I didn't think you would have a hero. I'm sorry. It wasn't fair for me to send you unprepared. I should have done better."

Claine paused, as if waiting for Rina to turn it into a fight. Rina supposed it wasn't an unreasonable assumption given their relationship over the last few years. They focused on training and avoided anything related to "should." It had been a long time since either had said "I'm sorry."

At the moment, Rina had negative interest in a fight. In addition to the activity of talking taking her away from eating, Rina really didn't want to break the burgeoning thing building between them. It felt fragile and precious. Rina took advantage of her mouthful of food to mumble something purposefully unintelligible in a tone that conveyed acceptance of Claine's apology.

Claine's smile was relieved. She retrieved Rina's uniform from where it hung on the back of the door. "I also washed and pressed your uniform while you were gone. We can go to the ceremony together."

It took Rina a moment to understand. With the day of sleeping, it had been a week since Syrana's death. Her funeral would be today. Rina would have been able to hold back the tears if not for the look of pure empathy Claine gave her. Rina wanted to imagine that no one understood her pain and her loss, but it was a self-serving lie, and it wasn't even that self-serving. Claine had been almost as much of a mother figure to Syrana as she was to Rina. If she could accept Claine's pain, she could accept her support as well. Rina stood from the table and buried her face in Claine's shoulder once more, finally letting the pent-up sorrow flow freely.

They finished breakfast in silence.

Keddeth was already in the chapel when Rina and Claine arrived. His eyes were puffy and the whites around his purple irises were more red than white. He greeted both with a painfully tight hug as if afraid to let go. After each lit a candle and prayed to the Goddess, a priest led them from the nave to an auxiliary chamber where Syrana's shroud had been prepared. The thin linen fabric was woven back and forth across a giant slab, presenting the entire surface area for decoration. Around the slab, cushions were set on the ground for mourners. Rina, Claine, and Keddeth each took an offered charcoal pencil, found a cushion, and began to write.

The words poured out of Rina. She couldn't wrap who Syrana was to her into a single word, but here she didn't have to. She would run out of time before she ran out of words.

Rina wrote until her hand ached. Stories of love, adventure, and childhood filled the layers of the shroud. These were the ways Syrana had touched her life and thus would never be forgotten.

Other guardians filtered into and out of the room as the day passed by, adding their own candles to the nave and anecdotes to the shroud. Rina glanced up at each, wanting them to know her pain, but also wanting to receive and recognize theirs.

For a moment, the constant scratching of charcoal over linen halted around the room. Rina looked up to see Eryn give the collection of guardians a sympathetic nod, accept charcoal from the priest, and take a seat next to the slab. Her pencil was the only sound in the room for a long moment aside from the breathing of nearly two dozen guardians and a single priest. Several lines later, Eryn glanced up, smiled at the group again as if to reassure them that she was indeed in the right place, and went back to writing.

Around the room, guardians gave each other bewildered looks before going back to their remembrances. Rina had only been to a few funerals in her life, all them guardians, and all of them attended only by guardians. As a rule, guardians didn't interact with the other castes much. Even heroes who had served with their guardian for a decade rarely attended their guardian's funeral, and Eryn had known Syrana for a day.

The muscles in Rina's legs twitched with the desire to rise, to rush to Eryn and embrace her. She wanted to thank her, praise her, admire her. But her mind quickly snuffed the flame growing in her heart. How dare she be here? Rina couldn't quite say that Eryn had caused Syrana's death, but she certainly hadn't saved her. She had known her for one day, watched her die, and then thought it was appropriate to write her remembrances on Syrana's shroud. What did she even have to write about? Sorry I let you die?

A gentle elbow in her side interrupted Rina's glaring. She glanced over at Claine, barely fighting the urge to growl at her. "What?" she whispered.

Instead of answering, Claine took Rina's right hand in her own and slowly pried the broken charcoal pencil from her grip. She handed Rina her own pencil and motioned back at the shroud before rising and trading the broken pencil for a new one.

Rina's face burned with embarrassment. This was about Syrana. More words were believed to garner more of the Goddess's favor for the deceased in her journey to the afterlife. She should be appreciative of any additional people around the table, and she certainly had no right to stop writing. Rina lost herself again in her memories and her stories. She pretended not to notice exactly how long Eryn was there before she handed back her pencil and left.

Rina wrote until sunset, when the priest gathered the shroud and carried it into the deeper recesses of the chapel where Syrana's body lay waiting. Rina followed the remaining guardians to the nave and waited for the final presentation of the body to the Goddess.

Everyone who had been there throughout the day returned over the course of the next hour, mingling and sharing some of the stories, remembrances, and wishes they had written on the shroud. Rina did her best to avoid Eryn, unsure which side of her temperament would win when face-to-face with her hero. She really didn't want to think about why she wanted to hug Eryn and punch her in the face.

The room fell silent as a door off the nave opened and singing spread from the head priest outward, enveloping the crowd. Four priests followed, carrying the shrouded body to the ichor fountain in the center of the nave. The crowd followed, singing to the Goddess, asking for her blessings for Syrana as her spirit made the journey to the afterlife. The priests laid Syrana's body into a jut-out of the fountain designed for this, careful to not touch the ichor they could feel but not see.

Rina watched Syrana's body rest there for several seconds, looking like she was floating on shimmering, swirling air. Ichor always looked like the haze over a fire to Rina. Looking at the woman she had grown up with, the woman she had grown to love so deeply, felt just as surreal as the fluid holding her up.

The head priest stepped forward and gently directed Syrana's body toward the center of the ichor fountain. As Syrana's head reached the center, she disintegrated and rose like purple ash blown from a fire. The words and drawings from her shroud lifted into the ichor column, projecting their contents onto the wall of the nave like artwork on a lantern, rising slowly up the curved walls until they floated out of the roof. Blank shroud material collapsed onto itself as the form it had been surrounding disappeared, leaving a wad of linen to float through to the other side of the fountain and be gathered by the priests.

Outside, the whole of the Community would be able to see the black markings and purple sparkles drifting down the dome like rain on a window. They would be too small and distant to read outside the confines of the chapel, but everyone would know a guardian had passed into the embrace of the Goddess.

Rina read what she could as the words traveled up the wall, far too plentiful to take them all in. She picked out Claine's and Keddeth's handwriting easily. Tears of sadness but also of catharsis spilled down her cheeks as she relived Syrana's triumphs, kindness, and amusing blunders.

Just before Syrana's feet passed under the fountain, taking the last of her physical form, a short paragraph of unfamiliar handwriting caught Rina's eye. "I want you to know that I'm sorry, sorry I couldn't save you, sorry for pushing forward like I wasn't grieving, sorry I almost lost the token you gave me. You told me that you were proud to be my guardian, but I want you to know how proud I was to be your hero. We had so little time together, but I felt like we had something special and not just a foresight. We would have done amazing things together. Thank you for all the ways you gave to the Community and may you rest in peace. May the Goddess hold you and keep you."

Rina jumped to the next much longer paragraph of the same handwriting and skimmed through the only story Eryn had to tell— Syrana's last day. Rina's heart ached as she read. Eryn's remorse was evident in every line. Her takeaway was just as clear. She would serve the Community in Syrana's name. "And I will protect her in your name," Rina whispered to the last disappearing remnant of Syrana.

CHAPTER FIVE

Sinking and Synchrony

Eryn breathed a sigh of relief as she stepped through the dome and into the Dark Lands. She'd always imagined that trips outside for ichor would be invigorating and exciting, but she'd never expected them to be a breath of fresh air. The air itself was musky, heavy with the scent of decomposition. But, for the first time in three weeks, Eryn was back where she was meant to be, where she could be in her element.

For the last three weeks, Eryn felt like everyone was walking on eggshells around her. It didn't matter what she was doing or with which caste, everyone seemed to know that the Community's golden child had lost her guardian and her foresight. Everywhere she went, people were overly welcoming, complimentary, and excited to have her help them. She hated it.

Being alone with her restless mind was worse.

They kept a brisk pace throughout the day, pushing deeper into the foothills. She was determined to cover as much ground as possible. The sooner she reached the true depths of the mountains, the sooner she might find ichor, but it was more important to not let an accident or lack of attention cut her trip short. This trip and all future trips, she would have ten days to find ichor.

Eryn found herself smiling at the grim scenery. She would hum if it wouldn't attract attention. The life around her thrummed with anticipation, and she could feel her own heartbeat pick up to match its rhythm. Every step felt like a conversation, the Dark Lands questioning her and her answering confidently.

Every sense was tuned to her surroundings. She could hear the creaking of trees breathing in her scent and know whether her current path would put her within their range from the sound alone. She could smell the rot of worm piles long before the ground grew slick with their traps.

Eryn basked in the feeling of exertion. The sweat beading at her brow and on the back of her neck beneath her braid was intensified by the humidity of the air. There was a pleasure in long hours of pushing herself to the height of her abilities.

The day was defined by steady progress to each landmark Eryn set for herself. She didn't know where exactly she needed to go besides deeper and farther, but she reached every goal she set no matter what the Dark Lands threw at her. Instead of hacking her way through the carcass of the land around her, she made a single, efficient cut and moved forward. Each challenge of the Dark Lands, whether monster or terrain, gave her a springboard to move forward.

This felt like the thing she was meant to do.

It wasn't until Eryn felt sufficiently spent, unable to continue operating at peak performance, and called it a day that she even noticed Rina's presence. Throughout the day, when Eryn needed something, it simply appeared within her reach. She didn't ask Rina for it, just held out her hand and food, water, a handkerchief, or retrieved arrows were placed in her open palm. Rina was like a seamless extension of Eryn's will. She was actively sinking into obscurity as they passed through the Dark Lands, and it was everything Eryn could have asked for.

When Eryn announced it was time to camp, Rina had their site blocked-out with equipment by the time Eryn started the ichor lantern. As she stepped out of the tent, Rina handed her a bowl of stew, and as she took her last bite, Rina undressed her. Sinking into the pleasure of having Rina between her legs for the second time, Eryn couldn't remember a day that could compare to this one. She let the thought drift away. She didn't want to think about the past or plan the future. She only wanted to be in this moment, where everything felt perfectly right.

For four days, Eryn progressed deeper into the mountains with Rina always one step behind. Once they were deep enough, Eryn climbed to the top of a ridge or peak to look for auras whenever the opportunity presented itself. It was on one such climb that Eryn first caught sight of an aura.

The golden glow was almost lost behind an expanse of yellow-orange leaves, like those of the Community in the days before Frost Night. Eryn couldn't make out the vaguely humanoid shape older heroes had described, but the glow was unmistakable. She was seeing a product of the Goddess.

"I see one," she called down to Rina, masking none of her excitement. "Over past the mangrove." Her words trailed off as their meaning sank in. The aura was in the middle of the bog.

Eryn knew tales of the bog, but they were all from before living memory. She rappelled down, a plan already forming in her mind. As soon as her feet hit the ground, she moved to enact it, unfinished as it was. "We're going to the bog."

"The bog?" Rina said, her tone making it very clear how bad an idea she thought it was.

Eryn stripped off her climbing gear. "Yes. There's an aura in there, and so there might be ichor. Think about it, with heroes scouring the Dark Lands, doesn't it make sense that an untapped ichor source would be where no one else is looking?"

"Sure, but how are we going to get through the mangrove?"

Eryn rolled her eyes. "The mangrove isn't like a normal tree. It grabs food from the water with its roots. We just have to stay out of the water."

"And the dire alligators?"

"I'll shoot them in the mouth, and if any get close enough, you'll stab them in the gullet with your spear." It really was straightforward and not that different from anything they had already faced.

"And the dire fish?"

"Like I said, stay out of the water. You can manage that, right?" Eryn let the challenge hang. She'd known from the moment she met Rina that she had something to prove. Perhaps her low score and sense of inadequacy was exactly what Eryn needed to use to motivate her.

"Eryn, I think this is a bad plan. Was the aura headed toward the dome?"

"I'm going to follow that aura and find ichor. I'm going into the bog, and if you want to protect me, then you'll have to come too." Eryn felt more than prepared. This would be the culmination of a perfect trip.

Rina gave a huff that Eryn took as a resigned yes. So, she set off in the direction of the bog.

The smell of blue moldy cheese wafted over Eryn as she made her way closer, getting fouler with every step. This close, Eryn could just see the glint of the aura on the other side of the mangrove, which swayed slightly from side to side like an antsy child shifting from one foot to the other. The ground grew more sodden and unpredictable as the marsh changed from pockets of water amid the moist ground to islands of squishy dirt and yellowed grass poking up from the water.

Eryn reached the end of one such island and stopped, out of land and momentarily out of ideas. She felt Rina tense behind her and followed her gaze to what looked like a piece of land about five feet wide floating toward them. The top of a head, like a chunk of granite, was just visible beneath the surface of the water. Eryn looked back in the direction the creature had come from to see a hoard of similarly shaped islands bobbing near a chunk of real land.

As the crest of the dire snapping turtle's head surfaced, an idea bloomed. She thrust out her hand. "I need bread."

A few seconds later, Rina placed a large hunk into her hand and Eryn began to tear, tossing chunks into the water. The snapping turtle changed direction, rushing toward the closest piece of bread instead of Eryn. She whispered a "yes" of triumph as the bale of turtles sailed toward them, all attempts at stealth gone.

Eryn continued to tear and throw chunks, casting them as far across the divide between her and the mangrove as she could manage in a straight path from herself to the trees. As the last of the turtles arrived, heads bashing the water and each other to get at the bread, Eryn threw the last pieces into the water right in front of her.

"This is a bad plan," Rina grumbled.

Eryn bounced on the balls of her feet, waiting for her moment, and then sprang.

The first turtle took no notice of Eryn's weight pushing it deeper into the water as she sprang off its back onto the next turtle. The bread was enough of a distraction. By the fourth turtle, the bread was down to crumbs that barely served as a distraction. There were at least another dozen leaps from where Eryn was to the mangrove, but there was no way she was turning back. She leapt and leapt.

A turtle head shot out of the water, its heavy jaws snapping just shy of her ankle. Slightly to the right and she'd have lost that foot to its crushing jaws. A small noise of alarm escaped her lips before she could stop it. All around her turtle heads popped out of the water to look at her with hungry black eyes.

Eryn ran.

She'd been leaping with care, making sure to land in the center of each shell. Now, she moved as quickly as her legs could carry her. Her path was still there, but it was quickly dissolving into a mess of snapping jaws.

The turtles closed in, hissing and fighting each other to get to her. They pulled their heads back into their shells before shooting forward almost two feet, the snapping sound providing a thunderous clap after their lightning speed.

Eryn avoided one snap, almost landing inside the mouth of the next turtle. She jumped to the next turtle's back and yelped as her foot slipped in the mushy dirt on its back. She toppled forward straight toward the jaws of the closest turtle. One arm flailed while the other drew her short sword. Her flailing hand came down on the turtle's snout, inches from its razor-sharp beak. She held on and swung her sword at its head. Her sword pinged off the side of its head and the turtle's eye seemed to glint with amusement before it tossed its head, dislodging her grip and dropping her face toward its mouth.

Something grabbed the back of Eryn's gambeson, pulling her from the jaws just as they snapped in front of her nose. She stared in horror as the beast pulled back its head into its shell. She knew what would come next. The point of a spear struck past Eryn's face to lodge in the turtle's eye. It thrashed once before beginning to sink.

The turtle didn't have a chance to sink far before a root snaked out of the water. The root split like the fingers of a hand, wrapping itself around the dead turtle's shell and wrenching it under the water. The other turtles hissed and snapped in the direction the root had disappeared, clearly warning it that they would not be taken so easily.

"Go!" Rina said, taking advantage of the momentary distraction to right Eryn. Her spear struck over and over at the turtles pressing in closer and closer.

Eryn didn't pause. She leapt forward again and again, swinging her sword like a club in hopes of knocking aside a well-timed bite. Ahead of her, turtles snapped and hissed. Behind her, she could hear the splash of turtles being yanked under the water.

As she reached the end of her path, she realized too late that her path had dissolved. There was no way she could jump from the last turtle's back to the mangrove. She would have to go in the water and there was no telling what was waiting for her, assuming the mangrove didn't grab her first. As if to confirm that last thought, half of a snapped turtle shell floated to the surface of the water, the grasses on its top plastered to the hallowed outside.

"Go!" Rina said again, right behind her.

Eryn had to try. There was no other way. She bent down to jump and felt a hand grab her gambeson at the butt and under the arm. Eryn sprang up with all her might and launched forward, propelled by Rina's throw as much as her own jump.

She grabbed at the spindly mangrove trunks, wedging herself in their tangles to keep from falling backward. Eryn heaved a sigh of relief that was cut off by the continued sound of snapping turtles. Rina.

She slashed a vine dangling between two trees and turned back the way she had come. "Rina, jump," she said and threw the vine as hard as she could.

Rina jumped when commanded.

Eryn's throw was perfect, but Rina's jump was not. With her shorter legs and giant pack, she barely made it three feet. She managed to grab the vine before plunging into the water up to her armpits.

Eryn grabbed the vine, reeling it in as quickly as she could while Rina scrambled hand over hand to pull herself through the water. She was moving faster than seemed reasonable, each hand grabbing feet ahead of the last one, and for a moment, Eryn thought they had a chance. It took her that moment to realize what was happening. Rina wasn't pulling herself along, a mangrove root was pulling her in.

Several feet behind Rina, the water churned with roots. The mangrove had claimed its prey and was fending off competition.

"An axe, Rina. I need an axe." Eryn gawked at her reliance on her guardian. If she was going to do anything but slash at the mangrove with her sword or stick it with arrows, Rina had to provide Eryn with the tools while trying not to die.

Rina thrust one hand up, continuing to get higher and higher holds on the vine. With her other hand, she grappled with her pack. Her hand emerged with a hammer. She tossed it aside. She was moving faster now, down as well as toward Eryn. Rina was up to her shoulders in water.

Her hand disappeared into the pack again. It emerged with a collapsing tent pole. She threw it toward Eryn as her head sank beneath the water. Eryn let it sail past. She yanked on the vine, feeling it pull tight. The mass of wet, red hair moved appreciably closer to her, but also toward the mangrove's underwater mouth.

Eryn pulled again. Rina was so close now. She could almost reach her.

The mangrove jerked, almost pulling the vine from Eryn's hands. Rina sank another few inches. Eryn's strength couldn't compare to the tree's. She turned to the tangled trunks around her and weaved the vine through them. She knotted it and turned back to Rina in time to see the glint of an axe poking just above the surface of the water.

Holding the vine for support, Eryn leaned as far over the water as she dared and snagged the axe. She began to chop, hitting the above-water part of the root holding Rina as hard as she could. She got four good whacks in before she caught movement out of the corner of her eye. A root from the adjacent tree rose like a long spindly arm. It grabbed for Eryn, who struck it in the joint between two finger-like roots.

The root retreated underwater and Eryn got two more swings on Rina's root before a different pair of roots slithered out. She hit the first, cleaving a root finger off. The other smacked into her, not even bothering to try to grab her. She hit the tangle of trunks hard, almost dropping the axe.

Eryn pulled herself to her feet. This wasn't working. Even if she cut through the root holding Rina, there were so many more. Eryn drew her bow, took a moment to aim, and shot a snapping turtle in the eye. She didn't wait for the mangrove's reaction before firing again and again.

The churning water in front of the snapping turtles ceased as the roots rose from the water to grab dead turtle after dead turtle. Eryn kept firing. She reached for her quiver and came back empty-handed. She'd killed almost two dozen turtles in the span of thirty seconds. Rina had been below water longer than that. Eryn grabbed the axe again and gave another blow to the root holding Rina.

The root spasmed, not broken, but clearly injured. Eryn raised the axe again. The root spasmed once more and Rina came sputtering and gasping to the surface. She had a moment to breathe before the root threw her at Eryn and launched toward one of the sinking turtle bodies.

Eryn and Rina collided in a gasping, clutching heap, each trying to keep hold of the other and the mangrove trunks.

"Thanks. Whatever you did, it worked," Rina said. She pulled herself to her feet, bringing Eryn with her.

Eryn looked at the broken-turtle-infested waters and nodded grimly. They'd come far too close to being bits of gambeson and pack floating as refuse. "I'm sorry. I didn't mean to put you in danger." She hadn't been thinking about Rina at all, and she was fairly sure that was worse.

"The Dark Lands is danger," Rina said with a half-smile. "But maybe next time we can do it together?"

Rina retrieved the thrown tent pole while Eryn refilled her quiver with arrows from Rina's pack. Then they scrambled deeper through the mangrove, avoiding damaging any of the trunks or vines to not spur another attack from the roots. They reached the other side in a matter of minutes and looked at the center of the bog.

Where the outside of the bog had been a marsh of dirt and water, the inside was a giant, mostly submerged plateau of basalt columns. Littered throughout the landscape, columns rose from the water three inches to three feet, and on the center was the aura. The mangrove ringed the entirety.

"We need to jump again," Eryn said, pointing to the closest basalt column. It wasn't nearly as far as she'd jumped from the last turtle's back, but it was still going to be difficult for Rina.

"Can we wait until the mangrove gets closer to the columns?" Rina asked.

The whole center of the bog seemed to be rotating slowly and it took Eryn a moment to realize that it wasn't the bog, it was the mangrove. She'd thought the mangrove was swaying. It wasn't. The roots deep underwater were rising and falling, walking the mangrove slowly forward like a centipede.

"It's all one creature," Eryn said. She'd assumed each tree was working cooperatively with those around it, not that it was one continuous tree.

More importantly, ahead, the mangrove drifted closer to the center of the bog to within a few feet of the basalt columns. "Perfect," Eryn said. She and Rina were already working more in concert for the betterment of the team.

"What does the aura look like?" Rina asked as they waited for the mangrove to meander far enough forward.

"Well, vaguely like a kneeling person covered by thousands of golden spikes of light." The brightness this close was difficult to look at directly, and Eryn found that every time she blinked, the shape of golden light was burned into her retinas. "It's like a person stepped into the ichor fountain and started to dissolve, and when they got out, the ichor all started to evaporate off them. I suppose you've never seen ichor, so that's probably not a helpful description and it doesn't get across how beautiful it is. What does a shadow look like?"

Rina thought for a moment. "Like a person with tremors trying to cut a human shape out of darkness, then kind of giving up on the legs and just giving the figure a jagged, pointy bottom."

"Interesting," Eryn said. She was glad she saw auras instead.

"Do auras come inside the dome?" Rina asked as they prepared to jump.

Eryn leapt from the mangrove. "I don't know. Auras don't talk, so unlike shadows, there's really no way to know since presumably they can't become corporeal within the dome. Although legend says that when an especially successful hero dies, an aura is there at their deathbed. It's what gave rise to the belief that auras may be the spirits of heroes, sticking around to help other heroes find ichor." Eryn wanted the afterlife designed for them by the Goddess, but sticking around for a bit to continue serving the Community sounded pretty epic.

Eryn and Rina stepped from column to column toward the center where the aura hovered.

"Do you see ichor?" Rina asked as they reached the center.

Eryn held in a frustrated breath. "No."

"Is it going anywhere, leading us anywhere?"

"No." Eryn got down on her hands and knees. There had to be ichor here somewhere. That's what auras did. She scraped the lichen from the basalt column and found only rock. Surely, the aura didn't expect her to be able to get ichor from inside the rock. She stood up and pushed her frustration down. She said politely, "Where can I find ichor?"

The aura's head turned toward Eryn, seeming to notice her for the first time. It floated around them, drifted around the bog a few times, and returned. Eryn found this less than helpful.

"Is there ichor here?" Eryn asked it.

The aura gave an almost imperceptible shake of its head before drifting back the way Eryn and Rina had come from, through the mangrove, and out of sight.

"There's no ichor here," Eryn said. Somehow saying it aloud felt even more painful and defeating.

"That must be frustrating," Rina said.

Eryn expected Rina to be angry, to call her out on the way she had endangered their lives for nothing, but Rina sounded genuinely empathetic. "You're not upset?"

Rina shrugged. "Exploring the Dark Lands is what we do. You would have been kicking yourself for months if we hadn't checked. It could have been our cohort's first ichor find. I'm not upset."

Eryn smiled. She was still upset with herself, but Rina's reaction gave her a reason to move past it. She'd learned something and they'd survived. Now to get out of the bog. "There's a spot that almost touches the mangrove over there." She pointed to the other end of the bog and paused in case Rina wanted to contribute anything. Rina nodded and they both set off toward the mangrove, stepping carefully from column to column.

They'd almost reached the mangrove when Eryn froze. The rock that was barely above the surface of the water blinked again. "Dire alligator," Eryn whispered, moving her lips as little as possible.

The dire alligator's body was just visible below the surface of the murky water. The part Eryn could see was more than fifteen feet long. She imagined it was safe from being consumed by the mangrove based on its sheer size.

For a long moment, Eryn and Rina stared at the alligator and it stared back, each waiting for the other to act. The alligator broke the standoff. It reared up, displaying a mouth full of dagger-sized teeth.

Eryn moved the second the alligator did, drawing her bow and firing three arrows at the beast's scaled gullet. Each bounced off with barely a tinking noise. So much for stab it in the gullet, Eryn thought as the alligator continued to show off its teeth. If it was attempting to intimidate its prey, it was working.

"We'll have to go for the inside of the mouth," Eryn said. She had another arrow drawn. Now, she just needed the alligator to tip its head down ever so slightly.

A blur of orange dropped from the mangrove above the alligator onto its open mouth. A dire crab the size of a barrel lid held the alligator's jaws open with its eight legs. As if it had listened to Eryn's directions, the crab twisted its giant claw down and snipped the alligator's jaw all the way to the second joint. The alligator reeled, thrashing its head, but the crab barely seemed to notice. Its many feet rotated it around to sever the other side of the alligator's jaw.

As the crab disappeared inside the alligator, more dire crabs fell onto its dying body. Several followed the first inside the corpse while others swarmed the underside, their claws severing joints along the way. Mangrove roots held the alligator in place and prevented it from sinking any further. With their large claws, the crabs chopped bits of the alligator into pieces they could shove into their mouths with their smaller claws and severed larger parts that the crabs allowed to be pulled away by the mangrove. A swarm of dire fish were gathering at the edges, waiting for their share of what was left behind.

Eryn stared in shock. The alligator had seemed like a very risky challenge. How should she categorize a group that could take down that challenge in a matter of seconds? How about one that seemed to be collaborating with the mangrove that they'd only survived by giving it an easier alternative. Eryn looked at Rina and motioned for them to back away slowly, a task that was easier mimed than done.

As they moved away, Eryn watched Rina's feet, sure she would misstep. Eryn's heart sank as her own foot slid backward and she felt a rock skitter away and splash down into the water below. At the sound, many dozens of obsidian black eyes turned to stare at her.

Mandibles clicked and claws snapped as the crabs observed their new prey. Their long, many-jointed legs curled under them, then sprang them across the distance between the dire alligator's corpse and the basalt columns. Dozens of dire crabs scuttled up and around the columns, surrounding Eryn and Rina.

Eryn fired at the eyes of the closest but had as much effect on the crabs as she'd had on the alligator. She slung her bow onto her back and drew her short sword.

Eryn felt more than heard Rina shift onto the columns beside her. "Have you seen any weak spots?" Rina said.

"When their mouths are open, their mandibles draw back. Otherwise, they seem entirely covered. Even their joints have thick exoskeleton," Eryn said as the crabs crept in closer, still clearly evaluating their prey's threat level and weaknesses.

"Then we have to get them to open their mouths." Rina's free hand went to the pack.

Eryn shook her head. "I have an idea. Cover me." She looked below her into the murky waters and the ripple of activity she'd been expecting. As quickly as possible, Eryn squatted, adjusted her grip on her sword, and thrust out, spearing a dire fish. The dire fish spasmed for a moment, its tiny, spiked teeth flailing before going still.

Eryn heard the crunch of stone as a crab launched off its current column and felt Rina step onto her basalt column. There was a scrape of steel on chitin and a splash as the crab was knocked into the water. Eryn ignored it. She trusted Rina to have her back. She quickly unstrung her bow, keeping one end firmly attached to the wood, and tied the fish to the other end.

"I can't hold them off for long. One good hit from a claw and my spear shaft will be toothpicks." Rina was fully standing above Eryn now, striking crabs aside with her spear as they launched themselves one after the other at her. Each crab that splashed into the water immediately climbed the nearest basalt column to engage Rina again.

"Ready," Eryn said. The crab to her right jumped to the column next to her. She could see its mandibles working as it clicked at her. But the gap was too small. The crab shifted its weight between its eight legs as if it couldn't decide whether to attack Eryn directly or go for the fish dangling from her bow string.

"This one," Eryn said, and flicked her wrist as if using a whip to jerk the fish within reach of the crab's mandibles.

The crab opened its mouth reflexively, mandibles reaching into the empty space that had held a fish less than a second before. Instead, it received Rina's spear, killing it instantly. The body crashed into the water, a frenzy of fish beating at the carapace.

Eryn watched only long enough to confirm that her plan worked before twisting under Rina's extended torso to flick the fish under the crab that was clearly attempting to flank them.

Rina's body twisted, bringing her spear around to stab the newest crab and forcing Eryn to duck under the human-sized pack. As she did so, a crab launched at her, its giant claw extended and ready to snap her from ear to ear. Eryn's vulnerability sank in as she raised the unstrung bow. It was about as useful as any stick. Crouched under the pack, she had no ability to dodge.

Rina's spear struck the crab in the face, knocking it into the water. Before Eryn could recover, she heard the splash of another blocked crab. Rina's spear was a blur of thrusts, but she wasn't going to get anywhere without Eryn's fish trick. And Eryn wouldn't be able to go far without Rina's protection.

Eryn stepped onto a new basalt column, flicking her fish, then pivoted her back foot to a new rock. Rina's foot joined hers on the forward column as she stabbed the most recent crab and twirled to knock another aside. Eryn stepped to a new column and flicked her fish. She felt Rina join her and heard the satisfying squelch of steel into meat.

Eryn's movements became fluid, a dance more than a fight, and Rina was the perfect follow. Everywhere Eryn stepped, Rina was a moment behind her. Every crab she taunted received an immediate death. Eryn ducked when Rina twirled, and Rina sprang when Eryn squatted.

Their dance was imperfect. Rina couldn't cover all sides at once and Eryn didn't have the equipment to defend herself. Eryn received a long but thankfully shallow gash down her calf from a crab that came at her from below and a scrape of skin that felt like she'd run a cheese grater over the curve of her shoulder several times from another.

With every step, Eryn felt exhilarated. No, she hadn't found ichor, but this still felt like the culmination of a perfect trip. She was at the peak of her abilities, fighting in perfect sync with her guardian. She was mastering the bog. No, *they* were mastering the bog, and the achievement felt all the more fulfilling because it wasn't her victory alone.

It took several minutes for the decrease in crabs to become noticeable, and the change was dramatic from there. The crabs seemed to notice their dwindling numbers and began to retreat. The initial retreat was slow and hesitant, as if the draw to food was almost too much to ignore. By the time they were too far for Eryn's fish to trip their automatic reflex, it was clear that the fight was over.

A quick glance told Eryn that Rina's damage was also superficial. She took a step toward the place where the mangrove almost reached the basalt columns and watched the crabs shrink away. "Let's get out of here."

Rina's grunt of approval was breathless but determined.

Eryn all but ran through the mangrove, not wanting to give it or the crabs a chance to change their minds. They threaded through the mangrove to a spot where they could jump to squelchy marsh, and only stopped moving when their boots landed on consistently solid ground.

Eryn turned to Rina, her heart still racing. "That was amazing. The way you moved. The way we moved. The way we moved together." She watched Rina's chest heave beneath her gambeson and felt her mouth go dry. She licked her lips and tried to remind herself that they were still in the middle of the Dark Lands and barely out of the bog. She felt like she was vibrating. Her fingers twitched as if they would take on a mind of their own and try to tear Rina's clothing off right here, unprotected and anything but alone.

Rina closed the space between them. She buried her fingers in the hair above Eryn's braid as she pulled Eryn's face down to her and kissed her deeply.

Eryn was drunk on the feeling of Rina's mouth against her own and high on adrenaline. More, she needed more. She snaked her tongue into Rina's mouth and moaned as Rina shifted a thigh between her legs.

Just enough of Eryn's logical mind pushed to the surface of the waves of desire roiling through her to pull her back. "Not here," she gasped.

"Camp?" Rina's single word raised goose bumps up Eryn's arms.

"Yes," she said and then, against her worse judgment added, "but farther from the marsh."

❖

Rina needed Eryn and she needed her now. She needed to feel the warmth of her skin, hear her moans, taste her pleasure. She all but ran the mile or so that Eryn so reasonably insisted on and had the tent pitched enough to accommodate them by the time Eryn finished lighting the ichor lantern.

Eryn sprang from the lantern, knocking Rina back and almost taking down the poorly constructed tent in the process. Eryn barely seemed to notice. Her lips assaulted Rina's as Rina undressed her. Every touch, brief and rushed as it was, sent jolts like static shock through Rina's nerves.

Rina kissed Eryn's exposed skin, taking a nipple into her mouth and moaning at the way it made Eryn arch into her. She needed more.

Eryn's body radiated desire and it wasn't enough to feed that flame, as she had on previous nights. It wasn't enough to bask in the warmth of Eryn's fire. She needed to feel it on her skin directly, to thrust herself into the fire and let it consume her.

Rina tore her own clothing off, stripping before Eryn for the first time during sex. "I want to show you the way we can move together."

A deep, guttural noise escaped Eryn. "Goddess, yes." Her gaze raked over Rina's body and Rina felt a glow of pride at the lust in Eryn's eyes. Eryn rose from her bedroll to meet Rina halfway, their bodies colliding like two magnets accelerating together at the last moment. Rina's heart fluttered as their bodies melded, Eryn pushing up into the connection as much as Rina pressed her down.

Rina nudged her tongue into Eryn's mouth and groaned at the welcome reception she received. She draped her body against Eryn's, savoring every point of connection. The sting of adrenaline still pumped through her veins. The heightening of her senses from the preceding battles made every sensation staggeringly powerful.

On the basalt columns, she and Eryn had moved as a single entity. Now, every flicker of Eryn's movement still told her exactly how Eryn was going to move next. Eryn's body rose in waves and Rina met every ebb and flow.

Rina pressed Eryn into the bedroll. She slipped her leg between Eryn's thighs and ground herself against Eryn's thigh. She melted into the sensation, the pent-up tension in her muscles releasing like floodgates. She let herself sink into the carnal sensation of wanting and being wanted in return and drown herself in the heady aroma.

Feeling Eryn's pleasure, her wetness, her need directly against her skin was overwhelming. Her lips went to Eryn's neck, kissing a trail of goose bumps. Eryn's movements beneath her were desperate and Rina found herself just as desperate for release. There would be plenty of time later, after she tended to Eryn's wounds and her own and made dinner, to take it slowly and bring Eryn to the pleasurable kind of climax that would send her blissfully into sleep. Now, she wanted the kind of orgasm that would explode, reverberating between their melded bodies. She wanted to leave Eryn gasping, spent but still on fire.

Rina slipped her fingers between their entwined bodies, sliding into Eryn like a satin glove designed for her hand. Everything felt right. She was at the peak of her abilities, moving in perfect sync with her hero. She knew exactly how to protect her, how to support her, and how to love her.

Eryn jerked beneath Rina, a quaking that began between her legs and radiated out until her whole body was shaking with orgasm against Rina's bare skin. Her short nails dragged down Rina's back, leaving stinging pleasure in their wake.

Rina felt like a glass hit by the perfect frequency to shatter. Every nerve exploded simultaneously in a full-body orgasm that threatened to swallow her whole. She collapsed onto the bedroll beside Eryn and pulled Eryn onto her chest. They lay there for several long minutes, Eryn's head cradled between Rina's breasts as they both tried to catch their breath.

The voice inside her head told Rina that as well as she had done, she needed to get up and make dinner and tend to Eryn's wounds. The scrape on Eryn's shoulder was still weeping blood, and who knew what might have gotten into it during the trip through the mangrove. Rina did her best to ignore the voice. All she wanted, all she needed, was to be right there with Eryn.

Finally, Eryn pushed up, her golden eyes full of appreciation bordering on awe. "Thank you," she said. "I have trouble letting other people take care of me or even help me. I'm not trying to ignore you or push you out. It's just that working independently comes so naturally. It can be hard to remember to, well, to let you in. So, thank you for always coming in exactly the way I need you whether I reach out or just start to fall."

"I will always be there for you," Rina said. Dedication. That night she sat vigil for Syrana, Alba said Eryn saw dedication as love. That was what Rina wanted to give her and what she felt uniquely prepared to do, not just as a guardian, but as a person whose dedication had been questioned more times than she could possibly count.

In the Community, she felt constantly overlooked and dismissed. She felt a constant undercurrent of frustration at everyone and everything. Out here, she was surprised by how easy it was to let go of Eryn's mistakes, even in the moments when Eryn was committing them and the moments when Rina was paying the cost.

"Now, let's see to those wounds. I'm sorry for not protecting you from them," Rina said, pulling the pack toward herself to keep her position under Eryn as long as possible.

Eryn chuckled as if it were a silly apology. "You saved my life over and over again. You have nothing to be sorry for. I'm the one who should be apologizing. I put us in that mess for nothing."

"It wasn't nothing. We searched for ichor, and we didn't find it. That sounds like every other day." She had sworn to protect Eryn, not to find ichor. So, she had succeeded at her job in the toughest circumstances and was proud of the results. Her job was to support Eryn whether she found ichor or not. Even more, perhaps, when Eryn did not. "Plus, it was exhilarating to fight by your side like that, and that's not even mentioning the aftermath." She gave Eryn a wink and received a kiss in return.

Rina treated Eryn's shoulder before finally admitting that they had to move if she was going to tend to the cut on Eryn's calf, despite Eryn's attempted acrobatics to try to provide her leg without leaving Rina's chest or her lips.

After dinner, Rina gave Eryn what she called the lullaby kiss, a slow and gentle orgasm that drifted Eryn to sleep. "Thank you," Eryn whispered again.

CHAPTER SIX

Unrequited and Randy

Rina was surprised when she and Eryn were one of the first pairs back from the Dark Lands. Based on the way they'd pushed in the past, ten Eryn days were more like thirteen Community days. But the second half of the trip hadn't been like that. Days searching for ichor were the interludes between time in the tent, curled in each other's arms. Rina kept waiting for Eryn to stop shooting her lusty sidelong glances and go back to sprinting toward danger.

Instead, Eryn found excuses to be close, to pull Rina in for a kiss, and to call it a day early. They fought their share of monsters, but the trip after the bog felt far more focused on each other than on the Dark Lands. Rina was far from complaining.

"Thank you for a great mission," Eryn said as they left healers' hall. She rested her hand on Rina's shoulder and gave it a squeeze before winking and heading home.

Rina stopped by the guardian cafeteria on her way home and grabbed one of the packages of bread loaves, raw chopped vegetables, and ham hock. She'd never understood why anyone would want to make a meal that took a day just to cook. As she dropped the contents of the package, minus the bread, into a pot on her stove with a slow-burning fire and then collapsed into bed, Rina wondered what other simple miracles she'd overlooked.

When Rina woke, she snarfed down her soup, soaking up the last drops with bread, and headed to find Claine, who had promised her an updated schedule when she returned. She found Claine in her head guardian office with Henna, moving small rectangles of slate across her desk into pairs and triples.

Claine looked up from her desk and smiled. "Rina, I see you are adjusting well to transitioning between trips into the Dark Lands and being home. You look well rested and fed. How was your mission?"

"Really good." Rina gave Henna a friendly nod, and approached the desk, looking over the names of six-year-old guardians and recently retired guardians scrawled in chalk on the slate pieces. The pairing of mentors would be the next important guardian event of the year. Rina wondered if Henna would get a mentee already or if she would wait until her cohort retired. "I feel like Eryn and I are really connecting. We had a really successful trip. No ichor, but we got from one end of the bog to the other mostly unscathed."

The piece of slate Henna was holding clattered to the desk. Claine and Henna stopped to stare momentarily at Rina, as if waiting for her to say she was kidding. When Rina did not, Claine pursed her lips and nodded as if impressed. "I assume that was Eryn's idea?"

"I tried to talk her out of it, but she saw an aura and was determined. But it gave us a chance to perform at our best. Usually, it's just Eryn doing basically everything, at least in terms of fighting and forging forward. This time, I really felt useful, you know. Like I got to show her my best self and not just because I knew exactly what to hand her when, which also went really well."

"You always were very good at anticipating needs," Claine said absently, her attention on the pairings once more. She nodded as Henna swapped two slates.

Rina was glad Claine was looking down and missed what she was sure was a very skeptical look. Much of Rina's practice anticipating needs had been done with Claine acting as her pretend hero. All day, she followed Claine around with her giant pack, even more oversized on her teenage body. Claine would pause in what she was doing and thrust out her hand, and Rina was expected to know what she wanted. When she didn't provide it, or took too long, Claine docked her points. When she didn't open doors for her or preempt her hunger and thirst, Claine docked her points. To hear that Claine thought she had done well was news to Rina.

"You, uh, said you'd have a new schedule for me," Rina said when she knew her voice wouldn't betray her momentary frustration.

Claine paused to draw a paper from her desk drawer. "Any plans for the evening?" There was the smallest tinge of sympathy in her voice as she added, "Keddeth and I are having dinner late. You could come over."

Her days in the Community since Syrana's death had been worst in the evenings when she didn't have training of herself or others to distract her, when she lay in an empty bed in an empty house. But dinners with Claine and Keddeth only seemed to highlight that the fourth person in their group was gone.

"Thanks, but I think I'll check in on Eryn." Her mood brightened at the idea. Maybe she wouldn't have to sleep in an empty bed in an empty house for at least one more night. She ached to be near Eryn again, to touch her, to love her. After so many days spent together, every hour without her felt lonely and lacking.

"Don't," Claine said sternly, pulling Rina from her thoughts of curling up with a very naked Eryn.

"What? Why not?"

Claine's expression bordered on harsh. She gave Henna a look that made Henna grab her cane and amble out without further conversation. For a moment Rina thought she was about to lose points before remembering that her score was no longer active. "Rina," Claine said with a frustrated sigh.

It took a moment for Rina to realize that Claine's frustration was with the situation, not Rina. "There's something else you haven't told me about being a full guardian," Rina said.

"I knew it would only make you angry. If you weren't going to have a hero, why fight about it? You can't change it, so there's no reason to be angry. It's just the way it is. It's part of being a guardian and it's part of having a hero."

With that kind of preface, Rina could already feel her temper rising. "Just tell me."

Claine gave Rina a look as if Rina were the one being impertinent. "When a guardian is bonded to their hero, it creates an inseparable bond. It's the reason guardians die when their heroes do and it's also the reason guardians fall deeply, irrevocably in love with their heroes. But, Rina, it only goes one way. Heroes do not love their guardians. They never have and they never will. Outside the Community, it's just you and Eryn and she will turn to you for support, protection, and pleasure.

But inside the Community, Eryn has her own friends and lovers. Going to see her will only make that painfully clear and, knowing you, risks an awkward and possibly relationship-damaging confrontation. So, I say again, don't."

Rina's temper warred with a rising epiphany. "That's the reason for the voice in my head."

"What voice?" Claine seemed intently interested.

"The part of me that's thrilled every time Eryn seems pleased with me, that can't wait to do something else to make her day better or, Goddess willing, earn me a smile. That voice." Rina wasn't sure if she was more relieved or irate to finally understand.

"The puppy dog," Claine said.

"The what?"

"I think of it as a puppy dog. Overly excitable, eager to please, distractingly yappy." Claine had gone back to her slates, which Rina found entirely dismissive.

"You're telling me every guardian has this, this puppy dog voice in their heads?" Rina tried to keep her voice from rising. She didn't need a repeat of far too many conversations when she was a teenager in which Claine refused to say more until she calmed down to the degree Claine deemed sufficient.

Claine shrugged. "Yes, all guardians with a hero, that is. Though I don't think most guardians identify the puppy dog as being separate from themselves. They just are overly excitable about their hero's happiness and eager to please them. They know going into the bonding that they will love their hero unconditionally, so it's simply part of the relationship."

Rina's mind whirled as the meaning of it sank in. "So, you're saying I'm not really in love with Eryn. The fact that her smile fills me with joy, that I orgasm just from getting her to climax. It's not real?"

"I wouldn't say it's not real. It's just not your choice. Heed my advice. Cherish those orgasms while you can. They are the best ones and possibly the only ones you are going to get."

"What!" Rina couldn't contain her outburst. Why hadn't Claine told her any of this? The worst part was knowing that Claine wasn't finished. She could feel the true revelation just around the corner. Part of her wanted to slam her hands on the desk and demand the whole truth. Another part thought perhaps it might be best to walk out before she heard something she couldn't unhear.

Claine sighed as if this was quite the imposition, but she was the kind of person to rip the bandage off. "I said it the day you were bonded to Eryn. Nothing in the lands can compare to the feeling of having a hero. That much love makes everything else pale in comparison. Nothing will ever make you feel the way Eryn does and it makes all other love, all other sex, passion, or affection seem watered down. Even if Syrana were still alive, you would not be able to have with her what you used to because it would be in all ways lesser. When you were with her, you would wish you were with Eryn instead."

For a long moment, all Rina could do was stare at Claine in disbelief. "But…" She couldn't think of a counter except that this couldn't possibly be true.

"Why do you think guardians can't get married?" Claine asked. Her tone was infuriatingly calm as if she could force her calmness on Rina through extreme demonstration.

"Because they're sterile." Rina's answer puttered out as she realized it didn't make sense. A couple was not required to conceive a child for the Community to adopt a two-year-old. Even the fact that guardian children were raised in the garrison instead of by a family didn't explain it. Hero children grew up in the haven, but heroes got to marry and raise children from their spouse's caste.

"A guardian could never truly love their spouse. It would be destabilizing to the family and to society."

"But you and Keddeth?" This wasn't just a question of her future, but how Rina understood her life up to this point and her place within it. Claine and Keddeth weren't married, but they lived together and, as far as Rina had understood it, loved each other. They'd trained and raised Rina and Syrana together since becoming their mentors. Rina liked to pretend they were a family: a mother, a father, and a child from each parent's caste. She imagined family dinners to be like what she had with them, minus losing points for pushing her peas onto Syrana's plate when she wasn't looking and having to go back to the dorms at the end of the night.

More than that, Rina had always imagined herself having something like that with Syrana. Now, Claine was telling her she'd never have that with anyone.

Claine shrugged again. "Keddeth and I care very much about each other, we have since we were juniors, but we both know that the way we feel is nothing by comparison. I call him Ardon in bed and he calls me Tessy. It's the reality of being a guardian."

Rina stared at Claine. How could she simply accept an existence without love as if she somehow deserved it after a life dedicated to the Community? "How can you live like that?" Rina wasn't sure if she was accusing Claine or asking for real advice.

"I serve the Community, and for ten years, I served my hero. That is enough." Claine gave Rina a pointed look that was meant to end the conversation. "It is enough for all guardians. It is enough for you."

But what if it wasn't enough for her? The mild heartache that had felt like a weight in her chest since waking up alone, felt as though it was seeping into her bones. She would never be free from desperate, unrequited love and it would haunt her every moment she was away from Eryn.

"You have your schedule." Claine waved at her dismissively and went back to her slate pairing. When Rina didn't move, she added as if none of the last few minutes had happened, "And you're still invited to dinner if you change your mind."

Fuming, Rina turned and left. Claine had never been especially good at emotional support, but this felt like a new low. How could Claine just expect her to figure it out and what, be happy?

Was Claine even happy? She had a relationship that seemed devoted, she was highly respected and head guardian, but was she happy? Was it so easy for her to accept Rina's unhappiness because it was all she expected any guardian to achieve?

But Rina wasn't like other guardians, and she certainly wasn't like Claine. Maybe love would be different for her. A block from home, Rina changed directions. She wasn't Claine and she would never become her—driven, devoted, and destitute.

Her sharp knock at the door interrupted the laughing coming from inside, making Rina feel even more like an outsider. Was every other guardian carrying on with their days, their friendships, their lives as if nothing had changed, when in fact everything had changed? Did they know that they could never go back to normal lives?

The woman who opened the door gave Rina a pleasantly surprised smile. Jesta and Rina had never been that chummy as juniors, running in different circles with friends who did not like each other. Nevertheless, Rina considered her to be one of her closest friends. Syrana had once asked her why she liked Jesta. She wasn't particularly good in any area of training, she couldn't keep up with Rina physically or mentally, so what did Rina get from their friendship? Rina had tried to explain, but how could she make Syrana understand that sometimes it was nice to be with someone who didn't push her to be her best, but just enjoyed her company without pressure to be anything but a warm body.

"Rina, what brings you by?" Jesta said. The twinkle in her purple eyes told Rina she'd knocked on the right door.

Syrana had always been Rina's first choice lover, but there were nights when living together, training together, and sleeping together became too much and each had sought comfort in the bed of another. Any guardian was happy to accept Syrana into their bed, but it was Jesta who always took in Rina. With Jesta, Rina's feelings didn't have to be validated, conversations weren't debates, sex was passionate without being a competition, life was simple and straightforward.

Rina didn't bother with words. She closed the space between herself and Jesta, pressing her lips to Jesta's before slipping her tongue inside Jesta's welcoming mouth. Jesta's moan made the hair on the back of Rina's neck stand on end. I'm not broken, Rina told herself, smiling into the deepening kiss. Rina pulled back triumphantly.

For a moment, Jesta looked like she was going to tip over. Her expression was that of having eaten something far spicier than she'd expected. "Pietra has friends over," Jesta said as if she hadn't quite wrapped her head around why this fact was important.

"Shall we go to my place, then?" Rina offered her hand. Jesta took it immediately, skipping down the steps and swinging their intertwined hands as if they hadn't a care in the lands.

They exchanged brief anecdotes of their second missions as they walked the short distance to Rina's home. Rina's recounting of the bog drew many impressed oohs and ahs from Jesta, while Jesta's story of avoiding a dire bear was bland and showed no attempt to outdo Rina. Tonight was going to be exactly what Rina needed.

Once inside the house, Rina wasted no time pulling Jesta into her bed and out of her clothes. Jesta might not have anything to prove, but Rina did. She would pleasure Jesta the way she had so many times before and Eryn would be the furthest thing from her mind.

Jesta was so much more expressive in bed than Eryn, which made it so much easier to know she was achieving her goals. She didn't need to feel herself rising to orgasm off Eryn's pleasure when she had someone who openly moaned and urged her on.

Climbing between Jesta's thinner legs was so much easier than Eryn's strong, toned thighs. Loving Eryn was just something she did when they were outside the Community. Rina didn't need her sweet, metallic taste or her silky soft skin. Jesta felt good against her naked body. She didn't need to compare Jesta to Eryn because pleasuring them each was as different as fighting and debating. She could enjoy each in their own way.

Rina tipped her head up to take in Jesta's quivering, keening body splayed before her. She was beautiful even if she didn't have Eryn's glow. Jesta's right hand was buried in her long curls, while the other clutched at the sheets. Her back arched off the bed like the curve of a bow and her eyes were clenched shut in rapturous joy.

Aside from her nights with Eryn, Rina didn't think she'd ever put this level of dedication into the act of pleasuring. Even in her competitions with Syrana, Rina had been more focused on winning and proving her abilities than doggedly providing pleasure.

See! Rina wanted to yell. Not only could she still have passionate sex, but so could Jesta, who was as middling a guardian as there was. *I will make her orgasm harder than her hero ever can and then I'll know,* Rina coached herself. *Just because Claine can't love doesn't mean we can't.* Rina could feel herself rising with Jesta. Only with Eryn had the orgasm of her partner been enough to make Rina come undone, but she could feel herself riding that edge now. Everything was going to be okay.

As Jesta's body rose further and further off the bed, her cries became wilder, her head thrashing. "Yes!" Jesta yelled as she came. "Yes, Kalia, yes!"

With that single word, Rina's bliss turned hollow in her chest. Kalia. Jesta hadn't had her eyes closed because the sensation of Rina on her had been too intense. She had been imagining that Rina was her hero. Jesta had orgasmed for her hero and Rina was nothing more than a proxy.

After a long moment, Jesta pushed up and pressed kisses to Rina's dumbstruck lips. "My Goddess," Jesta said breathlessly between kisses.

"Rina, that was so amazing, I could imagine it was Kalia doing it to me. Eryn has such a treat in having you to warm her bed."

Rina flinched back, the words cutting her as if Jesta had sliced into her with her sword. Jesta knew everything Claine had said. Whether or not she knew the long-term implications, Jesta knew that Kalia would be the only thing that would ever satisfy her and yet she spoke of it so cavalierly, as if calling out another woman's name in bed was a compliment.

Jesta traced her hands over Rina's bare skin, trying to entice her, but where they had once left goose bumps in their wake, Rina felt only the chill of lost comfort. Rina refused to look at Jesta as she fought back tears. Jesta wouldn't understand. She would listen without judgment, then apologize for the role she had played in Rina's pain and try to use sex to alleviate Rina's burden. But sex was only going to make things worse. She would spend every moment thinking about Eryn and trying to decide if it was better to just give up or to give in and pretend it was Eryn between her legs like every other guardian did, apparently without question.

As Jesta's lips moved to Rina's neck, clammy against her unmoving skin, Rina didn't think she could go through with it. She'd just have to let Jesta down as easily as she could, send her home, and try to fall asleep in an empty bed. Rina opened her mouth, still unsure what she was going to say. A sharp knock at the front door cut off the words as they formed. Thank the Goddess, Rina thought, slipping from between Jesta's sweaty arms and grabbing a robe before hurrying to the door.

❖

The rhythmic knock on her door filled Eryn with self-satisfaction as her libido spiked. "Right on time," she said before pulling the heavy door back to reveal Henk standing on her doorstep, grinning. He'd had the expression plastered on his face since she'd caught his eye and winked at the end of the impromptu storytelling game she'd invited her cohort to do in the obstacle course rather than lazing around in the common room. The simple gesture was all it had taken to get him hard right there standing on top of a balancing column and to get Henk plenty of thumbs up from the rest of her cohort when they thought she wasn't looking. His golden eyes glittered in the light from her porch lantern and his almost golden locks ruffled in the light breeze.

Eryn didn't bother inviting him in. Instead, she turned her back on him and strode to her sitting room, reveling in the sound of the front door clicking behind her and the feel of Henk close at her heels. Eryn stopped in the middle of the room, turned to Henk, and raised a single index finger, pointing it at the spot between her feet.

As commanded, Henk sank to his knees before her, swallowing hard as Eryn unbelted and discarded her robe. His look of unadulterated lust filled Eryn with pride. This was just how she liked it—the strongest, manliest hero in her cohort on his knees, desperate to pleasure her.

Eryn sank into one of her chairs, presenting herself to Henk's raking gaze. Eryn held back her shiver as his gaze dragged over every rise and valley of her body. He shuffled forward on his knees. After his eyes came his lips.

Eryn relaxed into the feeling of being worshipped physically. Displeasure interrupted her enjoyment as the feel of his rough stubble scraped across her knee. She'd always found his mostly shaved facial hair to be a turn-on, so why did it make her want to kick out at the feeling? Eryn sighed and focused on the feel of his lips caressing up her inner thigh.

Henk followed his typical path from toes to fingertips to breasts. By the time he was done, Eryn didn't think she'd ever grimaced so many times during foreplay. Even their first time together, when she'd taught Henk how to pleasure her through trial and error, had been better than this. The worst part was that she couldn't put her finger on what was so wrong.

His upper lip was too prickly, but that had never bothered her before. His progress was slow but that had always been enticing. He pulled just a little too hard when he suckled her nipples, but that had always sent an enjoyable shock to her groin. This time, she just wanted to smack him away from her like a pesky bug.

I'm just tired, Eryn thought as she wished his kisses weren't so wet. She kept her lips closed when he tried to push his tongue into her mouth as he carried her to bed. His breath wasn't great and if she already thought his kisses were too wet, having his tongue stuffed in her mouth was not going to help anything.

As Henk buried his face between her legs, Eryn couldn't help thinking Rina had done it better. Rina had been trained in the art of pleasuring her hero, after all. Rina didn't look up the plane of Eryn's body with carnal craving as if she was about to claim the prize of her hard work. She looked at Eryn like nothing else in the lands mattered, as if the Community could crumble around them and all that counted would be right there beneath her tongue, as if Eryn's pleasure was the air she breathed. Eryn felt her body reacting to the memory.

Devotion had always been her fetish, but what Henk provided was only the imitation of devotion. He respected her, but the worship he provided to her body was the necessary step to reach his ends. The way Rina looked at her and touched her made it clear that she was so much more than just the best hero. By the Goddess, she orgasmed just from the experience of Eryn's climax.

Henk groaned as he climbed up her body. "You're so wet." He was ready for his reward.

No! Eryn's mind screamed at her as Henk placed himself against her. She told the voice it was overreacting. Rina was her guardian and clearly loved her, but Henk was a hero. He was powerful and fabulous in bed. He could give her what she wanted and take her mind off Rina.

No! Eryn's body insisted again, pulling away from Henk, despite her intentions to the contrary. Her hips had always risen off the bed to meet him and she would make them do so again. Now was not the time for thinking about her guardian.

Henk repositioned himself and smiled at her, excitement radiating off him.

"No!" Eryn called out, squeezing her eyes shut against the impending feel of his body entering hers.

"What's wrong?" Henk said, pulling back.

An overwhelming wave of relief washed over Eryn. "No," was all she could manage. She didn't understand what was happening, but one thing was starkly clear—she did not want to have sex with Henk.

"Do you want me to use my tongue some more?" Henk asked, confused. He was clearly trying to process the odd mixture of fear, revulsion, and relief she felt and was surely displaying. "You were so wet, I figured you were ready and didn't need any more, but I can do more."

"No," Eryn said. What she needed was for him to leave. She tried to tell herself that what she needed was a woman, but that was only half true. She needed Rina. "I have to go," Eryn said, "I have a previous engagement."

For a long moment Henk just stared at Eryn, his sticky, glistening lips, spread halfway between a pout and an attempt to speak. "Now?" he finally asked.

"Yes, now," Eryn said, crawling out from under him and grabbing one of her wrap dresses. She didn't have any undergarments, but where she was going, she wouldn't need any.

Eryn didn't bother to wait for Henk to dress or leave. He could see himself out as he had done on so many mornings when she had left in the wee hours to train. Right now, she just needed to be away from him.

"Thanks," he called after her. There was no sarcasm or malice in his voice. He always thanked her for their time together. Even if he didn't get the climax he'd been expecting, the perception that he slept with her would be enough to get him any other hero with an interest in men. Apparently, that isn't me anymore, Eryn remarked to herself, wondering what in the Dark Lands was wrong with her.

Once she'd left the hero quarter, Eryn found herself slinking along in the darkness, across the training fields. She'd always walked through every part of the Community with her head held high. It was part of who she was to be seen with all walks of life. But tonight, she didn't want anyone to see her seeking the pleasures of her guardian. Everyone talked about how good it was, but not inside the dome.

Eryn supposed she could always claim that she wanted to speak with Rina about their last mission or the next. She could be providing feedback on Rina's performance or a training regimen for improvement. Rina was the lowest ranked guardian after all. It would stand to reason that she might need extra coaching or attention.

The ridiculousness of that statement caught Eryn by surprise. The rest of her cohort had suggested that perhaps she could get Rina to a place of competency, but Rina was already leaps and bounds ahead of any of them. In the game she'd designed for them, they took turns as the story master, leading the group through a reenactment of their latest missions. As she skipped across the tops of the balance poles, telling her story of the bog, heroes around her fell left and right or simply gave up trying to keep up with her. Her movements were barely equal to what she and Rina had performed, in sync, while being attacked. Plus, Rina had done the whole thing with a pack so large she expected any of her cohort wouldn't be able to stand on a beam with one, let alone jump and fight. Even Henk had been out of breath and many obstacles behind her by the middle of her story.

To be seen slinking around in the dark would make the argument she wanted to train Rina that much harder. But Eryn just couldn't find the confidence that had always defined her. She felt deflated and needy, so how was she supposed to project otherwise?

"Rina is my guardian. Her job is to fulfill my needs," Eryn said, though the thought made her feel worse, not better. She wandered up and down the paths between the blocks of identical guardian homes, looking at the nameplates above the doors. She could knock on any door and receive directions that would have been happily provided without question, but she'd wander all night to avoid it. She would have to remember what number Rina's home was when she found it so she wouldn't have to search next time.

"There won't be a next time," Eryn said before wincing. She tried not to make a habit of lying to herself and certainly not so blatantly.

"Syrana and Rina," the sign above the door read.

Roommates? Had her first guardian and Rina been friends? Or perhaps Rina had been placed with Syrana as a form of tutelage in an effort to fix Rina's deficiencies.

Before she had a chance to stop herself, Eryn marched up to the door and knocked. She had a right to be here. She would have her needs met and deal with the storm inside her mind once the present situation was dealt with. Her calm would be restored, and she would be able to process whatever was going on with her in a clear and logical way.

Rina's expression was etched with an odd mixture of relief and startlement as she opened the door, but the look melted away upon seeing who was on her doorstep. Eryn watched with satisfaction as her guardian's pupils dilated and her chest rose with excitement at her unexpected visitor. "Eryn," she said as if the word were the Goddess's true name.

When Rina seemed too dumbfounded to say more, Eryn stepped forward and Rina stepped back, offering her entrance to the place Eryn would make her own for the time she was here. Her doubt and fragility were gone. This was where she was supposed to be, and her confidence filled the space.

Eryn strolled to the common area in the center of the house, her mind picking up small details without her having to pay her surroundings true attention. The space did not matter in that moment, only how she would use it.

With deliberate slowness, Eryn turned to Rina, who had followed her from the door so like Henk and yet so much more endearingly. Rina sank to her knees without command and looked up at Eryn in awe. The way she stroked Eryn's calves felt deeply intimate and Eryn got the sense that if she never disrobed, but simply stood here all night, Rina would happily continue her ministrations without end, never demanding more than to give Eryn whatever she wanted or needed.

Eryn looked down into Rina's adoring expression and felt her chest tighten with a feeling she didn't recognize. As she stood there, trying to remember the way normal breathing felt, one thought kept running in her head: "It wouldn't be enough for her to just give me what I want."

It was an incredible turn-on that Rina didn't need or expect a reward, but Eryn wouldn't truly feel fulfilled if Rina didn't get a great deal from the encounter as well. She'd never truly cared about Henk's climax or that of any of the heroes she slept with, but Rina's mattered.

Eryn removed her dress and smirked at the lust that played across Rina's face. Rina stroked higher before pausing halfway up her thighs. For a moment, Rina's expression shifted, and she looked indecisive and almost angry, as if she hadn't meant to be doing what she was doing. The look was only there for a moment before the stroking began again, both tender and energetic. Rina looked decisive and even at peace in the moment before she buried her face between Eryn's legs.

Eryn and Rina moaned. This was what Eryn had needed, what Henk couldn't give her, what in the back of her mind she was starting to fear no hero could give her. She tried to push the thought away, to be fully in the sensation of Rina, but the thoughts came anyway, drowning her normally clear mind.

A small gasp drew Eryn from her racing thoughts. A woman her age with long, curly brown hair stood naked in the doorway to one of the two bedrooms, staring at them. "You're not alone," Eryn said, her chest aching in a whole new way.

"Eryn," the guardian said, her cheeks reddening. "I'm so sorry to have interrupted. Please ignore me." She scuttled across the room, her left shoulder rubbing against the wall the whole way as if she wished she could simply sink into it and cease to be there faster. Within three seconds, she had made it to the door and slipped into the night.

"She didn't even get dressed," Eryn said, more to herself than to Rina, who was posed a few inches from her previous position, staring from the door to Eryn's body and back. Her frustrated expression was back but she didn't seem annoyed at having been interrupted. Eryn didn't have the mental capacity to question the source of Rina's feelings. Her own were bubbling up wildly.

"You were having sex with her," Eryn said. She was angry, embarrassed, and confused. She'd left Henk in her bed to be here, but that didn't matter. It mattered that Rina had found pleasure with someone else. For reasons she could barely scratch the surface of, she didn't want anyone but Rina, but Rina didn't feel the same way.

"I'm sorry." Rina's instant apology seemed to make Rina frustrated rather than embarrassed.

How dare she be upset! Eryn was the one who had been betrayed. If Eryn couldn't get Rina out of her head while in bed with someone else, how could Rina share her bed with someone else? It wasn't fair. It wasn't right.

I'm jealous, Eryn realized. She'd never been jealous of anyone. She was the best. She was what everyone strived to be. But here she was, not only jealous of Rina for her ability to bed whomever she wanted, but jealous of some random guardian who had turned Rina's head.

Eryn grabbed her dress from the floor and tossed it on. She couldn't be here. Not now, maybe not ever. In a matter of seconds, she'd gone from owning the space to not belonging. She'd run away from Henk and her home to be here and now she was running from her own guardian.

I'm supposed to be, what? The best? In control? Worshipped? Needed? A hero?

She fled into the dark of the night. There was only one place she belonged, where she might find the answers she needed to get back to the future she had built.

CHAPTER SEVEN

Repression and Revelation

For several minutes, Rina just stared at the empty couch in front of her, keenly aware of the silence around her. She was specifically trying to prove she didn't need Eryn, but when Eryn had shown up at her door, her resolve immediately failed and all she could do was fall to her knees and worship her.

Rina knew how she felt—angry, frustrated, and betrayed by everyone and everything, but the feeling was not new. The justification for her feelings was deeper than it had ever been, but besides sexually frustrated, the feelings themselves weren't that different from the way she'd felt since the first time she'd told a guardian that shadows told her the truth and been told she was wrong and bad. What she didn't understand was Eryn.

The hurt that had been apparent in Eryn's eyes cut into Rina even now. Her drive to take away that pain had driven her resentment higher, but the longer she knelt, staring at nothing, the more her resentment was replaced by regret. No matter what had been done to her and all guardians, Eryn was still her hero and Rina had hurt her and their relationship. Rina was bitter, but damaging her relationship with the person she was meant to serve and love served no one's good. It wasn't Eryn's fault. All Eryn wanted to do was help people…and always be the best.

Eryn needed her and she needed to be there for her hero.

Rina made it all the way across the training field between the hero and guardian quarters before she knew she was going the wrong way. Eryn had lost her first guardian and been hurt by her second. There was only one place she would go.

In the middle of the night, the spacious nave of the chapel was empty save one kneeling woman woefully underdressed for the grandeur of the building around her. Rina gathered her own robe tighter around herself, giving a silent apology to the Goddess and assuring Her that she meant no disrespect. She joined Eryn on the kneeling cushion at the front of the room. Only a matter of weeks ago, Syrana had knelt in this same spot and pledged her life to the Community and to Eryn. Rina felt like a sorry excuse for a replacement.

For a long moment, they stared at the fountain in silence. Rina recited the prayer she had learned before she was even able to talk. She thanked the Goddess for all that was her life, for the Community, for the Goddess's sacrifice that had saved them all. Her prayer done, Rina waited, silent and present.

Several minutes later, Eryn broke the silence as Rina had known she would. Her voice was strained as if she was just barely holding back tears. "The priest said Syrana and I were going to save the Community. The Goddess gave him a foresight. It was supposed to be the culmination of everything I have worked for, everything that my life has meant, and then she died. She swore to be by my side, to protect me, to help me achieve everything I was destined for, and then she died. She left me and all I have is you."

"She left me too," Rina said. Eryn's words stung, but she couldn't hold on to anger at Eryn, and it was easier to be angry with Syrana than herself. "She was my best friend, my confidant, my lover."

Eryn gave a tearful snort. "She pitied you?"

"I was her only equal." Rina barely kept her voice to a respectful volume.

"She was the best guardian since Claine. You are the worst guardian in your cohort. What were you possibly her equal at?"

"Everything. History, philosophy, pleasuring, swordsmanship, defense, archery. We trained and trained until we could outshoot everyone in our cohort just because we wanted to beat each other." With each word the anger slipped from her voice. Rina could remember the smile on Syrana's face every time Rina outshot her. Nothing made Syrana happier than a true challenge.

"Then why are you the lowest-scoring guardian anyone can remember?" Eryn sounded as if Rina's score was a personal affront.

So much for my score not mattering anymore, Rina thought. "Because I used to argue that shadows didn't always lie, that if we listened, we could use what they said to prevent bad things from happening." Rina told herself she wasn't lying to Eryn. Sure, her beliefs hadn't changed, but she no longer argued about it.

Eryn's look of horror made Rina glad for the lie of omission. "I don't understand how that made you the worst."

"I lost points, hundreds of points sometimes for arguing about it. It didn't matter how well I did in every other aspect of training, I lost everything I gained every time my mentor pushed me on the topic or I couldn't keep my mouth shut." Rina wasn't trying to blame Claine. She was fairly sure Claine gave her fewer points for successes and took more points for failures than other mentors. In group training, she always received fewer points for equal or better performance if Claine was instructing. Not to mention the ways Claine noticed everything Syrana did well and everything Rina did poorly, from individual training to setting the dinner table. Syrana swore it was just Rina's imagination.

Eryn nodded though she didn't seem particularly comforted by the explanation. "You aren't the problem. I'm the one who lost my foresight. You've guarded me well, done everything I asked, kept up with me when I felt like I was performing my best. I'm the one who has to do better. You can't find ichor. We haven't found it yet and that's on me."

"We've only been on two missions. One real mission."

Eryn ignored Rina's interruption. "I've allowed my feelings to distract me."

Feelings? Rina wanted to ask. Eryn had come to her home with obvious desire, but had there been something more?

"The Community and ichor are the only things that matter. I always said that I wanted a guardian who would protect me against monsters, not perform in our tent at night. You are fabulous at both, but I've let one distract me from the other. After the bog, all I could think about was getting to the next campsite. That's not how I'm going to be the hero I've been training all my life to be. I lost my foresight; I have to try all the harder. I can't let anything distract me." Eryn nodded again before announcing to the empty room as if she were proclaiming it to the Goddess, "No more sex. Not in the Community, not in the Dark Lands. We're going to find ichor and serve the Community."

Rina watched Eryn sigh as if releasing an incredible weight and felt it land squarely on her own chest. The Claine in her brain kept repeating, "enjoy it while you can" as Eryn's words stabbed deeper.

Eryn smiled at Rina and laid a hand on her shoulder. "Thank you for telling me about your score. I'm glad that you don't try to listen to shadows anymore. I'm sorry for judging you based on it before. I think we can still do great things together and I'm looking forward to our next mission." With that, Eryn left the chapel.

Rina groaned, her forehead sinking to rest in her palm. So much for not being driven, devoted, and destitute.

Over the next three weeks, Rina threw herself into her regimen, showing up at the courses that had been reassigned to other guardians to assist, and attending dinners with Keddeth and Claine just to have something to keep her mind occupied and her hands busy. Claine seemed especially happy, clearly taking Rina's actions as both forgiveness and acceptance. Rina was far from either accepting or forgiving. She'd found there was a big difference between resignation and acceptance.

As Rina donned her gambeson and pack for their next mission, she was anything but excited. It would be nice to get to feel useful again, but the memory of the heartbreak that first night Eryn rejected her advances haunted her. She knew now why it was so soul crushing but was sure the knowledge wouldn't help her any. Her puppy, as Claine referred to it, didn't control her actions, but it had an iron grip on her emotions.

Rina met Eryn at the dome and returned her smile. At least Eryn seemed excited. Rina's job was to turn that excitement into joy, and joy into pleasure, and pleasure into ecstasy and success. Or so the puppy said. Rina tried to tell it that there would be no pleasure, but it listened as well as Rina understood all puppies to listen.

Most of the first three days Rina spent trying to keep her melodramatic and borderline manic-depressive puppy in line. Her emotions fluctuated between extreme insecurity and quixotic optimism. Rina could feel herself slipping, half her attention on providing for Eryn's every need and keeping them both safe and half her attention trying to preserve enough of her sanity to keep doing so. On the bright side, she didn't have any brainpower left to spare on shadows.

Nights were the worst. Within the Community, she found it hard falling asleep in an empty home, alone. Falling asleep, desperately needy for the woman several feet away while her mind insisted that she was a failure, was impossible. She lay awake telling her body that if she didn't sleep, she wouldn't be able to protect Eryn, but her puppy yowled on.

Rina lay staring at the tent ceiling, listening to the even cadence of Eryn's breathing and willing herself to sleep. It had been an especially bad day. While Rina struggled to focus on keeping her eyes open and her senses alert, Eryn had forged forward. She'd traipsed across a wide, open field which had fared fine under her light weight but crumbled under Rina's. An entire field of dire prairie dogs had taken it upon themselves to seek revenge for their destroyed home, popping out of the ground and shrieking at the top of their tiny lungs to try to draw predators to take care of the humans for them.

A twisted ankle and a barely satisfactory fight with a dire boar later, Rina stumbled her way through dinner and into her bedroll, miserable and exhausted. She just wished any of it would lead to sleep.

Trouble sleeping? The hissing male voice sent a shiver up Rina's spine and her half-lidded eyes sprung open. She reached for her spear. Shadow voices were only ever so clear and sharp when they were corporeal, which they couldn't be within the ichor lantern's shield. Had the shield gone down?

The dim light filtering through the tent ceiling told her the lantern was still above them. No shadow was visible within the tent either. Was she just hallucinating after days without sleep?

I felt it was time we became acquainted, you and I.

Rina froze, her breath caught in her throat. Shadows never referred to themselves. They simply spouted negativity about others. In her fifteen years of listening to shadows, never once had a shadow used the word "I."

"Who are you?" Rina asked, her words barely more than an exhale.

I have gone by many names. I call myself the Commander of Shadows.

Humble, Rina thought. As if shadows listened to anyone, even their own kind. "Why are you here?"

Like I said, I thought it was time we met. We have a unique opportunity, you and I, to speak to someone who will actually listen to us. Someone who will believe us. Someone who is not blinded to reason by fear. Kindred Spirits.

How does he know I listen to shadows? Rina wondered. She supposed it was possible he wandered the Dark Lands whispering in every guardian's ear waiting for someone to react, but this felt too targeted for that.

Rina bit her lip. The Claine in her brain was yelling at her to shut this shadow out. Had Rina not caused enough pain and suffering by listening to shadows? To speak to one was a new low. She knew he was trying to manipulate her, but Rina couldn't deny what went far deeper than curiosity. He was right. She would listen and she was starving for someone who would listen in return.

"Then speak," Rina said. Shadows spoke to her all the time, so really, she wasn't breaking any rule or taboo she didn't already break daily.

Rina could hear the self-satisfaction in the Commander of Shadow's tone and wondered if shadows had the ability to smirk. *You are a bright young woman, Rina. So, I'll start with a question. What is Furin's postulate?*

Rina had been waiting for his question to set off alarm bells in her gut, but Furin's postulate? It was basic philosophy, the kind of topic you brought up at a party to try to look smart. "Does the Goddess foresee fate, or does She shape it?"

The Commander chuckled, causing the hair at the nape of her neck to stand on end. *Now, Rina, I thought we were going to be honest with each other. A postulate is not a question. It is an answer. So again, I ask. What is Furin's postulate?*

Rina's heart skipped a beat, and she felt a wave of cold wash over her as the blood drained from her face. How could he know? Rina hadn't even told Syrana her true belief. For a moment, she considered not answering. She'd listened to a shadow—worse, she was having a conversation with one, but she hadn't committed heresy, not yet. Rina glanced over at Eryn, moving her head as little as possible to confirm she was still asleep. Was it heresy if no one heard her? It wasn't like the Commander could tell anyone.

This is my chance, my only chance to speak what I have hidden inside, Rina thought. The Commander had offered her an ear not clouded by fear. How could she not take it? "Furin argues both options equally because the answer to does the Goddess foresee fate or shape it is yes. If both are true, then the Goddess must see multiple options, possible futures, and use the powers She has left to try to shape the future toward the possibility She wants. Foresights then are Her sharing a possible future with a priest to try to get the result She wants. But Furin could never write that. It would be heresy to suggest that events are not dictated by fate or by the Goddess but by our choices. It would put us above the Goddess, according to some. And it could suggest…" Rina bit her lip, willing herself not to say the last part, the truly damning part that she had to assume even Furin hadn't considered. "It suggests that what shadows say aren't lies, but other possible futures as well as demoralizing statements."

The Community desecrates itself in its fear of the profane. Imagine if a mind like Furin's, a mind like yours, were set free. Imagine the future that could be shaped. Brilliance, innovation, and progress are not heresy. They are using the gifts the Goddess gave us to shape a better future. Would She truly want them squandered for fear of insulting Her? Is that the Goddess we truly believe Her to be? I will leave you with two things to ponder.

As he spoke, Rina felt a prickle of ice creep across her forehead from left to right as if the Commander were stroking her with a chilled dagger. She followed the motion, looking again at the sleeping form of Eryn. *Heroes do not care about anything but themselves, whether they have what they need, whether they find ichor, whether they are living up to their potential. When you both return with ichor it will be her who found it and when you return without it, you will be to blame. She will not hesitate to let you take the fall. So, get what it is that you want and need on missions because you will always be an afterthought.*

Rina grimaced as he stroked her face back the other direction. She looked at the tent ceiling just to keep him from repeating the action. *And now, I leave you with this final thought to fill your sleepless nights. If foresights are the gift of the Goddess to priests, who is to say that the words of shadows are not the Goddess's gift to guardians?*

With that final word, Rina felt his presence recede. It was as if the entirety of the Dark Lands receded with him. Colors regained their vibrancy. The chilly, musty air was replaced by the smell of smoke and reconstituted pot roast rather than death and decay.

For several minutes, Rina lay perfectly still, breathing slowly and silently as if she were afraid of waking reality itself. She imagined the ground opening up below her and swallowing her whole as the Goddess took it upon Herself to end such apostasy.

By morning, Rina was about as sure what constituted blasphemy as she was that any of the conversation had actually happened and wasn't a figment of a delusionally tired mind.

❖

Eryn didn't like the way Rina looked. There were dark circles under her eyes, and red rimmed the whites of her eyes. She blinked slowly as her gaze moved across the landscape.

If Rina was distracted or slow, it put both of their lives in danger, but it wasn't concern for their mission that drove the ache in Eryn's chest. She didn't want to tell Rina to wake up and get her head in the game. She wanted to hug her.

"Are you okay?" Eryn asked.

"I'm fine." Rina's tone was clearly sharper than she'd intended. She bit her lip and shook her head as if to clear it, then said again in a milder, more confident tone, "I'm fine."

"Do you need more time to rest?" Rina had been awake and preparing breakfast when Eryn awoke, so she'd figured she was ready to go. Perhaps she should have asked.

"No, I'm ready." Rina gave Eryn what was clearly meant to be an enthusiastic smile. Eryn gave her a half-hearted one in return. Should she insist on making camp again and waiting until Rina was in a better state? Perhaps they ought to just head back. What if Rina was ill? "Rina, I need you to tell me the truth. Are you well enough to go on?"

Rina closed her eyes and took a breath that made her whole body expand and contract. When she opened her eyes again, the spark that had been one of the first things Eryn noticed about her was almost back. "I am well. I promise."

Eryn nodded. She had to trust her guardian. "Then let's go find ichor."

Throughout the day, Eryn could feel Rina making a concerted effort to seem chipper. Anything Eryn wanted Rina provided, as she had during the last trip, but this time it felt more forced. Eryn found herself trying not to need anything just to keep Rina from having to fill those needs.

A snapping branch drew Eryn's attention. She drew her bow and spun toward the noise, but not in time. She used it as a shield more than a weapon as a blur of beige sprang from the bloodberry bush to her right. Her bow was slammed from her hands, knocking her back enough to save her from the creature's second paw.

Eryn hit the ground and looked up into oversized feline eyes. A dire cougar stood before her, its glistening, rippling muscles straining beneath its hairless skin. Where the dire dogs and the dire squirrels looked like they barely had enough sinew to hold their rotting corpses together, the dire cougar's skin appeared oiled with a dark web of vascularity throbbing on top of its muscles. Those muscles flexed, launching the cougar over Eryn's body, narrowly missing Rina's spear.

It landed ten feet up a nearby dead tree, its curved claws digging deep into the bark. A chill worked its way down Eryn's spine as the cougar's head rotated 180 degrees to stare at Eryn and Rina with its huge owl-like eyes. It hissed at them, extending its jaw wide enough to fit Eryn's entire head inside.

"You go left, I'll go right." Eryn scrambled to retrieve her bow. Before she could, the cougar leapt again. Claws came at her face and Eryn had nothing to defend herself. She launched backward, knowing it wouldn't get her far enough away.

The cougar's path veered as Rina slammed into it with the full weight of her body. The cougar sprang away and back again. Eryn watched in horror as it hit Rina. Its claws slashed at her gambeson. Its head rose and fell with her arm gripped between its teeth.

She's dead, she's dead, she's dead, Eryn thought. She couldn't lose Rina. She needed her. She didn't need her to place bread in her hand or even to save her from dire cougars. She needed her by her side. Realization flooded Eryn. It wasn't the Dark Lands that made her feel alive. It was Rina. It wasn't ichor that gave her purpose and made her feel like she could do anything. It was Rina.

Eryn drew her sword and ran at the beast. She sank her blade between its ribs with all her strength. The cougar screamed, high-pitched and eerie. Its head flickered to look at her, Rina's arm still in its mouth. There was a sickening cracking noise and the muffled sound of Rina groaning, long and breathless.

She's alive! Eryn tried to pull her sword out. She had to save Rina. But the blade didn't budge.

The cougar's eyes shone as if with a light of their own. It opened its mouth, dropping Rina's arm. The sight of Rina's metal gauntlet around her left arm gave Eryn a moment of relief before the cougar hissed. Its legs flexed to lunge. Its back muscles rippled with anger. It bared its teeth and a murderous rumble resonated from its chest like a dreadful purr.

She'd stabbed it through the chest, and it was excited to kill her for it.

The sound cut off in a single wet crunch. Eryn tore her gaze from the cougar's dulling eyes to Rina's hand at the underside of the beast's chin. Rina pulled back, removing her utility knife with a spray of burgundy red blood. She'd stabbed with enough force to punch directly through the soft palate into the cougar's brain.

The cougar slumped onto Rina, who gave another guttural groan of pain. Eryn put both hands on the cougar, glad for the gloves that kept her from feeling its hairless skin, and shoved. It took several tries to release Rina from its weight.

Rina lay on her back, her gambeson shredded. Splashes of crimson interspersed the burgundy. Eryn was encouraged to see that the crimson of Rina's blood wasn't spreading. The claw and biting damage appeared to be mostly superficial. Her left arm lay across her chest at an unnaturally low angle, and purple bruises were blossoming across the skin beneath the metal frill of her gauntlet.

"Rina, are you okay?" She was breathing, but Eryn had no idea how deep the damage went.

"Fine. Just—just dislocated my shoulder." Rina's words came out with a hiss of pain. "I can reset it. I just need—" She started to sit up, but Eryn pushed her back down with a firm hand on her good shoulder.

"Oh no you won't. You're not resetting your own shoulder. I was trained to do this by the healers themselves, so just lie there and try to breathe normally." She removed the gauntlet, which had protected Rina's arm nearly flawlessly. Slowly, she rotated Rina's arm across her chest until it was held straight out from her body. Eryn anchored her feet against Rina's side and pulled, smoothly but firmly.

"You need to relax your muscles." Eryn wished she had the herbs the healers gave patients.

"I am relaxing them," Rina said through gritted teeth.

"You're clearly not." Eryn pulled harder, trying to keep her pressure even and level. She was rewarded with another loud popping noise as the joint went back into the socket.

Rina's head sank to the ground and a whoosh of air slipped through her lips.

"You're not going to pass out on me, right?" Eryn could get the ichor lantern lit before anything else came to bother them, but she would much prefer to move away from the corpse first. And while she knew how to treat shock, it had a concerning habit of looking awfully like dying. She already thought she'd lost Rina once today. She didn't want to do it again.

"No," Rina said, though she didn't open her eyes. "It doesn't hurt so much anymore. I'm just catching my breath."

"We should make camp and take care of your injuries."

"Not here. The corpse will—"

"Attract other creatures. I know. We'll move if you're able."

"I'm able." Rina tried to sit up, made another guttural noise, and slumped back down. "If I were already standing, I'd be able."

"Let me help you," Eryn said, reaching for Rina's good arm.

Rina pulled away. "I can do it."

"Not if you don't let me help you." Eryn let some of her pent-up tension and fear slip into her tone. "Rina, I need you to make it to a safe place to camp. To do that, I need you to let me help you. I need you to tell me where you are hurt and how badly, and I need you to be truthful."

Rina sighed and sank back once again. She took several deep breaths before answering. "I have a couple of cracked ribs, but my breathing is fine and when I don't move, the pain is minimal. The cuts on my chest are shallow thanks to the gambeson and they don't burn, so I don't think the dire cougar's claws were infected. I just need to get up such that I don't have to bend."

Eryn helped Rina remove the nearly torn pack straps and helped lift her to her feet. When she was sure Rina was stable, Eryn hefted the pack. For a moment, she almost buckled under the weight. How in the lands did Rina carry that thing all day every day, running, jumping, and fighting?

Eryn and Rina ambled away, Eryn providing additional support where she could. They didn't go far before Eryn called it sufficient. Rina sagged more with each step, and there were slowly increasing blotches of red across her tunic.

"Sit," Eryn ordered her once as she lit the lantern, three times while setting up the tent, and twice more as she got Rina situated on her bedroll and pulled the medicaments from the pack. "Dark gods be damned, Rina. Would you just hold still, please? No, you cannot patch yourself up. No, you don't need to show me where each ointment is. I know what I'm doing, so just lie down and hold still."

Eryn removed the shredded gambeson and torn tunic, wetting and removing shredded pieces imbedded in Rina's cuts. She was relieved to see that nothing needed stitches. She'd done them before, but never outside the sterile environment of healers' hall. There were in fact several ointments and creams that she didn't know, but she didn't dare ask Rina. If she did, there would be no chance of Rina acquiescing to being cared for, and that was more important than using all the resources at her disposal. With each wound Eryn treated, she sent a silent prayer of thanks to the Goddess that Rina's armor had protected her and the damage was not more severe.

When she finished, Rina told her where to find the painkillers. "You didn't want those, you know, while I was putting sterilizer on open wounds and rubbing ointment on the skin that is over your cracked ribs?"

Rina shrugged sheepishly. "They'll probably put me to sleep, and you might have needed me."

"I needed you to relax and trust me," Eryn said, her patience running thin. She gave Rina the painkillers and water and left the tent to figure out dinner. She'd watched Rina set up, cook, and clean enough times, but she'd never been a very able cook herself. Her home had a kitchen, but she spent most meals in the cafeteria or, more accurately, grabbed something from the cafeteria as she moved from one task to another. The first step was a fire, and she felt very competent at that.

Rina woke a few hours later and ate her burned, cold stew without complaint. Eryn appreciated the lack of criticism, but it felt like yet another page in the library of things Rina wasn't telling her.

For the first time, Eryn woke up in the Dark Lands without the scent of fire and breakfast. She lay watching Rina's chest rise and fall for several minutes before rising to make a slightly better breakfast than the dinner she'd crafted. When Rina awoke, Eryn gave her a bowl of nearly solid, thankfully not burned, oatmeal and informed her that they would spend the day resting and repairing Rina's armor. Then back to the Community. The shorter trip would give them enough ichor to leave the lantern lit throughout the day so they wouldn't have to worry about monsters or shadows.

Rina accepted with clear irritation. Eryn wanted to tell Rina that it was okay. These things happened in the Dark Lands. Rina had said something similar to Eryn on their last trip, but Eryn had a feeling it wasn't a welcome sentiment. Rina would take it as condescension or coddling.

They worked in silence, Eryn stitching the straps of the pack while Rina jabbed new stuffing and boning into her gambeson as if the need to do so were a personal afront. When her task was done, Rina stood, donned her gambeson, and reached out to Eryn for the pack. "I think we should go. Staying in one place too long could attract attention. We don't want to have to fight multiple monsters when we take the lantern down."

"You need more rest." Eryn wasn't about to make the mistake of letting Rina tell her she was fine again.

"That's not how my body works. While I'm out here, I can endure. I can push through. I don't even really feel the pain." Rina bent forward fluidly. Only her gambeson prevented her from reaching her toes. "When we get home, I'll crash, but I'll have the healers, time, and my own bed. The longer I stay here, wallowing in my injury, the longer my body has to ignore itself with nothing else to focus its attention on. It'll only make recovery harder. So, please, can we go?"

Eryn was torn. She wished she knew whether Rina was telling her the truth or saying what she thought Eryn needed to hear to agree. "All right. But we make it a short day, agreed?"

Thank the Goddess, the day passed uneventfully. As they ate their evenly cooked stew that did not have clumps of uncooked flour in it, Eryn was relieved to see Rina did not look any worse for the day of travel. Either she had been telling the truth or she was a very good actor.

This isn't working, Eryn thought as she lay in her bedroll. Their last trip had been so perfect. Minus her almost getting them both killed and then spending the second half more concerned with each other's bodies than finding ichor. But they'd moved together as a team. She had trusted Rina and Rina had followed flawlessly in her footsteps. This time, things hadn't felt the same from the moment they stepped outside the dome. Their connection was gone.

I hurt her, Eryn realized. How had it taken her so long to understand? After her first mission she'd realized perhaps her rejection of Rina's sexual advances might have felt personal. She'd tried to explain her reasoning for ending their sexual relationship, but she'd been too inside her own head to consider whether solving her own identity crisis wasn't just passing it off to Rina. She'd hurt Rina, and how could she expect to move as one entity with her when she dug the wound deeper every night?

Eryn had always imagined that sex would be the least of her concerns, and in doing so she'd ignored that it might be important to Rina. Eryn's libido could handle not having sex, but she missed the look of adoration on Rina's face. She missed the sound of Rina climaxing against her. Most of all, she missed the feeling of Rina's warmth.

Eryn climbed out of her bedroll as silently as she could and crawled over to Rina's side, dragging her bedroll behind her. Since her moratorium on sex, Rina had stored her stuff between them as if she'd needed a physical barrier. They'd been able to see each other, but that was all. Eryn shoved the pack out of the way and laid her bedroll down in its place. Rina's back was to Eryn and her knees were pulled toward her chest. Eryn couldn't imagine it was a comfortable position for a person with cracked ribs.

Eryn reached out a tentative hand and ran a finger down the purple bruises left by her dislocated shoulder. Rina stiffened under her touch. "Rina?"

Rina sucked in a long sniffling breath before rolling over slowly. In the dim light cast by the dome, Eryn could just make out Rina's bloodshot, swollen eyes. She'd been crying. "I was thinking," Eryn said, unsure how to begin. She didn't really want to explain her reasoning. That was what got them into trouble in the first place. Talking and not listening. "If you want to, if your body is up to it, do you want to have sex with me?"

"But you said—"

"I was wrong and I'm sorry."

"You want me to?" Rina's look was pure vulnerability.

"Please, Rina. If it's what you want, I want it too."

The look of glee that spread across Rina's face left Eryn with no question as to what either of them wanted. Rina tore her bedroll covers back and pulled Eryn to her, their lips and bodies meeting.

This, Eryn thought, this is how I always want to be with her. It was so much more than sex. It was the feeling of being whole with Rina. Eryn fell asleep in Rina's arms to the sound of Rina's sleep-steady breath.

Eryn woke to the familiar smell of delicious breakfast. Rina's smile was hesitant as she held out the bowl of oatmeal that smelled of pear juice. Eryn leaned in for a long kiss before taking the bowl. She wanted there to be no question of her intentions or whether last night was indicative of the nights to come.

A kiss wasn't good enough. "Rina, I care about you a lot. I like who I am when I'm with you. I like the way we fight and move and yes, have sex, but it's more than that. You told me that you will always be there for me, and I need you to know that it goes the other way too. I need you to know that I will always have your back and I need you to know that I trust you to always have mine. You don't have to hide when you're hurt, physically or emotionally. You clearly consider it your job to make sure I feel good. Well, I consider it my job to do the same, and I can't do that job if you don't tell me. Can we do that, be honest with each other?"

Rina nodded, worrying her lip with her teeth. After a moment of silence, she took a deep breath. "It felt really lonely without you."

"Yeah, it did. How about we don't do that?"

"I can get behind that plan." Rina chuckled.

"You know what else feels lonely," Eryn said, wondering why it hadn't occurred to her before. "Walking through the Dark Lands silently, not talking to you."

"But we don't want monsters to—"

"Anything that's going to hear us talking was going to hear us breathing. It's been two months and I barely know anything about you, and I don't like it. Could we not do that too?"

Rina chuckled again. "All right, but you have to tell me about yourself as well."

"Deal. You can start by telling me what it's like to have the head guardian as your mentor." Eryn picked up her spoon and smiled around her first mouthful at the way Rina puffed out her cheeks, as if that was a very loaded question.

"Oh Goddess, where to begin? Well, I guess at the beginning. I remember being so excited the day Claine announced the pairings. It wasn't even about bragging rights or the prestige. I felt like Claine must have seen something in me that none of the others saw. That she wanted me; she did the pairings, after all. I didn't get that sense from any of the other guardians. To this day, I don't know if it's true. Was she the only one willing to take me? Sometimes I get the sense she just wanted to prove that she could fix me, that every time she docked my score it was as much about her as it was about me."

Rina looked away, stamping out the fire as she said, "But Claine is amazing. I got to be trained by the best swordswoman in the Community. She never held back, and I owe who I am to her. One time we were training on the obstacle course in the dark. It was late and I kept falling and she said, 'We won't stop until you finish the course.' I told her that I wouldn't finish the course until she did. She grabbed a pack and ran halfway through before falling. We were there until daybreak, both of us running it over and over again, cussing up a storm every time we fell."

Eryn laughed. There was so much more to the story Rina had started to tell, but she could wait to hear that part. Right now, it just felt good to laugh and to have Rina be the one making her laugh.

CHAPTER EIGHT

Blame and Belief

Eryn lifted onto the toes of her new boots and tried to see around the heads of the heroes celebrating around her. The boots really didn't fit the aesthetic of her outfit and she hated breaking in new boots, but if they were going to be ready for ten straight days of walking in just under three weeks, she needed to start the process now. Her golden dress was far too thin, small, and flowy to be very practical and so low cut she'd fall right out of it if she did anything more strenuous than walking. But it was a gift from an artisan for filling in for his wife during calving season so the pair could care for their ill child. She had so few opportunities to wear it that it felt like a shame to not on occasions like this.

Around her, heroes and guardians were dressed in their best, though the showiness of the heroes' outfits identified them long before seeing the color of their eyes or even the consistent purple coloring of the guardian clothing. Eryn wondered if it was a matter of ostentatiousness or that guardians simply didn't feel the right to acquire impractical finery. Eryn searched the crowd, excited to catch sight of Rina in something showier than a gambeson and tunic.

In one corner of the large community hall, an eclectic band of tinkerers and artisans blared upbeat music on unique instruments. Through a double-wide arch, Eryn could see into the kitchen where kegs of mead and bottles of hooch were slowly being spread into the masses. The whole front half of the hall had been turned into a game of foot the ball, and someone was going to break a bone by the end of the night. Lewd noises came from the little rooms that were used by day as small group gathering places. Eryn wondered how many people would still be here in the morning, disentangling themselves from the hungover bodies of the people they'd slept with.

"Goddess keep the contraceptives coming," Eryn said. She often wondered how they would possibly avoid overpopulation if not for the herb that grew like a weed. "Maybe people would learn a little self-control." Around her, neither moderation nor self-control were welcome party guests.

At the center of it all, on top of a table covered in food, Nim danced, his arms thrown wide and singing at the top of his lungs. Eryn could just make out Lairdin looking up at him with an even mix of envy and pride. There'd be no living with him after this, and Eryn guessed this was the beginning of the end for Nim and Lairdin.

Eryn adjusted the draping of her dress, wishing it covered just a little more of her chest. She was looking forward to the look on Rina's face, though. If it was anything like the look Rina gave her when she stripped during missions, Eryn was fairly sure she'd have to see what those side rooms had to offer.

She'd been reticent to seek Rina's attentions while inside the dome since the night she'd slunk around looking for Rina's house three months before. Everyone talked about sex with their guardians, but never within the dome. She told herself that she was making their times together outside the dome more special. It kept her from having to wonder whether there was something wrong with the fact that she didn't go a day without thinking about Rina and wishing she were there.

But here, their coupling would be lost amongst the mixing of hero and guardian bodies.

"Look no further, I'm right here," a masculine voice whispered at her ear before prickly lips danced over her neck.

Eryn fought back a grimace and pulled away, her shoulders trying to protect her neck. "Hello, Henk."

"You are ravishing, my dear. And ravish you, I shall." He gave her a charming smile to match the affectation of his voice.

"That word really isn't the one you're looking for." At least Eryn hoped it wasn't the right one because she indeed had no interest in sleeping with him. He'd never pushed her on a no, but she'd been saying no to him a lot lately. She was surprised by how much she still found his body attractive while being repulsed by the idea of having him on top of her.

"The only word you're going to need is 'Oooh.'" He did a rather demeaning impersonation of an orgasm and winked. "Plus, I was thinking my guardian could go down on you while we do it. Pretty great, right?"

The guardian standing at his heel smiled at Eryn. Her look screamed, "it's my honor to serve." It made Eryn want to barf. This wasn't having sex; this was abusing his position to make his guardian into a sex object.

"No. I'm not interested," Eryn said. This was not the time or the place to tell him how she really felt. Even if her feelings toward him hadn't already soured, that suggestion had ruined any chances they'd ever get together again.

Henk's expression changed from charming idol to petulant boy in a matter of seconds. "What's the deal, Eryn? It's been three months. Are you hooking up with someone else?"

"No, I've just been busy." Eryn wasn't lying by Henk's standards. He wouldn't count sex with her guardian. Somehow, not counting it felt worse.

"Busy not finding ichor!" Nim inserted himself into the conversation, bringing the crowd with him. Eryn wondered how long he'd been waiting for just such a moment.

"Nim," Henk said. His tone was equal parts warning and chivalry.

"What? I just thought it was worth noting that I found ichor first, not Eryn. It took five trips, but it was me, not her." Nim walked up and put a heavy hand on Eryn's shoulder. She had half a mind to pull away and let him fall. He was certainly drunk enough to land on his face. But aside from being mean, it would be immature and unsportsmanlike. They all served the Community. Eryn should be happy for Nim and happy for the Community.

"I'm proud of you, Nim." She meant it. The Community was more important. This party was for all heroes and guardians in their cohort, but it was because he had found ichor.

"Plus, he used your method of climbing and looking for auras," Lairdin said.

A look of betrayal flowed slowly across Nim's drunken face. If their relationship hadn't been done before, they were done now. Lairdin seemed just as happy to be the one knocking Nim from his high horse. Eryn could understand Lairdin's frustration with Nim's inflated ego and the way it was turning his head and sexual interests around the room like a weathervane in strong winds.

Kalia jumped in, ever the peacemaker. "And no one can blame you for not finding ichor yet, Eryn. You do have the worst guardian in history. She's slowing you down. We know that."

The people around Eryn nodded. Eryn couldn't find her voice. A blush was creeping up her neck. Rina's idea had found Nim the first ichor in their cohort and yet Rina was the one being blamed. Why was everyone staring at her? Why couldn't she just say, "No, Rina's great actually"? Why hadn't she been the first person to find ichor?

"That's why you've been distracted and busy," Henk said, as if this explained everything.

"There's only so much you can do," Kalia said.

"You must be exhausted carrying the team." Henk jumped in again.

Around her, the crowd exploded into statements of support.

"This is why the best hero is supposed to be with the best guardian."

"Nim, you really shouldn't go after Eryn. She already lost her foresight."

"…wonder she brings her guardian back alive every time."

"…death of her first guardian."

"Even Claine couldn't…"

"…can't be blamed."

"…fault…"

They were pressing in on all sides. Eryn couldn't speak, couldn't think, couldn't breathe. "It's not my fault," she yelled into the chaos. The guilt over Syrana's death came surging back. Feelings of inadequacy and loss. Judgment of herself, her feelings, her reactions, that were far harsher than anyone else could thrust upon her.

The room fell silent.

Henk placed both hands on Eryn's shoulders. "No, it's not your fault." He lifted his gaze and glared poignantly over Eryn's shoulder.

Eryn turned slowly to follow the gaze of the entire room. Rina stood in the middle of what had been the foot the ball game. Her silky purple button-down and black trousers looked stunning. Her red hair was pulled back from her shoulders by clips, giving the entire room a good view of the blush that ran from her neck to her forehead. Silently, Rina turned and left.

"Rina," Eryn said before hurrying to follow.

Behind her she could hear Henk call after her, "Yeah, you send her home. She shouldn't even be here. We'll catch up later."

Eryn pushed past the leakage of the party onto the road and hurried after the quickly disappearing figure of Rina. "Rina, wait."

Rina didn't slow.

"Rina, I know you can hear me. Just stop and let me explain."

Eryn saw more than heard Rina's sigh as she stopped and waited, still turned away. "Rina, listen, I'm sorry. I wasn't saying it was your fault. I just got overwhelmed." Tears stung her eyes and she fought to keep her voice steady. "It's not—"

"It doesn't matter." Rina spun to face her with a mask of indifference. "Everyone thinks I'm the worst guardian. Even among the other guardians who know how skilled I am, I'm a pariah. Syrana was the only one who got me. The only one who was interested in anything from me besides a fun night."

Eryn tried not to take the statement personally. This was about Rina, not the fact that Rina had just entirely discounted who she was to Eryn. Nor was it about how she felt every time Syrana was the topic of Rina's stories. "That's not—"

Rina interrupted again. "People are going to think the worst of me no matter what. At least you get to benefit from it. My job is to protect you. It's what I swore to do. So let me protect your reputation too. I'm no worse off. If it saves you from the vultures, then something good has come from it."

Eryn didn't like it. It wasn't fair. It wasn't right. "But—"

"Just let it go, Eryn. You can't fix it. When we find ichor, you will get the credit. When we don't, I'll get the blame. That's just the way it is."

"But it shouldn't be."

Rina shrugged. "It is. I'm going home. You should have fun." She pointed over Eryn's shoulder toward the party.

"I don't want to go back. Walk me home?" She didn't think she could face Henk without punching him in his charming little face.

Rina shrugged again but set off in the direction of the hero quarter.

They walked in silence until they reached Eryn's porch. Eryn made it up the five steps before realizing Rina wasn't following her. "Do you want to come in?"

"I should get back." She turned to go.

"You look really great," Eryn blurted.

Rina paused to look Eryn up and down. She'd gotten plenty of attention throughout the night, but it was this appraisal that Eryn had been waiting for all night.

"You always look beautiful, Eryn." Rina turned and left.

❖

Rina wouldn't quite describe waking up in the Dark Lands as refreshing. Even inside the lantern dome, the smell of decay leaked out of every thread and pore. But she did get to wake up with Eryn's body half in her own bedroll and half in Rina's, warm and naked.

In the Dark Lands, no one questioned Rina's value. She'd put in a request with Claine to shift to training younger guardians. If she could get to them before scores defined their lives, maybe they would define her less by her score. It was hard to get a fifteen-year-old to respect her and improve his form when his score was higher at fifteen than hers was at twenty. Claine had said her score wouldn't matter anymore, but she was wrong.

Rina dressed and crept from the tent to start a fire and make breakfast. As the flame burst to life, a wave of cold dread spread over Rina. Like the wind on Frost Night, she felt his presence sweep through the lantern dome to rest at her shoulder.

Hello, Rina.

Rina suppressed a shudder. It wasn't just the cold, the smell, or the dimming colors that the Commander brought with him. It was the feeling of being angry and adrift. The truly wretched part was that the emotions didn't feel pressed upon her but instead brought out from inside, as if he were digging into her soul and bearing her worst truths.

Have you thought about the two things I left you with last time?

Rina groaned inwardly. She had in fact spent most of her waking moments thinking about what he had said. The majority was spent trying to walk the wishy-washy line between thinking perfectly respectable things about the Goddess and reaching what must certainly be heretical conclusions about the lies of guardian philosophy and the truth of shadows. It was hard to focus on teaching young guardians how to make excellent camp breakfasts while trying to figure out if she was being poisoned or cured.

She'd been relieved when he hadn't come back during the last two missions, but he'd clearly just been waiting for something to prove his words correct.

While the question of shadows had occupied her thoughts, it was his warning that had occupied her heart. Her puppy demanded that she ignore any words against Eryn. It was willing to admit that heroes as a generalization were rather full of themselves, but didn't they have reason to be? In addition to being literally the purpose of guardians, they collected the lifeblood of the Community. But Eryn was different. She was the best. She cared about Rina. She'd said so herself.

The pain of the first-ichor party came rushing back as the Commander lingered at her shoulder waiting for an answer. She'd been honest when she told Eryn that being blamed by everyone else didn't matter. She'd known they would blame her. But Eryn?

Rina was a distraction. Hadn't Eryn made that clear when she'd said they shouldn't have sex? She'd come back because the difference in their performance was obvious. It was clear where Eryn's priorities lay—ichor and her own reputation.

The weight of darkness swelled and ebbed as if the Commander were nudging her. "Yes," Rina said. She turned away from his presence and went back to setting up her cooking tools.

Ah, I see my warning has cut deeper than you expected. Trust me, the heartache of realizing the truth is much less than living in delusion.

Rina made a noncommittal noise. What possible future did he see for her? And why speak of it in a veil of warning rather than just spouting it the way other shadows did? They had never held back.

Well, I can tell when my presence is not welcome. It has been a pleasure speaking with you, nonetheless. It is always nice to have someone who gets you. For me, Rina, that is you. Who is it for you?

The darkness of the Commander lifted, but Rina found her anger and loneliness didn't leave with him this time, like a glob of sap that wouldn't wash out. How dare the Commander try to use her words against her. But she wasn't just angry with him. She was angry with Eryn, who had proven him right. Eryn, who Rina wanted to be the person who got her. Eryn, who she couldn't help but love, who said she cared about Rina but made it very clear that she cared about everyone in the Community, especially herself.

For two days, Rina followed Eryn through the Dark Lands. The majority of their conversations focused on the differences between their schooling. Heroes went to school with the children of other castes to learn reading and writing from priests and math from the judges, while guardians were educated in the garrison by guardians. Rina fell asleep each night with Eryn, trying to savor every moment.

Rina!

Rina grunted, pushing at the edges of her dream.

Rina!

She sat bolt upright on her bedroll, spear in hand. Next to her Eryn rolled away with her own grunt.

Rina, a hero is about to break a natural dam farther up the mountain. It will flood the valley in which you are camped.

Rina gave a final grunt and lay back on the bedroll. "The dome will protect us." She was going to have a terrible time falling back to sleep and she had a marsh to look forward to in the morning.

From the water yes, but there will be a colony of dire ants that floats down with it. They will see the dome as higher ground and climb on top. When Eryn brings down the dome, they will rain down upon you.

Rina could feel their thin, stabbing legs crawling all over her and imagine them stinging over and over.

If you get moving now, you can be gone before the water gets here.

Rina hesitated. Could she trust him? Was he trying to lure her and Eryn into a trap, groggy and unsuspecting?

If I wished you ill, there would be easier ways to do it. The Commander's tone was clipped. *I have bigger things in mind for you and for us. Things that will make a real difference. If you stay, you will prove me right, but I am not here to be proven right. I am here to help you.*

"Eryn." Rina shook her shoulder. She would rather feel foolish waking Eryn for nothing than risk a battle with an entire colony of dire ants. "Eryn, you need to wake up. I heard something. We need to break camp and move to a safer location."

Eryn swatted her away. "The dome will protect us."

"Not if we're surrounded. Eryn, this could be important. Please, get up. I need you to trust me." The fact she was really saying Eryn needed to trust a shadow felt deceptive, but there was no way she could tell Eryn the truth.

As if she'd pedaled her brain into motion, Eryn's eyes flickered open and she sat up. "What do we need to do?"

"Pack and move to higher ground."

Eryn moved with the same efficiency and grace she used to fight monsters. She trusts me without question, Rina thought, handing the thought to her puppy so it could roost on that rather than yapping about whether she was betraying that trust.

It took them barely over a minute to break camp and extinguish the lantern. Rina couldn't hear or see any changes. Were they early enough to beat the flood? Was there even a flood?

"Which direction will it come from?" Rina said in a whisper to the prickle of stinging cold at her shoulder. They were outside the lantern dome, and the feeling of the Commander intensified though he was still incorporeal.

Rina led Eryn out of the valley as the Commander indicated. They'd only made it a few minutes when a booming crack broke the near silence around them. Rina watched from their higher vantage point as a river of churning, grimy water spilled down the mountain to their right. It was only about ankle deep, but Rina knew well the kinds of dangers opaque water could hold in the Dark Lands. The remnants of their campfire were easily swept up and disappeared into the debris.

Next to her, Eryn cleared her throat, but Rina hadn't yet seen what she was watching for. She could see Eryn out of the corner of her eye evaluating her. She would have to explain herself. Would that be easier or harder if the last part of the Commander's prediction came true?

As she watched, a raft of living, squirming ants bobbed over the churning waters. Each was the size of her hand and discernible clambering into and out of the water to share the surface with the members of its colony. A small sound escaped Eryn and Rina couldn't help but agree with the not quite relief, not quite concern it expressed.

"Rina, how did you know that was going to happen?"

Rina had been relying on saying she'd heard the dam break, but they'd both heard it clearly minutes after Rina had lied. Now what? She chewed on her lip reflexively and turned in the direction of the Commander's presence.

Tell her the truth or lie. The choice is yours. You are safe, and that is what matters to me. With that, he moved away, not gone but far enough that his absence was a physical relief.

"Rina?" Eryn said again. "You agreed to be honest with me."

Rina turned to her with nothing better or more believable than the truth. "A shadow told me."

For a long moment, Eryn was silent. Her face was an open book of emotions as if she turned the page at the end of each thought. Confusion. Anger. Betrayal. Fear. "You said you stopped listening to them."

"I said my score was low because I used to listen to them. But yes, I implied it, and it wasn't true. I still listen to them."

The look of betrayal and horror only increased as Rina spoke.

"I'm sorry. I should have told you, but please listen. Shadows don't always lie. I have proof. That right there. That's proof." She pointed at the flooded ground where their campsite had sat minutes ago. "There's no other way I could have known. A shadow told me, and it was true and not because I made it come true. I couldn't have caused the dam to break. I couldn't have caused that mat of dire ants. I certainly couldn't have caused it to happen to our campsite. And it's not the only proof. I've been listening to them the whole time."

Eryn flinched back but Rina couldn't stop. She needed Eryn to understand. "I stopped us from walking under a hive of dire bees. I kept us away from a rockslide. I knew about the dire raccoons moments before they attacked not because I heard them, but because a shadow told me. Shadows see possible futures, and we can use that to avoid bad futures."

"You...but...how?" Tears were collecting in Eryn's lower eyelashes, and she looked on the verge of turning and fleeing. "Are you sabotaging us?"

"No! Eryn, I would never. Everything I've done has been to protect you and help you find ichor. I just want to keep you safe, and listening to shadows helps me do that."

"You're supposed to block them out! You're going to get us

killed!" Eryn was on the edge of hysterics. Rina had expected Eryn to be angry, but not to scream at her. "How am I supposed to trust you when you hid the truth from me? How am I supposed to ever trust that what you're telling me isn't straight from the mouth of a shadow?"

"I haven't betrayed you. I just saved you." This panic was a side of Eryn Rina hadn't seen and didn't know how to manage. Normally, Eryn was logical and pragmatic.

I can lead you to ichor. The Commander's sudden return felt like a plunge into icy water. She gasped, filling her lungs with painfully cold air.

Rina opened her mouth and then quickly closed it again. Was this the path the Commander was lining up before her? Each step was a choice to follow him, but broken up, each could feel reasonable. She still didn't know what he wanted, and she didn't like playing a game where she didn't know the rules.

Eryn refused to look at Rina. She looked pale even in the dim light. She seemed more lost than angry and as unsure what to do next as Rina. Rina had no doubt that were they in the Community, Eryn would have run away from her by now, possibly never to return. But out here, where could she go?

There was only one real way forward, though Rina didn't like it. She wanted to handle one crisis of trust at a time. "The shadow says it can lead us to ichor."

It? Rina, I'm hurt. His voice was taunting, and Rina had no time for it.

She watched Eryn's expression flip through emotions waiting to see where it would end. The book of emotions snapped shut as if Eryn had decided to simply turn it all off. "You said shadows don't always lie. How do you know it is telling the truth this time?"

"Because it wants me to believe it, and if it lies, I won't trust it again." Whatever the Commander was building her toward would be bigger than leading her to false ichor. She had no doubt that this was an early step in what he wanted to be their shared journey.

"And that's enough?" Eryn fixed her with a hard stare and Rina knew it wasn't just the Commander staking everything on this, it was Rina too.

"I know it's telling the truth." There was no other way forward.

Eryn seemed to have come to the same conclusion. "If I think we are in danger, we will turn back and leave. If we do not find ichor, we will turn back and go home. Rina, you need to understand that if we return without ichor, you and I will never leave the Community together again. Are you sure?"

Rina couldn't hesitate. She couldn't seem unsure. "Yes."

Her puppy lost its mind.

CHAPTER NINE

Love and Lesser Creatures

Panic lapped at Eryn's ankles. She shoved it back, but there was too much of it creeping in from too many sides. Syrana listened to shadows. Syrana died. They were following a shadow. How could this possibly not lead to death?

Part of Eryn wanted to turn back. She was supposed to trust her training and her own gut, and both told her she should run the other way. But if she did, she would be running from Rina. She couldn't go on missions with Rina if she couldn't trust her, but going on missions with her was the highlight of every month. When she was in the Community, she longed to be in the Dark Lands with Rina, and she knew it had much less to do with the excitement, the challenge, or the chance of ichor than it did about time with Rina.

She started to pray that they would find ichor and then quickly cut off. Was it blasphemy to ask the Goddess for a shadow to lead them to ichor? She felt even more blasphemous for the fact that her desire wasn't really about returning with ichor. She wanted Rina to be right. She was hinging everything on this single outcome, and she wasn't sure she was willing to follow through no matter which way it went.

With every step, Eryn expected the ground to open up and swallow them whole or for a swarm of creatures to leap on them. As they crested a hill, Eryn gripped her bow and prepared to fight to her last breath.

Eryn stepped into a rocky clearing, her gaze drawn to the towering tree at its center. Its colossal trunk pulsed with an ominous rhythm, and its threat radius stretched forty feet in all directions. Boulders scattered around the outer edges testified to its relentless growth. Fire moss flickered on the ground, while roots broke through like bulging veins. Beneath two such roots, Eryn got her first sight of ichor in the Dark Lands.

The strip of golden liquid looked just like a vein of mineral gold. Just the sight felt like hope and joy, like coming home. It was enough to bring tears to Eryn's eyes. "Ichor."

Next to her, Rina breathed a sigh of relief. So, she hadn't been so sure after all.

Eryn pointed out the location to Rina who wouldn't be able to see the ichor even after Eryn scooped it into bottles. "How are we supposed to get to it?" Eryn said. The shadow had led them to ichor, but within the tree's reach, it was useless.

"We'll have to distract it. Blind it." Rina's willingness to see this as a challenge to be overcome rather than a deterrent surprised Eryn. It was usually Rina trying to rein in Eryn's proclivity to take risks. Eryn supposed Rina had far more invested in this outcome than wandering into a bog or climbing one final mountain before turning back. So did Eryn.

"Trees don't see, they smell, taste, and feel their prey."

Rina nodded. Her fingers danced over the alchemical vials in the bandolier across her chest. "Smoke it out, overstimulate its senses. I'm going to need wood, as moist as we can find it, and a lot of rocks. I'll distract the tree and keep it busy while you focus on the ichor. Get as much of it as you can, then drink it and we'll run."

When they had finished preparing, Rina handed Eryn the smaller pack within her giant pack, filled with glass bottles for just this purpose. As Rina squatted next to the first unlit bonfire she'd prepared, she paused and turned back to Eryn. "If you don't want to leave the Community with me again, I'll understand. All you have to do is let Claine know what I told you and she'll make sure I don't leave again. But if you do want me to stay your guardian, Claine can't know, and no one who would tell Claine can know, like the head hero. I just wanted to let you know before you drink the ichor since I don't think I'll have a chance until we're back in the Community once we start."

The thought made Eryn's heart ache. It would be so easy to lose Rina. She could lose her here and now trying to fight a tree for ichor.

Rina was about to risk her life without even knowing if she was going home to celebration or rejection.

Eryn leaned down, buried her hand in Rina's red hair, and pulled their lips together. She kissed her long and hard, savoring it. "I want you, Rina. Be safe."

Rina's smile was all triumph and determination. "Let's do this." With her metal gauntlet, she scooped up a pile of fire moss and mashed it into the center of her unlit bonfire. The wet logs burst into flame and gray smoke billowed forth almost immediately. Rina poured one of her vials into the fire and the air was filled with an acrid scent that burned at the hairs in Eryn's nose.

In the center of the clearing, the tree's expansion slowed, then it twisted shut with violent speed. Rina was already moving, one of the burning logs in her hand. She used it to light the other bonfires around the circle.

The tree remained shut, seemingly unaffected. Rina grabbed a rock off one of her many piles and rolled it across the ground as if she were playing a giant's version of Ichor and Shadows.

A thick limb swung across the field, long thin branches like fingers raking the air above the rock. Rina rolled another rock and another, drawing the tree's focus and exposing it to the acrid smoke. When grabbing at the air failed, the tree began to slam the ground along the rolling rock's path with enough force to make the whole hill vibrate.

Rina smiled. Her rolls slowed slightly as she began to aim. The tree struck the ground again, this time hitting a patch of fire moss and exploding in flames. The limb flailed back, whipping through the air with blinding speed. While the tree tried to put itself out, Rina refocused on the fires, fanning the smoke toward the tree.

Rina went back and forth between her rock piles and fires, waiting for the tree to almost resolve a crisis before switching to another. She gave Eryn the signal.

Eryn hunkered down and ran. She scurried under a raking limb, zigzagged away from a scooping branch, and dropped next to the ichor shining just below the surface. Now, all she had to do was retrieve the ichor without causing any disturbance.

The whirling golden light from the ichor seemed to be flowing in a root all its own just below the surface. She pulled a small blade from the pack, made an incision into the ground, and was rewarded with a thin fountain of ichor spouting from the hole she'd made.

"Eryn!"

Eryn looked up just in time to see the branch coming for her. She rolled to the side, narrowly avoiding the crash of multiple limbs. The tree whipped its limbs back and forth, searching the ground and air.

"Hey!" Rina yelled. The thunk of rocks striking the tree's thick trunk quickly followed. The branches changed direction, searching for the source of the rocks. Eryn sidled back to the spurt of ichor as softly as she could and began to fill the first bottle. She corked bottle after bottle as Rina ran from rock pile to bonfire and back around the circle.

As the stream of ichor became a trickle, Eryn looked up in time to see the tree pull itself to its full height and slam down in Rina's direction. A creaking noise as loud as a crack of lightning reverberated from the tree as it leaned into the strike, pulling its trunk with it.

Rina stumbled backward, tripped over a pile of rocks, and landed hard on her back. The tree reared up and slammed again, bending until its trunk nearly touched the ground. Its finger-like branches closed around Rina's torso and snatched her into the air. She flailed and struck at the branches holding her, to no avail. The tree wrapped more branches around Rina as she struggled to fight back. All the while, it brought Rina closer and closer to the opening in the top of its trunk where it would attempt to consume her.

"Rina!" Eryn grabbed a rock from the ground and threw it at the tree. She had to distract it. There was no way she could damage it.

The tree smacked Eryn full in the chest with one of its many limbs, throwing her several feet to land sprawled across roots and rocks. She sent a small prayer of thanks to the Goddess that she didn't land on any fire moss and ran back toward the fray.

Eryn scooped up rocks and flung them as she ran. She made it halfway back toward the tree, dodging limbs, before one connected and sent her flying again. She hit the ground hard this time. It took concerted effort to draw breath. Her whole chest ached. That didn't matter, though. The tree had Rina's thrashing body directly over its trunk, and she didn't know how to stop it. Her feeble attempts to attack it didn't even distract it. She had to try something else.

"Eryn, drink the ichor!"

The ichor! Holden always said there was nothing like the feeling of having the blood of the Goddess pumping through his veins. He felt like he could do anything.

Eryn picked herself up and tried to run. Her body spasmed in pain and she fell. Her left hand landed palm-first into a patch of fire moss and she screamed as flame engulfed it. She smothered the fire with her scarf and tried desperately to ignore the pain. Rina needed her. She scrambled, her bad hand held to her chest. A branch came for her. She dove over it, grabbed one of the bottles, uncorked it, and downed the contents.

Eryn threw her head back as her body went rigid. She could feel her blood vessels expanding to accommodate the Goddess's blood. Her muscles seared with heat. Her clothing felt constricting and she flexed, popping threads in the layers beneath her gambeson. The lacing of her gambeson pulled tight as she took a deep breath, marveling at the feeling of near invulnerability. Power felt good.

In the background, a small voice was yelling. Some lesser creature was struggling for its life. That was the way of lesser creatures.

Eryn scooped up the bag of ichor. She would take this back to her den, and she would have power. She would be a higher creature and when her supply ran low, she would find more. She would feel like this forever. The draw toward home was unmistakable. She could feel it calling her. She turned to run.

"Eryn!"

The lesser creature was calling to her. Eryn looked over her shoulder. It stood no chance against the tree it was fighting. That was unfortunate.

She turned away and felt a rush of sadness. She didn't want the lesser creature to die. That lesser creature was important to her. Very important. It would take so little to save the creature.

Eryn sprinted to the closest boulder. She hefted it above her head and ran at the tree. A limb swung toward Eryn, slow and predictable. She jumped over it. Another forced Eryn to duck. The third she climbed, running toward the lesser creature. She landed, her feet straddling the tree's mouth, and looked down into its cylinder of grimy, gnashing teeth. An acrid smell rose from the dripping, digesting fluids within.

Eryn set the boulder under the lesser creature's body, blocking the mouth. She grabbed it around the waist and pulled. The lesser creature whined. The tree didn't want to let go, and together they were pulling the lesser creature apart. Idiotic tree, Eryn thought. It too was a lesser creature. She slapped away the branches that tried to grab her, then grabbed the branches holding the lesser creature and snapped them one by one.

Something sharp scratched across Eryn's arm and she looked down to see blood dampening her gambeson. A moment later, she felt a sting of a fresh cut across her face. She looked down at the lesser creature. She looked scared. Her attention flicked around them as if she was scared of the air.

Silly lesser creature, Eryn thought. If this tree dared to harm her, she would kill it. Nothing could harm her, not really.

Eryn clutched the lesser creature to her chest and jumped on the rock with all her strength. Her legs strained with power, and it felt good to flex it.

A sound like the ripping of cloth brought Eryn joy, even as another cut dug deep into her gambeson. But she wasn't ripping, the tree was. She jumped again and again, slamming the rock deeper and deeper into the insolent tree while it dared to try to hurt her. The trunk ripped open more and more.

Against her chest, the lesser creature pulled her head away and started talking. Her words were desperate and breathless. "You said you're the commander, so can't you tell the shadows to stop or something?" The creature's words didn't make sense, so Eryn continued stomping. She was so close.

With a final, satisfying tearing sound and a squish of fleshy juices, the boulder hit the ground. The tree split, its branches and trunk collapsing onto the ground in a splay around Eryn.

She leapt down to the ground triumphantly and placed the lesser creature next to her giant pack. She was damaged. Her gambeson was sliced with trickling blood beneath. A deep scratch down her face was oozing blood. She was a pitiful creature, but she would likely heal. Eryn turned and ran. She had ichor and she needed to get it to her den where she could hoard it.

Something was following her. Eryn looked over her shoulder to see the pitiful creature running after her. One hand was held to her side and the other to her chest as if it pained her to be running. She was a silly, pitiful thing to think she could keep up with Eryn, especially with that giant pack. But she was giving it everything she had. Good for her. Eryn turned back toward home and picked up speed.

The same sadness rose in Eryn. She turned back to look at the pitiful creature. She was trying so hard. It was adorable really. She liked this adorable creature. She didn't want to leave her behind.

Eryn stopped. Despite the overwhelming urge to get back to her den, Eryn turned around and jogged back to the adorable creature. She was about a head shorter than Eryn and looked like she was about to fall over. Eryn took the pack off the adorable creature's shoulders and slung it over her shoulder next to the pack of ichor. She bent down and scooped the adorable creature onto her other shoulder, then turned back toward home.

Joy flooded her as she took off toward home. Her power and strength, the thrill of pushing her body past the point she'd ever been, felt good. Defeating the tree had felt better. To have this adorable creature over one shoulder and a bag full of ichor on the other felt glorious.

The adorable creature whimpered as she jostled back and forth on Eryn's shoulder. She couldn't have that. She certainly didn't want to hurt her. She changed her gait. It slowed her pace slightly, but it was worth it.

She would take both the adorable creature and the ichor back to her den. The ichor would keep her strong and the adorable creature would keep her happy. She would protect the adorable creature, feed her, and love her.

Realization dawned on Eryn. That was why the adorable creature had felt so important to her, why it filled her with joy to have her close and sadness to watch her struggle. She wanted to love her. She did love her.

"Everything will be all right," she said to the adorable creature. "I've got you."

She crested a final hill and looked down at the glow of her home in the center of the flatlands. She longed for it. Home!

As she approached, her pace slowed again. She tried to push faster, but her legs didn't respond. The weight on her shoulders grew until she simply couldn't manage it all. She set the adorable creature and her pack down. "Follow," she said, stumbling forward.

Her head ached, but everything would be okay. She just had to get into her den and then she'd be able to drink more ichor. She would feel the power again and nothing would stand in her way. She clutched the bag of ichor to her chest. She would have the adorable creature to love and ichor to drink. She would be powerful. She would be invincible.

Eryn stumbled through the dome and collapsed at the edge of a line of fruit trees.

"Eryn." Rina was there, looking down at her. She really was adorable. Though perhaps beautiful would be a better word for it. "Don't worry. We're home. You're going to be all right."

Eryn smiled at her. Why was Rina concerned? Everything was great, even if her head felt like it was splitting open, and her legs felt like jelly. She held up the bag of ichor bottles before her arms gave out as well. "We did it." Her eyes drifted shut and she tried to repeat the line but wasn't sure it made it out of her mouth.

Eryn moaned as consciousness seeped back into her. She felt like she was being shoved headfirst through a hole that was much too small for her.

Holden chuckled next to her. "Like the worst hangover of your life, isn't it? Luckily, it passes much faster than a regular hangover. You'll be back on your feet in an hour or two."

Scrunching her face didn't make her feel any better, but she hoped it got the message across. It wasn't just her head either. Her whole body felt like someone had been beating on it for hours.

"Where's my guardian?" Eryn asked. She remembered Rina had been injured.

"I sent her home a couple of hours ago. She did not want to leave." His tone made it clear he found her reluctance annoying rather than endearing. "Ichor stories are always my favorite, especially first-time ichor stories. So, since you're going to be here for the next hour anyway, do tell and please don't spare any details." Eryn could imagine the smile on his face and the gleam in his eyes.

Personally, Eryn wasn't sure how she felt about her story. Living it had felt amazing, but now she felt empty without the ichor and lonely without Rina. She didn't just have a hangover. This was withdrawal, and it was miserable.

Eryn could feel Holden shifting in his seat expectantly.

She started with the trip up the mountain from their last campsite, making sure to leave out the flood, the shadow, and her ultimatum to Rina. In her version, they'd simply come across the tree, and she'd seen ichor amongst the roots. She described Rina's methods for distracting the tree and her own retrieval of the ichor. Holden made noises of agreement as she described the feeling of drinking the ichor, the surge of power, and the drive to bring it back. She also skipped the part about her intention to hoard the ichor for herself to feel that powerful forever.

"I grabbed a boulder and ran to save my guardian. I smashed the boulder into its mouth until I split the tree open—"

"Wait, you drank ichor and then went back for your guardian?"

Eryn opened one eye to take in Holden's shocked expression. He looked equal parts incredulous and impressed. "Yes," she said hesitantly. Was she not supposed to?

"I have never heard of anyone having the self-control to do anything but run back to the Community after drinking ichor. That's why heroes are supposed to put on their guardian's pack before drinking, because there's no way they would have the wherewithal to do it after. You are truly one of a kind, Eryn." After a moment's silence, Holden said, "Do go on."

So, Eryn told the rest of her story in a mostly accurate way. Instead of going back for her guardian a second time, she combined it into simply carrying her after the tree attack. She described the joy of pushing her body beyond its former physical limits and skipped any revelations to do with Rina.

By the time she was done, her head indeed felt almost normal. She could keep her eyes open without squinting and she bet she'd be able to sit up without the room spinning.

Holden looked exceedingly satisfied. "Excellent work, though I would expect nothing less. Next time if you don't exert yourself so much on the return trip, you'll make it all the way into the Community before you finish metabolizing the ichor. I'm proud of you, Eryn. Get some rest. You've certainly earned it."

He left, leaving her at the part of her story she'd left untold. "I want to love her," Eryn repeated inside her head. Except that wasn't how it was supposed to go. Heroes didn't fall in love with their guardians. Guardians didn't even date anyone but other guardians. But

Eryn couldn't look at her actions or her feelings and come to any other conclusion. She groaned. Didn't her body hurt enough without adding heartache and confusion to the mix?

She wished she could ask Holden or any of her instructors about it, but she already knew how they would react. They would dismiss it, attributing her emotions to the lingering effects of the ichor high, and insist that she was confusing her love for the Community, success, and adventure with love for her guardian. But Eryn had spent enough time with Rina on missions to recognize the truth. It was Rina who stirred these emotions within her. There was only one person who might truly understand. Eryn had to cling to that hope because carrying this unspoken burden felt as heavy and painful as ichor withdrawal.

That night, Eryn wandered through the crowd gathered in the middle of Alba's neighborhood. One of Alba's neighbors had adopted their first child, and the whole neighborhood was gathered to celebrate. Maybe if she wandered long enough, she would find the words to ask the question she needed.

If she was honest with herself, Eryn knew she was scared. Alba's opinion mattered to her more than anyone else's, even Holden's. What would she do if Alba told her something she didn't want to hear? Alba was the only person in Eryn's life who was able to be both nonjudgmental and brutally honest at the same time. What if Alba thought less of her for loving the wrong person? And Goddess, if she ever knew that Rina listened to shadows, Eryn couldn't imagine what she would think of Eryn loving her anyway.

Finally, Eryn spotted Alba seated at the edge of the dance circle, cradling a baby and swaying to the music as she tapped her foot. As Eryn approached, Alba gestured towards the empty spot on the bench beside her, wearing the warm smile that never failed to fill Eryn's heart.

"I wanted to ask you a question," Eryn said. She wished she didn't sound so uncomfortable. "Well, maybe it's not a question but a statement. I haven't quite figured it out." She gave Alba what she was sure came across as a self-deprecating smile and tried not to wince.

"I am here when you're ready," Alba said, turning to her with the full depth of her attention.

Eryn bit her lip before finally uttering the words that weighed on her. "I think I'm falling in love with my guardian."

Alba seemed unfazed. "And?"

She'd been afraid of what Alba might think, but she hadn't expected her to—what? Accept it with a single word that at the same time was entirely unfulfilling? "And...I don't know what to do about it."

"Is it really what you should *do* that's making you uncomfortable?" Alba asked.

No, but the thought of delving into how she felt was like a rock in the pit of her stomach. She didn't want to admit she was scared of being judged; it was deeper than that. "I want to know if there's something wrong with me for feeling this way." She hated the way admitting it felt right and horrible at the same time.

"Tell me more. What about loving someone makes you feel wrong?"

It wasn't about loving someone; it was about loving Rina. "Heroes don't fall in love with their guardians."

"Sure, but you aren't like other heroes."

"I fail to see how being the best makes me more likely to fall in love with my guardian." Eryn felt her impatience bubble up. Why didn't Alba understand that this was a big deal?

Alba placed a reassuring hand on Eryn's shoulder. She did understand. She always understood, but she was reaching at something deeper, Eryn realized. "I wasn't talking about being the best. I'm talking about caring about people that the rest of the heroes wouldn't deign to give a second thought. Your instructors are too busy teaching you all to be heroes to teach you how to be people. I'm talking about compassion, humility, empathy. Before me, no one had taught you that. I don't take credit for the woman you've become. You did that all on your own. So, perhaps other heroes aren't the best measuring stick for what's right or wrong for *you*."

Eryn had wanted to know if she was less of a hero for loving Rina. It was overwhelming to consider that maybe she'd been asking the wrong question the whole time. Over the past five months, she'd tried not to be uncomfortable with the way other heroes talked about Rina. It wasn't just Rina either. They treated all their guardians that way. The look on Henk's guardian's face when he'd suggested they all hook up had made it all too clear that Henk's treatment was not new or surprising to her. Possibly most damning was Eryn's own shame that she loved Rina and the deep fear that someone might see it or think it. She was embarrassed to even tell Alba.

"What if I'm just confusing love of getting ichor with love for her?" It would be so much easier if it wasn't real.

Alba let the question linger, creating a moment of space for Eryn to recognize it as an excuse. Then, she redirected it with a curious expression. "How do you feel about her when you aren't getting ichor?"

A feeling of longing washed over Eryn. "I want her with me. I want to bask in the way she looks at me and the way I feel when I'm with her. When I'm with her, I feel like it doesn't matter if I find ichor because she'll still be there, she'll still care about me and want to help me succeed."

"It sounds like you're willing to be unguarded with her."

Perhaps that was part of the problem. At the same moment Rina was making Eryn feel accepted, she made her feel vulnerable to the judgment of others, to herself, and to shadows. "But there's more about my guardian that you don't know."

"I won't unless you tell me," Alba said.

Eryn looked around, scared someone might overhear. Should she even be telling Alba? She just wanted to feel vindicated for her hesitance and even shame at falling for her guardian. She wanted to be told she was allowed to feel those things or at least that she should be confused about how she felt. "She listens to shadows. She believes them."

"That must be terrible." Alba's tone was soft and sad.

"Right? How am I supposed to trust her?" Vindication was within sight.

Alba's expression was filled with sympathy, but she wasn't looking at Eryn. "Actually, I meant that must be terrible for your guardian. As I understand it, shadows say horrible things meant to make the guardian feel bad about themselves and predictions about the future full of death, failure, and pain. We say that all the castes are equal, but, well, I shouldn't admit this, but I'm sad when a baby's eyes turn purple because I know they will never have the life everyone else gets. I've always wondered how young guardians make it through their formative years like that before they learn to block shadows out. Can you imagine what it would be like to never learn to block them out? Can you imagine being told horrible things about yourself and the future every day, and worse, believing them?"

Eryn's heart sank. No, she couldn't. All her life people had told her how wonderful she was and all the wonderful things she would achieve. She'd nearly caused the death of herself and Rina when she thought she'd lost that future. At the first-ichor party, she'd panicked when she felt like people were telling her she was a failure, and they'd been blaming Rina, not her. Rina said everyone was going to blame her anyway, that she was a pariah. How in the lands did Rina hear nothing but negativity from shadows, heroes, and guardians, and yet get up every day ready to serve Eryn and the Community?

"She's all by herself," Eryn said, more to herself than to Alba. Maybe, in the end, this wasn't about Eryn. It was about Rina.

"She has you."

She will, Eryn thought. She hadn't gotten the vindication she wanted but perhaps she had gotten what she truly needed—permission to see Rina as a person deserving of her compassion and love.

❖

The head priest's words floated by Rina unheard. She was supposed to be worshipping, echoing the priest's words in her heart and mind, but her mind kept drifting back to watching Eryn drink the ichor, pick up her pack, and start to leave without her.

Telling Eryn to drink the ichor had been the Commander's idea. But if he saw negative futures, how could he have known it was a good idea? Unless he'd seen Eryn leave her. Had he been waiting for Eryn to abandon her, to show where her true priorities lay?

Everything Rina knew about ichor-imbued heroes was second-hand, as it was unthinkably dangerous to have a hero drink ichor inside the Community when they didn't have a sack full of ichor to run home with. To see Eryn transform had been exhilarating and terrifying. Physically, she hadn't changed much, but seeing her with a boulder held above her head, running with the speed of a dire cougar was truly intimidating. She'd treated Rina with alternating tenderness and indifference. The animalistic and eventually possessive look in her eyes still sent shivers up Rina's spine. She wasn't sure if she was more distracted by the fact that Eryn had almost left her multiple times or by the fact that she hadn't.

The Commander's role in it all only added an additional layer to wrangle with. He'd led them to ichor, saved them from the dire ants, and banished the shadows attacking them, but Rina still had no idea where he was leading her or why. How many more times would he give her what she wanted before he took what he wanted?

When the service ended, Rina paused to give a quick prayer of apology for her distracted mind before following her caste-mates out of the chapel into the bright, warm afternoon.

"May the light of the Goddess be in you this day, Eryn." Rina straightened as she heard the name from a guardian ahead of her. She pushed through the crowd to find Eryn standing outside the chapel, clearly waiting for someone.

Between herself and Eryn, the line of guardians all slowed to bow their heads in acknowledgment and say, "May the light of the Goddess be in you this day, Eryn." Rina took her place in the ad hoc receiving line and waited her turn, antsy and impatient.

When she reached Eryn, the smile she received made her heart melt. There was no question that Eryn had come here and waited just for Rina.

"Rina, are you free this afternoon? I wanted to show you something."

Rina was indeed free, but she would have happily skipped any training to spend time with Eryn. The only times she really felt seen or wanted were when she was with Eryn. Being in the Dark Lands with Eryn was so much better than being in the Community without her, so what would being in the Community with her be like?

Eryn led Rina down one of the main roads from the chapel into the market. From the main road, smaller roads branched out, curving in concentric circles parallel to the dome with alleys connecting them.

People milled around Rina and Eryn, chatting with friends and dipping into shops. The buildings around them were some of the tallest in the Community, though nothing compared to the spire of the chapel. Above each shop were two to three floors of workshop or storage space for the creation or maintenance of what was offered below. Glass blowers with orange glowing balls of molten glass, bakers kneading dough, alchemists mixing volatile blends, and weaponsmiths hammering stood next to open windows, showing off as much as airing out their workshops. Behind closed windows, tinkerers could be seen leaning closely over their work while the silhouettes of people moved behind darkened windows meant for storing perishables.

Rina rarely came into the market. Most of her needs were met in the garrison, which received its own deliveries of food, basic clothing, and household effects. Weaponsmiths and armorers came to the garrison every month to discuss any new equipment needs and deliver special orders. She carefully maintained each of her things so she wouldn't have to acquire new ones. When she did come to the market, it was always with a clear destination and goal, whether it was new boots or a better pot.

Next to her, Eryn strolled as if she had nothing better to do than window-shop. So, Rina figured she might as well too. It was nice to just have Eryn nearby.

Eryn slipped her hand inside Rina's to pull her toward a specific shop, and Rina felt her heart leap. Rina couldn't deny a spark that had nothing to do with her puppy. It wasn't superficial and overly ecstatic the way her puppy always was. This feeling was like the hot coals simmering at the bottom of the fire, hotter and longer lasting, less bright and showy. The puppy's happiness was always followed with what Rina needed to do to keep Eryn's happiness or success going. This felt like contentment.

Their destination turned out to be an oil and candle shop. Eryn pulled her past the front displays of scents meant to purge the smell of the Dark Lands from returning mountain folk and heroes and scented oils that were good for soothing fussy babies. Near the back was a small section with a linen sign that read, "Scents of the Kitchen." Eryn grabbed one and held it in front of Rina's nose with a wide smile.

Rina inhaled deeply, and closed her eyes as the smell of sausage, eggs, and beans filled her nostrils. It smelled like waking up in Claine and Keddeth's house on the rare occasions when training went late enough that Claine let Rina and Syrana sleep on the couch rather than back in their dormitories. It smelled like childhood, Keddeth's big morning hugs, and fork-sparring with Syrana for the last sausage.

"It reminded me of what you said about the smell of eggs in the Dark Lands reminding you of home and what you were fighting for. I wake up to that smell the first few mornings and I know that you are there waiting for me with breakfast. I thought we could get some for our trips for after the eggs are gone. We could still have the smell."

Rina felt like her whole chest was expanding, and she knew she must have a smile as large as Eryn's. It wasn't just that Eryn had listened and remembered; she recognized and appreciated Rina's effort and wanted to be a part of it. "I would love that."

Eryn grabbed several candles and thanked the artisan for her exquisite work. She was thanked in return for "helping my mother with her crops when she busted her knee, so she would feel useful and use the knee but not too much."

Eryn never ceased to impress Rina. When she'd first met her, Eryn's ego had been apparent. But the more Rina learned about Eryn, the more obvious it was that she'd misjudged her. Yes, she was proud, but she managed to be the perfect balance of self-important and selfless. She knew how great she was, but she used it to make the lives of everyone in the Community better simply because she wanted to.

The artisan paused as her attention turned to Rina in her purple guardian tunic, and she raised an eyebrow in question.

"This is my guardian." Eryn's smile faltered as she added, "I'm helping her get supplies for our trips outside."

Rina's heart sank as the artisan gave her a judging look and nodded as if she now understood everything. Eryn was compensating for Rina, helping her fulfill one of her central functions as a guardian. Rina knew that wasn't what Eryn was doing, but it was what she wanted everyone else to think. It was the thing that would explain why the best hero and the worst guardian were spending time together inside the Community. Rina was relieved when Eryn bustled them back onto the street.

"Do you want to get lunch together? I know a great place a few blocks over the makes amazing grain bowls." Eryn's eagerness told Rina this wasn't just a nicety. She nodded and tried to lose herself once more in Eryn's excitement, but she couldn't help noticing the extra space Eryn left between them as they walked down the road. Her gaze wandered around the crowd as if checking to see if people were looking at them.

Rina shifted easily into a subordinate position behind Eryn's left shoulder and watched Eryn's posture relax. She doesn't want to be seen with me, Rina realized. Eryn did want to be with Rina, and that was a whole new level of happiness, but it didn't truly soften the blow.

Lunch was exquisite. The guardians who cooked in the garrison were very good, but they simply couldn't compare to artisans who spent their Goddess-given powers crafting flavor and nutrition combinations.

Halfway through the meal, Eryn even stopped looking around their street-side table at who was observing them, though she did make sure to direct their conversation toward their last mission whenever anyone approached their table.

When the meal was done, Rina stood and stacked their plates to take inside, but Eryn interrupted her.

"They'll collect those."

"I'm going to go do dishes to put in for this meal."

"You don't need to do that."

She wants you to get in trouble. She wants you to fail. She will tell everyone you took more than your share, that you are lazy, that you are worthless.

"Yes, Eryn, I do." Rina tried to keep the frustration out of her voice. It wasn't Eryn's fault that she didn't understand or that a shadow was spinning lies. "I haven't dug trenches with the artisan's wife or taken care of his children. I can't just acquire whatever I like. I have to put in." People are judging me enough as it is, she added silently.

"Rina, you just brought back ichor. So, unless you went on some massive acquiring spree yesterday, you've paid in." Eryn made it sound so easy. It was for her after all.

"You brought back ichor."

"We brought back ichor. We all pay in by doing our jobs. Your job is to protect me and help me find ichor. You did that. You did it exceedingly well. You have paid in."

Rina sighed. Why couldn't Eryn just let this go? She lowered her voice and tried again. "Everyone is looking at me. If I leave without paying in, people will talk. It will look bad for all guardians. Eventually, it will get back to Claine and she will be very angry. I need to do this whether it is reasonable, whether it is fair, or not. Can you just let me do this, please?"

Eryn chewed the inside of her cheek, but nodded. "I'll join you."

"No. That will only make it worse. It will look like you are paying in for me. You could go window shop and I'll find you when I'm done."

Eryn looked very displeased but nodded. "I'll meet you farther down this road."

Rina took the dishes and reported to the kitchen. Plunging her hands into cold, soapy water brought with it a shot of relief. This was something she could do that everyone would accept as right and reasonable. She was just out to lunch with her hero, talking about missions, and then paying in her due.

She met Eryn outside a weaponsmith's shop. "What did it feel like to drink ichor?" she asked, hoping it was an appropriate public conversation because she really did want to know.

The ghost of a smile passed over Eryn's face. "It's indescribable really. I felt unstoppable. I wasn't afraid of anything. Everything was lesser compared to me." She looked at Rina and looked away quickly, blushing.

"I've heard that after drinking it a hero only thinks about ichor and home." But clearly Eryn had thought of her as well, twice.

Eryn nodded. "It was intense. I don't fully remember all of it, just the need to protect the ichor and get more so I could always feel like that." She blushed again.

A new question sparked in Rina's mind. "Do you still feel that desire for more?" Did heroes get a taste and always need more?

Eryn shrugged. She seemed genuine when she said, "No. I mean, I'm excited to feel it again, but that's it. Even when I was recovering, I felt like I was in withdrawal, but I didn't feel like I needed more. While full of ichor, it felt like an inextinguishable thirst, but once that fire burned out, it was out. Honestly, I want to have more because I want to help the Community again."

They wandered the market for another couple of hours, moving from one safe topic to another. Rina loved the feeling that Eryn was trying to drag the day out as much as she was. As afternoon turned to dusk, they followed the crowds slowly departing for their homes. They took the road that divided the hero and guardian quarters, each step coming a little bit slower than the one before it.

As they reached the point at which it was most logical to go their separate ways, Eryn turned to Rina, swinging her hands at her waist as if too full of nervous energy to hold still. "All the other heroes will be at dinner. Lunch was so great. I really don't feel like having dinner. Do you want to come home with me?"

Rina wished the whereabouts of the other heroes wasn't the chief concern in this plan, but it barely tarnished the offer. She did indeed want to go home with Eryn very badly. It was so hard to go from spending all day with her in the Dark Lands, talking, exploring, and kissing when the situation allowed to not seeing her in the Community. It was just as hard to go from nights cuddled together to her lonely, empty bed. "I do, yes."

Eryn took Rina's hand and led her across the heroes' training field. Rina loved the feeling of her skin on Eryn's no matter how innocent the touch. She tried to ignore the way Eryn's head scanned the hero quarter as if she were in the Dark Lands watching for threats. Mentally, she felt her puppy prod her. If Eryn was worried about being seen, so should Rina. She should be ready to leave at the first sign that Eryn was uncomfortable. Rina shushed the voice. She was going home with Eryn and that was that.

As Eryn led the way over the threshold and into her home, Rina was struck by how similar it was to her own. A hallway led past the water closet on the left to a large sitting room. Eryn's sitting room was sparsely furnished, leaving a large empty area in half of the room, which Rina assumed Eryn used for calisthenics. On the left was the kitchen in the same location, only a little smaller than Rina's. To the right was the bedroom door.

Eryn pulled Rina to her lips, kissing her as if she'd been fighting the desire all day. The feeling was mutual. They stumbled through the door to the bedroom. Rina took in the room in a single glance. It was almost twice the size of hers since hero houses weren't designed for a roommate. The only aspect Rina particularly cared about was the location of the bed. She gripped Eryn's butt, pulling her up until she was straddling Rina's hips. Eryn's couple of inches more of height didn't matter to Rina. Eryn was lighter than the pack she carried on missions, and no matter how well she adjusted the pack, it didn't cling to her like it was made to be against her body the way Eryn did.

Eryn's arms wrapped around her head, pulling her harder and deeper into each kiss. She wasn't sure which of them was burning hotter as she carried Eryn to her bed, but it only increased her need. She stripped Eryn while Eryn yanked at Rina's clothing, their lips never parting. Eryn's skin felt so soft, and she loved the goose bumps that rose under her fingertips.

Rina pulled off the clothing Eryn hadn't managed to remove and climbed onto the bed, pressing her naked body onto Eryn's. There was no one around to judge them or hold them back. She could be with Eryn as if it were just the two of them in the Dark Lands, but without the gloom and sense of dread that the lantern dome diminished but never truly eradicated.

A shadow voice was there, trying to whisper at her ear, but Rina ignored it. Here, everything was right. She rose and fell with Eryn, feeding her fire and being fed in return. Here, Eryn was putty in her hands, and she wanted nothing but to make her come undone again and again.

Eryn lay on her side facing Rina, her eyelids heavy with post-coital drowsiness, and ran a fingertip down Rina's jawline, over her collarbone, and around her breast. She looked at Rina's hands cupping her breasts and smiled lazily. "I missed this," she said.

"I missed it too. I always miss it when we are in the Community."

"Today was really fun, though." Eryn yawned and rolled over, then scooted back into Rina until she was cradled against her front.

Rina kissed the back of Eryn's neck and enjoyed Eryn's small shiver. "It was."

"I'd like to do it more often. You could come to the other castes with me, if you want to and you aren't too busy."

"I would love that." She meant it. Even if Eryn had to come up with excuses for why they were together, even if everyone thought the worst of her, she would still be with Eryn. It was nice to have someone to share her days with and value her contributions.

Her puppy woke her before dawn. The feeling of Eryn in her arms was almost enough to ignore its yapping and pestering. Rina sighed and slowly withdrew. She gave Eryn's cheek a final kiss, dressed, and slipped into the empty night. Eryn wouldn't have to figure out an excuse for why her guardian had slept in her bed and maybe, just maybe, they'd get to do it again.

CHAPTER TEN

Scars and Origins

It was odd to find a place in the Dark Lands that didn't produce its own uniform light, which made the twin caves all the more ominous. Eryn raised her lantern and stared into the slanted teardrop-shaped cave entrances. Stalactites and stalagmites covered nearly every surface, oozing yellowish-green goo. A light breeze, the only one they'd encountered in the Dark Lands, brushed Eryn's face, emanating from deep inside the two caves.

The walls shimmered with hidden ichor. Unlike the spring that had been ready to pop like a pustule, this ichor looked like a thin layer of golden webbing just below the rock face.

Eryn retrieved a stick and brushed it against one of the stalactites. The goo ran down the stick, far less viscous than Eryn had anticipated. She dropped the stick and watched as it melted onto the cave floor. "Well, I don't think we're going in there."

"Is there much there?" Rina asked. She was staring at the goo a little too closely for Eryn's comfort.

"Not really, no." Unless the strands of web connected to some deeper source, Eryn doubted there would be enough to make it worth drinking and running back. She'd been so excited to find ichor only two months after their first find, that it was hard to turn away. They were five days out, and it was time to head home empty-handed.

As they turned toward home, Eryn lamented how short missions felt. Of course, now that they were spending some nights together in the

Community, it wouldn't really be three weeks before she was able to be with Rina again. But here, they were free.

Since their first night together within the Community, almost two months prior, Eryn had invited Rina on weekly outings that she couldn't help but think of as pseudo-dates. They hadn't been very romantic. The sewage trench had been the worst, but the laborers needed all the help they could get, and it had been an opportunity to work beside Rina and a great excuse to bathe together afterward. Even if it had taken multiple rounds of water before bathing was fun and not just necessary.

In the trench, no one had questioned Rina's presence. They were just happy to have her strong arms. But everywhere else, just as Rina's purple tunic had stuck out like a sore thumb, the reactions around her bordered on unwelcoming. While transcribing old texts from yellowing, degrading linen to new cloth, every priest, even those who couldn't see, had stared at Rina. No one had ever questioned Eryn's presence in any part of the chapel or the crypt, but Rina was met with disdain everywhere she went.

She's here to help you! Eryn wanted to scream. Instead, she repeated the same thing over and over. "Everyone serves the Community. My guardian is joining me in doing that." It was the same phrase she told the pastorals when she and Rina showed up at dawn to milk cows, the tinkerers whose machines they had oiled, and the mountain folk they'd help split wood. And Goddess, Rina looked good swinging a splitting maul.

The phrase was innocuous enough, but Eryn couldn't pretend she didn't know exactly how everyone else was taking it. She'd meant that her guardian was no different than herself. They were serving the Community together. The nods of understanding told Eryn they accepted Rina's help as the extra work such a bad guardian needed to do to pay in her due. Everyone accepted and appreciated Eryn's service, so why was Rina any different?

The worst part was not knowing what to do about it. Rina seemed to take it all in stride, but Eryn could tell it made her uncomfortable. Yet she ended each pseudo-date telling Eryn during pillow talk that she was looking forward to the next time.

Eryn wondered if the treatment of Rina had more to do with

her being the worst guardian or simply being a guardian outside the garrison.

As they worked their way back to the Community empty-handed, Eryn broke the silence, prompting Rina with a question as she often did. "Tell me about listening to shadows."

Rina looked startled. She opened her mouth and closed it again. Her fingers tapped nervously on the shaft of her spear. "Um…"

"I mean how did it start? My understanding is that all guardians hear shadows when they are little, but they learn to stop listening. What made you decide to listen?"

"Oh." Rina visibly relaxed, but her voice was still tight as she spoke. "I suppose I was always worse at blocking them out. A lot of guardian children cry a lot about the things they are told when they are very young, so learning to block them out is a necessary coping mechanism. As early as I can remember, I just wanted to understand. It made sense to ignore shadows if they lied, except that left me with two problems. One, if they always lied, then couldn't we use what they said, knowing the truth was the opposite? But more importantly, because I was listening and trying to understand, I heard truths also. But I guess that was more of the foundation. What made me *decide* to listen to shadows was Jemmy.

"We were all on the training field learning early calisthenics and watching some of the older guardians practicing. There was an issue with some of the equipment and everyone rushed over to help, including our instructors. Jemmy announced to the group that he was going to cross the balance poles and ran off toward them. I wasn't going to say anything. Jemmy used to make fun of me for being heavier than the other kids. It's not that I wanted him to get hurt. I just wasn't going to open myself up for him to say I would break them or anything. So, I just watched.

"As he got to the top of the ladder, a shadow whispered to me that he was going to fall, he was going to crack his head open, and he was going to die. I felt relieved. A shadow had said it, so it was a lie. Jemmy would be fine. I watched Jemmy make his first two leaps before he missed. I remember it to this day as if I were watching it in front of me now. The tip of his toes brushed the top of the pole, and for a moment it looked like he might recover, but he didn't. He fell hard and fast. The back of his head hit the ground first, and I remember staring at him, waiting for him to scream and cry, but he didn't. He just lay there. The other kids started to scream but I just stared. Our instructors told us Jemmy was dead.

"Later that day, after all the other kids had settled, I told my instructors what had happened. They told me that I was wrong. They didn't know how I had caused Jemmy to die, but by listening I had caused his death. They'd been arguing with me for over a year, and I think they saw it as an opportunity to drive home the point. I had killed him.

"As you can imagine, that was rather devastating to be told by the people who, yes, I'd questioned, but were still my entire support system. They wanted it to bring me back in line, but it did the opposite. I couldn't just accept that I had killed Jemmy. I had to prove I was right. So, I listened. I didn't act on it. I just listened, and every time a shadow was right and there was no way I could have caused it, I brought it to my instructors. I wanted them to listen. I wanted them to understand and to absolve me, but of course it only made it worse. Not only was I listening, but they were also afraid I was going to convince other kids to listen too. But worst of all, from their perspective, every bad thing the shadows correctly predicted, I had caused. It wasn't just something they told me. They believed it. All guardians do.

"When Claine named herself as my mentor, I thought maybe I would finally have someone who would listen, someone I could convince. Everyone told me that she was stern, unemotional, logical, practical. Plus, she had chosen me. Maybe she understood already. Of course, that wasn't true. The shadows told me she would grow to despise me, that she would never be proud of me. I don't think she hates me, not really. But I know that I constantly disappoint her."

Throughout her story, Rina had seemed dispassionate, as if relaying someone else's story. But Rina stumbled over the last part, trying to keep her voice free of emotion. She wanted Claine to be proud of her, but Rina's story made it clear that she was trapped. If she accepted what Claine and the other guardians said, she also accepted killing someone and all the other things that had gone wrong. But trying to prove herself right only made things worse.

"Wait," Eryn said, "you said that Claine became your mentor after you were blamed for Jemmy's death. How old were you when Jemmy died?"

"Five."

"You were five years old!" Five was about the age Eryn had been when everyone started telling her how wonderful she was and how they expected great things from her. It had become a part of who she was. She couldn't imagine telling a five-year-old that they had killed someone, especially when she'd done nothing but listen to a voice she hadn't yet learned to block out.

Rina just nodded.

In that moment, Eryn didn't care if listening to shadows caused bad things. She cared about the small child Rina had been. Alone. Body shamed. Desperate for someone to hear her, to see her and what she wanted to contribute to the Community.

"I'm sorry," Eryn said at last. She stopped and turned to Rina, who looked on the verge of tears. She opened her mouth and closed it again. There was something more. "What is it? You can tell me."

Rina hesitated. Her teeth were dug so deeply into her lip that Eryn was surprised she wasn't drawing blood. Finally, she said, her voice a whisper as if saying it quietly could make it less true, "Shadows told me Syrana was going to die."

A feeling of deep empathy filled Eryn. She wasn't the only one who had spent the last seven months trying to convince herself that she hadn't caused Syrana's death. "It wasn't your fault." Eryn knew she was speaking to herself as much as Rina.

"I know." Rina shook her head and rolled her eyes as if to say that her tears were silly. "She was already on her deathbed when they said it. I tried so hard to say it wasn't true. But there was nothing I could do."

"There was nothing you could do." Again, Eryn meant it for them both.

Rina gave her a dejected smile and another nod. She looked plenty ready to be done with this conversation, but it didn't feel like any sort of conclusion to Eryn. Rina needed more than just agreement. Eryn placed a hand on Rina's shoulder and looked deeply into her eyes. She needed Rina to internalize what she was going to say as much as she'd clearly internalized the words of her peers, mentors, and shadows. "You have protected and saved me many times by listening to shadows, so thank you."

A real smile spread across Rina's face and in the dim, flat light, she seemed to glow. She pulled Eryn to her for a lingering kiss. "Thank you, Eryn. You don't know how much that means to me."

❖

Rina lay on her back, Eryn cuddled against her chest, and stared at the tent ceiling. She should be getting up to make breakfast, but she wanted to hold on to this moment for as long as possible. These were the times, while her puppy was telling her to leave, that she felt most sure of her true feelings. It wasn't just her bond to Eryn that made her love her. Somewhere along the line, from being ignored by an over-eager Eryn who only believed in herself to Eryn being the only person who really saw her, she'd fallen hard.

There was no denying that the puppy still pulled many of her strings. There were times when she couldn't help but think Eryn was the greatest being to come after the Goddess even when she was openly implying to others that Rina needed to do more to serve the Community. But she could cite just as many times when it was all her own feelings of respect, appreciation, and love.

Hello, Rina.

Rina held in a groan. She much preferred when he joined her while she made breakfast. This trip she'd told him about her mixed feelings about spending time with Eryn in the Community, and he seemed to be taking far too many opportunities to interrupt her enjoyment of moments like these.

Careful. Holding a leech that closely is bad for the health.

With that comment, Rina had even less interest in letting him disturb her. "Why are you here?"

He tsked as if she were a misbehaving child. *Well, I was going to discuss the origin of shadows with you, but since you clearly have better things to think about, like that floozy in your arms, I guess I'll leave you to it.*

Why did he always seem to know exactly what to dangle in front of her? She hated being manipulated. Her own mind and body were doing enough of that without him adding to it. "What did you want to tell me?"

No, the Commander said in disdain, *if you aren't going to bother to even pretend to care about what I have to say, I'm not going to waste my time. You can find the answer yourself. The texts were last copied some two hundred years ago, so they will need rewriting soon. Let's see if you can put the two disparate parts together without help.*

Rina felt him leave and released a frustrated sigh. Everyone knew that shadows had come from the Dark Lands beyond the mountains. They were the creation of some dark god. So, why was his challenge so enticing? She wanted to have the library of texts in front of her now, poring over every linen scroll. "Dark gods damn you," Rina said to the darkness.

Rina spent the rest of the trip back to the dome half listening to Eryn's story about a childhood of being told how amazing she was. She understood that the moral of the story she was supposed to walk away with was that Eryn had been shaped by how people treated her and so she had greater sympathy for how Rina had been shaped by her childhood. Rina didn't need to pay attention to the random anecdotes to understand. Instead, she spent the time trying to figure out a reasonable way to ask the priests to let her copy the two specific texts she wanted and somehow figure out which two she needed.

Rina waited until Eryn took a breath between stories to interrupt. "Can I ask you a question?"

"Of course." Eryn seemed pleased that Rina was finally engaging with her story.

"You've done all this work with all the other castes." Rina tried to make it seem like her question related to the current conversation in some way. "When you work with the priests, how do you know which texts to copy next?"

"Oh, the priests mark items that need to be rewritten with a ribbon. All texts are recopied every two hundred years, so I always get items that are two hundred, four hundred, six hundred etc. years old. I try to make sure that when I'm working with any of the castes that I'm doing what is most useful to them, not necessarily what I would pick. It took a bit at first to convince people to give me the dirty, hard tasks, especially as a child, but I kept asking for harder and harder tasks until they gave me the things they really didn't want to do."

Eryn seemed ready to keep going so Rina interrupted again. "Do you know if they sort them any specific way, like are they stored based on topic?"

Eryn tipped her head to the side as they walked, clearly wondering how this line of questioning related to anything. "Well, they're sorted chronologically by topic and caste of the author, so you don't have to be a priest to find the scroll you're looking for. Priests are there to help, but in general if you want to read about the crop yield of barley three hundred years ago, you'd just go to the agricultural section and look at texts from three hundred years ago by judges."

"Wait, so can anyone go read scrolls?"

"Of course. It's the Community's archive. The priests maintain it, but it's not just for them. What are you looking for?"

Rina had known that this would eventually be Eryn's question. If Rina lied to her about this and Eryn found out, she wasn't sure she would be able to repair the damage. "I want to find out more about the origin of shadows."

"Shadows come from beyond the mountains." Eryn's answer felt too quick. Rina felt an almost instinctual dislike for any answer that felt more like a mantra. She didn't like the many, many aspects of her life that were based on ideas she wasn't supposed to question.

"But where? Why? How? It just seems odd to me that we just go with that explanation. Shadows are growing in number and making it harder and harder to get back to the Community after the hero drinks ichor. So, why is no one more interested in where shadows come from?" Why did no one else ask these questions? Eryn was the first person she'd been able to talk to about it without being told she was trying to make trouble or even that she was being disrespectful to the Goddess Herself.

"We can't travel beyond the mountains, so why does it matter where shadows come from or why?" Even as Eryn said it, she seemed less sure of her words. Eryn didn't seem like the kind of person who questioned authority very often, but she was smart. Maybe all she needed was for Rina to plant the kind of seeds the Commander so loved to sow inside Rina's head.

"The more we know, the better our chances of fighting them."

"I thought you wanted to listen to them, not fight them." Eryn shot Rina a skeptical look, rife with concern that Rina was keeping something from her.

"Not when they are attacking us. If we knew what they were after, maybe we could just avoid them altogether. Imagine how much better it would be if no one died trying to get back to the Community with ichor."

Eryn nodded thoughtfully. "There's a section on the Dark Lands written by heroes, guardians, and mountain folk over the centuries. I used to ask to transcribe those when I was younger. I figured I could learn more about the Dark Lands and aid the priests."

"Could you show me?"

"How about I help you instead?" Rina watched Eryn puff up with excitement and loved every part of it. The Commander was trying to drive a wedge between her and Eryn, but Rina saw no reason she couldn't have both.

Rina met Eryn in the crypt two days after their return to the dome. According to Eryn, they were researching "topics most beneficial to our survival in the Dark Lands." Rina understood the looks she got from the priests. They would give Eryn free rein to attempt to fix the inadequacies of her guardian. Rina supposed she should be more insulted. Realistically, anything that got her what she wanted without having to explain that a shadow talked to her was a win.

Eryn led Rina through room after room of underground archives. The air was stale with the scent of old parchment and well-maintained dirt floors. There was no breeze to carry new scents or cover the sound of whispering voices and scratching quills. The walls were lined from floor to ceiling with columns of uniform metal lockers. Each locker door, about a foot and a half tall and wide, had a series of numbers imprinted on it and was sealed tightly to keep out moisture and light. Eryn opened one to show Rina the scrolls within, rolled and stacked neatly. Eryn drew one out gingerly and ran her finger over the numbers.

"The first number tells the topic, the next is the date it was written, then the caste of the author, and finally the date it was most recently rewritten. Everything in this locker deals with monsters and was written in 900 PD, about three hundred and fifty years ago, by a mountain folk. The oldest texts start over there and they work their way to the present here, then everything farther on is empty waiting for future writings."

"Fascinating," Rina said as she ran her finger over the imprint of numbers on an empty locker.

"Right? I suppose it shouldn't be surprising that the priests would have the foresight to build the crypt with the future in mind. Get it? Foresight." She chuckled quietly at her own joke. Rina found Eryn so adorable when she was being clever and laughed along with her. What she really wanted to do was kiss her, but far too many people lingered or drifted nearby.

"The hero section looks quite large," Rina said.

"Yeah, retired heroes come down to write their memoirs. I'd be lying if I said I didn't think about that while I'm transcribing. Sometimes, as we're walking back home, I even think about how I would write one of our adventures down."

This didn't surprise Rina in the least. It wasn't just the ego of it either. In the stretches of silence between their chats and discussions, Rina couldn't imagine Eryn's mind holding still and savoring the silence the way Rina did. Eryn was always moving, always thinking, always planning. Rina admired it, even if it did make her roll her eyes sometimes.

"So, shadows," Eryn said in a barely audible whisper. "What time period should we start with?"

The Commander had said the pieces she was looking for had been rewritten almost two hundred years ago, which narrowed it a bit but not much, since everything was rewritten two hundred years after it had been rewritten. "Maybe we start at the beginning of missions for ichor, the first years Post Death? There wasn't any need to go into the Dark Lands before that. So, I guess we could start around twelve hundred years ago in 50 PD with guardian authors."

Eryn nodded and led the way. They each grabbed a handful of scrolls and headed to the nearest empty table.

Rina found herself constantly distracted and annoyed. She didn't want to read about Dark Lands flora and fauna being described in excruciating detail. She wanted to get to the parts about shadows. Why couldn't they just have a shadows section? Rina tried not to scowl. "This is going to take forever."

Eryn chuckled softly. "Yes, but at least we get to do it together. Plus, we're just reading. Can you imagine if we had to copy these?"

Rina's hand cramped at the thought. After the last time they'd been here, she'd had to soak her hand for an hour just to get it to stop curving into the shape of holding a quill.

"Next time, if you write at a steady pace and don't grip your quill like you might have to use it to stab someone at a moment's notice, you'll be able to write for a lot longer."

Rina smirked and reached her hand under the table to give Eryn's thigh an appreciative squeeze.

After two hours, she and Eryn had worked their way through twenty-six scrolls and Rina had training to lead. They hadn't found a single mention of a shadow.

"Do you have plans tonight?" Eryn gave her a suggestive wink, and the frustrations of the morning quickly disappeared.

"I could make you dinner at my place." What Rina didn't add was that no guardians would judge Eryn's presence whether she chose to leave after dinner, after some post-dinner fun, or even if she decided to stay until morning. Rina regretted not adding it many hours later as she lay in her empty bed after a very nice dinner and screwing around on the couch. She would see Eryn the next day, and perhaps they would have a greater success to celebrate.

CHAPTER ELEVEN

Stability and Change

"Oh Goddess," Eryn said, pausing her reading. After two days of reading very dry descriptions of everything from the growth patterns of trees in the Dark Lands to the hibernation habits of dire bears, Eryn switched to priest authors. If anyone was going to theorize origins, it was priests.

"What?" Rina sounded excited. They hadn't found a single mention of shadows in 50 PD or 250 PD, and were a couple of hours into 450 PD.

"This is just so graphic," Eryn said. No one compared to the descriptive prowess of the priests. "There used to be enough ichor that priests kept casks of it in storage during especially fruitful times and then used it to refill the fountain during lean times. Apparently, there was a group of priests who were in charge of protecting the casks from heroes who wanted to drink it to feel all that power. This scroll is about a fire in the chapel that reached the ichor storage. The priests tried to save the casks, eventually even by opening one of the casks and using cups to throw ichor onto the flames. The ichor vaporized, and they breathed it in. All the ichor was lost, and the priests involved all died over the next few days coughing up blood. The author says that they kept moaning about how they had failed, that they had ended up basically drinking the ichor they had sworn to protect."

"Eww." Rina read a couple of lines over Eryn's shoulder before grimacing and returning to her own scroll. "This one is yet another thrilling explanation of the life cycle of fire moss. It seems like when ichor was more plentiful and shadows hadn't yet shown up, guardians used to sit and journal about their surroundings whether they were on ichor missions or protecting mountain folk. I think the guardians expected later generations to really engage with what the Dark Lands had to offer besides metals, minerals, and lumber. This author suggests best life stages for the collection of fire moss for using in ovens and cook fires."

"Well, I can attest to the power of fire moss," Eryn said, trying not to remember the searing pain of burning flesh. She could only imagine how her hand would look if she hadn't been able to immediately drink ichor.

No wonder there had been a time when priests had protected extra ichor from heroes. She wanted to imagine that no hero would put themselves before the Community, but in the moment, it might be near impossible to resist just a sip when the Community had so much.

But no hero would do that now. The stories of the few who had done it hundreds of years ago were enough. No one would risk the damage to the Community or the chance that they would simply run into the Dark Lands, completely unprotected and unprepared, and never return.

"Eryn," a tear-choked voice said from across the room, breaking the near silence. Eryn looked up from her own thoughts to see Oraina, one of the heroes from her cohort, standing next to a blind priest who had clearly guided Oraina to this room. She stood in nothing but a healing gown, wavering on her feet. There were actively bleeding scrapes across her face and spots of blood on her gown. Eryn dropped her quill and rushed to her.

Oraina collapsed into Eryn's embrace. "My guardian is dead. I almost died. I—" Her sobs interrupted her.

"Pietra," Rina whispered from behind them. Eryn assumed that was the name of Oriana's guardian. There would be more than just Oraina who would mourn her guardian. It would be the third loss of a guardian that year: Syrana and the hero-guardian pair from the cohort above them that had simply never returned, presumably killed by shadows after finding ichor.

"I'll never go out again. I'll never taste ichor. I'll never bring it back. I'll never…" Eryn tried to hold Oriana steady as her body racked with sobs.

"Let's get you back to healers' hall." She shot a look at Rina, who nodded solemnly. Rina would finish and clean up before going to support whoever it was on the guardian side who needed support.

"What am I going to do, Eryn?" Oraina moaned as Eryn laid her back in her bed, surrounded by relieved healers. "How did you do it when you thought you weren't going to get to go back out?"

I didn't, Eryn thought. I nearly fell apart. Rina was the only thing that kept me from being *this*. She looked over Oraina's injured form with a rush of empathy. "I knew I would still serve the Community," Eryn said. It was what Oraina needed to hear.

"But you did. You have a new guardian. You've brought back ichor. You've felt it. You've tasted it. You've served. I'll never."

"Shhhh." Eryn petted the stray brown hairs from Oraina's sweaty brow. "Everyone serves the Community. When you are well again, we will find you something you love that serves." Oraina was right. Unlike Eryn, she would never seek ichor again. She would eventually get to leave the Community to protect mountain folk with a guardian who wasn't her own, one whose hero was busy, like Holden. But she would enter early retirement and shift to a life of training. "Sleep now, we'll talk more when you wake up."

"You'll be here?" Oraina's voice cracked with desperation.

"Yes, I will be here."

Eryn requested a pile of clean laundry and folded it while she waited. It was nice to have something to do with her hands as her mind jumped from one possibility to the other. What if Rina hadn't become her guardian? What if Rina died? What if she was all alone in the Dark Lands, scrambling to get home knowing she'd lost the person she cared about most? Eryn tried to push the thoughts away. Bringing herself close to tears repeatedly wasn't helping anything.

Oraina woke a couple of hours later, stronger, but just as morose. Eryn didn't ask for the story of what had happened, but it bubbled out of Oraina nonetheless. She and her guardian had fallen through loose ground into a dire snake nest. Her guardian had thrown her out of the pit before succumbing to the swarm of slithering, biting snakes. Oraina had watched her die before turning and running. She'd run for two days straight.

It's not me, Eryn kept reminding herself as her own breath hitched and her heart hammered. It was hard not to relive dragging Syrana.

"Everything is going to be okay. You've always been so good at explaining and storytelling. You will be a wonderful instructor."

"You don't understand, Eryn. This was my life and it's been taken from me. You've brought back ichor. Henk brought back ichor for the first time on this trip. Even damned Nim has brought back ichor. I never will. I'll spend the rest of my life training heroes to do what I will never be able to do."

"You are alive. Your life has not been taken from you. Your guardian saved you." Eryn reminded herself to be patient and empathetic.

"But now she's dead and I will never get another chance."

"There will be time to grieve your guardian. It's okay to grieve multiple things at once. You didn't fail her. She would want you to move forward and to serve the Community in her absence. I recommend going to your guardian's funeral. I found it very cathartic."

Oraina's eyebrows furrowed in confusion. "I'm not talking about my guardian. I'm talking about me. Who is going to listen to an instructor who hasn't brought back ichor? What can I possibly teach anyone?"

"I know that it can be hard to recognize the need to grieve, but if you don't allow yourself to grieve your guardian it will sit with you, you'll drive yourself crazy trying to figure out if it was your fault—"

"My fault! My guardian couldn't get herself out of a damned snake pit! I'm the one who ran back home, alone. She's dead and I have to live with the consequences. I thought you would understand. I thought you would be on my side."

"I am on your side. How are there even sides? I just want you to be able to work through what you're feeling without hiding behind anger or frustration."

"I'm not hiding. Why are you trying to make this my fault somehow?" Oraina's yelling had drawn a small crowd of healers.

"I think you ought to go," a healer said, pulling gently on Eryn's shoulder.

"But I'm just trying to help," Eryn said, directing it at the healer and Oraina.

"You're not helping!" Oraina collapsed back on her bed, sobbing.

Eryn hurried out, her face hot with embarrassment. She'd just wanted to help Oraina avoid her mistakes. She'd just wanted to be Alba for someone who didn't have an Alba. Apparently, this was why no one ever went to Eryn with social or emotional questions. Training, yes. Emotions, no.

Eryn wasn't surprised when she got a summons to Holden's office.

"What were you thinking?" Holden's voice reverberated off the walls and Eryn thought she could even hear the decanters shaking. It was the voice he used when addressing the whole of the haven and was not designed for a room this small.

"I was just trying to—"

"Oraina almost died. She managed to get back all by herself. And did you tell her how well she'd done? Did you assure her that she would still serve the Community? Did you absolve her of any wrongdoing? No! You told her she needed to grieve her guardian." His face was red as he paced behind his desk. He'd been mad at Eryn before, but never this mad.

"I did tell her she would still serve—"

"Her guardian is dead. Her guardian did what she was supposed to do and that is the end of her story. How could you make this about Oraina's guardian when Oraina needed you?"

"She asked me what it was like for me. I needed to grieve my guardian. I just thought—"

"You thought wrong, Eryn. Your situation was different. You redirected your grief of losing your foresight into grief for your guardian. Heroes don't grieve their guardians, certainly not after less than a year together."

"Why not?" Eryn knew she shouldn't yell back. But how dare he accuse her of not truly grieving Syrana. "Guardians are people too. Everyone serves the Community. Why are they any lesser when they literally give their lives to the Community? Oraina's guardian threw her out of the dire snake pit. Everyone should be grieving her. Especially Oraina."

"That's not how it works."

"Why not?" Eryn leapt out of her chair, her anger too great to live inside her anymore.

"Guardians are meant to serve. They shouldn't cause distractions. They shouldn't cause problems. Their only role is to serve. That's why we don't grieve them. That's why we sterilize them."

"What?" Eryn asked, her anger compounded by confusion. She had always assumed guardians were naturally sterile. It was simply an attribute of being a guardian: incredible strength, endurance, dedication, ability to see and hear shadows, and sterility.

Holden sighed. "I suppose you'll find out when you become head hero one day. We sterilize guardians when their eye color sets."

"Why?" Eryn clutched desperately to her anger. It felt like the only thing grounding her.

"Because the Goddess's contraceptive doesn't work when it dries out. It's easier to sterilize guardians than to try to enforce abstinence outside the dome. Abstinence doesn't work. We can't have heroes and guardians in their prime getting pregnant all the time." Holden said it so matter-of-factly. As if these weren't people who might have wanted to give birth if it had not been taken away from them.

"There are a lot of same-sex pairs." Eryn grabbed at a logic that Holden seemed to promise but was just an illusion.

"We don't know which guardians will need to be sterilized, and if we wait until they are paired, they will know their sterility isn't Goddess-given. It is a small change to the Goddess's plan but a necessary reaction to a shrinking dome. Everyone serves the Community, guardians just have to carry a bit more of the burden, but it's what they are born to do. The Community is stronger for it and guardians never miss what they never had."

"It's not inequality if no one notices."

Holden nodded. He seemed relieved that Eryn finally understood.

Eryn couldn't just stand here and listen. It wasn't just the new information. Holden wasn't embarrassed by what the Community did. To him, it was logical, it was necessary.

Eryn turned and left.

"You understand why this is sensitive information," Holden called after her.

"The Community is stronger for it," Eryn muttered under her breath as she stormed out of the haven.

She headed back toward the center of the Community, veering down one of the main roads and straight into the nursery.

Alba gave Eryn a warning look as she burst into the room. Sleeping babies lay in neat rows of cribs with childrearers meandering between them. Alba stood with her hand on a baby's chest, whisper-singing a lullaby. She took a deep breath, raising her hand in front of her abdomen and then lowering it with a long exhale. Eryn mimicked the gesture and found it easier to stop dancing from one foot to the other, but no easier to pause her racing mind.

Alba repeated the gesture several more times until Eryn went back to acting like a small child that needed to go to the bathroom. She gingerly lifted her hand from the baby's chest and nodded to her castemates before leading Eryn from the room and into a room full of small wooden structures for crawling on and in, but empty of children.

"Did you know guardians are sterilized? Not sterile, but sterilized," Eryn burst out.

Alba took a slow breath, centering herself as she had motioned for Eryn to do. When she spoke, her words were slow and her tone even. Eryn could tell it took effort to keep them that way. Where Eryn was angry, Alba seemed almost heartbroken. "No, but it doesn't truly surprise me. When babies get their eye color, they go to the healers before they are paired with their family. Guardian babies are with the healers longer before they go to the garrison than heroes to the haven or other castes to families. I never really thought about it, but now that you say it, I'm sure that is what is happening. How hard for them to have that choice taken from them." Alba had given birth three times, and even though the babies she had birthed were mixed in with all the other babies so that even she wouldn't know who had come from her, she said the experience was life-changing to literally give life to another.

"How can they do this? And everywhere I go with my guardian people look at her like she shouldn't be there. Every time we help a caste, they act like this is somehow a penance for her when it is a gift from me. How can they treat guardians like this?"

"Who is they?" Alba asked, her tone had a forced calm.

"I don't know. The healers who sterilize guardian babies. The heads of castes who know about it. The artisans who expect my guardian to bring them back ichor and then to wash their dishes. The priests who whisper behind our backs. The heroes who feel their lives are ruined when their guardians die." The list didn't end there, but Eryn was out of breath.

"So, everyone?"

"Yes. I guess. Even the guardians who allow it. Why doesn't the head guardian fight for her caste? Isn't that what heads are supposed to do? But she doesn't. She gets mad at guardians who step outside the expectations set on them." Even Rina allowed it because it was easier to clean a dish than upset people.

"Maybe she thinks it's the way things are supposed to be. Everyone serves the Community to the extent they can. People notice when someone isn't putting in enough, but it takes a lot before people recognize someone who is putting in more than their share."

"Just because the rest of us don't notice it's happening doesn't mean it's any less wrong."

Alba nodded ruefully. "True, but it makes it a lot harder to change. The most important things to the Community are the Goddess and stability. Stability comes from doing the same thing in the same way whether it is the best way or not."

"But that's not how we grow."

"Look around you." Alba spread her arms wide and shook her head, eyebrows raised. "The Community isn't growing. It's shrinking."

"Then now is when we need to do things differently."

Alba's patient expression hardened, and she placed both hands on Eryn's shoulders, dipping slightly to put them at eye level. "Eryn, I'm not saying you are wrong. You are right. But people are scared. People don't try new things when they are scared. They don't seek to treat people better when they are scared. People like you, Eryn. People respect you. Be careful they don't become scared of you. People are fickle when they are scared."

"I can't just sit back." Eryn could barely hold still. How was she supposed to pick stability over growth?

"I'm not saying you have to. I'm just saying to be careful. I'm saying don't make people choose between you and stability."

"What other option is there?" Eryn wanted to scream and shout. She wanted something better. But she wasn't willing to hurt the Community to do it.

"That's the question." Alba's expression softened back into the rueful smile. "Give *them* a better option, whoever *them* is."

Eryn's mind was back to whirling. Now it had a problem to solve, not just a problem to rage against. She was already doing something by spending time with Rina in the Community and showing the other castes how hard-working and unassuming she was. Perhaps she could do more.

"Thank you," Eryn said. She felt her anger flow out, purpose taking its place. It was only then that she took in her surroundings fully. "I barged in on you while you were working. I'm sorry. I can stay and help with diaper changes and naps, or help with the older babies."

"It's okay," Alba said. "You're a little too lightning-y at the moment. Next time try to come after you've breathed a bit more, eh?" She gave Eryn a kind smile and ushered her out of the nursery. "Come by for dinner if you want. You can tell me how things are going with your guardian."

Eryn nodded. If she was right, she had a good deal of goodwill to rebuild with her cohort as well as Alba. She wasn't entirely sure the best way to go about it, but showing up seemed like a good first step.

❖

Rina stared at the scroll she'd been looking for over the last two weeks. After skipping forward to 650 PD, she found a plethora of descriptions of shadows, reports of the slowly shrinking dome, and a distinct lack of diatribes. By then, everything about shadows was the same: dark omens and hateful statements that one must ignore or risk causing. So, Rina returned to 450 PD, at least feeling somewhat confident she was in the right era.

Finally, she'd found the first mention of shadows—a multipage, step-by-step description with diagrams of everything from appearance outside the dome in their corporeal form to the exact phrases they spoke. According to the research of one prolific author by the name of Jonaban, there were seven shadows in total, which they had determined by comparing the slight variances in hissing voices and corporeal forms. All appeared to spend their time near or within the dome. Predictions ranged from death by monsters to debilitating accidents to a consistent description of the shrinking of the dome starting with the slow but methodical death of heroes.

Rina scoured the lockers, pulling everything by Jonaban. She was struck by his consistent reference to a "she" who was never given a name or title. He would reference her opinions on his notes, and the sentences often seemed slightly out of context, as if Rina were missing the sentence before. Rina had to assume it was Jonaban's hero.

Rina followed Jonaban through the first shadow attack on a hero and guardian pair when the hero drank ichor for the return trip. Shadows had shown no violent intentions before that moment, but according to Jonaban's interview of the surviving guardian, his hero was killed by all seven shadows swarming them deep in the mountains, all repeating that this was not the Community's ichor.

Rina stopped.

There had to be a transcription error. It wasn't possible for the guardian to be reporting on the death of his hero. Somewhere along the line, some priest must have accidentally swapped the hero and guardian titles and it was the hero relaying the story. Except that the descriptions were too complete for someone providing the information secondhand. There was no way a hero, who could not see shadows, could have told Jonaban that level of detail. Had Jonaban simply embellished based on his own understanding of shadows?

But the stories continued. Guardian after guardian reported on the death of their hero. Jonaban provided short notes about hero-guardian pairs who did not return. The dome began to shrink as fewer and fewer heroes returned with ichor or at all. Crops and orchards were lost and became carnivorous trees that cannibalized each other outside the dome. Inside the dome, community areas were converted into new crops and pastureland. Diets shifted to less and less meat to save valuable land for crops. The judges requested fewer and fewer pregnancies to prevent overpopulation. The shadows' predictions came to fruition.

The last entry from Jonaban explained simply that things had to change. Underestimating the shadows, listening to their predictions, and using a doddering academic approach to the Dark Lands had led to these problems, so a stricter, more dedicated approach would be necessary to prevent the destruction of the Community itself. There was no doubt in Jonaban's mind that shadows were the antithesis of the Goddess and that the act of listening to their predictions, analyzing them academically, and trying to prevent them had caused the decline of the Community exactly as the shadows had predicted it.

That was the end. No more scrolls from Jonaban.

Rina skimmed scroll after scroll finding similar, less detailed accounts of those same seven shadows, but nothing that year describing what was being done about them or the dome.

More concerning was the gap. At first, Rina just thought she was reading the dates incorrectly, but the closer she looked, the more pronounced the gap became. For twenty years, there was not a single scroll written by a guardian about the Dark Lands. Almost two decades to the day the scrolls picked back up again, but the tone had changed. Gone were the long, technical descriptions and diagrams. Rina couldn't even accurately describe them as stories anymore. They were more like the strategy documents Rina had grown up reading—succinct, accurate, boring. No one talked about the lifecycle of fire moss, only how to avoid it and ways to treat your hero's burns should you fail to avoid it.

Jonaban had already hinted at the need for such a change, but why the gap?

Rina moved over to the hero section, located the dates in question, and found the same gap. What had happened in those twenty years that no one had written about it? How could they not even reference what had happened once they started writing about the Dark Lands again?

As she skimmed the hero scrolls before and after the gap, Rina found a similar if opposite shift in the writing style and tone. Pre-gap scrolls were pithy explanations of dire creatures, their habitats, habits, and best strategies for fighting them. Post-gap, the scrolls became stories bordering on epics. The flowery language that the guardians abandoned, the heroes seemed to adopt. They weren't just hunting, they were adventuring. Shadows went from a horror to something that their guardian dealt with. And most subtly, their guardian, who was rarely mentioned in either, went from being the second person in a hunting strategy to the kind of loyal companion a mountain folk might consider their dog.

What had changed?

Rina went to the final section of the Dark Lands archives, to the mountain folk. Here, there was no gap. Rina grabbed everything she could hold and rushed to her table, spreading them across every surface. But the more she read, the more disappointed and confused she became. There was no mention of a change. The only discernible shift Rina could find in twenty years of scrolls was a single mountain folk who mentioned in passing that a guardian had told him shadows didn't spend their time so close to the dome anymore which was a relief.

She was still staring over the scrolls when Eryn arrived after four days of absence. Just the sight of her brought butterflies to Rina's stomach, and for the first time in hours her mind didn't feel like someone with a very large wooden spoon stirring an overfull pot. She wanted to rush to her, to embrace her, to kiss her. Instead, she stood, gave Eryn what she was sure was a goofy smile, and stated the obvious. "You're back."

"I'm sorry. I kind of said the wrong thing to a few different people and needed to put in socially. I don't really do that, the social part, so it took a while. And then harvest. I always help with this last harvest of the year. Did you find what you were looking for?" Eryn seemed unusually uncomfortable, as if she was afraid Rina was going to be angry with her. Rina wasn't sure she had the capacity to be angry with Eryn and not just because her puppy would forbid it.

"Yes, sort of." Rina dropped her voice from soft to barely audible. "Maybe we should discuss it somewhere else."

"Your place?" Eryn gave her a wink that set her puppy and body on a whole new round of butterflies.

"I have a roommate actually. Jesta. She used to be roommates with Pietra, so when Pietra died, Jesta moved in with me." Rina hadn't been there for the move. It didn't matter that Syrana's room had sat empty for almost eight months. It still felt too soon. She didn't want to see Syrana's clothing removed from the closet, her unreasonably large weights returned to the garrison, or her identity stripped from the walls. Rina kept one unwashed undershirt that she could hold to her face and pretend still had the slightest musk of Syrana. Everything else was just stuff, and she didn't want to watch it leave, didn't want to question if a shirt was enough or if she had any right to hold anything that could be used by another guardian.

"Oh." Eryn seemed to sense that there was more there, but didn't delve. "You can come back to my place, then."

The evening air was brisk as Rina and Eryn left the chapel. The trees would lose their leaves soon in preparation for Frost Night. The roads were crowded with people. It didn't matter that Frost Night came at the same time every year, it was Rina's experience that people thrived on waiting to acquire warm clothing, food, and gifts until the first day temperatures dropped. She supposed there was festiveness and camaraderie in it. Who didn't want to sip hot wine while admiring the wares made for just such an occasion?

If she'd ever gotten to participate, Rina guessed she would understand. Instead, Rina had stopped by the garrison's storage before their last trip outside the dome to get a well-fitting pair of underlayers, gloves, and a hat. She'd almost finished carving and wood burning the personalized fitness dice for Claine. The only thing she had left to do was figure out what in the lands to make or get for Eryn and how to get out of spending Frost Night with Jesta.

Beside her, Eryn tensed and untensed every few steps as people she knew drew close and then drifted away, distracted by one festive thing or another. They'd made it most of the way down the road when someone called out to Eryn. Rina didn't think she'd ever felt Eryn tense that tightly.

The blond man who had pointed at her at the first ichor party and accused her of being the source of all blame jogged over to Eryn with a wide grin. Rina wondered if that smile looked anything but smarmy to other people. She imagined it must or he would stop doing it.

"Eryn, so, your place or mine for Frost Night? I've already put in a request with the kitchen for that spicy apple dish that always makes you horny." Unsurprisingly, Rina's presence didn't seem to register with him in the least.

"Oh, I um…" Eryn looked like she would rather dive into a sewage trench than be in this conversation, let alone spend Frost Night with him. "I haven't made my Frost Night plans yet."

Smarmy man's brow knit in confusion. "But you don't need to make plans. We always spend Frost Night together. We go to service with your farmer friend—"

"Childrearer," Eryn corrected him.

"—have dinner, and spend the rest of the night going heavy. It's like the only time each year we go more than once in a night."

Rina held in a scoff. She could just imagine Eryn pushing his postcoital body off herself and leaping out of bed to go do something else. Frost Night was probably the only night a year Eryn didn't have something more interesting to do than continue to marinate with his warmth.

"Well, I don't want to do that this year."

"You're doing Frost Night with someone else?" smarmy man said incredulously. "Who?"

"I haven't decided. I mean, I might help the childrearers. They are always grateful for families to take an additional baby for the night." Rina could tell Eryn was making a concerted effort not to look at her.

She wants to spend Frost Night with me? Eryn couldn't say it and she most likely wasn't going to do it either, but just the thought was enough to make Rina puff up with pride. For once, she was glad that people like smarmy man completely ignored her. She didn't have to hide her smile.

"You're not seriously going to spend a chaste Frost Night with some squirmy baby in your bed. That doesn't even make any sense." His voice rose with his temper, and Rina hoped she wasn't going to have to intervene. There was no way a confrontation ended well for her. "What in the lands is going on with you? We haven't even had sex in like seven months."

"I said I haven't decided, just don't plan around me. There are plenty of other heroes who would love to have you. You certainly haven't been celibate without me. Go spend Frost Night with Yetta. You always love to show off when you're with me to get her hot and bothered. She'd go all night for the chance to spend it with you."

"You're missing the point, Eryn."

"No, you're missing the point. I'm not spending Frost Night with you. Go ask someone else." Eryn sidestepped smarmy man and marched down the road. Rina had to jog to keep up. "The nerve," she kept mumbling.

"Did you still want to…" Rina asked, drawing Eryn out of her mutterings as they reached the point to turn off the road toward Eryn's home.

Eryn looked surprised. "Yes. I still need to hear what you found, and also yes to wanting to have you over."

They walked in silence across the training field, Eryn still lost in her annoyance and frustration. Rina found herself down an entirely different path of thought. If she was right, she might know exactly what to get Eryn for Frost Night whether they spent it together or not.

As Eryn let them both into her house, Rina went straight to the kitchen. She had a feeling that seeming distracted and busy was going to make the conversation she wanted to have a lot easier. "Eryn?" she asked, as she prepped the wood for the stove. "Do you like men?"

"I uh, I mean…it's not like…it's just…" She went silent for a moment. Rina looked over her shoulder to see Eryn, lips pressed together, trying to fight the flush in her cheeks. When she saw Rina looking at her, she opened her mouth, paused, and shut it again.

"Obviously it's fine either way, I just didn't ask when we were paired almost eight months ago, and that guy made me wonder." Rina stuck her head unnecessarily far into the stove, pushing ash from the last meal she'd made Eryn into the trap and setting the kindling for another fire. She looked at the black soot on her fingers and smiled before purposefully wiping it across her forehead. When she looked back at Eryn again, she got the chuckle she'd been hoping for.

"I like you. How's that for an answer?"

Rina's puppy told her she liked it very much. A shadow in the room told her it was a lie. "Not actually an answer to my question. Though I do like it very much." She moved to the icebox, pulling out whatever looked like it hadn't spoiled. "You can like me and men."

Behind her, Rina heard Eryn slump into a chair. The idea that she could hear Eryn's posture amused her. Inside, her puppy warned her to back off. If Eryn didn't want to talk about this, why was she pushing? Outside, the shadow pestered Rina nonstop about how she paled in comparison to a man, Eryn simply didn't want to admit it.

"I don't know. I guess I never really thought about it. I've always liked manly men. I like strength. I like broad shoulders. But then again, I don't particularly love naked bodies, you know. At a party, I'm not really looking at naked men or women. I'm looking at their actions and movements, whether they're doing the things I like. I've probably been with as many women as men, but only in groups. One-on-one, I've only been with men and you. And, well, you're better."

Rina felt herself puff with pride again. She didn't turn around as she chopped vegetables and asked, "So you like penises?"

Eryn sighed, audibly sinking lower in her chair. "Yes, but obviously it's not necessary. If it answers your question, I'd much rather spend a night with you without one than a man with one. Not even just Henk, but any man. Rina, I haven't had sex with anyone but you in seven months. That night I came over and you were having sex with that other guardian, I haven't been with anyone but you since then and I don't miss it."

Rina pushed the chopped veggies into a pot of water and walked over to where Eryn was slumped so far in her chair it looked like she was about to melt onto the floor. "I haven't been with anyone else since that night either. I only want to be with you." She kissed Eryn, pressing their foreheads together and rubbing.

"Did you just rub soot on me?"

"Yep. You seemed like you needed a little something to lighten the mood. Plus, you shared with me, it was only fitting I share with you." She gave Eryn a second kiss before asking, "So, did you want to hear what I found in the crypt?"

CHAPTER TWELVE

Them and Us

Eryn woke in her empty bed and stretched her arms into the space that Rina had occupied only hours before. It was the only thing Eryn could say Henk had on Rina. He was always there in the morning. She didn't care about his morning erection, she cared about his warmth, his presence, his desire to be near her as long as possible. She liked slipping out of his arms to go do something else. What was Rina always leaving her to do instead?

At dinner with Alba, she'd brought it up. She hadn't realized until she'd voiced it, just how much it hurt that Rina was gone. Even in the Dark Lands, Rina was always making breakfast. Eryn woke up alone every single morning.

"Have you talked to her about it?" Alba had asked.

"No. I don't actually want to hear that she gets antsy holding me and would rather do something productive."

"How do you know she would rather do something else?"

"Because she's gone. Because she doesn't stay. She leaves and does something else."

"What does she do after she leaves?"

"I don't know."

"Well, have you talked to her about it?"

Eryn groaned, then clarified, "I'm not upset with you." She was supposed to be having dinner with Alba to apologize for bursting in on her, but of course Alba was more interested in hearing about how things were going with her guardian, than being apologized to. "I guess I need to hear this. I just don't want to do it."

Alba smiled. "I know when you're standing in your own way. It's just about getting you to see it too."

"I'll talk to her." But then she hadn't. Rina gave her the perfect opening by asking her about Henk, but she'd been too wrapped up in her own insecurities, her own attempts to answer what in the lands it was she wanted, to tell Rina that what she wanted was to wake up next to her.

"Tonight," Eryn promised. They had plans to meet in the fields to help with the harvest and then investigate the scrolls for the gap years from other castes, which meant skimming through dozens of lockers and hundreds of scrolls. Shadows had clearly become more prevalent in those twenty years, and someone had to have made guesses if not the guardians.

In the cafeteria, Eryn grabbed fruit and sat at a table with Kalia and two heroes from the cohort above hers. Moments like these seemed like an easy, quick way to put in socially when she was just going to be eating anyway.

"I'm getting him this really great hat. The artisan who makes them says it keeps off the rain and that it'll suck the sweat right off his head," Kalia said. She was currently romancing a farmer whose strong biceps and soft fingers filled most of her stories.

"Are you getting your guardian anything?" Eryn asked.

The three heroes exchanged contemptuous looks before turning back to her and shaking their heads in unison. "No."

"Oh, I just wondered since I've heard guardians often get something for their heroes." She was sure she'd heard heroes talking about what they'd received in the past.

"Sure," one of the older heroes said. "Most do, but I've not heard of a hero giving one back. I don't really think it would be appropriate. It feels like leading them on, you know."

Eryn nodded. No, she didn't know, but she doubted asking was going to get her anywhere. Instead, she finished her pear and left. She wondered if she'd been saving herself a lot of headaches over the last fifteen years by avoiding her peers.

Her day working alongside the farmers in the fields was long and her back ached by the end, but Eryn left with a feeling of accomplishment that went deeper than the pain or the bruises. It was nice to hear people talk about their families and their traditions beyond just exchanging gifts and getting naked. Frost Night was about more than staying warm. It was about letting go of the past and looking to the future together.

After their research in the crypt, Eryn talked Rina into strolling through the market with her to discuss what they'd found. Eryn procured them both hot wine, but of course Rina refused to drink any of it.

"Why don't you wear something other than purple when you are leaving the garrison?" Eryn asked. She knew she sounded huffy, but it seemed silly to draw undue attention to herself. It seemed like a better solution to change than to deny herself every small luxury.

"Everything I have is purple. All my tops at least. It's just tradition. Guardians wear purple. It's what people make for us, so it's what we wear."

Eryn hid her smile behind a mug of hot wine. She knew exactly what to get Rina for Frost Night. Screw tradition.

As they wandered the market, they exchanged anecdotes from their research, which had been rather fruitless. Crop yields were down because the land in which they were growing crops had held schools, houses, and community centers in prior years. Fruit tree seedlings would take years to bear fruit. There were so many mouths to feed. It would take a generation for the decreased birth rate to have any impact, so everyone was simply expected to make do.

Artisans filled scrolls with recipes for stews and soups that would feed more with less. Priests wrote about the light of the Goddess that would carry them through this dark time. Laborers sketched diagrams for more space efficient, uniform homes that could be built with the materials pulled from older, larger homes. Everyone found ways to adapt. What the scrolls didn't contain was any mention of what the heroes or guardians were doing.

They ate dinner at an artisan's shop and Rina did the dishes while Eryn chatted with the artisan about her children. Eryn still didn't like that routine, but she did like that she and Rina had found a rhythm inside the Community the way they had outside. Now, Eryn just had to figure out how to break the pattern they'd established for the end of the night. Dinner, surrounded by people wasn't the right time to talk about it, but neither did making out on the couch feel like the right time. Eryn didn't want to interrupt being carried to bed, and there was no way she was interrupting Rina when she was between her legs.

Eryn lay in Rina's arms trying to convince herself that there was literally no other time. If she didn't say something now, she was going to wake up alone again. Frost Night was three days away and she still hadn't made plans. What if Rina said she didn't want to spend it with Eryn? What if she said yes, left in the middle of the night, and got hypothermia?

This is silly, just ask!

"You leave in the middle of the night. You aren't here when I wake up. You aren't there when I wake up in the Dark Lands either. Do you not want to be here?" Eryn hated the way it sounded, hated the ability for Rina to break her with a single word. Eryn was practical, she wasn't driven by emotion, so why did the concept of Rina not wanting to be there make her chest ache?

Rina hesitated. She kissed Eryn's neck before answering, as if she needed to soften the blow. "I want to be here. I like waking up with you in my arms."

Eryn released her held breath. Thank the Goddess. Though, that still didn't address the issue at hand. "I want that. I want to wake up with you in the morning."

Behind her, Rina stiffened. "We can't do that."

"Why not?" Eryn made a great effort to keep the desperation out of her voice.

Again, Rina hesitated. Eryn hated it. She wanted to spin around and demand honest, blunt answers.

"Because staying overnight is something couples do. If people see me leaving in the morning, it will invalidate the image you've created. You can't parade me around the Community like an incompetent puppy and then treat me like a partner. Everyone is happy to accept my incompetence. They expect it. I don't even mind it. It means I get to spend time with you. But people won't just accept it if we act like a couple. There's a reason we don't quite stand next to each other in the market or hold hands or kiss in public or wake up together. I'm trying to preserve what you've created because I want it. I want this with you."

Eryn closed her eyes against the prickle of tears. She'd wanted to know how *they* could treat guardians like this. She had truly believed she was not part of *they*. It was everyone else. They assumed the worst about her guardian, having nothing to do with the way she worded her explanations. They saw her guardian as lesser than her, which had nothing to do with the fact that she felt more comfortable when people saw Rina walking at her heel rather than next to her.

She rolled over and pushed words out around the knot in her throat. "I'm sorry."

Rina drew her in closer, petting her hair and shushing her as their bodies pressed together. "It's okay. It's not your fault. It's just the way things are. I still get to be with you. I can even wake you before I leave so we can wake up together."

Eryn shook her head against Rina's shoulder. She didn't want that. She wanted Rina like a partner. She wanted another option.

She pulled back from Rina's shoulder and rubbed the tears from her eyes. "No. I want you to stay tonight. I want to wake up with you in the morning, have a roll between the sheets, eat breakfast together, and leave the house hand in hand. I want you to be my Frost Night date and I want everyone to know it."

"Are you sure? Are you absolutely sure?" Rina looked as desperate for a yes as Eryn felt.

"Yes."

There was a difference in the way they moved together that night. It wasn't a roll between the sheets. This is what it feels like to make love, Eryn thought as she lay tangled in Rina's limbs. I love her and that doesn't scare me anymore. She held in a snort. That was a lie. It scared her a lot, but it no longer embarrassed her.

Eryn had expected to love the feeling of waking up in Rina's arms, but the warmth, the feeling of skin on skin, and the pressure of arms around her only gave credit to one sense. She loved the smell of Rina pillowed beneath her head. She loved the sound of her holding nothing back as she brought them both to orgasm. She loved the look of her standing naked in front of the icebox and stating that if they were going to make this a regular thing Eryn was going to have to learn to properly stock her kitchen. She loved the idea of a regular thing.

As promised, Eryn left her house that morning with Rina's hand held in her own. She was ashamed of the fear that bubbled up as she opened the door and by how hard she gripped Rina's hand just to make sure she didn't pull away as they descended the steps to the stares of all her hero neighbors. How had she been naive enough to think this would be easy? But every step got easier. The first time she leaned over and kissed Rina in the fields, she was sure her heart would explode if it beat any faster. But by the fifth kiss, the morning of Frost Night, Eryn found she was able to keep from averting her gaze to avoid making eye contact with the people around her. People weren't staring any less, it just didn't bother her as much.

"So, are you ready for your Frost Night gift?" Eryn asked as they meandered through the market.

Rina gave her hand an appreciative squeeze. "Yes, and then we get to go and get yours." Eryn wasn't sure she had a good feeling about the glint in Rina's eyes. She trusted her nonetheless.

Eryn took the lead, making sure to pull Rina along like a lover and not like a pet. Rina seemed surprised when Eryn pulled her into a clothing shop and directly to the counter. "Layula, here is my guardian for the measurements we discussed." She'd made sure to present the request the day before. She didn't need to go back and forth on whether it was appropriate to make a guardian something in beige in front of Rina. She also didn't need Rina to know exactly the size of the favor she was calling in to get it done. Eryn was finding it was easier for people to choose her over stability when she sweetened the pot.

When her measurements were done and the fabric chosen, Eryn and Rina left the shop with Layula's promise that it would be completed within the next three days. "I hope you like it. I thought it might be nice for you to be able to go places and do things without people immediately identifying you as a guardian. It's not that I don't want people to know I'm with you. I want to walk hand in hand with you." She held their hands out entwined to make her point. "I just figured maybe I could hand you a drink and you could enjoy it without people looking at you and wondering if you paid in for it."

"I love it. Thank you for giving me this and for wanting this for me."

"I do. Rina, you do so much. You should get to have this without a new outfit. I just hope this makes it easier."

"I appreciate that, and I think it will." She came to a stop and an impish grin spread across her face. "And now, it is time for your gift."

Rina led her across the threshold into a shop Eryn didn't think she had even seen before. It smelled like the oils and candles shop, but silkier and headier. Throughout the shop stood small tables with artfully placed collections of oils and glass, metal, and glazed clay objects Eryn couldn't identify. The signs didn't help much either. "Massage." "Beads." "Heat." "Eggs." Eryn caught sight of the table they were headed to and pulled to a halt. "Is this a sex shop?"

Rina's grin only widened as she nodded. "Guardians are taught how to use everything in this shop, but female guardians receive specific training with these." Rina rested her hand on a glass replica of a giant, vein-popping erection. "That way if they are paired with a female hero who prefers men, they can still pleasure her the way she likes it."

"Welcome, ladies." The sudden voice behind her made Eryn jump. She spun around to see a pair of artisans smiling at them. Eryn was pretty sure it was the first shop they'd been in where the artisans had welcomed them both with smiles. "Here for a fitting?" the woman asked Rina, who nodded. She directed Rina a few feet away from the table and began to take measurements not too different from the ones Layula had taken.

"Have you used one before?" the other artisan asked, running her hand along the table of options.

"No." Eryn's voice came out as a squeak. She wasn't entirely sure why the question made her face burn and her neck seem to shrink inside the collar of her shirt, but she felt very out of her element.

"Then let me help you pick one. What do you like in a penis?"

"I, uh…"

"Do you have experience with penises?"

"Yes, I uh, I do." It shouldn't be this hard to talk about sex…with the woman I want to be my partner clearly eavesdropping.

"Let's talk size." There was no way out of the conversation that was less awkward than just having it. It's only awkward if I make it that way, Eryn coached herself. Goddess knew this woman wasn't going to judge her. It was literally her art to create these. So, the artisan walked Eryn through everything from size and shape to feel and durability, all while Rina silently listened in.

"All right, I think we have a winner." The artisan lifted the glass penis from the table and handed it to her fellow artisan who was clearly her wife. The second artisan took it to the counter along with the leather strapping she'd been wrapping, cutting, lacing, and buckling around Rina's groin throughout Eryn's discussion and wrapped the two items carefully before handing the box to Rina. "Have fun," the artisan said with a wink.

"Thank you," Rina said.

"The pleasure is all yours," the artisan said, earning herself a groan and an elbow in the side from her wife.

Outside once more, Eryn looked at the sky where smudgy, black words were drifting down the golden glow of the dome and groaned. "We have to get to the chapel, or we'll be late." There was no time to store the package anywhere, especially not if they wanted to use it that night, and Eryn had no interest in waiting. There would be other services throughout the day, but she always went to the second service with Alba. It was one of the only services all year in which castes didn't attend services as a unit. She liked reflecting on what the next year might hold with her chosen family and she liked the idea of kneeling before the Goddess in thanksgiving with Alba on one side and Rina on the other.

As they slid into the pew next to Alba, Eryn kept waiting for someone to ask her what was in the box Rina was very conspicuously trying to shove under the pew in front of her. Next to her, Alba chuckled at the embarrassment that Eryn knew was radiating off her. "I'm not going to ask," Alba whispered, "I'm just going to laugh." Eryn wasn't sure if that was better.

"Frost Night," the head priest said from her platform beside the ichor fountain, "is a time to remember that from the greatest struggles of our life can come the ripest fruit. Without Frost Night, there would be no apples, no cherries, no lavender for our bees, no echinacea for the healers, and no dyes for the artisans. The Goddess gives us this night together to bear fruit, to bear children, and to bare ourselves to the people we love. As we begin the next year, let us look back on the one we have completed with thanks for what we have learned and what we have experienced together."

Throughout the chapel, priests passed baskets of fallen leaves and charcoal pencils through the pews. "We each come here with sorrows in our hearts, those spoken and those unspoken. Tonight, we turn over a new leaf. From our pain will grow something new, something beautiful, delicate, and precious. Our sorrows are no less real, not forgotten, but put to a greater purpose. Every year we undertake this exercise to commit to ourselves, to each other, and to the Goddess to fill the gaps in our lives with flowers. Please write on one side of your leaf a word to represent a sorrow you bring from the previous year and on the other side a blossom that you will cultivate to grow out of that sorrow."

The content of Eryn's leaf each year had always been a struggle. She almost felt bad for the lack of adversity in her life. But this year, she knew exactly what to write. She scrawled her two words and turned to Rina, ready to share. "Them." She flipped over her leaf and smiled as Rina ran her finger over the charcoal word "Us."

Rina set her leaf next to Eryn's. "Syrana," it said. Delicately, she flipped it over and ran her finger once more over the word "Us."

They dropped their leaves back into the passing basket and watched as priests tied the leaves to a large wreath and slowly lowered the wreath into the ichor fountain until it began to melt. Flame licked up the wreath, igniting the leaves and sending a puff of heat that fought back the chill of the air. As the wreath melted and turned to ash, the charcoal words floated on the surface of the ichor, casting hundreds of words onto the walls. Names of loved ones, accidents, hopes, and dreams all caught in single words strewn throughout the chapel. The words rose through the column and out onto the dome above, a testament and a promise made to the Goddess in Her blood.

Eryn pulled Rina in for another kiss, longer and more tender than the pecks they'd exchanged in public thus far. She was very much looking forward to spending her Frost Night with Rina and only partially due to the contents of the box at Rina's knees. What they had was new and it was delicate, but it was precious, and it was beautiful.

❖

How adorable. The sarcasm in the Commander's voice was not lost on Rina. She didn't really know why she was telling him about her Frost Night, except that, as he had said, who else did she have to tell. It was nice to wake up in Eryn's arms in the Dark Lands and not immediately feel the need to get up and make breakfast. Filling the time until Eryn woke by reliving the last week of acting like a couple made it all the better.

What she should be talking to the Commander about was the

research his prodding had led to. She had a strong feeling he knew what had happened in those gap years, but every time she brought it up, he simply said, *You have all the pieces, I cannot put them together for you.*

"And the way she looked at me that first time with the glass cock strapped to me. I was freezing, standing there naked, but I could have done it for hours just to savor that look. She wanted me. She wanted everything I was offering and nothing more. She told me I was sexy. She said I was the sexiest person she had ever seen and if I didn't come get under the covers with her right then and there, she would be forced to come to me, and we'd freeze there like some beautiful mid-coital statue."

And did you become a statue of unending bliss?

Rina rolled her eyes. How sad was it that he was the best listener in her life? "No. I blew her mind over and over again and she told me she loves me. She loves me!"

Rina was thrown from her reverie by waves of emotion roiling off the Commander. She had felt her emotions change with his arrival and departure, but this was an entirely new sensation. She still felt joyful, but she could feel the Commander's ire, his wrath, and an underlying sense of betrayal washing over her and beating at her joy. *She does not love you!*

Rina gripped her joy, trying to protect it and herself.

She loves the way you make her feel. She loves that you give her everything she wants without question. She loves that you subserviate yourself before her every whim. She does not love you. She will betray you.

Rina fought back the fear that the Commander and his words were trying to push inside her. "Leave me alone," she yelled, startling Eryn awake in her arms.

"What is it?" Eryn asked, her hand immediately going to the sheath of her sword beside their bedroll.

"Just a shadow," Rina said as she felt his presence withdraw.

"What did it say?" Eryn's grip didn't loosen on her sword or Rina's hand.

"It told me we wouldn't find ichor and that everyone will say I'm a failure. I'm sorry I shouldn't have yelled. It just got me riled up." She didn't like lying to Eryn, but it felt like the only way to protect the glow of happiness she felt every time Eryn looked at her.

"It must really suck to have to hear them all the time, even if it is useful."

Rina nodded and kissed Eryn's head. "Do you want to sleep some more?"

"No, I'm awake now. Breakfast?"

The Commander's words replayed in the back of her mind again. *She loves that you subserviate yourself to her every whim.* Making breakfast was her job, so why did it feel so demeaning?

The Commander kept his distance over the following days. She could feel him waiting just at the periphery. It wasn't until they were almost back to the dome that the Commander drew near again.

You do not want to hear it, but I must put you and your safety before your feelings, Rina. I will not, however, tell you how to feel. It is not my way to provide answers, only to lead you to your own and to warn you of what I see in your future. So, I will leave you with a warning and a question. Beware the golden boy and consider, you give pleasure to her all the time, but does she give it to you?

Rina tripped over a branch and barely caught herself from stumbling into a patch of bladed grass. She liked that the Commander listened, but she did not enjoy listening to him.

"Are you okay?" Eryn said, helping steady her.

"Yeah, just tired I guess." She was looking forward to being back in the dome where the Commander left her alone. "You make me happy," she said, directing her statement at Eryn, but it was an answer to the Commander.

"You make me happy too," Eryn answered.

Not what I said. The Commander stood there, incorporeal as always, and rather than withdraw, simply let Rina walk out of his sphere of influence. The relief of passing through the dome felt like warm summer rain. No more Commander for three weeks. Just the memory of his whispers and jabs and questions.

But he was wrong. Rina had been concerned that perhaps the social pressures, the stares, and the whispers would change Eryn's mind about acting like a couple. They'd been staring since Rina started spending time with Eryn inside the dome, but Eryn hadn't been the target before. She had let their judgment slide past her to Rina. Now, she accepted it with her head held high.

"She loves me," she reminded herself as she touched the smile that had felt constantly affixed to her face over the last week. Rina couldn't remember a time when she had smiled this much. She felt like she had to—this much happiness couldn't be contained.

Rina breezed through the door of her home, already untucking her purple tunic from her pants. She needed a quick bucket shower to rinse off the smell of archery training, then into her beige tunic for an evening feeding vegetable mush to babies who were just as likely to grab the food with their hands and spread it in their hair as they were to open their mouths.

It was frustrating, it was tedious, but she got to watch Eryn, with a baby in her arms, smile that tender smile over and over again as she rocked the babies to sleep.

"Jesta, I'm just—Claine." She skidded to a halt just outside her bedroom door. Claine stood from the couch and fixed Rina with a stern gaze. Of course, Rina thought, just when things were going well.

"We need to talk," Claine said, indicating for Rina to take a seat.

"About what?" Rina asked, though she was fairly sure she knew.

"Your relationship with Eryn," Claine said, never one to beat around the bush. "The word is that the two of you are acting like a couple."

"And why shouldn't we?" Rina could feel all the anger that had been absent for the last week about to boil over. It was as if the anger hadn't been gone but was only lying in wait for just such a moment.

Claine gave Rina a pejorative look. It was a look she had received many times over the last fifteen years. It said Claine was about to impart wisdom that Rina was to follow whether she agreed with it or not.

Rina had no interest in hearing it.

Rina spoke before Claine could. "You told me to love her. You told me to put her before all else. You said and I quote, 'Eryn is the best trained hero we've ever seen, do everything she says, and everything should be fine.' So, I've done that. I love her and she loves me. What could possibly be wrong with that? Things are finally going right for me, why do you want to ruin that? Why do you want me to be unhappy? Why do you want me to fail?"

Claine blew out a long breath and her whole body seeming to deflate as she took a seat on the couch once more. Her stern expression was gone as she silently rested her face in her hands as if defeated. "Please sit," she said without looking up.

Rina took a seat in the chair, wondering if Claine had finally reached the end of her rope.

"The hardest day of my life was Ardon's wedding," Claine said, her face still hidden by her hands. "I had to watch the man I'm desperately in love with dedicate himself and his life to someone else. He was so happy and so in love and I knew I should be happy for him, but it hurt so much. Most guardians don't go to their heroes' weddings, but I was head guardian by that point and thought it was my duty to be there. I had to stand there with a neutral expression through the vows, the dedication, the promises, and kisses, all while I felt like a shadow was clawing into my chest, finding anything soft and vulnerable, and tearing it out.

"My point is this, Rina, I knew Ardon didn't love me. I was his guardian and that was it. And yet despite the fact that I had known for over ten years that he didn't love me and would marry someone else, that day I truly wanted to climb into a hole and die. I can only imagine what that pain would have been like if I had thought Ardon loved me.

"Guardians can't get married. Eryn will eventually find someone she loves and move on. It doesn't matter how much she cares about you now or how much she enjoys pretending to be a couple, one day she will want a family and she can't have that with you. That is simply the truth of being a guardian and the unrequited love that comes with it.

"I know that sometimes it seems like I want you to fail, but it's exactly the opposite. I love you, Rina, and all I've ever wanted from our relationship is to protect you. From monsters, from shadows, and from yourself. I'm here because now I want to protect your heart. Acting like a couple, believing that she loves you, can only end in terrible heartbreak."

For a long moment, all Rina could do was stare at Claine. Claine had never spoken about her feelings and certainly never with such vulnerability. Her weapon of choice was cajoling and guilting, not sincerity.

Rina didn't doubt a word of it. She could try to ignore the Commander, but the evidence was right in front of her. Eryn didn't just look good with a baby in her arms, she would want to have one of her own one day. She would want a family and a house with little paintings on the side. She would want a life that she couldn't have with Rina, and it was going to break one of them. Rina didn't believe that Eryn would betray her, but she would move on, and Rina never would.

But the question was what would she do with this truth? It wasn't as if she could simply stop loving Eryn. Loving her had felt like the only light in her life. Was going back to the darkness truly better? Not to mention that loving her hero wasn't a choice she had made.

"What am I supposed to do?" Rina said, feeling just a taste of that inevitable heartbreak. It felt like a knife to the chest just to think about losing Eryn to someone else one day. In her life, Claine had always had an answer for all Rina's questions. They weren't always the answers she wanted, but surely Claine would know what to do.

Claine rested her hand on Rina's knee. "You have always questioned everything you are told and never taken anything for granted. Use that. Recognize that Eryn's love is fleeting, so enjoy it while you have it but don't become blinded by it. Question your own feelings. What is simple enjoyment of the moment, what is the uncontrollable love of a guardian? What are the aspects that you can control and limit? You can still be an amazing guardian and serve your hero without succumbing to your feelings. If anyone has the introspection and the vehement belief in logic over what they are told that is necessary to separate how they feel from what they think, it is you."

CHAPTER THIRTEEN

Truth and Confrontation

Eryn parried and spun, using her youth and dexterity to outmaneuver her instructor. Mattian stroked his well-trimmed white beard with one hand and rotated his quarterstaff with the other, blocking her blade easily. "Move less," he said. "Yes, I will wear out faster than you, but not if I can simply stand here. You won't always be young. Learn to fight like an old person early and you will be young longer."

"That doesn't make sense," Eryn said. "Acting old will make me old sooner." She danced out of his reach and lunged back in. He smacked her attack out of the way with a twist of his wrist and caught her in the back of the knee with the other end of his staff. Eryn fell to her knees, panting.

"And that is why you will not beat me for another ten years. Conserve your energy for when you need it, and you will be able to fight forever. Dive headfirst like a fool into everything, and you will be on your knees panting when the real fight begins." Mattian wasn't most heroes' first choice for a weapons instructor. He was very good at most weapons, but he held nothing back in either his attacks or his commentary.

Eryn pushed to her feet and readied her blade. It was the thing he liked best about her, and she knew it. It didn't matter how many times he struck her down, she always got back up and she never blamed her failure on his actions. Eryn liked him because he was blunt, and he didn't particularly care what people said or what they did when they didn't have a weapon in their hands.

He was exactly the person she wanted for the question she needed to ask. "Heroes fall in love with people from any caste. Has a hero ever fallen in love with their guardian?"

Mattian's chuckle became a snort. His snort became a laugh. His laugh became howls of laughter. He gasped between a mixture of words and peals of laughter. "Now that is a strategy. Jokes don't work very well on monsters, but distraction is often an excellent option."

When Eryn didn't take advantage of his distraction, his laughter died. "You're serious? No, I have never heard of a hero falling in love with their guardian."

"Why not?"

Mattian pursed his lips in thought before a smirk spread across his face. "Gravy," he said with satisfaction. "Guardians are like gravy. Gravy is delicious, but gravy is not a meal. Potatoes are a meal. Now, potatoes and gravy are a great meal. Why would a hero ever choose gravy when they could have potatoes and gravy? The gravy is always there, always waiting to please. So go find yourself some potatoes and together, you'll have a real meal."

Eryn hadn't understood when the hero said, "It feels like leading them on," until now. It was leading them on to think they were anything more than a side dish in their hero's life.

Pain shot through Eryn's hand as Mattian's staff smacked the back of it. She dropped her sword to clutch her aching hand to her chest.

"See," Mattian said with a smirk. "Distraction."

"Yeah, thanks," Eryn said blandly. "Thanks for the session."

Eryn hurried home, her right hand still cradled in her left. The back was already starting to turn purplish-blue. After a session with Mattias, she ought to be glad nothing was broken. A good long soak in cold water seemed like just the thing. Rina had afternoon training to lead, so maybe by the time she came by, Eryn's hand wouldn't be swollen.

She'd just gotten her hand into a bucket of water when there was a knock at her door. She knew that knock. It filled the pit of her stomach with the feeling of eating rotten pork. But she couldn't just hide inside pretending not to hear. He wouldn't be dissuaded so easily.

Henk's charismatic smile was distinctly absent when Eryn opened her door. "Hello, Henk," she said. She could tell him to leave, but this conversation was going to happen one way or another, and it was better to have it without an audience.

"Great, so at least you haven't forgotten who I am." Henk smelled like sweat and chalk. He'd clearly come immediately from training, something that had once turned her on.

"I've never forgotten you, Henk. I just don't want to have sex with you anymore."

"Well, that's a relief," he said sarcastically. He didn't wear a scowl well. "We had a good thing. You can't just treat me like this. After everything I put into our relationship, you're going to throw me away for what? To pretend to be in a couple with your guardian? You look pathetic."

"We never had a thing. You don't care about me. You care about being seen with me. And what did you put into our relationship besides your cock?" She was glad she hadn't let him inside her home to have this conversation more privately. She was looking forward to closing the door in his face.

"I pleasured *you*!"

"And you always got what you came for." The climax of every encounter was his own.

"You were always running off to spend time with other people, other castes."

"I invited you to come with me so many times, but you never showed, even when you said you would. But you know what, I'm glad because you would have spent to whole time complaining about how you were above doing that work."

"I didn't need to go help the other castes. I'm not like you. I'm not…" He raised his arms slowly from his waist to over his head while jittering his hands like he was too jumpy to hold them still. "I'm normal. But I'm sure your guardian doesn't complain. I'm sure she bends over backward to make you feel loved. Not everyone gets to be with me. It meant something when we were a couple. I'm the second-best hero. People respect me. My love means something."

"You don't love me, and you never have. The only person you've ever loved is yourself." She didn't really want to make this a fight, but he had started it. Normal? He wasn't normal. He was a jerk.

"Don't you get it, Eryn? Her attention, her love doesn't mean anything. She's just doing her job. You're so desperate to be the center of attention that you're willing to look like a fool clinging to someone who has no choice but to make their life revolve around you. She will always be there. Having her doesn't mean anything."

"Rina isn't gravy!"

Henk stared at her slack-jawed. It took Eryn a moment to realize it wasn't because he had no context for why Rina wasn't a food topping. She had just called her guardian by name. They stood there in silence for a moment processing that.

Finally, Eryn broke the silence. She wanted to be very clear and then she wanted to be done. "I like that Rina is always there. I like that she loves me. I like her. There is no us and there never was. Let it go." She closed the door with a satisfying thunk and slumped against the wall. "People respect me," she whispered. People would learn to respect Rina too. She deserved it. People didn't think Eryn was a fool, they just didn't understand. They were too focused on the way things had always been to see the way they could be. It would take time, but they would get there. It wouldn't always feel this crappy.

Rina's knock a few hours later brought a lift to Eryn's spirits. There had been a time when Henk's knock had brought her excitement, but he'd never brought her joy.

But there was something different about Rina that night. She seemed distracted and distant. In their few months of serving other castes together, Eryn often caught Rina staring at her, but usually when she did Rina smiled as if embarrassed and looked away. But tonight, it was Rina who caught herself staring, frowned, and stopped. Whenever Eryn drew near as she rocked a baby to sleep, Rina shooed her away as if she were a disruption. They didn't always go home together after such an outing, but Rina usually seemed disappointed when they didn't. Tonight, she seemed relieved. Taking care of babies was exhausting and Rina's excuse of being too tired was realistic. It was the feeling that exhaustion was an easy out rather than a letdown that concerned Eryn.

For a week, their interactions felt strained. Sometimes, Rina was fully present and happy. But those moments felt more and more like Rina was distracted into being happy than genuinely enjoying herself.

The distance was most striking on mornings when she woke up in Rina's loose hold, received a kiss, and was asked what she wanted to have for breakfast. She'd expected things to get better. Why were they worse?

A real date seemed like the place to start. So, when Eryn was invited to a neighborhood dance to welcome a newly married couple, she invited Rina to be her date.

All night, Rina seemed to have a chip on her shoulder. She'd fall briefly into the revelry before leaping out as if from an overly hot bath and sit sullenly again, observing the other participants with an odd mixed look of jealousy and apathy. The looks she gave Eryn were the worst part of the evening. Eryn never knew if she was going to get an expression of unadulterated love, or the frustrated expression Rina might give a petulant child.

Eryn found herself taking every opportunity to dance with others, as if a bit of distance could make Rina's expression grow fonder. It didn't. Her dance partners simply became targets of Rina's capricious expressions. Eryn knew Alba would tell her to talk to Rina about it. Open communication had been the key to starting to act like a couple. It seemed reasonable to at least try it first rather than trying to grin and bear it, waiting for something to magically change again.

She plopped down on the bench beside Rina at the edge of the impromptu dance floor. "You seem distracted." It seemed like an innocuous enough statement.

Rina shrugged. "No, just tired I guess."

Eryn set her hand on Rina's inner thigh and watched her features cycle like a miller's water wheel. "We promised that we would be honest with each other. Something is different. You're frustrated with me or something and I want you to tell me what it is."

Under her hand, Rina shifted uncomfortably. "I'm not frustrated with you."

"I said or something. Please tell me."

"Okay. I just…maybe not here." She waved her hand at the crowd dancing, laughing, and drinking around them.

Eryn took her hand and pulled Rina through the crowd to a more deserted edge of the neighborhood.

This was the most uncomfortable Eryn had ever seen Rina. She picked at her cuticles with one hand, and her posture made her look small and scared.

"What is it?"

"It's going to sound bad, okay? So, I need you to promise me you'll listen to everything before you get upset."

It had to be something about shadows with the way Rina's emotions flitted back and forth without any clear cause. "Okay."

"Claine came to talk to me about us acting like a couple and why it's a bad thing."

"Ugh, Henk tried to do the same thing—" Eryn cut off. She just promised to listen.

"She's worried about me. She says that one day you're going to want to get married. You're going to want a family and you can't have those things with me. She says you'll find someone else, and it'll break my heart. And I'm not saying that you will mean to. She's not saying that either, just that you will because you'll want that, and you'll deserve that. You deserve a family. It's just that you have the ability to love whomever, and I don't."

"But I don't want to love anyone else." Eryn had to interrupt this line of reasoning. Other heroes might consider her statement of monogamy this young to be foolish, but she had always found them to be rather foolish. "I don't want a family if it means not being with you."

"You're just saying that because you're twenty. You have no idea what you want with the rest of your life outside of seeking ichor."

"You say from the wise old age of twenty-one?" Why was everyone treating her like she was a child? It was really pissing her off. She expected better from Rina.

"No, I say from the young and inexperienced age of twenty-one. I don't know what I want from the rest of my life, but I know that no matter what happens, I will love you—"

"I will love you too, Rina." This moment felt like it ought to be romantic. Why was Rina so anxious and cagey? She seemed on the verge of simply running away from this conversation altogether.

"No, you don't understand. I physically can't love anyone else. I have to figure out how to distance myself or when you inevitably move on it'll break me."

"Why do you keep assuming I'm going to move on? I mean, who's to say you're not the one who will move on? This goes both ways."

"No, it doesn't. No matter what you do, no matter how much you break my heart, I will always be forced to love you." Rina's expression shifted again from exasperated to stricken. She clearly hadn't meant to say that last part.

"What do you mean forced?"

Rina took several steps back as if afraid of Eryn's reaction.

When she didn't speak, Eryn stepped into the space Rina had vacated. She needed to know. She'd put her neck out in so many ways for this relationship. What did Rina mean by forced? "You promised to be honest with me."

Another moment of silence stretched between them before Rina whispered, "The ceremony to make us a hero-guardian pair, it made me fall in love with you."

Rina's words hit her as if she'd rammed her with a cart rather than simple words. She'd thought Henk was just being hateful. He'd been a cad, but he'd also been right. She thought Rina loved her, but she'd made a fool of herself clinging to someone who had no choice but to act out a false love. She'd done it in front of the entire Community, parading her naivete around for everyone to see. No wonder they had stared.

Rina was saying more. Eryn watched her mouth move, but all she could think about was all the people who were probably laughing at her. How many times had their kisses become the butt of a joke?

Rina reached her hand toward Eryn with an expression of concern. Eryn couldn't let Rina touch her. Not after everything. How dare she?

Eryn turned and bolted into the crowd. She weaved through happy couples laughing and wondered just how many were laughing at her. Had they seen? How much more would they laugh now that she had finally figured it out?

She was a hero. She wasn't supposed to fall in love with her guardian.

The ceremony. Maybe Rina hadn't been the only one affected by it. Eryn pushed through the crowd and headed to the center of the Community. Maybe everything could make sense again. Maybe there was an excuse that everyone would accept.

Eryn slipped through the open doors of the chapel and past the few people near the back lighting candles of prayer. A door off the main nave near the ichor fountain stood open and at her desk sat the head priest, who looked in Eryn's direction when she knocked on the doorjamb. "May the light of the Goddess be in you this day. How can I help you?"

"And you. It's, um, it's Eryn, the hero that you paired to a second guardian."

"I remember."

"Well, I was wondering, did you do anything differently the second time you paired me? The pairing makes a guardian love their hero, right? Did you do anything that might have made me fall in love with my guardian?" It all made sense. All she needed was the priest to confirm it to other people and no one would be able to blame her for being irrational. All she needed was a yes.

"Yes, it makes a guardian love their hero, but no, I didn't do anything that would have made you fall in love with her. You were unconscious when it was done, so if anything, you should love her less because you never experienced the brief glimpse of love before it wore off on your end. Anything that you feel is your own."

Eryn's heart sank. She could remember that brief sense of awe for Syrana when they had been paired. She'd chalked it up to excitement for their foresight, but it had been the ceremony. She didn't feel that way for Rina. She'd wanted the future she and Syrana would achieve. She wanted a future with Rina.

"I'm sorry I couldn't give you the answer you wanted."

Eryn shook her head, trying to fight off tears as much as express that it wasn't the priest's fault. She can't see you, she chastised herself. How many more times could she make a fool of herself. "Thank you," she said instead. It wasn't the heartfelt thank you the priest deserved, but it was the best she could muster.

She wandered out of the chapel and headed toward the housing district. She repeated the same line inside her head until she was standing on Alba's doorstep saying it through tears. "I love her, but she doesn't love me."

❖

"Dark gods damn it." Rina swore as she watched Eryn flee into the crowd. Had Eryn even heard her say she really did love her? The forced part was just the part she couldn't get rid of. There was so much more to the way she felt.

Eryn had promised to listen to everything, but she'd jumped to conclusions instead.

Inside her head, her puppy yelled at her. This wasn't Eryn's fault. Rina had been the one to say that her love was forced. It had been a bad idea and she knew it. How was Eryn supposed to take it except as a statement that she didn't really love her?

Rina tried to catch up to Eryn, but Eryn's slim frame slipped through the throng in a way Rina could not. By the time she reached the other end of the party, Eryn was gone. Rina jogged the two miles to Eryn's dark, empty house before realizing that she'd made a poor decision again. Eryn wouldn't go home. There was no one for her there. The first one she would go to was the Goddess. Rina turned and ran to the chapel.

As Rina entered the nave, the priests sweeping the floors and oiling the pews for the night looked up, some blind and some sighted, and nodded at her. In the center of the nave, the head priest sat on the edge of the ichor fountain, moving her lips and hands silently. They were the same kind of movements she made while giving a sermon. Rina had once asked a priest about it and he told her that since the head priest couldn't write down her sermons, she used mnemonic devices like hand movements to remember them.

Rina hated to interrupt, but if Eryn had spoken to anyone, she guessed it would be the head priest. Knowing Eryn, she had probably rescued the head priest's husband's dog out of a tree once and got to speak to her like an equal.

"May the light of the Goddess be in you this day, guardian. How can I help you?"

"I'm looking for my hero, Eryn. Is she here?"

"No, she left several minutes ago."

If only she'd realized to come here first. "Do you know which way she went?"

The head priest waved a hand in front of her face and chuckled. "No."

"Sorry, I just meant…" Rina trailed off. A thought occurred to her. "When I leave, you'll know which way I go, won't you? All the priests know I'm a guardian, even when they can't see me. They know where all adult guardians are. I've seen it during services. How?"

"We can feel ichor, move it a little as well. It's one of our Goddess-given skills. We feel the ichor throughout you." She drifted her hand above the surface of the fountain, making ripples and swirls of glittering air in the invisible liquid without touching it.

Realization dawned on Rina. "In the ceremony, the golden thread has ichor in it. That's what melted into my skin. It's what makes me love Eryn, isn't it?"

The head priest nodded. "You ask insightful questions. Be careful they do not get you into trouble."

Rina couldn't help a chuckle, no matter how inappropriate. "They do. All the time. Thank you for your wisdom and your answers."

She stood up to leave but the head priest spoke again. "Love is a gift from the Goddess whether it is placed upon you or given freely. To waste it is as blasphemous as wasting ichor."

Rina nodded and wondered if the head priest had the precision to sense the ichor in her head nodding with her. She thanked her again and left, headed for the housing district. After the Goddess, Eryn would go to Alba. The problem was, Rina had no idea where Alba lived. She couldn't just start knocking on doors. There were over a thousand houses in the housing district. Unless she happened to pick the right neighborhood, even the people who lived here weren't likely to be able to point her to Alba's home. She wandered around the empty roads between houses for almost an hour before giving up and heading back to Eryn's house. Eryn would return eventually, and Rina wanted to be there when she did.

She climbed the steps of Eryn's porch and slumped down against the door. The rocking chair seemed too presumptuous, and she certainly wasn't going to let herself into Eryn's house without her there. At some point, when her eyelids became too heavy to hold open, and against her will, she fell asleep, hunched against the door.

A hand on her shoulder woke Rina just as dawn was breaking. She looked up into the wrong golden eyes surrounded by the wrong blond hair. The man who had asked Eryn to spend Frost Night with him looked down at Rina with a look of contempt. His grip on her shoulder was uncomfortably tight and he didn't quite focus on her as he glared.

"What are you doing here?" he demanded. His breath reeked of whiskey and his touch felt clammy. Rina was sure Eryn had mentioned his name, but she didn't remember what it was. She hadn't much cared.

"I'm waiting for Eryn."

He is going take her away from you, a shadow hissed at her ear. Rina reminded herself that Eryn had chosen her over him already.

"She doesn't want you. You're a joke, you realize that right?" His words were slightly slurred, and his grip kept digging deeper into her shoulder. "Everyone laughs at you. She laughs at you. She tells us how bad you are in the bedroll, you know? How you didn't even pleasure her that first night. You're a failure and she's just too nice to say it to your face. But we all know it. She says it behind your back."

She goes to him for what you cannot provide.

"Shadows aren't the only ones that lie," Rina said under her breath. She'd spent her whole life parsing lies from truths. This guy was an amateur.

"She doesn't care about you. She doesn't love you. She talks about you all the time, how awful you are."

Rina couldn't help smiling. Of course a hero wasn't in love with her guardian, so the only reason he would feel the need to say so was if he thought Eryn really did love her and he was jealous. "That's funny. It sounds like she talks about me a lot. She's never mentioned you."

Fury flared in his bloodshot eyes. He pushed back, releasing her shoulder. "Stand up."

He wants to fight me, Rina realized. She had no interest in fighting a drunk, jealous hero. "Go away."

"I am a hero and I told you to stand up, guardian."

"No. You are not my hero. You do not get to tell me what to do. Go away." Rina wondered if anyone had told him no before. From the bewildered look he gave her, Rina guessed it was rare if ever.

"I told you to stand up!" Rina watched him shift his weight onto one foot and saw his foot coming for her face before he'd even lifted it off the ground. She caught his boot inches in front of her face. She was surprised by the speed with which he was able to move given how much alcohol he must have consumed. There was no doubt he'd consumed a great deal, it leaked out of his pores, but he wanted her to think he was even less competent than he was.

Still sitting, she twisted at the waist, and caught him in the back of the knee with her own foot. Then she threw his foot back in the direction it had come.

Rina's move would have felled an adept, sober fighter. The drunk hero fell hard, slamming into the railing of Eryn's porch stairs. He clawed the air as the railing buckled under him and flesh and wood collapsed onto the dew-covered grass.

He's going to try to kill you for that. The shadow seemed almost gleeful.

"How dare you?" He scrambled out of the wreckage. "You dare attack me? I'll teach you a lesson you won't soon forget!" As he yelled, he was caught for just a moment in the glint of the rising light and seemed to glow.

He's the golden boy, Rina realized. He grappled around in the pieces of broken railing and pulled out a makeshift spear that had once been a railing post. As he leveled the spear at her, Rina laughed inwardly. In what possible future did she need to worry about him?

But that wasn't the future the Commander had warned her about. There was a future in which she responded to his slovenly attempts with real ones, and he died. If she accidentally killed him or even just injured him badly enough, it was likely she would never be allowed to leave the Community again. She would lose Eryn.

"Leave me alone," she said. She could hear doors and windows opening around her as heroes looked to see what was happening. She would sit there. She would not be a threat.

"Stand up!" the golden boy yelled again. The threat of an attempted skewering was clear.

"Leave me alone."

The golden boy ran at her, spear held in a sloppy underhand grip. He was once again faster than he looked but still no match for Rina. She brought her foot up in an almost perfectly timed kick to the hand. The piece of post clattered to porch as the golden boy wailed in pain and stumbled back down the steps.

"She attacked me. You saw it. She attacked me. A guardian in the hero quarter." He looked like a yellow chicken running around the pasture squawking at anyone who would listen.

"You're drunk. Go home and leave me alone." Why wouldn't he just go? She scooped the piece of post off the porch and, without standing up, chucked it off the side, away from herself and the golden boy.

A small crowd was gathering, watching in confusion. One of the older heroes who looked as though he had been preparing for a mission outside the dome approached. "Henk, what's going on?"

"She attacked me. She kicked me down the stairs. She tried to stab me with a piece of railing." He seemed crazed, but would the other heroes see it that way?

"She seems like she's just sitting there."

"That's what she wants you to think. She's manipulating you, just like she's manipulating Eryn. I'll stop her, even if you won't." He grabbed the sword from the older hero's sheath and launched himself toward Rina.

The stakes changed in that moment. He was no longer holding something that was laughable. He had the weapon of a hero, and she had nothing but sobriety. Rina leapt to her feet. "Don't kill him. Try not to hurt him," she said silently. Around her, heroes called for him to stop while shadows egged her on.

As the golden boy reached the top of the stairs, Rina was ready for him. She grabbed his sword hand in her right hand and moved with his momentum like a swinging door, putting pressure on his wrist in hopes he'd simply drop his weapon. When he didn't, Rina moved forward instinctively. She brought her left arm to his elbow and used the strength of both of her arms to bring his sword arm down across her knee as if she were breaking sticks for firewood. The golden boy's arm snapped as audibly as a stick. He collapsed down the stairs once more, yowling and writhing on the ground.

"Dark gods damn it." She hadn't meant to break him. Not really. Why was he so damned fragile?

"Get a healer," a hero said.

"Get the judges," another hero shouted over the rising din.

Rina sank back down against the door and kicked the hero's sword farther away from herself. The golden boy was carried off to the healers shouting, cursing, and moaning. Multiple heroes made sure to tell Rina not to go anywhere as she sat there waiting for the judges to come retrieve her. It hadn't mattered how careful or measured she had been. She'd attacked a hero in the hero quarter, and she would pay for it.

A burly man with hazel eyes and the greenish-gold robes of a judge came to collect her almost half an hour later. He appeared prepared to wrestle her to the ground to subdue her and seemed pleasantly surprised when she greeted him and followed him unquestioningly to the judiciary.

She stood before three judges who sat at a long table on a short platform and took notes as she told her story. She provided every detail of her encounter with the golden boy as exactly as she could remember.

All the while, her heart sank more and more. It would be her word against the golden boy's, and she could only imagine what lies he would come up with. It wouldn't matter that to lie to a judge was considered a blaspheme against the Goddess. It would be his jaded truth and it would be what the judges would believe. No one would ever take the word of the worst guardian over a hero.

When they were done with her, the burly judge led her to a small room with a single window from which to watch people enter the judges' chamber. She would be able to see who had come to testify for or against her and then would be given one last chance to amend her testimony before the judges conferred and made their decision.

She watched many of the heroes who had stood around the golden boy as he yelled and yowled go into the judges' chambers, followed by Claine, the head hero, and finally Eryn. Eryn didn't look in Rina's direction as she walked into the chamber, though Rina was sure Eryn would know where she was. She longed for Eryn to even spare her a glance so she could try to read Eryn's expression. Was she still angry? Hurt? Sad? She wished the door to her room wasn't one of the only locking doors in the whole of the Community. She needed to know if Eryn was okay, if she would ever forgive her.

You will lose your hero. The judges will never let you leave with her. They will never let you see her again. Rina wished the shadows couldn't sense her dismay. It only made them louder.

When the judges called her back, Rina had nothing to add to her testimony. She'd told every detail, so she went back to her little room to wait.

The short deliberation time did not bode well. Rina shuffled into the judges' chambers along with everyone else who had testified, minus the golden boy, who was still in healers' hall having his bones set. Claine was at her shoulder, stiff and indignant. Somewhere in the crowd was Eryn. Between them, it seemed that every hero who had been nearby had shown up to hear how Rina would be punished for besmirching their self-hallowed ground. All around they whispered possible options. The shadows were much darker in their predictions.

The center judge clapped a single time, the sound reverberating around the room, drawing everyone to silence. "In alignment with the principles of the Goddess as set down by the Community Covenant, it is decided. We are one people, and we thrive or struggle as one. It is for that reason that violence is not tolerated."

Rina took a deep breath and closed her eyes. She wouldn't cry. Not in front of everyone. Even if they took Eryn away from her and she never got a chance to say she was sorry, she would not cry.

"For attacking an unarmed member of the Community—"

Rina held her breath.

"Henk's penance is a two-month prohibition from alcohol…and a broken arm."

Around Rina, the crowd mumbled in a mixture of disbelief and agreement. They quieted quickly. They knew as well as Rina that the judgment wasn't done.

"For causing destruction of property and personal injury, Eryn's guardian's penance is to fix Eryn's porch."

For a moment, Rina didn't breathe. What would be her version of "and a broken arm"?

"A laborer will drop the necessary materials and tools this afternoon." The three judges all clapped in unison three times, finalizing their judgment and dismissing the crowd.

It wasn't until Rina felt Claine sigh next to her that she released her own pent-up breath. That was it? They believed her?

Claine led her out of the chamber to a secluded side room where the crowd of departing heroes would not hear them. "I'm proud of you, Rina. Based on the judgment and the stories everyone is telling, you showed great restraint. You have grown up so much in the last nine months. I know there have been some setbacks, but I'm proud of the way you have set aside being right to serve the Community and your hero."

The pit of Rina's stomach squeezed uncomfortably, and she forced a smile. She wished Claine's words could bring her happiness. Claine had said she was proud of her. But her pride still rested on the lie that Rina didn't listen to shadows. Not to mention that Claine had just referred to learning she was forced to love her hero and that when Eryn moved on it would break her as nothing more than setbacks.

"I should go take a nap before I have to fix Eryn's porch," Rina said. "I didn't sleep much last night."

Claine gave Rina's shoulder a last squeeze of approval before leaving.

"I didn't lose Eryn," Rina whispered to herself. She needed to focus on the bright side, not all her emotional backlog with Claine.

But it won't be long, a shadow said before Rina heard their voices diminish from her brightening mood.

She still had a chance to make things right.

CHAPTER FOURTEEN

Commitment and Jealousy

Rina dropped her hammer on her foot as Eryn's front door opened. She'd been jumpy since the moment she arrived and started work, waiting for Eryn to come outside.

"Ow! Eryn, hi." She felt silly for her words, her uncertain tone, and her boot held in her hand.

Eryn's expression warred between amused and concerned. "Are you okay?"

"Yeah, I just haven't done much carpentry. It's not really on the guardian curriculum." Building a tent she could do; a railing was an entirely different matter.

"Let me help you, then. I've helped repair several houses in the last few years." If she was willing to help, Rina had to guess she wasn't too hurt or angry.

"No, this is my penance. It wouldn't be right for you to help me. Though I do appreciate the offer." She gave Eryn a smile she hoped conveyed her appreciation for Eryn's presence as much as the offer.

"Oh, okay." Eryn shifted her weight from one foot to the other. "Well, I could make you some lunch."

Rina grimaced. "Fixing your porch is enough of a penance, thank you." She felt comfortable with a little teasing and hoped it would lessen the tension.

Eryn laughed, a blush creeping up her cheeks. She was clearly insecure in a way Rina rarely saw, but she definitely didn't seem angry.

"We should talk," Rina and Eryn said at almost the same time.

"Maybe not out here, though," Eryn said. She looked embarrassed for having said it. "I just think it's a more private conversation than my front porch. I could go get us food that someone besides me has cooked, come back, and we could eat inside when you're done."

"That sounds perfect," Rina said. She picked up her hammer and pretended not to notice the way Eryn looked at her admiringly as she swung her hammer with pushed-up sleeves. She struck her finger, yelped, and felt distinctly less sexy.

It took her far longer than she had hoped to finish fixing the railing. Their lunch was cold and more dinner by the time they sat down at Eryn's dining table. But Rina was in Eryn's house sharing a meal, so she certainly wasn't going to complain.

"Eryn, I—" Rina started.

"Can I go first?" Eryn interrupted her. She didn't wait for confirmation. "I'm sorry for running away. You asked me to listen to everything before getting angry, but I didn't. Well, I guess I got upset, not angry, but I'm sorry all the same. And I'm not just sorry for my reaction. I'm sorry that this was done to you. No one should be forced to love someone else. There are so many ways that you are treated poorly that aren't fair. It's not your fault that you don't love me or that I do, love you that is."

Rina couldn't let these statements go unchallenged. "Eryn, I do love you. That's the part I was trying to say when you ran away. Yes, there's a part of me that is forced to love you. But I also love you as me. I love you despite being forced to love you, and for me that's a really big deal. I hate things that are forced on me. I beat against them until I've lost more than I could gain, just on principle. But not with you. I tried to fight it, but you stirred something real in me and I love you as me."

"How can you know that?" Eryn's expression said she wanted to believe Rina, that she was desperate for it, but she'd clearly come into this conversation with a wall around her heart and she wouldn't let it down so easily.

For the first time, Rina was glad of the endless hours she spent debating with herself and her puppy about where her true feelings lay. From them she'd been able to script her answer while she hammered nails into wood, pulled them out, and tried again. "The part of me that's forced to love you loves when you need me, when you are vulnerable, when you are lost. *I* love you when you are strong, when you are determined and unflappable. Those are the times when we flow, when together we are unstoppable. I'm forced to want to build you up, but *I* love that you're already there. The part that's forced makes me overjoyed to serve you, cook you breakfast, fill your every need, and pleasure you. *I* really love the moments we spend together just talking, cuddling, and being present. Those are the times when the forced part of me is restless for me to do more, to be more, to somehow put you first better. That's how I know it's me."

Eryn gripped the underside of her chair. She looked like she was holding herself back from leaping from her chair into Rina's arms. Rina wished she would let herself. Why was she still hesitant? "But you said you have to distance yourself because I'll eventually move on?"

"I can't give you the life you deserve. I want you to have a family, but guardians can't get married because they could never love anyone like they love their hero. So, I want to enjoy these moments with you, but I have to be ready for you to turn to someone else." It physically hurt to say it, but losing her to someone else was going to hurt far, far more.

"I know you think I'm saying this because I'm young, but look at my record. When I decide something, I commit to it, and I never go back. I love you, Rina. I want to be with you. What if I could get an exception for you and me to get married when we retire? We could petition the judges to let us. The rule shouldn't apply to you because you'd be marrying your hero."

The naivety was endearing. "The judges would never approve that. Claine would never allow it. Would the head hero? The Community doesn't allow exceptions. It's destabilizing." She spit out the last word, Claine's word.

"Then we have ten years to convince them or come up with an alternative. I'm not giving up on you or us. Please don't give up on me." She let go of her chair to take Rina's hand.

Rina couldn't deny Eryn. She did want it. Resigning herself to an introspective existence of half love might be Claine's thing, but fighting for Eryn could be Rina's thing. "I won't."

"Good. Now for the other part."

"The other part?" That didn't sound good.

"You said the ceremony makes you want to serve me, make me

breakfast, and pleasure me. Do you not want to do those things? You always seemed so happy to do them. Is that just the love that's forced on you?"

Rina hated the Commander for planting those ideas. She had enjoyed those things, even as her. But now it was hard to not notice the ways in which even sex subserviated her. "I do want to do those things. It's just that I also *have to* do them. It's hard to explain. But there's a difference between getting up early to make you breakfast in the Dark Lands and choosing to come home with you and make us dinner."

"And pleasuring?"

Rina paused. Repeating the Commander's words felt disastrously dangerous. "I like pleasuring you a lot. It's just that you've never pleasured me." A shadow took this opportunity to inform Rina that Eryn never would pleasure her after that comment.

"What do you mean?" Rina could hear the defensiveness rising in Eryn's voice. "You always orgasm."

"Yes, but I orgasm because of the connection between us. I cum from the euphoria of making you cum. You've never, you know, it's always me pleasuring you."

For a long moment, Eryn was silent. She didn't look at Rina when she finally spoke. "I don't think I've ever pleasured anyone. I've never made that distinction. As long as they finished, I figured that was enough. I've never pleasured you. Goddess, I'm sorry." She looked ashamed and truly miserable.

"It's okay," Rina said instinctively.

"No, it's not. We have two days until our next mission, so tomorrow is about you. After your training, I want to take you on a real date. One where you get what you want."

Rina smiled. Even a date that was about her came with the words "I want" from Eryn. "That sounds lovely, but you don't need to do that. It doesn't have to be all about me, I like to give, it would just be nice to get sometimes too."

"I want it to be all about you. I've got nine months to make up for, after all."

Rina wondered if Eryn would ever notice how often she said "I want." She wondered if she would have noticed without the Commander pointing it out. He'd planted the kind of Dark Lands seeds that burrowed under her skin, but with Eryn they'd sprouted flowers.

Eryn was oblivious to so many things, but when they were pointed out to her, she apologized and strived to do better. It was one of the many things Rina loved about her.

The next day, Rina couldn't finish her training fast enough. Every question from a junior guardian seemed like an unreasonable burden. Why couldn't they just listen to her breeze through the instructions the first time, succeed, and go back to the dormitories?

She bounded up Eryn's steps in her beige tunic and raised her fist to knock. Eryn opened the door before she could. She was wearing the gold dress that left very little to the imagination. The one that managed to drape and cling in all the right places, and Rina took a moment to appreciate all those places. Rina forced herself to exchange only a brief, chaste kiss. If she did any more, she'd find herself entwined with Eryn in her bed, pleasuring her until she screamed, and that was not the point of the evening.

They walked hand in hand to the market, just two women on a date, and it felt right. She savored these moments when Eryn was so much more than her hero. She was the woman who wore a sexy dress in public with her and for her. It was a statement to Rina and to everyone else who would see them together. Being with Eryn made the Dark Lands bright and the Community feel like home.

They'd barely made it to the market when a child's voice carried over the din. "Eryn!" Alba's children, whom Rina had met briefly at the Frost Night service, came bounding through the crowd. The boy, who Rina guessed was about seven, skidded to a stop in front of Eryn and thrust out his hand. "Eryn, I won a game of Ichor and Shadows. I played just like you taught me. Look at the marble I won."

"Benji." His sister sounded exasperated. She looked to be about nine and her frustration turned to excitement as she said, "He's just trying to outdo my news. I saw my first birth today. It was so exciting… and gross. It was kind of gross."

"Come play a game of Ichor and Shadows with us," Benji insisted. "I want to show off the spin it can do."

"That's so great, Peyna. You're growing up so quickly." Eryn turned from one child to the other as Alba appeared out of the crowd. "And I'm very proud of you, Benji. Rina and I are hanging out, so I can't play now, but maybe when I get back from my next trip outside the dome?"

Benji's crestfallen expression pulled at Rina's heart. Everyone loved Eryn and for good reason. She was generous and caring. But it was the fact that Eryn could have anyone and chose Rina that meant the most to her.

"That's okay," Rina said to Eryn. "If you want to play a game with them, I can wait. It'll only take a few minutes and you won't see them for another couple of weeks."

"But today is about you and what you want," Eryn said.

"What I want is to date you, and part of that is spending time with your friends. Plus, it's cute to watch you play with the kids." Rina looked from Eryn to Alba. She hadn't spoken to Alba since the night they'd sat vigil, and she wanted to know more about the woman who came up in Eryn's stories more than anyone else.

"Yes, please." Benji grabbed Eryn's hand and started to lead her into the crowd.

"Benji," Alba scolded him before turning to Rina. "Can I offer you tea? My sister has a tea shop around the corner, and she'll make space for them to play."

"That sounds lovely," Rina said, her words sparking excited jumps from both children, who immediately took the lead.

Rina knew she was supposed to be spending teatime engaging with Alba. She'd arranged for it to be that way, but she kept finding her attention drawn to Eryn instead. Benji's idolization of her was clear, but so was the reason. Eryn didn't let Benji win. Every shot she took shone with her typical acuity, but she wasn't trying to win either. When a marble was perfectly lined up for Benji during Eryn's turn, she let him go instead, utilizing every shot as a learning opportunity and giving praise as often as advice.

Rina caught Alba watching her out of the corner of her eye. "Sorry, I didn't mean to ignore you."

Alba shook her head with a smile that radiated graciousness. "I like the way you look at her." She followed Rina's gaze back to Eryn and chuckled as Eryn leapt up and chased Benji around the open area before catching him and tickling him until he released the marble in his hand, all while managing to keep her dress in place. "I envy her that much energy."

Rina laughed along with her. It was one of the things Rina loved about Eryn. She could keep up with Rina in so many ways—mentally, physically, and in dedication to others. Perhaps most importantly, it wasn't a competition to keep up.

"She's so great with kids," Rina said. There was far more melancholy in her voice than she meant to let on. She enjoyed watching Eryn, but it was also a reminder of the inevitable heartbreak in their future one way or another.

When Rina looked back at Alba, she had a surprisingly knowing expression. Eryn always talked about how Alba understood her emotions long before Eryn did, but Rina hadn't expected that to immediately translate to herself as well. When Alba didn't say anything, Rina filled the silence. "She deserves to be happy."

"You don't think you make her happy?" It was clear from Alba's tone that she did think Rina made Eryn happy. It was relieving to feel like at least someone supported their relationship.

"I can't give her the future she deserves."

"You have nine years before Eryn can have any of that. What she wants is you. What makes her happy is you. You are her guardian; I'm sure you give her everything you can and more." Alba took a sip of tea and let her words sink in. "Can I give you some advice?"

Rina nodded. After all Eryn's stories, there was no way she was going to turn Alba down.

"Healthy relationships are a give and take. Eryn is like a member of my family, not because I take care of her or give her what she needs, but because we take care of each other. What Eryn needs isn't someone who gives her everything she deserves. What she needs is a partner who loves her and wants to serve the Community alongside her. Happiness isn't just something you give. It's something you make together."

Alba was silent as Rina took in her words. She hadn't looked at it that way. She wanted to build a life with Eryn. They didn't just have nine years to figure out how to have a life together, they had a life together for the next nine years despite the limitations put on Rina's future.

Rina gave Alba a smile. She wished she had something more substantial to offer in thanks. "I can see why Eryn speaks so highly of you."

Alba beamed. "I would say the same about you."

Eryn trotted over, Benji and Peyna close at her heels. "We'd better get to dinner before I'm up to my eyeballs in won marbles."

"I won," Benji complained. He smiled when Eryn ruffled his hair. "Come by for dinner when you get back, Eryn?"

"And bring Rina," Alba said.

For a moment, Rina stared at her, stunned. Alba didn't say "bring your guardian" like anyone else would have. The sound of her own name had never made her feel so seen.

Eryn took Rina's hand in her own and nodded enthusiastically before practically skipping off toward dinner.

During dinner, Rina couldn't help but notice the difference in the way people looked at her. It was as if they no longer questioned her presence. A few people even smiled at her. The artisan addressed them both as he took their orders, even taking a moment to comment on how nice they both looked.

"They're afraid of me," Rina said, keeping her voice low. "Do they think I'll attack them like Henk?"

"They're not afraid of you. It's kind of the opposite, I think. I overheard some farmers when I was in the fields today. The judges wiped your slate clean when they gave you your penance. It was more than just your actions against Henk that were on trial. The judges consider all the defendant's actions and character when making their judgment. Your only penance for a potentially grievous act was to fix my porch. It was a statement to everyone that your dues are paid, at least up to this point. People will probably still expect you to pay in more for your meals or if you want to acquire anything, but any service you do now is above and beyond your due."

A clean slate.

After fifteen years it didn't seem possible. But she couldn't deny the smiles that had never been directed her way or the attention that was beautifully neutral.

After dinner, Rina led Eryn to one of the obstacle courses in the guardian training field and gave her a more practical outfit in which to leap through obstacles. Since becoming a full guardian, she'd been on it several times to train herself and others, but there was something distinctly different about training with someone who could keep up with her, and she'd missed it greatly. A day all about her wasn't one in which she was the best, but one in which she was challenged to do her best, and Eryn was the only person who could truly bring that out. She wanted to move with her the way they had in the bog, and she wanted to feel the burn of pushing herself to the height of her abilities.

It was dark by the time Rina called an end to their session and put their equipment away. Every brush of Eryn's hand or body against Rina's own in the process of moving through the obstacles was getting harder to overlook. It didn't help that they were getting more risqué with each pass. It was thrilling to be able to flirt and exert at the same time, knowing Eryn wasn't trying to distract her, but to make it part of the game. But she was more than ready to move on to the next activities of the evening.

"Can I just tell you how awesome it is that you wanted to spend our date like this? You're so sexy." Eryn sounded out of breath and not just because of the obstacle course.

Rina couldn't help a chuckle. "I'm glad you think so."

"I do." Eryn closed the space between them, dipping her head to capture Rina's lips with her own. Her heat was undeniable, and Rina felt her own rising to meet it. Her puppy, whom Rina had relegated to the back of her mind to do nothing more than watch, leapt to the forefront. It was time to pleasure Eryn.

She wrapped her hands around Eryn's rib cage and pulled her closer. She pushed her leg between Eryn's thighs and savored her moan.

"Stop." Eryn pushed her back. Her chest heaved and the gold of her irises was almost completely gone in the combination of darkness and lust. "Don't pleasure me. This is about you."

Rina nodded. She didn't trust her voice. Mentally, she banished her puppy back to its corner. She wanted to pleasure Eryn, but she wanted this to go her way, not her puppy's way.

Eryn stepped back into her space, rousing the fire that was all Rina's own. She grabbed the collar of Rina's tunic and pulled her in again, kissing her with equal parts passion and fierceness. Rina found she liked having Eryn in control very much.

Eryn wandered her hands over Rina's body, aggressive yet indecisive. She pulled at Rina's tunic before switching tactics to go for her belt, then got distracted by trying to position her leg between Rina's.

"You don't have to do everything at once," Rina said at Eryn's ear before kissing her neck and enjoying the goose bumps that rose in its place.

"I want you so badly. By this point you've always gotten all our clothes off and I can't even get started." Her tone was lust-filled, but there was an undercurrent of self-consciousness that played at Rina's resolve.

"You're doing great. It's not about how fast you do it. It's about the fact that you are the one doing it. Also, telling me things like how badly you want me is an excellent turn-on."

A smile spread across Eryn's lips. She sank to her knees on the practice field and used both hands to undo and remove Rina's belt. "You don't just want to hear it, though, right? You want to see it." She looked at Rina with pure desire that made Rina's mouth dry up. She pushed Rina's tunic up and dusted kisses across her stomach. "You want to feel it."

She grabbed the waistband of Rina's pants and underwear and pulled them down to her ankles. "You want to know that at any moment, a guardian could walk across this field and see you with your hero on her knees." She stroked her tongue between Rina's legs. "Going down on you."

It took all Rina's willpower not to finish right there. Her hero was between her legs, and it felt blessedly good. She had served her hero so well, earned her love so well—

She cut the thought off. This wasn't about her hero or her service. It was about Eryn. It was about the woman she loved, loving her in return.

Eryn looked up, her tongue swirling in ways that made Rina's legs threaten to collapse. "Good?" she asked.

"So, so good." She pushed down the urge to lay Eryn out on the field and return everything she'd received and so much more. The act drove her own heat higher, as if she were teasing herself, drawing out the pleasure by denying herself what she itched to do.

Rina could feel Eryn's smile against her skin. Eryn watched Rina as she brought a hand up Rina's inner thigh, stroking her stance wider, before slipping two fingers inside Rina.

My hero is inside me. Eryn is inside me, Rina corrected herself.

Her hips bucked no matter how much she tried to hold them still. It felt so, so, so good. There weren't enough sos in the whole of the lands for how good it felt.

"Cum for me?" Eryn said, an invitation, not a demand, not a request.

No amount of willpower could hold Rina's body back. She could no longer feel the touch of a gentle breeze on her face or the press of the ground beneath her feet. All that existed was the feeling of coming undone and the look of passion on Eryn's face. She was exhilarated and dizzy, faint and...

Rina didn't open her eyes. The feeling of Eryn holding her, the smell of Eryn's sweat mixed with her own pleasure, the touch of the grass on her naked legs, and the knowledge that she'd been more than brought to her knees, were things she wanted to bask in all night. "By the Goddess," she said.

"You look different, you know." Eryn sounded relieved as she brushed damp hairs from Rina's brow. "It's the way you looked at me that time after the bog and on Frost Night. Your eyes look different when you are just you, enjoying us rather than you pleasuring me. I like it a lot."

"Me too." Rina pulled Eryn down for a languid kiss.

"Do you want to come home with me?"

"No," Rina said reluctantly. "Tonight was perfect. If I go home now, I know this night ended with just me in control, because there are a lot of parts of me that want to say yes. So many parts, not just the part that's forced. If I go home with you, I won't be able to stop myself because I want you very badly. I'm sorry, I know it's not fair to you."

Eryn scoffed. "You have been more than fair to me. It's time I paid into our relationship."

Eryn helped Rina get to her feet and gave her a good night kiss that tested Rina's resolve to the limit. "Good night."

Rina woke early the next morning, still sated and smiling. She wanted the future Eryn promised. What she needed was a path to another option. Claine said she wanted to protect Rina's heart. If there was any chance she would truly side with Rina's heart, she had to try.

Her best chance was to catch Claine during breakfast, before the weight of responsibility truly settled on her shoulders each morning. Instead, she found only Keddeth in his and Claine's home. "Let me make you some eggs," he said, ushering her into the kitchen before she could turn him down. "It's been too long. How are things going?"

Rina supposed Keddeth had always been a better source of emotional support than Claine. So, as he cooked and served her an omelet, she laid out the state of her relationship from finding out about being forced to love Eryn to revealing that fact to Eryn. "She wants to find a way to marry me, to spend her life with me, and I want that too. I just don't see how we can. I want to protect myself, but not at the cost of failing to fight for what could be."

"Have I ever told you about Melia?" Keddeth asked as he scrubbed the egg pan.

"No," Rina said. She kept the question of why this was relevant to herself.

"Melia was a guardian in the cohort above me, and she was my first love. She was beautiful and kind and she had a laugh like birds singing." He smiled, and Rina could almost see the enamored teenager he had once been. "But she didn't feel the same about me. My love for her didn't die when she told me she only liked women. She simply became my first unrequited love. Wanting her was what got me to start looking at the other women around me. Because of her I decided to pursue Claine."

"This was before you got your hero?" Rina asked.

"Yes. We knew that how we felt about each other would change when we got our heroes, so we decided to become really good friends instead. But I fell in love with Claine. I fell in love with my hero as all guardians do, but it didn't make me stop loving Claine, just as being rebuffed didn't make me stop loving Melia. I just loved her in a different way. I know that there is a ceiling on how I can feel about Claine. Claine has never taken my breath away. I've never been infatuated with her. I don't look at her and think she's the most beautiful woman. But that doesn't keep me from loving her. No love can compare to how I feel about my hero, but that doesn't mean I don't love other people. And I have loved someone as much as my hero—Syrana and you. It's just a different love."

Keddeth abandoned the dishes and took a seat across from Rina. "Claine thinks of the part of her that's forced to love her hero as being a puppy. It is separate from her. It's not her at all. To me, it's no different from my teenage love for Melia. It's a part of who I am, but it's only a piece. It limits me but it also guides me to the people and things that matter, just as my love for Melia led me to Claine."

"What if I'm not like you? What if I'm like Claine?" Rina said.

"You are however you choose. You and Claine are more alike than either of you would like to admit. When you decide something is some way, you make it that way, often even in the face of conflicting evidence. You also have to consider the source. Eryn treats you with love. Claine seeing the part of her that loves Ardon as not a part of her is as much a coping mechanism as a fact. Ardon is an irredeemable asshole."

Rina gawked. Keddeth didn't use language like that. He was soft-spoken and overly polite. The fact that he said it about a hero, and more specifically about Claine's hero, was shocking.

"Ardon goes out of his way to hurt Claine. He treated her worse than dirt when they were an active hero-guardian pair. He was always jealous that she was better than him. But he didn't stop there. He made her go to his wedding, made her a part of his wedding party and played it off as him being magnanimous, but he knew exactly what he was doing to her. And that's nothing compared to the day she became head guardian." Keddeth cut off, dipping his head as a blush rose under his graying beard.

"What did he do to her?"

Rina winced as a different voice answered from behind her. "He came to the house. For a moment, I actually thought he was there to congratulate me. My prestige could be his prestige after all." Claine's face was a statue of emotionlessness as Rina turned to look at her. "We had sex for hours. I almost missed my own swearing in. My puppy loved every moment of it even as he told me I was worthless, that I was nothing without him, that no matter who I became or what I achieved, I would always be on my knees for him, begging for more."

Rina tried to keep the horror and the pity from her eyes. Claine wouldn't want either.

Claine shrugged. "When I'm with him, my puppy is in charge. The rest of the time it's not."

Rina didn't want that. There were other ways to be unbroken than to become dispassionate. Eryn wasn't like Ardon. Eryn wasn't what Claine predicted, and she wasn't what the Commander insisted she was.

Claine wasn't looking at Rina but over her shoulder at Keddeth. There would be words when Rina left. She had no intention of staying.

"I'm sorry," she mouthed to Keddeth with her back to Claine.

He pulled her to him for a hug and kissed the top of her head. "I love you, Rina. Remember, just because you start with eggs doesn't mean you have to make a scramble."

Rina spent the rest of the day with Jesta, swapping stories of the Dark Lands and preparing their packs for the next morning's trip for ichor. Jesta had taken their new chastity, despite three years of infrequent romps, exceedingly well. What made Jesta a good guardian wasn't any of her skills but her desire to make others happy. Knowing Rina was sleeping with her hero instead was about as good as it could get, Jesta told her.

As she and Eryn made their way into the foothills of the Dark Lands, Rina turned to Eryn. "We said we'd be honest with each other. Was the other night okay? Was it okay that I didn't go home with you and that you didn't get to finish?"

"Yes!" Eryn was practically skipping. "The other night was wonderful. Yes, I was hornier than I've ever been, but it was because I really liked pleasuring you. I loved it actually. It was hot. I've seen women go down on each other at the same time. I was thinking maybe we could try that tonight if you want that too."

"That sounds wonderful." Rina was going to spend the next several hours reminding herself to pay attention to her surroundings that wanted to kill her and not her mental images of the night to come.

The wave of despair that Rina knew all too well washed past her. She felt as if her happiness were a dome of its own against his effects.

I see you've been busy since we last spoke. You eat out of the palm of her hand, and she eats—

"I don't need you." Rina spun to face his incorporeal presence. "I'm tired of you saying mean things about her. I'm tired of you planting rotten seeds and waiting to see what will grow. Go find someone else."

Beside her, Rina felt Eryn draw her sword. "I'm here if you need me."

Rina set her jaw and took Eryn's hand in her own, though she ended up getting mostly gambeson sleeve. "I need her, not you."

Rina felt the Commander's ire rise, and a spike of fear shot through her. He was clearly very powerful, and she didn't doubt he could end her life if he truly believed she wasn't useful to him anymore. Those would have been useful thoughts before she'd mouthed off.

His ire faded quickly to annoyance. He was clearly reining himself in. *Oh, Rina, that's far from the truth. But I must forgive youth its naivety. So, you don't want to hear the truth about the true villain in our midst. I can hold my proverbial tongue. But you do need me. More than that, the Community needs me. Don't you want to know how I knew where the ichor was?*

"You foresaw her leaving me. But she didn't."

I've decided to see it as cute, the level to which you underestimate me.

Rina held back from rolling her eyes. His ego was ridiculous, but she also knew a veiled threat when she heard one. She bit back her own pride instead. "Please, I would like to know how you knew where to find ichor."

Much better. Rina could hear the self-satisfaction in his voice. *The answer has been in front of you the whole time, you've simply been too indoctrinated to see it. Of all the things they took from you, your dignity, your chance for love, your ability to have children, I think the most grievous was taking away your ability to think for yourself. It wasn't always this way. You have a Goddess-given mind for analytical thinking. Use it.* The Commander paused. He'd planted more seeds and Rina could feel them growing in her mind.

"My ability to have children?" Rina said aloud and felt Eryn stiffen next to her.

The Commander gave a haunting and distasteful laugh. *She knows. Ask her.*

Rina turned to Eryn with a raised eyebrow. She hated when the Commander was right, but she also knew this was one of those cases. She trusted Eryn to tell her without demanding the truth.

"I only recently found out."

Lies.

Rina raised her eyebrow higher.

"Okay, it was a couple of months ago. Holden told me that the Community sterilizes guardians so that heroes and guardians won't get pregnant during missions. It's not a natural sterility from the Goddess." Eryn did seem ashamed both of the truth and for not telling Rina sooner.

Rina turned back to the Commander. "That's beyond the point. What do you want me to use my mind for exactly?"

The Goddess became the mountains. You've been walking on Her body for months. Surely you have noticed what your predecessors saw before the priests called that line of thinking heresy. A cliff that looked like a crumbling finger. Twin caves that seemed to breathe.

"Her nose." The teardrop-shaped entrances should have been obvious but only if she were walking on the body of a giant human, not the body of a god. "That's blasphemy."

To think that a god could have a nosebleed? To think that a goddess has a mangrove in the bog of her nethers? The chapel is built from Her excavated bones. The dome is sustained by Her blood. You cannot choose to see Her as having a body only when it is religiously useful. The Goddess provides Her body to the Community. To tread on Her without direction, without logic, and without purpose is a degradation of that sacrifice.

"How does this help us find ichor?" Rina had no interest in letting him ramble on another one of his diatribes. They were on the cusp of something that could change the way the Community found ichor.

How does blood flow through the body?

"In veins and arteries." Could it really be that simple? "But those would be far beneath the surface."

The Goddess pushes a part of one of Her blood vessels to the surface. What heroes find is like a self-inflicted blood blister.

"So how do we know where She has pushed a vessel to the surface?" Rina's heart was pounding in her ears. In nine months, they'd found useful ichor once. The typical hero found ichor two to four times a year. What if they could find it every time?

You don't. Rina's heart sank. *But you have a trail to follow that will eventually lead to ichor. Rather than wandering aimlessly in the dark, you pick one of twelve paths and follow it until you reach the blister. It can take a few days, but it does not take months.*

"Can you show us?" Rina thought better of her request and added, "Please. This is brilliant." The addition was a good choice. She could feel his vanity expand to fill the space.

Yes.

❖

"Are you sure we can trust it?" Eryn wasn't sure if whispering was effective.

"He would prefer you call him 'he.'" So apparently, he could hear her when she whispered. "And can we realistically turn this down? If what he's saying is true, this could change everything." Rina turned to her right and addressed the empty space. "Yes, I'm saying 'if.' I realize there's false indoctrination at play, but you are still a shadow."

The way Rina said "false indoctrination" made Eryn assume they were the shadow's words, and it didn't make her any more comfortable. Apparently, he said mean things about her and "planted rotten seeds." That didn't seem like someone they should trust, even if he had led them to ichor and was promising to do it again.

Perhaps the most disturbing was confirmation that Rina had been speaking to the same shadow. Every time Rina turned to speak to him, it brought back vivid memories of Syrana doing nearly the same thing.

Then again, they risked their lives every day they were in the Dark Lands in search of ichor. Was this really all that different from following an aura into the bog? Except that it might work.

Eryn felt entirely ignored as she and Rina worked their way up hills and through a gully. Ahead of her, Rina seemed to step in all the right places, while Eryn's boots sank further into the mud and slime. She tried to step in Rina's boot prints, but she was having enough trouble keeping up with Rina's pace. Was this how it had been for Rina when it was Eryn who was forging ahead toward the hope of ichor without engagement or consultation? She hoped not. This sucked.

Rina's constant conversation was perhaps the most isolating part. Eryn simply couldn't put together what they were talking about from half the dialogue. Rina was constantly pointing out aspects of the geography around her and occasionally referencing body parts.

After grueling hours of squelching through endless gullies broken only by impassable flora that forced them to climb steep hills, Eryn called a halt to the day. It was demoralizing to realize how much she was the weakest member of the team. She couldn't keep up with Rina and her shadow friend, and they were the ones who might actually find ichor.

Dinner was plagued by more conversations between Rina and her shadow. Eryn had hoped the ichor lantern would earn her a temporary pause, but no. She kept waiting for it to end, for Rina to take her to bed, but the discussion of anatomy continued long past Eryn's food had run out and her patience was quickly following. Sexually, physically, and mentally frustrated, Eryn placed herself in Rina's lap and drew her in for a long kiss that promised so much more. She felt Rina react below her for a moment before pulling back.

"I really should stay up and learn as much as I can about the Goddess's veins. You should go sleep, though. I'm sorry. I know I'm letting you down, but you can understand why this is more pressing than tonight's pleasuring."

Yes, a way to consistently find ichor was far more important than pleasuring each other, so why did she feel so personally slighted? It wasn't like Rina was choosing her shadow friend over Eryn, so why did it feel like it? It was just hard to get used to the idea that doing what Rina wanted was leaving her horny and alone more often than she wanted.

Eryn woke to an empty tent and the sound of Rina talking.

"Were you up all night?" Eryn asked, not bothering to come up with alternate words for a nightless existence.

Rina looked up from her cross-legged position on the ground and smiled as if this were any normal morning together. But there was no fire, no breakfast, no undivided attention. "No, I slept for a few hours."

"Shall I make breakfast?" Eryn said, hoping to get the morning moving. No one really wanted her to make breakfast.

"Oh, I was thinking we could just have some trail rations so we can get back to finding the ichor faster." Rina reached into her pack and held out a handful of dried fruit, veggies, and meat. Eryn took it and ate by herself while Rina broke down the tent and waited for Eryn to unlight the lantern.

As they transitioned from mud- and thistle-ridden terrain to traversing the sloped face of a mountain that made Eryn's ankles ache, she turned her focus to how great this was for Rina. Rina lived in a constant state of believing the terrible things shadows said about her and her future, reinforced by people questioning her worth and telling her she was a terrible person. And here she was, forging the way to not only finding ichor, but a new way to finding ichor in the future. And she seemed happy.

The thought brought a smile to Eryn's lips and an ache to her chest. Rina was happy, but it was entirely due to an entity that in so many ways was openly trying to replace her. He was Rina's conversation partner, her source of finding ichor, and her source of joy and self-worth.

Eryn was as relieved as elated as they moved from the slope to a gully once more and the feeling of nearby ichor struck her. She surged forward, skirting past Rina and peering into the dense brambles in her way to the shimmer of ichor just below the surface. "Machete," she said, holding out her hand. It took several seconds for Rina to place it in her hand. Eryn tried not to notice and hacked through the brambles with unnecessary zeal. It was nice to have something to destroy.

Rina held out bottle after bottle to be filled. This whole process was so much easier when they weren't being attacked by a tree. When they were done, Eryn donned Rina's pack, gave her a kiss, and downed a bottle of ichor.

The feeling was exquisite. The rush of power felt like the return of a cherished toy to a young child. All thoughts of jealousy or self-doubt were gone. She was the second most powerful being in these mountains, after the Goddess of course. If lesser beings couldn't see that, it was their loss. She would show who was the slow one and who needed who. She had ichor, nothing else was necessary.

Eryn looked back to see the source of her former jealousy almost keeping pace with her. She snorted. Not for long. She flexed, widening her stride until she was leaping as much as running. Her muscles sang. Her heart pounded. She felt alive.

She looked back and smiled at her triumph. The lesser creature was far behind her now. Her muscles sang. Her heart ached. She felt unsatisfied.

She didn't want to win. She wanted this lesser creature, who didn't matter compared to ichor, who had made her angry and so didn't deserve consideration, to succeed as well. They weren't really at odds after all. The lesser creature was not a threat. She was something to be desired and to be cherished.

Eryn slowed down. As the lesser creature drew near, Eryn held out her hand to it and gripped the smaller creature's hand in her own. They ran like that all the way to Eryn's den with its golden warmth and protection. She passed through the barrier, and for a long moment all she could do was stare at all the creatures milling about in her den picking at silly little plants. What were they doing here? This was her place.

The lesser creature with her hand in Eryn's was petting her arm and speaking to her. "Eryn, you should run some laps to help your body process more of the ichor." But Eryn didn't want to run laps. She wanted to know why other people were in her den.

"We could go to your house instead. Do you want to take the ichor to your house?" The lesser creature's pitch was high and cadence slow. It was laughable that this creature would try to speak patronizingly to her. She should smoosh her for such insolence. But no. She would take the ichor to her house and leave all these creatures behind. They could not hope to get her ichor. She could overpower all of them at the same time.

Lesser creatures fled from Eryn as she sprinted to her house. She got to the stairs before she started to feel woozy. Rina was there to catch her as she fell backward down her porch stairs. "Sorry," she said, unsure if she was talking about needing to be caught, considering smooshing Rina, or all her less than generous thoughts even before drinking the ichor.

Even at my best, I'm far from the woman I want to be, she thought.

She was afraid, she realized. She didn't want to be hurt again. She'd invested her life into saving the Community. Then she lost her foresight. She gave up her relationships with other heroes for Rina. Then she thought Rina didn't love her back. After everything—life, heart, and soul—she feared no one would need her anymore. No one would want her.

In the light of the Community, somewhere between the ichor-driven titan she'd been and the scared twenty-year-old she was returning to, it was easier to see the truth through the fear. Rina loved her for being strong, committed, and someone she could be in sync with. None of that was related to finding ichor or being the most essential person in the Community. She didn't have to be the best or have all the answers to be relevant to Rina. She just needed to love and respect her, and being jealous and mopey was the opposite of that.

Rina took the pack and helped Eryn amble to the chapel to hand over the ichor and then to healers' hall to sleep off the aftereffects. The slower trip back, combined with a shorter overall distance, added up to a much subtler aftershock. Her head throbbed and her muscles ached, but it was no more than the frequent times she overworked herself in the training room or tried to keep up with the Goddess-given skills of the other castes.

"If what he says is true, we can find ichor without his directions," Rina said as Eryn sat on the edge of the healing bed and tried to rationalize lying down and resting when she felt jittery rather than tired. "We could even tell others how to find it. We have no proof that he didn't just foresee where to lead us. But next time we go out, especially if we can avoid him, we can test it."

"We have to go when he doesn't expect us. We could go now." Eryn could make up for the way she'd acted on the way to the ichor. She could help Rina prove she was right and get more ichor. "I still have some of the ichor power left. We could move faster. We could go at your pace. I'm not going to crash like last time. Holden said I wouldn't come down as hard after the first time and I'm processing the ichor more slowly this time. If we're going to go, if we're going to prove you right, we have to go now, before anyone can tell us no. Our trip took two days. We can restock empty bottles right here. Let's go." She threw open a cabinet of bottles meant for collecting bodily fluids and storing medicaments and started handing them to Rina.

Rina's face was entirely consternation. "What if going out causes your reaction to be harsher? What if you just aren't feeling it yet?"

"I'm fine. I promise." Eryn did a cartwheel, nearly knocking healing implements onto the floor. "We said we would be honest and that we would trust each other. I trusted you to follow a shadow to ichor twice. I want you to trust me. This is too important to not confirm."

Rina nodded hesitantly, putting the bottles into her pack. "Then we should go before the healers or priests get news back to the head hero that we returned. He showed up pretty quickly last time."

Once the bottles were loaded, Eryn bolted out the door. She was almost back to her normal speed, but with her added endurance, it would suffice. She was going to find more ichor. She would never have to feel the aftereffects of ichor if she always had it. She could just imagine it, an unending cycle of finding, drinking, and bringing back ichor, never holding still long enough to need to rest. She would regrow the dome singlehandedly. She would have ichor forever. The Community would have ichor forever.

CHAPTER FIFTEEN

Stealing and Stockpiling

This was a bad idea. How in the lands had she thought this was anything but a really, really bad idea. Rina ran along at Eryn's heel more to keep a full eye on her than to hold a position of inferiority. It made leading from behind more difficult. She was constantly having to grab Eryn's elbow to redirect her and try to point out the landmarks that the Commander had taught her for following one of the Goddess's twelve surficial blood vessels.

It wasn't just the path Eryn kept losing. Her footing was weak, her attention span was that of a fruit fly, and her sense of direction had her constantly veering off in the wrong direction.

Rina tried to focus on the bright side. They were making good time, going nearly twice their normal speed, and the Commander was nowhere to be felt. She'd never actually seen him, she realized, not in his corporeal form. But where shadows were roughly human sized, she could tell the Commander was much bigger.

She tried not to focus on the new seeds he had planted in her mind as he'd walked her through the Goddess's anatomy. She didn't care what evidence the Commander had provided; she hadn't been indoctrinated and she hadn't been brainwashed.

So what if guardians learned "your hero has two apples, you give them three, how many apples does your hero have" when everyone else had been learning "Hilna has two apples and Finty has three, how many apples do they have together?" Math was easier to learn when it was applicable, right? So what if heroes promised to put the Community before their pride while guardians promised to put their hero before their life. It was all part of the job. Everyone served the Community in the way the Goddess had set before them. But it was hard to deny that her sacrifice was encouraged by her instructors, her mentor, her training, and her puppy.

Integrating her puppy into just another part of herself was proving to be more difficult than Keddeth implied. It yelled at her every time she engaged with the Commander and was irate that Rina was unapologetically ignoring Eryn, her wants, and her needs. It didn't help that Rina could tell the Commander was actively trying to pull her away from Eryn at opportune moments and only drew attention to Eryn at her worst moments to point out how selfish and conceited Eryn was acting. This was the natural way of heroes, according to the Commander.

Rina was grateful for his help, finding ichor and casting off shadows that came to attack them after Eryn drank the ichor. It just felt like being a teenager again, not being able to be friends with two different people because they both hated each other.

Back in the Dark Lands without the influence of the Commander's emotions, Rina didn't find Eryn's bullheadedness egotistical or insulting. It concerned her.

"Maybe we should go back," Rina said, pulling Eryn back onto the trail once more.

"No, no. We're here to find ichor, to prove that we can find it without your shadow friend. It can't be too much farther, right?" Eryn's words tripped over each other in her haste.

"At the pace we're going we should find it today if he's right. But, Eryn, you're not acting like yourself. The ichor is still affecting you. Let's go back and we can try again in a week. My shadow friend, as you call him, won't be expecting us then either." She tried to grab ahold of Eryn's elbow, but Eryn tore off into the bushes ahead of them, her gambeson shredding on the thorns.

"Oh Goddess," Rina cried, pulling out the machete and trying to follow Eryn but with all her skin intact. Eryn was clearly failing on that front. Rina's machete hacked down branches filled with thorns that dripped with Eryn's blood and their own natural toxins.

"I feel it!" Eryn disappeared below the horizon ahead and Rina could hear the distinct sound of a body smashing down a hill, punctuated by almost maniacal laughter.

Rina ran down the hill full tilt to the spot where Eryn was lying face down, on the ground. Her knees were folded up under her chest with her butt up and she was petting the ground next to her face as if stroking a puppy.

"Eryn, are you okay?" Rina reached a hand down to Eryn's shoulder, with every intention of checking her breathing and heart rate, when a swell of emotion washed over her. The presence had nearly the intensity of the Commander's entrance, but the emotion was different. There was anger, resentment, and an odd feeling of triumph that weren't that different from the Commander, but underlying it was a crashing sense of being untethered and lost.

Just as I thought. Monsters are all too predictable and oh so easy to track. The hiss had a clarity nearly as sharp as the Commander's but almost an octave higher, still low, but almost feminine. It was the way Jonaban, the author of the pre-gap scrolls, had described the differences in the voices of the original seven shadows.

A shadow drifted down the hill, menacing even in its incorporeal state. *You will not continue to steal the Community's ichor. Not on my watch.* The shadow brought its hands together, its claws morphing together into vaguely the shape of a sword with a long, broad tip at the end. As it surged forward, rushing at Eryn, only its claws became corporeal. In this state, it would be impossible to strike and dissipate. Rina had never seen a shadow attack like this. What kind of shadow spoke of itself and fought strategically?

Rina raised her spear, but the shadow didn't seem to even notice her. It swung its claws at Eryn as if nothing stood between it and its target. The impact of claws on wood reverberated up Rina's arm. This shadow was stronger too.

The shadow leapt back, not floating, but jumping. *A shadow defending a monster? Curious.* The shadow sounded both incredulous and intrigued. *Maybe this will be an actual challenge.* It swung its claws in a wide, slow figure eight, less like a sword and more like a battle axe.

I'll have to tell Rina about this, it said before launching at Rina. Its claws were a blur. It took all Rina's attention and focus to fight off the flurry of blows. After the first few seconds, her mind slipped out of control and muscle memory took over. She met every strike, deflecting and attempting to turn it into a counterstrike. She had done this a million times before. Her opponent feinted right, and Rina jabbed left. She caught the shadow's claw strike and almost landed one of her own.

She could almost imagine the shadow's feet shifting stances and telegraphing its next move. Its shoulders moved in a way that gave its blows more strength but told Rina exactly where to block. It all felt so familiar, even the voice, laughing at each of Rina's attempts with an air of insult, but also exuberance to try to outsmart her.

Let's see how you like this. The shadow shifted its stance smoothly and put full force behind a single attack, sending Rina stumbling back. She almost tripped over Eryn's supplicating figure, still face down on the ground.

"A little help here," Rina said, getting her feet under her.

The shadow shifted stance again, returning to its original figure eights. Its claws gained more and more speed as it put the motion into its wrists and elbows instead of its shoulders. It rushed Rina, its claws moving so fast that the stark black of its claws blended into the dim black of its incorporeal body.

Rina moved on instinct. She thrust her spear forward, directly into the spot where the shadow's hands would be. "That won't work on a shadow," Syrana had always said when Rina did this move to break what she called her whirling bardiche.

But the shadow pulled back as if it expected the impact to happen. For a moment, it was confused. Shadows often seemed a little confused, but always mentally. This time, the shadow seemed confused by its own physicality, or lack thereof. *That won't work on a shadow*, it said slowly as if rolling the idea through its head.

Rina stared at the shadow as it stared at itself. "S-Syrana?" It was impossible. But now that she knew—knew, not guessed—it was impossible to deny. The hissing voice, the signature move, the comment about telling Rina, why everything felt so damned familiar. However, she clearly thought Eryn was a monster and Rina was the shadow. She'd said as much as she descended the hill.

The shadow looked up and straightened its stance again. *You again. I knew I hadn't seen the last of you.* She launched at Rina again, taking up Syrana's characteristic aggression when confused or embarrassed.

"It's me. It's Rina." She stumbled back further and further.

I told you the first time, leave her out of this. Rina could feel the fear and anger radiating off the shadow.

"Syrana, it's me, Rina. You, you're a shadow. It's why you don't have a body, why your bardiche is just claws." Fighting Syrana when she was mad was a good way to end up in healers' hall, and that was when she had a body to fight back against.

Shadows always lie! The shadow backed Rina up the hill she'd descended. Its strikes came slightly faster than Rina could defend. The claw bardiche caught her arm, leaving a shallow bleeding gash. Rina stumbled. The claw bardiche knocked her spear aside and nicked her cheek. She scrambled up the hill backward frantically blocking. Her mind spun. How was she supposed to talk down someone who thought Rina was a shadow? She was running out of time.

"Shadows always lie," Rina yelled.

The shadow froze. *What?*

"Shadows always lie," Rina said again. How could it possibly be a lie? Syrana couldn't cause it by listening to it, nor could she reject it. For a moment, the shadow flickered in and out of corporeality.

This was Rina's moment, perhaps the only one she would get. "The Community is the most important thing after the Goddess. When you were nine you broke your arm for the first time and refused to go to healers' hall until you put away all your equipment. You always cook your rice in broth even though salted water is basically the same. And you snore when you sleep on your back."

I do not, the shadow said, but her anger was acted this time. She emoted only confusion. She shifted stance, one last time, becoming fully corporeal. *Rina, what's happening to me?*

Rina didn't see the glint of steel until it was too late. Eryn's blade slashed through the shadow's corporeal body, and she puffed out like a popped bubble.

"No, Syrana!"

"It's Eryn, actually, and I hate how much you talk about her, okay? We found the ichor, now give me the bag." Eryn's head was tipped to the side and her eyes were open just far enough to start to bug forward. Bleeding, oozing gashes covered her arms.

"Eryn, you don't understand. That shadow was Syrana."

Eryn wasn't listening. If anything, she seemed angrier at the fact sound was coming out of Rina rather than actions. She grabbed a pack strap and nearly tore it, trying to yank it off Rina. "What part of 'ichor' do you not understand?"

Rina released the pack and followed Eryn to the spot of ground Eryn had been worshipfully petting. "Eryn, that shadow was Syrana. You dissipated her. We need to stay here until she reconstitutes so we can find out what happened to her."

"Stop talking to me like I'm a small child. You're crazy and I don't need you. I'm drinking ichor and taking it back to the Community. Stay here if you want." Glasswork clinked as Eryn pulled a shaking hand out of the bag and dropped everything she'd been holding on to the ground.

"Eryn, slow down." She reached for Eryn's hand but pulled away when Eryn bared her teeth at her.

"I need it." Eryn's words came out between jagged gasps. "I found it. I get it. That's the rule. That's how it works. I will never slow down. I will never stop. Everyone will love me. You will love me. You will love me more than Syrana. I will have everything. I will be everything."

Rina bit back the fear that roared inside her. Being afraid of Eryn or afraid for her wasn't going to help anything. "I love you very much. I just want to help you. Tell me how to help you."

"I need it."

"All right. I'll hand you bottles. You can fill them and put them in the pack. Then you can take the pack and drink the ichor. Sound like a plan?" Rina wished she could just fill the bottles, or at least hold them so they wouldn't be in Eryn's shaking hands. But without being able to see the ichor, she'd be guaranteed to spill on her hands and melt off some skin.

"I know how the process goes." Eryn grabbed one of the bottles, stabbed the ground with her knife, and set to work holding the bottles that Rina handed her in vaguely the same place before corking them and shoving them into the bag.

It occurred to Rina that it was possible there was no ichor and Eryn was acting out a hallucination. Unless she wanted to melt some skin, Rina wouldn't know until Eryn put a bottle to her lips and either bulked up and ran home or started running around as a slim, blond lunatic.

Rina watched as Eryn shouldered the pack and brought the last equally empty-looking bottle to her lips. Relief filled Rina as she watched Eryn's body grow as if the Goddess had blown power into her like a bellows.

A multitude of approaching hissing voices squelched her relief. The last two times they retrieved ichor, the Commander had been there to hold the shadows at bay. He was not there this time.

Eryn took off with Rina at her heels. She seemed faster this time and quickly outpaced Rina. Unlike the last two times, Eryn did not look back.

A claw sliced the back of Rina's calf, but she couldn't let it slow her. The most important thing after her hero drank ichor was to protect her hero by dissipating as many shadows as possible. They would all flow to where the ichor had been collected and then chase Eryn down. All they cared about was attacking Eryn, but any shadow would be happy to take Rina down along the way. Thank the Goddess, their frenzy made them corporeal. She swung her spear in a practiced wide arc sacrificing defensibility in order to strike more of them. Her own life was meaningless compared to Eryn's. There had already been a guardian death last month to shadows. Rina didn't want to be the next, but she would happily give her life for an increased chance that Eryn would live.

As the shadows streamed past Rina, slicing her gambeson and drawing blood more often than not, their hissing voices repeated the same general message as Jonaban had said. *Not the Community's ichor.* But if Rina listened closely as she had done for years, the author's interpretation was missing a couple of key words, words Syrana had provided as well: *Do not take the Community's ichor.*

By the time Rina hobbled through the dome, torn and battered, she was sure Jonaban had gotten it wrong. The shadows weren't trying to keep the Community from getting ichor. They were trying to preserve it for the Community. What Rina didn't know was whether the shadows thought that the ichor was being taken away from the Community rather than toward it, or that heroes like Eryn shouldn't be drinking it.

Rina stepped across the threshold of healers' hall ready to collapse. Strong arms grabbed her by the front of her dilapidated gambeson and for half a second, Rina thought she was going to receive assistance to a bed. Instead, she was slammed up against the wall as a beet-red face screamed inches from her nose.

"What in the lands is wrong with you? How could you let her go out again? I thought you were the worst guardian the Community has ever had. But you are worse. You are a disgrace to the very concept of a guardian. I will see that you never leave with her again." The head hero smacked her across the face and released her to crumple to the floor before turning and stalking away.

"She said she was okay. She promised." She couldn't lose Eryn. Not when they'd just figured out how to find ichor. Not ever.

The head hero spun on his heels and stomped toward her. Rina was too afraid to cower. She didn't care what he did to her physically. This was about her fear for Eryn. "She's supposed to be asleep during the worst part of the letdown, the part where she's willing to do just about anything for ichor. She would have been if you hadn't led her out of the dome again."

Rina opened her mouth and closed it again. She wanted to argue, but he was right. She had known it was a bad idea and had agreed anyway. She'd wanted so badly to prove that listening to shadows could save the Community that she'd been willing to believe Eryn was fine when she so clearly was not.

"What can you possibly have to say for yourself?" The head hero towered over her as she sat, propped against the wall, bleeding all over the floor.

"We brought back ichor twice." It was the only thing Rina could think of that might save her chance of leaving the dome with Eryn again.

"No. Eryn brought back ichor twice. You nearly got her killed." He turned and stalked off.

The Commander had told Rina that Eryn would get all the credit for their discovery of how to find ichor. He wanted Rina to be disgusted and disdainful, but she wasn't. Even lying on the floor, her hot cheek swelling where the head hero had struck her, she didn't begrudge Eryn that she would get the credit. It was the only way anyone would take it seriously. It was the only way they would save the Community.

❖

The effect of inactivity felt like a heavy blanket across Eryn's body. She'd been asleep long enough that the ache in her head had been completely replaced by the ache of desperate hunger.

A healer once told Eryn that the best patient was an asleep patient. They never complain, never argue, never try to use their body when it isn't ready. Eryn knew she was the kind of patient they were trying to prevent, but she hated waking up like this.

A familiar hand slipped into hers and squeezed once quickly. "I'm here because when she wakes up, she's going to be hungry, so I made her favorite soup," Rina said from beside Eryn.

"You're here because you want to make sure Eryn corroborates your story when she wakes up." Holden was sitting on the other side of the room, and Eryn could just imagine his expression of indignance. His arms would be crossed with one foot resting on the opposite knee.

"Why would I need her to? There's nothing to corroborate. I told you, she read about an old theory of ley lines in the crypt, and she's been tracking ichor finds for months. She seems to have figured it out because—"

"Shut up and get out. You won't be her guardian anymore if I have anything to say about it, and I do, so be gone before I have you brought to the judiciary."

Eryn continued pretending to be asleep as Rina pulled away and left the room. When she felt she'd waited long enough, she let out the groan that had been bubbling up inside her. Goddess, she was hungry, and the mention of Rina's soup certainly hadn't helped.

"Eryn, are you okay?" Holden was at her bedside in an instant, his hand in hers.

It was hard to be mad at Holden when he showed such clear protectiveness and compassion. "Yeah, how long have I been asleep? I'm starving."

Holden chuckled kindly. He helped her sit up and held out the bowl of soup, failing to mention Rina had brought it for her. "You were asleep for four days." Eryn nearly spit out her soup. How had she possibly needed that much time? She didn't remember getting grievously injured.

"What happened?" She remembered drinking ichor for the second time, though the memory was a little hazy, and running home. She'd made it all the way to the chapel with the ichor before falling down and being carried by several kindly people who had been worshipping.

"You left the Community again after drinking ichor. You had it twice in a row. Eryn, you're lucky to be alive. Not only is it dangerous to have more ichor so soon after drinking it, but if you hadn't found ichor a second time you would have fallen apart with need and withdrawal in the middle of the Dark Lands, and anything could have killed you."

"I didn't know," Eryn said, though she wasn't sure that was wholly accurate. She'd known it was a bad idea but the promise of ichor, not the potential but the promise, had been too good to resist while her mind was impaired with ichor-lust. She didn't question the fact that she would have fallen apart. She could remember lying on the ground while Rina fought something and not caring except that it was keeping her from releasing, collecting, and drinking the ichor.

"I didn't think you had to be told. I didn't think you'd be stupid enough to try." Holden always hid his fear in anger, but this was a new level of condescension.

So much for telling a hero it's not their fault and they did the best they could, Eryn thought. If this was how Holden was treating her, she could only imagine what he'd said to Rina. "Is my guardian okay?" she asked, realizing she shouldn't know Rina was up and about.

"She's fine," Holden said, his face instantly growing more bitter. "I don't want her to leave with you again. She never should have allowed you to leave."

"You can't do that." Eryn jerked up in bed, throwing soup onto her healing gown and the bed. "I need her. We've…I've found a way to find ichor, consistently, every time we look. You have to let us keep going out." Eryn knew this was as much about her time with Rina as saving the Community and she felt ashamed for it, but being with Rina filled both goals, so she felt justified for fighting as if it were about ichor and not love.

"How? How were you able to find ichor twice in a row?" The wonder and excitement Eryn had expected from Holden was absent. He sounded more like he saw it as an elaborate hoax than a huge breakthrough.

"I've been transcribing scrolls in the crypts for years and I came across a detailed entry about ley lines," Eryn said. She was glad for the extra time pretending to be asleep to figure out how to put Rina's words into her own version of the truth. "I know how you feel about them, but I got to thinking—"

"Ley lines are a bunch of hooey. Ichor finds don't follow specific lines of magical energy. You could draw straighter, better lines through the locations of trees in the Dark Lands than ichor finds."

"Exactly. Straight lines. I got to thinking, why would ley lines have to be straight? What if all ichor finds fall on one of many meandering lines? Then we would just have to follow the lines rather than wandering the whole of the Dark Lands." Rina had been right, no one would accept the explanation that the Goddess's blood ran in veins as simple as a human's. She was very grateful Rina had come up with an alternative that was as hard to believe but significantly less blasphemous.

"Ha! That would be even more impossible to chart. You'd just be drawing random lines and claiming a pattern where there wasn't one."

"But I'm not. I found ichor twice in a row in a matter of less than four days. And I can do it again. Better yet, I can teach others to do it. But you have to let me keep going out and you have to let me go with my guardian. Let me prove it to you. Don't you see what this could mean for the Community?"

"Of course I know what this would mean! Do you think I don't worry about the dwindling levels of ichor brought back? Do you think I don't worry every time a hero leaves the Community? When I found out you'd left a second time, I didn't think I was ever going to see you again. Your guardian didn't keep you safe. That's her one job."

"I made a dangerous choice. This isn't my guardian's fault. In the state I was in, she could not have stopped me from going out. She did her job by coming with and protecting me." She could remember the insatiable drive for ichor, though she felt none of it now.

Holden looked skeptical. "You'll show me these ley lines and explain how to find them. You'll teach a hero from the cohort that heads to the Dark Lands in a few days and see if this is anything more than fool's luck."

Eryn held back a sigh of relief. She wasn't sure what she would do if he asked her to describe the process right then and there. "May I go home?"

"Can I trust you not to go running off into the Dark Lands again?" He sounded like he wasn't really joking.

"Yes," Eryn said, though in truth she had no intention of heading home. She went straight to Rina's house, not caring who saw her in the guardian quarter. She knocked on the door and was greeted by the woman who had been naked in Rina's room that night so many months ago when she first left Henk for Rina. A bandage covered a fresh gash that cut diagonally across her face, but Eryn would never forget her face no matter how the Dark Lands changed it.

"Eryn, hello." The woman seemed both pleased and in awe. "Please come in. Rina is in her room."

It took all Eryn's willpower not to stare the woman down or demand to know what she was doing in Rina's house again. At least she was wearing all her clothing this time.

Rina met them in the sitting room. There were scabs across her face and a fading bruise on the peak of her cheekbone. She blanched as she looked from Eryn's raised eyebrows to the other woman's jovial smile. "Uh, Eryn, this is Jesta, Kalia's guardian and my roommate."

"Oh. I didn't realize she was your new roommate." Eryn worked very hard to keep her tone neutral. She'd displayed enough petty jealousy in the Dark Lands to cover her for a very long time. She changed the subject before her poorly veiled jealousy could draw a reaction. "You're back early and injured. Is Kalia okay?"

"Yes. She found ichor." Jesta seemed overjoyed to report the good news.

It was Kalia's first find. Eryn would have to remember to go congratulate her. "Congratulations," Eryn said to Jesta, almost forgetting to recognize the immense effort that went into an ichor find on the guardian's side.

Jesta beamed even as she blushed and shook her head. "Kalia gets all the congrats."

She does, but you deserve it too, Eryn thought. From Jesta's body language she doubted saying so would help. Eryn turned to Rina instead. "We should talk."

"Jesta, would you mind—" Rina said.

"Of course." Jesta turned on her heel and left the house.

At least she's wearing all her clothing this time, Eryn thought again. "Thank you for the ley line excuse. And for keeping me alive. And also for putting up with me being a whiny baby on the way to the first ichor and losing my mind on the way to the second."

"I shouldn't have let you go." Rina looked truly ashamed.

"I shouldn't have told you I was okay, and I honestly don't think you could have stopped me." Eryn held up a hand to interrupt Rina's retaking of the blame. "What matters is that I'm sorry and, most importantly, that you found a way to find ichor reliably. Holden wants me to teach it to others. Can you show me where the lines are and how to describe it to others?"

"Yes." Rina motioned for Eryn to wait, then disappeared into her bedroom and returned with a scroll. She unrolled the linen onto the sitting room table, revealing a rough approximation of the mountains around the Community.

Rina ran her fingers over her drawing reverently. Even a crude depiction of the Goddess was a sacred thing. "At a high level, we're essentially tracking one of twelve blood vessels that flow closest to the surface. Two in each leg, three in each arm, and two that run up the neck and branch across the chest and scalp." As Rina named each one, she pointed to where she had sketched it on the map. Next, she walked though how to find and track each of them, since the Goddess shifted over time. Some parts could be tracked by the discoloration of the ground or felt if you stood still enough in just the right places. The arms relied on tracking gullies, while the legs were tracked by ridges and swells. Along every line, the deep-rooted flora grew larger and beastlier while the shallow rooted plants withered.

"I can teach this." Eryn would have to use different language and come up with excuses for why magic ley lines affected the geography in different ways, but this was going to work.

"There's something else," Rina said. She hesitated before saying, "There was a shadow that tracked us and attacked us before you extracted the ichor."

Eryn vaguely remembered Rina fighting something and delaying getting the ichor. She remembered feeling incredibly annoyed and eventually very proud of herself. "Did it hurt you? Did it say something important?"

"It was Syrana."

"What? That's not possible. Syrana is dead. We both saw her dead body be sent to the Goddess. You mean it claimed to be Syrana?"

"No. It was her. She said things and did things that only she would do. She thought I was a shadow and that you were a monster. I think she could sense the ichor in you and tracked it. She wanted to keep you from stealing the ichor. She was more coherent than a normal shadow, but, Eryn, I think shadows may be dead guardians. When you drank the second ichor, the shadows that came after us wanted to keep you from stealing the Community's ichor."

"That doesn't make sense. We would know if guardians were shadows. They would tell us. They would defend heroes, not attack them." She was willing to accept that auras were the spirits of dead heroes, but it simply didn't make sense for shadows to be guardians.

"I don't understand it either, but I know what I saw and what I heard. It was Syrana."

"What are we going to do about it? It's not like we can go tell someone. You're not supposed to listen to shadows." That seemed the worst option, especially when everyone already seemed set on taking Rina away from her.

"No, we can't tell anyone, not until we have proof. For now, we, by which I mean you, teach the heroes about these 'ley lines.' We'll get the credibility we need one step at a time."

Eryn walked through each of the lines, how to identify them, and how to follow them once more to be sure she had everything correct and in a language everyone would accept. When she was sure her story was clear and compelling, Eryn rolled up the map.

"Rina, I really am sorry for acting so poorly in the Dark Lands. I want you to know I'm proud of you, but not in a pejorative way. I'm proud to be your hero and your partner."

Rina's whole body expanded with evident pride. "Go. Tell the other heroes how to find ichor, and let's make history."

Eryn's descriptions to Holden and the couple of heroes he had chosen to follow her preposterous non-linear ley lines were met with predictable skepticism. But when both heroes returned a few days later with ichor, no one questioned Eryn's method. Instead, she taught every active hero her methods. Over half the heroes of the third active cohort came home with ichor. By the time Eryn and her cohort were ready for their trip, it seemed like a guarantee that most of them would come back with ichor. As far as any history told, that had never been the case.

Eryn was even more pleased when Rina's shadow friend made no appearance. It took them four days to track ichor down the Goddess's leg, but Eryn wasn't concerned. They had plenty of evidence of their method, and it gave her more uninterrupted time with Rina.

Over the following week, Eryn watched the ichor pour in with a sense of true accomplishment. It didn't bother Rina that Eryn was getting all the credit. At least that's what she said. So, Eryn felt justified in feeling proud for the both of them. The dome would expand because of them.

Except that it didn't.

For almost two months, Eryn watched the dome. Its size didn't change. She started taking regular walks around the edge of the dome, marking the edge with sticks and rocks, but every day was the same.

"Why isn't the dome expanding?" Eryn asked as she accepted a celebratory glass of liqueur from Holden for the fiftieth ichor find in two months. She was due to leave the dome for her own mission for ichor the next day, and she couldn't stand to wait another month watching nothing change.

"We're building a reserve," Holden said, clinking her glass with his own as if she'd simply forgotten that piece of celebration etiquette. "The most important thing is making sure we have the resources to stay at our current levels. Once we have enough of a reserve built up, we can start expanding the dome little by little. It will take a lot of work to reclaim the land, and the dome has to be expanded slowly to remain stable. It will take time."

"But if it takes time, we should be starting now. The point isn't to hoard it. The point is to grow." She and Rina hadn't worked this hard and risked everything to create a big pile of ichor in the crypt.

"The point is to save the Community, is it not? Whether this new method holds or not, by building a reserve, we ensure that you have done that. You should be very proud of yourself, Eryn. You have managed to find a way to fulfill your foresight without your guardian. Now you have to trust the adults to use what you've provided us to the best benefit of the Community. Don't let your vanity get in the way of stability."

Eryn hid her disgust behind a swig of liqueur. She trusted "the adults" about as far as she could throw them. They were the ones who consistently chose stability over progress, and it was people like Rina who paid the price.

Chapter Sixteen

Hidden and Hallowed

So, are you the savior of the Community yet? Rina felt the Commander's presence the moment she stepped through the dome. It took several minutes to reach him, but as far as Rina could remember, this was the closest he'd come to the Community.

"It's working. This is going to be so great for the Community. It's brilliant." Rina decided to meet his jabs with appreciation. He was obnoxious, but it was a small price to pay for saving the Community.

Ah yes, look how much bigger the dome is. It'll be at the foothills in days.

"They are building up a stockpile," she said and slipped her hand into Eryn's as they walked. She wasn't nearly so upset about it as Eryn. She saw the logic even if she did think they ought to be putting at least a little extra into the dome to start the process of reclamation.

And who is doing that? The heroes and the priests?

"Yes." It felt like a Community decision, but she supposed it was the head priest and head hero with the final say. Everyone trusted them to do what was right for the Community.

And would you like to know why? Would you like to have the wool pulled back from your eyes? To have your misplaced faith corrected? After months with all the pieces waiting at your fingertips, it's time for the truth to be revealed.

"He says he's going to explain it," Rina said to Eryn.

"Explain what?"

"Everything?" Rina said, wishing the Commander would confirm or clarify.

Instead, the Commander led them silently across the flatlands until they'd nearly reached the foothills. *Have her light the ichor lantern here.*

Rina removed the materials from her pack and Eryn lit the lantern. The opaque shell spread above them and came down toward the ground until it connected with a structure that hadn't been there moments before. Instead of flowing in its natural arc, with its false sky, the ichor in that part trickled through the grout of a curved stone wall that now took up nearly a third of the lantern dome campsite. In the middle of the curve was a wooden door.

Welcome to disillusionment. The Commander pushed the door open with a single corporeal claw.

The dark room inside was circular and about twenty feet across with a wide staircase leading to an upper floor. The light of the ichor lantern illuminated two bedrolls to one side of the room and the setup for a campfire and cookstove in the center. An intricate chandelier hung from the high ceiling with unlit candles burned most of the way to the socket.

"Is someone else here?" Eryn whispered.

Not anymore. Shall we? He drifted up the stairs, Rina following in his wake and Eryn right behind her. *This tower marks the spot through which the Goddess brought Her people with Her to the Dark Lands. It is hidden from the dark gods and only corporeal within an ichor dome.*

"The dome used to reach this far?" Rina asked as she crested the stairs into a dim circular room. The were no windows at that level, but the dim light of the lantern filtered up the staircase. The stairs continued their journey on the other side of the room and spiraled around the outer edge of the tower all the way to the pointed ceiling fifty feet above. Cubbies of scrolls lined the walls, and a long table sat in the center with several scrolls unrolled on it. There were no chairs or places to sit, only open chests filled with yet more scrolls. Rina pulled a match from her bandolier and lit several of the candles from dozens of candelabras spread throughout the room.

Eryn gasped and moved to the part of the room that had sat in the darkness of the staircase until the candles illuminated it. There lay two nearly mummified corpses, the skin drawn tight and sallow, but not rotted or decomposed. Rina guessed that none of the bugs or corruption of the Dark Lands had been able to reach them, so only the bodies' own bacteria had touched them.

"A hero and a guardian," Rina said pointing at the guardian's clothing. "And they've been here a long time. We don't make gambesons like that anymore." The guardian was massive, larger than any person Rina had ever seen, and she'd seen Eryn full of ichor. Even his clothing seemed too small, as if the Community had been unable to make clothing big enough for him. His pack was spilled on the floor and uncorked vials for the ichor lantern laid at his feet.

"He killed him." Eryn's voice was barely audible. Her hand hovered over the hilt of a utility knife buried in the hero's chest as if she were afraid to touch it.

"But he would have been killing himself too." In addition to killing the person he loved. The thought of a guardian killing his hero turned Rina's stomach, and if she looked longer, she'd be truly sick. Rina moved away to investigate the rest of the room. The scrolls in the center of the table were much older than the scrolls in the crypt. The linen was yellowed and slowly deteriorating. She would have to handle them delicately to avoid damaging them.

Behind her, Eryn moved to the cubbies. "These are from the gap years," Eryn said, running her finger along the labels below the cubbies. "Though some are much older."

Rina glanced up for only a moment. As enticing as that statement was, the story playing out before her was much more astounding. The top scroll on the table was written not as a history, but as a note directed toward the reader. "They planned this," she said to Eryn as she read. "When the dome shrank enough to reach this tower, leaders of the Community decided something drastic had to be done. Whatever change they made, they decided that it was best to hide it. They agreed not to tell their children and to write it out of the histories. All of the scrolls that would have to be eliminated would be stored in this tower along with a full description of the change and initial outcomes. That way when the crisis was over and the dome regrew, the tower would be revealed, the change could be undone, and the history could be complete again. The Community could go back to the way the Goddess intended."

"What was the change?" Eryn said, reading over Rina's shoulder.

"I don't know yet. This scroll doesn't say, just that those who took the burden shouldn't have to carry it forever." Very gently, Rina rolled up the scroll and placed it to the side.

"Guardians. That's what changed." Eryn read aloud from the next scroll. "As mutually determined by the heads of the judges, priests, guardians, and heroes, someone must bear the burden of stopping the shrinking of the dome. As it is the heroes who are dying and whose numbers are dwindling, yet are essential to the retrieval of ichor, they must be protected. As it is the role of the guardian to guard their hero, the guardians, as represented by the head guardian and with the support of her people, have agreed to bear this burden. In the words of the head guardian, 'Until we have fulfilled our duty to the Goddess in protecting our hero, we shall take whatever measures necessary to further our dedication and enhance our ability to serve.'"

Eryn's eye's flitted over the page and she summarized as she read. "They found a way to make guardians fall in love with their heroes so they would do anything to protect them. Apparently, a long time ago people figured out they could give the tiniest amount of ichor to someone as a potent love potion. The practice wasn't just banned for misusing ichor, but because it was far too effective. If it didn't kill the person and was given at a time of heightened emotion, the person was irrevocably in love with the other person until death, and if the other person died first, the recipient of the love potion died as well."

"That's what happens in the ceremony. When a hero and guardian are bound, a tiny bit of ichor sinks into each. The hero metabolizes it, but the guardian does not. So that's what guardians agreed to?"

"Initially, yes. But it didn't take long before there were issues. It tore apart guardian families. Guardians who truly thought their heroes loved them in return were driven mad with jealousy if their hero strayed to someone else. My Goddess, Rina, this is our problem right here. Guardians gave up the right to marriage and heroes were told not to fall in love with their guardians in order to preserve stability and peace. Without a family structure, guardians were trained in the garrison so their curriculum could be 'better shaped to the role expected of them.' Apparently, it worked really well, so the heroes agreed to similarly separate their children."

"Guardians and heroes used to have families?" Rina felt decades of loneliness rise up and anger to match it.

"Yes, retired guardians served for the rest of their lives as trainers for the next generation They wore purple to remind them that they carried the weight of the Community and should not dillydally or share in the celebrations of those who had fulfilled their duty to the Goddess, 'excepting those celebrations of first ichor found by a cohort and those in celebration of the Goddess.'"

"And sterility?" Rina asked. She didn't want to read the scroll. She had to know but she didn't want to see the words that had created servitude for her and her entire caste for generations. None of it was truly new. Rina had lived with these limitations for her whole life. It was the knowledge that none of her suffering was the Goddess's plan and none of it had made a difference. The dome never regrew.

Eryn scanned lower. "Sterilization started when too many heroes and guardians started getting pregnant. Rina, this is horrible. How could guardians give all this up?"

"Each step probably didn't seem like such a big deal until they'd already given up so much. What did one more thing really matter." Rina could imagine Claine making that same decision in a heartbeat. How many times had those first guardians been assured that this was all temporary?

"But then they made it seem like it was part of the Goddess's plan. What they did isn't just wrong. It's sacrilege. And it's wrong!"

Rina nodded stiffly as she paced, her fists balled at her sides. "Is there anything about guardians becoming shadows? That's the last piece we need to explain everything."

"No," Eryn said at the same time the Commander, who had been silently watching from the periphery, spoke up. *So, you've already put that piece together. Keep reading.*

"He says to keep reading."

"And does he say which of the hundreds of scrolls to read?" Eryn asked, poorly veiling her annoyance.

"No." Rina drew out the word, hoping the Commander would interrupt and knowing he wouldn't.

"All right. Well, why don't you take the beginning of the gap years and I'll work on the oldest ones. I have a good deal more experience reading through the language they used in the oldest scrolls."

Rina and Eryn each took half the table, carefully unrolling, reading, and returning scroll after scroll and reporting on their findings.

Rina located an entire cubby filled with writings by Jonaban, who used detailed scholarly rigor in chronicling the rapid change in the role of guardians and heroes.

"The woman Jonaban kept referencing wasn't his hero, it was his wife. The sentences about her must have been left out when it was transcribed, but the references to 'she' were innocuous enough to be left alone. They literally wrote out the fact that guardians used to have spouses."

Jonaban's scrolls consistently remarked at how quickly not only the guardians had accepted their subservient position, but the rest of the Community had taken it to be natural and expected. Jonaban found it hard not to discount the younger guardians who he claimed acted like lovesick teenagers long into adulthood. They traded their intellectual pursuits and analytical minds for the dogged pursuit of their hero's happiness. "This explains the change in writing style," Rina said. "Guardians no longer had the time, brainpower, or interest to observe their surroundings, learn, or grow. If an observation didn't directly preserve their hero, it wasn't worth observing, let alone writing down."

"We sacrifice growth for stability yet again," Eryn said without looking up from her current scroll.

Jonaban was similarly fascinated by the speed with which heroes had risen to a place of prestige. The guardians' treatment of heroes as inherently better than themselves to the point of near worship seemed justification to the other castes to see heroes as superior. Heroes too promoted the idea of their natural importance to the Community. There were so few of them, after all. Superiority became indoctrinated into the lives of young heroes as much as subservience was indoctrinated into young guardians. By the time junior heroes reached the age to be paired, they fully embraced the idea that their guardian was meant to be an extension of themselves, given all the burden and none of the credit. Jonaban lamented that heroes had been allowed to become tyrants as much as he lamented the way guardians had so easily abandoned the pursuit of knowledge, joy, and love, for the "myopic prostration of themselves before their hero." Rina wondered when pleasuring had been added to the guardian curriculum.

At the end of the entry, he explained the decision to lock away the knowledge of the change in the tower in order to protect the system they had created. The Community had to believe everything was in line with the Goddess's plan or they might reject it. While the impact on guardians was harsh and shadow numbers were starting to expand, the problem was getting better. The dome had stopped shrinking at the time Jonaban was writing.

"Mine are all about different guardian customs and celebrations," Eryn said, as she finished another scroll. "Honestly, they were much more analytical like you, where they questioned everything as a matter of culture."

"Sounds promising. Anything about shadows?" It really would be nice if the Commander could give them a bit of direction. They could spend their entire ten-day trip here and get no more than a tenth of the scrolls read.

"No. This was before shadows existed. So, I'm probably not in the right section. Honestly, I think I need to sleep. I've read the same sentence five times and I still don't know what it says." Eryn looked exhausted. Rina felt bad for not noticing the signs earlier.

"Do you want to camp here or downstairs?"

"Hmmm, next to the dead guys or next to their abandoned bedrolls? I think I'll go downstairs. Do I need to worry about the ichor lantern?"

"He says you can take it down. You just need to be back in the tower by the time the ichor finishes running down the side." Rina translated. "I'll come help. I think I'm going to stay up a bit longer reading, but I want to make sure you get back in and asleep okay."

At Eryn's suggestive eyebrow raise, Rina shook her head apologetically. "It's super awkward in front of him, and if I ask him to leave, he'll stay and be all the more judgmental about it."

Don't deny your floozy on my behalf. I'm sure she won't mind my commentary.

Eryn waved a hand. "He led us to ichor, showed us the 'ley lines,' and took us to this tower. I'm not insulted." She sounded genuine, if disappointed. The Commander scoffed.

"Thank you. Now let's get you to bed."

Several drawn-out good night kisses later, Rina was back at the table unrolling a new scroll and skimming for anything about shadows. She was constantly distracted by yet another recounting of yet another thing guardians had lost, chronicled in hopes that one day their culture, heritage, and joy could be rekindled.

She was tired and fed up when she turned to the Commander, still lounging at the side of the room expectantly. "Do you want to just tell me where I should be looking?"

When did our relationship go back to you demanding things? He sounded more amused than angry, though there was an undeniable sharpness that reminded Rina who exactly she was talking to. After fighting Syrana's shadow, she knew what it was like to fight a shadow with the wherewithal to use their incorporeality to their advantage.

"I'm sorry, I'm just tired. I was hoping to find what you were referencing before going to sleep."

I didn't say "Keep reading and you'll find the section on shadows." I simply said, "Keep reading." I needed you to understand the depth of what you lost. The piece you needed you have already read, but it was months ago in the crypt.

"How do you know? You never go into the Community. Wouldn't I feel you?"

The Commander laughed as if at a child. *I am the Commander of Shadows. My shadows tell me what you say and what you hear. I do not have to be there to know.*

Well, that's mildly terrifying, Rina thought. What she said was, "Please, I'm tired and if I haven't figured it out for months, I don't think I'm going to without some help."

The piece you're missing, the one that has been waiting for you to connect it to everything else, is the original seven shadows. Seven shadows exposed to ichor who felt like they had failed the Community, whose souls were trapped here by ichor they could not metabolize, trying desperately to protect the Community's ichor from heroes trying to steal it, who knew exactly what they were supposed to do with the constant foresights they were given: tell them to everyone.

Rina felt her jaw fall open. "The priests who died trying to save the ichor from the fire. They were the original shadows who killed heroes, causing the dome to shrink in the first place. And then the Community reacted by giving ichor to guardians to fix the problem, which only exacerbated it. It's the ichor that traps the soul here?"

That and the inability to move on from a sense of duty to the Community that they felt they had failed. The original love potions didn't create shadows, but the victims' souls likely wandered the Dark Lands until their lover died and then moved on with them. They didn't have indoctrination binding them to something that does not die.

"So, auras are like the love potion victims. They get exposed to ichor, die, stick around helping heroes find ichor, and then move on with the hero they love when that hero dies. Auras are guardians too?"

Of course. Though rather than seeing dark possible futures, they see "positive" futures, namely heroes finding ichor. They foresee a hero finding ichor and run back to the Community with them to protect them. Then they run into that same hero who hasn't yet found ichor, realize they saw the future, and guide the hero to the ichor. They too are trapped in the endless cycle of devoting themselves to heroes. The only difference is that they move on with their hero, stuck as much to them in death as in life.

"But then why do shadows attack heroes?" Rina asked. That part still didn't make sense if shadows loved their hero and the Community.

The original shadows were just trying to stop heroes from stealing ichor. It was dedication to that purpose that trapped them here. Guardian shadows have no purpose without their hero, the Community never allowed them to have one. So, they latch onto the only one that exists for shadows—stopping the theft of ichor.

"But now we have a way to get ichor consistently and rebuild the tower. Things can go back to the way they were. We can stop making more shadows."

Are you really so naive, Rina? Through all this, even after you learned that guardians become shadows, you've failed to recognize the guardian right in front of you. Don't you want to know how I became not only a shadow, but the Commander of Shadows?

"Yes." For months, she'd silenced the part of her, puppy and logic, that said all of this was a terrible idea, by purposely ignoring the fact that he was a shadow. Every time she mouthed off to him, she was setting her own boundaries and pretending he was an anomaly, rather than the "Commander" of the things that readily and regularly killed heroes and guardians.

When the Commander remained silent, Rina acquiesced, "How did you become a shadow?"

About four hundred years ago, I was a guardian by the name of Traven. I didn't score well, as my talents for questioning authority and using my own brain didn't sit well with my instructors or mentor as you can imagine. So, I ended up with a lazy, self-centered, and cowardly hero. Perhaps he could have amounted to something if he had ever been told that he was expected to try.

On our second mission, he made it very clear to me what the next ten years would be like. We would travel just far enough away from the dome that no other pairs would notice us and camp there for the rest of the trip. During the days I was to protect him, while nights were for pleasuring him. I objected, of course, as we carried the weight of the Community on our shoulders, but he told me he had fallen in love with me and that it was more important that we stay together and safe. He couldn't stand losing me. The Commander's voice dripped with disdain.

Rina realized he'd been talking about himself when he said, *the heartache of realizing the truth is much less than living in delusion.*

We were camping in that fashion when we discovered this tower. He was thrilled to have a place safe from the monsters that didn't require ichor. He stored the ichor we saved here until we had enough to pretend to have found a small deposit.

"That's you!" Rina spun to look at the mummified body of the large guardian. The hairs on the back of her neck stood on end, and for a moment she half expected the body to react to her realization. "You killed—"

Rina. The Commander's sharpness cut her off. *I am deigning to tell you the story of my life, and you will listen.*

Rina nodded. She shivered at the thought of a claw through her own chest.

I never was much of a reader. I was always more interested in my own thoughts than those of others. So, I ignored the scrolls of the tower as thoroughly as my hero did. I spent my time at the top of the tower watching the guardians in my cohort search the Dark Lands for ichor and serve the Community as I never would. Here, I saw a greater distance than should have been possible. I saw almost the whole of the mountains and I watched as one by one my cohort found ichor. Over the months, I began to see patterns not just in the ichor finds, but in the terrain. It's so much easier to see the body of the Goddess for what it is when you are able to see the entirety of Her grandeur at the same time. The Commander paused expectantly.

"This is where you first mapped the Goddess's blood vessels,"

Rina said and felt the Commander's satisfaction with her following of the story.

You aren't the first guardian to listen to shadows, nor was I. I sat in this tower observing and listening. And I heard them when a hero found ichor. "Someone is stealing the Community's ichor" they would say before rushing off to attack the hero.

"That's how you figured out they were guardians?" It seemed like a rather large leap of logic.

Not yet. Like you, I learned that shadows don't lie. Eventually, I found a shadow who had also listened to shadows in life, and so she listened in death. She had no idea she was a shadow and believed me to be one instead. We spent days debating, the truth slowly driving her more into the darkness. She lost herself, but I gained the knowledge I needed. I began to read. Perhaps others had realized the truth as well. I read the scrolls here and in the crypt and what I discovered changed everything.

"You discovered how to become the Commander?"

No. Are you not listening? Have you not read the scrolls? Shadows don't lie. The Community lies. They present this debased version of the castes as the Goddess's plan and in doing so defile Her creation. But they wouldn't have to any longer. With the methods for finding ichor that I developed, we could grow the dome, reach the tower, and restore the Goddess's system. I too was naive. I told my hero what I had found.

Rina looked to the second body, the knife still sticking out of his heart. "He betrayed you." The Commander didn't foresee Eryn's betrayal; he projected his own history onto Rina's life and could see no other path for her than his own. She couldn't believe there was a future in which Eryn betrayed her.

He betrayed the Goddess! The Commander's ire hit her like a physical blow, and she stumbled back against the table. *He tried to burn the scrolls, for he would not allow a future in which the lowliest hero was not above the grandest guardian. I hated him. You only have the slightest taste of what it is like to love someone who is truly detestable. You are the first guardian I have approached who does not know what that feels like. In that moment, when he could have chosen to save the Community, chosen to take all the credit, for I would have given it to him, he chose to try to destroy it. I had no choice.* The last he said with perfect calm as if the burst of rage a moment before had never happened.

My body was meager, but my mind was strong. I drank the vials of ichor and used their power to kill him even as it melted me from the inside. That power, Rina, you have no idea what the raw power of the Goddess feels like. Yet heroes take it as if it is their right. As I felt my body dying, it was like a shell peeling off to reveal the true creature inside. My body was that of a lesser creature, but I was so much more. I wouldn't just take my mind with me into my new form; I would become something greater by choice. I tore my own soul from my body, and that is how I became this.

"What is it that you want?" Rina felt sorrow for the life he had lived trying to serve the Goddess and the Community, but the Claine in her brain kept repeating that emotion meant nothing, only what you did with it. With that kind of power, she had no question that he could have destroyed her after any one of her snide comments or dismissals. But he had not. He was so powerful, and yet he needed her for something.

I want you to save the Community. Tomorrow, I will lead you to the greatest ichor deposit. With it, you will have what you need to fix what the Community did almost eight hundred years ago. Now sleep. You'll need your rest.

Rina curled up next to Eryn with a sense of optimism that pushed back even the most pervasive of the Commander's temperament that always leaked into her in his presence. "Tomorrow," she whispered to a sleeping Eryn.

Rina woke and made breakfast over the fire that the Commander had prepared some four hundred years before.

It will take us six days at a quick pace to get to the deposit, and there will be enough to fill more than the bottles you carry. Your hero should take my pack and fill it with as many bottles from our stash as her inferior muscles can manage. Rina provided a more gracious explanation of the plan to Eryn, who filled the bag with as much glassware as she could run with.

For six days, the Commander pushed them to what Rina knew was Eryn's limit. Each night she fell over rather than lying down, and it took all Rina's cajoling to keep the Commander from waking her before she was ready. Breakfast and dinner were eaten while jogging, and rest breaks were almost nonexistent.

Rina pushed at every opportunity to take it easier on Eryn. She hated to see her slowly wearing down physically, mentally, and emotionally. Eryn wouldn't allow it. "I can do this. We're going to save the Community." It became her mantra, and Rina could hear her muttering it as they pushed harder and farther.

It will be worth it, the Commander continued to assure them, but with each hour, Rina felt a rising sense of dread. The dropping temperatures as they climbed higher into the mountains didn't help either.

On the sixth day, as they crested what Rina worried would be Eryn's last hill, she froze.

"Oh Goddess," Rina and Eryn said together.

Before them was a valley several miles across, and in the center was a dead tree whose splayed branches bowed all the way to the ground in a circle that was nearly a mile across.

"It looks like a dome," Rina said. But the sight of the tree was far from the most terrifying part. Large chunks of the tree's branching canopy had disintegrated with time, revealing the dark swirl within its dead embrace. "There are hundreds of shadows inside."

Nearly a thousand, the Commander said. *Welcome to the heart.*

"The ichor." Eryn sounded breathless. Rina looked over to see her dilated golden eyes wide with hunger. She'd never looked like that when she wasn't already high on ichor.

Control your pet, my dear, or this could go poorly for everyone.

Rina took Eryn by the shoulders and forced Eryn to look at her. "We will get the ichor, Eryn, but I need you to have patience, or the shadows will kill both of us. Can you do that for us, for me?"

As Rina watched, Eryn's pupils contracted, and she focused. A determined smile spread across her face. "I could walk away from it entirely for you."

How romantic, the Commander drawled. *You will stay with me every moment. If you are with me, the shadows will not think to attack you. We will walk slowly in, gather the ichor, and leave as slowly as we entered. When we return to this peak, she may drink the ichor and run home. Neither of you is to speak until we return to this spot. I will prevent the shadows from attacking so long as you follow this plan.*

Rina nodded and repeated the plan to Eryn. "Let's do this," Eryn said and gripped Rina's hand in her own as they descended.

Each step into the valley felt like wandering deeper and more fatally into an ice bath. Rina's lungs ached and she wondered if it was possible to drown without any water. She wasn't sure she'd be able to speak if she tried. She looked constantly over her shoulder, certain that the mountains were closing in on them.

As she stepped through one of the holes of decomposing tree branches, Rina nearly fell as her sense of balance shifted wildly. Being able to see didn't help. Everything around her was wrong. She didn't know where she was. She whipped her head around, trying to understand the multitudes of dark figures swirling around her. She was drowning. She tried to scream, but nothing came out. These creatures were surrounding her, suffocating her, dragging her into their depthless darkness. She was lost and she was cold, so cold.

Strong, warm hands gripped her shaking shoulders, trying to focus her, but she couldn't. She was supposed to do something, but she couldn't remember what. She was supposed to get out of here, but she couldn't remember how. The warm hands traveled up her shoulders and neck into her hair, pulling her in for a long, passionate kiss. Rina felt warmth breathed back into her core and bleed out to her limbs. The lips against hers pulled back, but she could still feel the warmth of a forehead pressed against her own. She waited in that moment a second longer, letting the warmth reach her toes and fingers before opening her eyes.

Eryn was staring at her with clear concern. Her eyebrows lifted, asking the question she could not say aloud, "Are you okay?" Rina focused on Eryn's lovely face, her gleaming eyes, the lips Rina could kiss for hours. She pushed out the shadow voices all around her, that mumbled in a constant drone of bewilderment and depression. They were lost with nothing but their dark visions, and they would bring her with them if they could. But Rina didn't have to listen. She had chosen to listen for so many years, but over that same time period she had been taught hundreds of techniques to block them out.

Rina nodded and slowly pulled back from Eryn, singing a jaunty tune in her head. The song's lack of sense had always annoyed her. Why sing a song that was just rhyming sounds? But the song wasn't supposed to make sense, it was supposed to make her bounce to the tempo, to form her lips into a smile, and to be exceedingly easy to repeat over and over again when everything around her threatened to swallow her whole.

At first, Rina thought Eryn's tight grip was to keep Rina grounded, except Eryn wasn't looking at her, but at her feet. The fingers of her free hand scratched desperately at her palm. I'm holding her back as much as she's holding me steady, Rina realized.

When the Commander came to a halt and pointed at the ground, Rina removed her pack and Eryn's, keeping one hand always entwined with Eryn's. Rather than handing Eryn the bottles one by one, she laid the glassware out and held both of Eryn's shoulders while she filled each bottle.

Around them, some of the shadows paused to approach them, but the Commander easily brushed them away. Rina could feel him exuding a sense of purpose and calm that both comforted and quickly dismissed the shadows.

When Eryn finished filling every bottle and placing the majority into her own pack, Rina helped them both don the enormously heavy packs and begin the climb back up the mountain. Physically, the trip was much harder with the added weight, but with every step, Rina's soul felt lighter, and her body felt freer. She was going to get out of this. They both were.

Rina and Eryn collapsed as they reached the top of the hill, laughing in relieved pants. "Thank you," they said in unison and smiled. Their lips were inches apart when the Commander interrupted them.

No time for dalliance. It is time for her to drink the ichor. She will need to have more than the normal amount if she is going to make it all the way back before running out of power and carrying both bags. Assuming she's willing to bear it rather than leave it on her beast of burden.

Eryn gave Rina one last kiss before downing two bottles of ichor. Rina could hear the threads of her clothing rip under her gambeson and the lacing of the gambeson snap to expand around her growing body. She ran down the mountain toward home without a glance backward.

A wave of shadows surged forward, streaming around Rina.

Rina spun toward the Commander, her heart in her throat. It didn't matter how fast Eryn could run; she could not outrun the shadows. "You promised!" Rina spat at the Commander, desperate and stricken.

The Commander just laughed. *They are not after her.*

It took Rina a moment to understand. They weren't going after Eryn; they were surrounding Rina. Without Eryn's hand in her own, she could feel their hopeless dread sinking back into her mind. She sank to her knees. She would be lost, but maybe Eryn would not be. Maybe the Community would not be.

The sense of hopelessness receded, and for the first time, Rina felt the Commander's presence calm and settle her. She looked up at him, longing for him to give her another choice. She wanted to get back to Eryn.

Rina, my dear, it is time for the last piece—the way you will save the Community.

She wanted it, whatever the Commander was offering.

It does not matter how much ichor you bring back; the heroes and the priests will never accept what is in the tower. You are not the first person since my hero that I have shown the contents in that tower, and my hero was not the last person to forsake its knowledge. Even guardians, who have everything to gain, are unwilling to accept the truth for fear that their beloved Community will crumble at the thought of rectifying their dereliction of the Goddess's path. Over the last four hundred years, I have learned that those with power will do anything not to lose it.

It does not matter how many times your hero kisses you or where. It does not matter what she professes about love or picking you over something else. She will not choose to destroy the system that has told her all her life that she is better than everyone else. And if she won't, how can you possibly imagine that anyone else will? They will burn that tower to the ground before they see a guardian climb out of the sewage drain of society that they willfully climbed into.

So, we will create a better society, one that does not forsake the Goddess in the name of power and pleasure but lives out her true vision for humanity. We will allow humanity to shed its mortal skin and ascend from lesser creatures into what we can be when we have divinity inside us.

The Commander's voice rose with divine fervor and intensity, which spread into the crowd of shadows and reflected back on Rina from every direction. She was lost in the power of his words and the allure of his offer.

My timing has been meticulous. Stewards Day is only two weeks away and the crypt has a pristine stockpile of ichor. While the priests are leading the supplication to the Goddess and the commitments of stewardship to Her vision, no one will be guarding the ichor nor the food for the feast. Everyone will be at the ceremony. You will enrich the feast with ichor, all the ichor, and as their dedicatory meal starts to melt them from the inside, you will take to the altar and you will tell them what they have done. You will tell them that they have failed the Goddess, that they have defiled Her body for their own gain.

"You want me to kill everyone?" Her exuberance turned to cold horror as his plan played out in her mind's eye.

Shadows never die. And we do not attract the dark gods. You will raise them from their humble humanity into creatures of the Goddess. We will create a new Community that has not desecrated the Goddess's plan. This is the will of the Goddess. We are Her true children. He swept his arm out at the shadows vibrating with religious zeal. *You will save everyone. Except, of course, the heroes who will watch the Community they leeched from until it was bled dry crumble around them.*

And you, Rina, will save the last bottles of ichor for yourself. When you drink, you will tear your mind and soul from your body, and you will be my protégé. We will lead our higher creatures together. We will be the heralds the Community needs and that the Goddess deserves.

Rina felt her bile rise up. She tried to hide her revulsion. The mania around her was still battering at her emotions, telling her that the Commander's way was the only way. It was justice. It was adulation. It was transcendence.

You are my perfect protégé. But know that if you fail me, if you fail the Community, I will target everyone who leaves the dome and kill them. No one can kill me. I will live forever. But the heretical Community will die one way or another. Save the Community, Rina. Start a new Community at the heart that will never die. We are the hallowed ones.

Around Rina the crowd broke into ecstasy.

You are the hollow ones, Rina thought before opening herself to the emotions beating down any barriers she could construct around her heart and mind. A feeling of pure delirium filled Rina and her face hurt from the size of the smile cracking her lips. "Yes," she said.

CHAPTER SEVENTEEN

Failure and Sacrifice

Eryn wondered if the knowledge of how horrible it felt to wake up after consuming ichor would ever occur to her in the moments before she drank it. She guessed not. At least not for the next ten years, until ichor lost its positive effects on her body.

"Oh, Goddess." She barely got herself rolled over and her head over the side of the bed before she vomited up the tiny bit of water and stomach acid that her weakened body could get up on an empty stomach.

Familiar hands caught her shoulders and slowly lowered her back to the bed. Rina took a moist rag from the bowl by Eryn's head and dabbed Eryn's mouth and chin clean. Eryn groaned her thanks, but Rina said nothing. She was silent as she cleaned the floor, disposed of the rag, and returned to Eryn's bedside.

When the room stopped spinning inside Eryn's head, she cracked one eye open, hoping to understand why Rina wasn't speaking to her. She hadn't been hurt, had she? That was another horrible part of waking up after ichor—remembering abandoning Rina and not knowing if she was okay.

Rina remained silent as she watched Eryn and simply held up a hand as if telling a dog to stay. She remembered Rina's shadow friend telling them to remain silent inside the creepy tree dome, but she didn't understand Rina's silence now. Was Rina okay? Was she mad about being abandoned?

Rina took Eryn's hand in her own, intertwining their fingers and resting their hands in her lap. With her other hand, Rina held a shushing finger to her lips, then reached into her bag and withdrew a scroll. Eryn took it, feeling the silence pull at her. What in the lands was going on? Whatever it is, Eryn thought, I trust Rina to have my back.

Eryn unrolled the scroll and began to read. It took all her willpower to keep silent as the story of Rina's shadow friend, whom she called the Commander, spread out before her. When she reached his plan for the destruction of the Community, Eryn couldn't help herself. She curled over the side of the bed and retched, her body trying to reject an intangible poison and only managing to cover the floor in more bile.

Rina cleaned the floor again while Eryn finished the last sentences of the scroll. The Commander would destroy them one way or another. The last sentence said, "We have a week and a half to figure out how to save the Community and they are listening to everything I say and hear to report back to him."

Eryn tried not to imagine someone ripping their soul from their body. Even with ichor, she imagined it would be hideously painful. Understanding dawned cold and frightening. "He killed Syrana," Eryn blurted.

It took a second to realize that Rina's bulging eyes were as much because she had spoken as what she'd said. For a long moment, they just stared at each other, the truth sinking in.

"You're lying," Rina said at last. Her tone had an odd lilt as if she didn't believe her own words. She made a motion for Eryn to keep going and it took only that motion to understand what Rina meant. The shadows could hear them.

Eryn nodded. She wasn't a very good liar, but at least she wouldn't technically be lying, just putting on a show. "No, I'm not. He's manipulating you."

"Of course you would say that. You're jealous that he's more important to me than you. He told me you would be jealous that I'm the one who's going to save the Community and not you. He told me you would turn against me."

"I'm not turning against you. I'm saying he killed your best friend. He's a monster." Eryn didn't like how realistic this fake fight felt, even if Rina was speaking as if teaching a child to read. Eryn *was* jealous of the Commander, and she hated how defensive she felt when accused of wanting to be the one to save the Community.

"You're the monster." Rina's eyes said she was sorry even as more insults streamed out. "You never loved me. You only love yourself."

Eryn gripped Rina's hand. It's not true, she told herself and Rina, even as she said what needed to be said. "No, I don't love you. Heroes don't love their guardians as anything more than a useful pet. And if you can't see that he is poisoning you, then you are no good to me. You aren't my guardian anymore, Rina. I'll save the Community without you."

Rina's grin was reassuring. "No, I will." She leaned back in her chair and held up a finger for Eryn to wait again. After a minute that felt far too long, Rina sighed and sank into the chair with relief. "I think that earned us some time alone. They ran to report back, which should take at least a day. This is the first time in a long time that I haven't felt a shadow at my shoulder in the Community. What in the lands are we going to do?"

"We have to talk to Syrana. He killed her. I'm sure of it. You said shadows don't attack in groups except after a hero drinks ichor. He was the shadow Syrana talked to. He ordered his shadows to attack her, and he ripped her soul out. She was dead before she ever reached the Community, and her body was like a chicken with its head cut off. It's the only thing that explains what happened to her and why her shadow feels stronger and more coherent than others. She may know how to kill him, and if nothing else, she's proof that we're telling the truth."

"But we have no idea how to find her."

"We don't have to." Eryn pushed up to a seated position and bit back another wave of nausea. Drinking two bottles had been necessary to make it all the way back to the Community, but it had also worn out her body in ways it wasn't truly built for. "She'll find us." The thought of finding more ichor turned her stomach even as it called to her. There was still enough ichor in her system to want it very badly, but the headache and nausea was just enough to convince her she should at least take it slowly.

"No." Rina straddled Eryn's legs, serving as a human blockade to prevent Eryn from rising. Eryn almost laughed at how unnecessary it was. A tap on her shoulder could knock her over.

"Rina, we are talking about the survival of the entire Community. That is more important than my health."

"You could die." Rina looked as sick to her stomach at the idea as Eryn was at the concept of standing and walking.

"We will all die." Eryn let that sink in before continuing. "We won't go far. We could even just circle the foothills until she tracks us down. We need to know what she knows. Will she talk to us? Will she help us?"

Rina looked skeptical, though Eryn wasn't sure if it was at Eryn leaving the Community or Syrana helping them. "I think so, but we have to be careful. The Commander said that he tried to convince a shadow she was a shadow, and it drove her into the darkness. But I more or less convinced Syrana and she just seemed confused and hurt, like she wanted to understand."

"We have to try. She's our only lead."

"We could tell someone. Maybe the head hero would know what to do. Maybe Claine." Rina looked very uncertain as she trailed off.

"And what would we tell them? That you've been listening to a shadow, and he wants you to kill everyone? I just don't see that going well." How many times had Holden threatened to take Rina away from her? Even with Eryn's testimony about the contents of the tower, there was nothing in there about guardians becoming shadows or the true destruction the Community was wreaking on itself. "We need Syrana, and I need you, or I'm not going to be able to get out of this bed."

Rina hesitated and all Eryn could think to offer her was a smile. She'd given her argument. This was about the survival of the Community.

"All right, but if you start to feel the urge for ichor—"

"I could ignore all the ichor in the heart for this. As long as you're holding my hand."

Rina took her hand and helped her to her feet and into a kiss. "Always."

They kept their weapons and Rina's bandolier but abandoned the packs. It took an entire lap around the base of the foothills before Rina signaled for them to stop. "It feels like her, but it could be another shadow or even the Commander sending weird signals. If I say to run, I need you to go back to the Community. You asked me to choose them over you. You have to do the same for me. You have to warn Claine."

This felt all too familiar, and Eryn had to make a conscious effort to fight back the panic threatening to blanket her mind. This time would go differently.

"Syrana?" Rina called into the empty dimness. After a beat, she said, "It's her, but I don't know what her state of mind will be. I still need you to be ready to run."

Rina started slowly, as if speaking to a scared child, and bit by bit explained what had happened and what the Commander proposed to do. According to Rina, Syrana had an incomplete memory of who she was, and Rina kept having to repeat herself to remind Syrana who they all were. She'd apparently been searching for Rina since the day Eryn dissipated her, but without Eryn's draw, she'd simply wandered for two months.

"She won't believe me," Rina said to the patch of air where Syrana apparently was, then turned to Eryn. "She says I need to tell Claine."

"What if we had evidence?" Eryn said, the pieces rushing together. She knew exactly what evidence they needed. "What if Claine wasn't the only person we told?"

"Who is going to believe us?"

"What if we told someone who wouldn't need to see it to believe it? Someone who even Claine will listen to."

"Who?"

"The head priest. Think about it. You told me she can feel the ichor in you. She should be able to feel it in Syrana. She'll be able to confirm that shadows are guardians. If she tells Claine it's worth listening, can Claine really turn her down?" Even Holden acquiesced to what the head priest said.

"But if she could feel ichor in shadows, wouldn't she feel them inside the dome?"

"Maybe she can only feel it when shadows are corporeal. Otherwise, it's not really there." Eryn hated how much even she wasn't fully convinced, but they had to start somewhere.

"We can try," Rina said.

When they returned to the edge of the dome, Rina stayed with Syrana, who Rina said was desperate to not be left alone for fear she would drift off into the oblivion of confusion again.

It took Eryn far less cajoling than she'd expected to get the head priest to follow her to the dome. She hoped that she had paid in enough over the years for the amount she was going to need to draw out in the faith of others, possibly from every person in the Community.

Eryn could tell the head priest was uncomfortable with the idea of passing to the other side of the dome for what Eryn was sure would be the first time, but to her credit and that of her faith in Eryn, she did it anyway. They would not be going far. If they traveled too far from the edge of the dome in a group larger than two, they would attract the dark gods, and that could guarantee the end of the Community no matter what they did.

As they approached Rina, the head priest dipped her head in acknowledgment, once to Rina and once to the empty spot to the left of Rina. "Guardians," she said. "What did you want to share with me?"

"You can feel them." Eryn couldn't contain her relief. Everything had just gotten so much easier.

"You already knew I could feel the ichor in guardians. Do not tell me that is what you brought me out here for." She sounded distinctly annoyed.

"How many guardians do you feel?" Rina asked.

"Two." The head priest looked ready to leave.

Rina nodded to her left and said, "How about now?"

The head priest's brow fell in confusion, and she no longer looked interested in leaving. "How did you do that? How did you hide your ichor?"

"She didn't," Rina said. "She went incorporeal."

The head priest's frown deepened. "That's not possible. Only shadows can go incorporeal."

"She's a shadow. Her name—" Rina started to explain.

"No, you tell me," the head priest said, turning to Eryn. "I trust you. You will not lie to me."

Eryn wanted to object, but this really did not feel like the time. "She's a shadow. Her name is Syrana, and she used to be a guardian… my guardian. The ichor in her has bound her soul to the lands, and she can't move on. When she's corporeal, you can feel her." Eryn signaled for Syrana to become corporeal, though she had no idea if she did so. "When she's incorporeal, you can't. We can prove it. The head guardian can hear her and see her. She knew Syrana well. But she won't listen, not unless you tell her to."

The head priest was silent for a long moment. Rina's scroll said the Commander lumped the priests in with the guilty parties for keeping the guardians subservient. For a terrible minute, Eryn wondered if they had chosen the wrong person after all.

"Go get the head guardian," the head priest said, directing her statement to Rina. To Eryn she said, "You will remain with me and explain how you came to this knowledge."

Eryn gave Rina a questioning look. Rina nodded and said, "We have to tell her everything if she's going to understand what is at stake."

"Go to Claine. I'll explain everything."

Claine stood like a statue in the large open field, her thick, muscled arms crossed and an ever-present frown on her face. Junior guardians swarmed around her, each in a group of three. Two guardians fought each other while one of them attempted to instruct the blindfolded third person in how to aid them. They were learning how to instruct their hero to fight shadows. Rina watched them with a new understanding. It was always just guardians fighting guardians, even when some of them were shadows. It was a cycle that only ended in more death and loss.

"I need to speak with you," Rina said after dodging through the swirling clumps of fighters. "It's urgent." She didn't want to risk the head priest deciding their story was apocryphal because Rina was too slow to provide the next piece in the puzzle. But at the same time, she couldn't tell Claine anything about what was happening in front of the junior guardians or Claine would be forced to denounce her in front of them.

"Dismissed." Claine's voice carried over the clanging of training weapons, without straining. The junior guardians around her hid their relief and tiredness as they hurried off the field. Rina could remember how great it felt to get a brief respite from Claine's judgment. She was much easier to get along with when she wasn't carrying the future of all guardians on her shoulders.

"What is so urgent?" She gave Rina the same look she'd given her as an impatient seven-year-old. It said you're either in trouble or you're going to be.

"I need you to come to the dome with me. Eryn and I have discovered something very important." She took several steps hoping that would be all it took.

"What?" Claine didn't move.

"I need to show you. Can you just trust me?" As the words left her mouth, she knew she'd said the wrong thing. Faith was the last thing she should be asking for.

"No. You will tell me what is going on or I will not be going anywhere, and neither will you."

Rina was still in her full Dark Lands attire including weapons, while Claine had only her utility knife, but she had no doubt Claine could keep her there if she tried. She was either going to have to lie very effectively or explain. Convincing Claine after lying to her seemed like the worse option. "I found Syrana. She's a shadow. Eryn and the head priest are outside the dome with her now. The head priest can feel her. She says she feels like a guardian, but she needs you in order to have proof that she's a shadow. Syrana wants to help us against what's coming, but she can't if no one will listen."

Rina had expected confusion or denial. What she got was a complete lack of emotion. "You've been listening to shadows."

"Yes, but, Claine, that's how Eryn knows where to find ichor. I've learned really important information that I need to share with you." Oh Goddess, she was digging herself a deeper and deeper hole.

Claine tipped her head to the side with the kind of interest she might give to a message from the council. "I'm willing to listen. Come to my office."

"But Eryn and the head priest—"

"Can wait. My presence will signify my agreement, and I will not agree to anything until I know what I am agreeing to. Come to my office or the answer is no." Claine walked away as she said the last sentence.

Each time Rina tried to speak, Claine raised her hand for silence. Finally, Rina simply hurried ahead, opening doors and shooing people out of her way until she ushered Claine into her own office. "There's this shadow—"

"Take off your weapons when you are in my office." Rina hated how easily Claine made her feel like an impolite child.

"But I need to tell you—"

"There is the rack for your gambeson and weapons. There is the chair." Claine walked to her bookshelf, not deigning to give Rina her attention until her demands had been met.

Rina pulled the items from her body, threw them onto the rack next to Claine's sword, and flopped down into the chair. "There's this shadow. He told me a lot of things including how to find ichor. But he also killed Syrana and he wants to destroy the Community. He ripped her soul out and now Syrana's like him, well kind of, and we're hoping she can help us figure out how to stop the Commander. She said we needed you."

"The dire shadow," Claine said without turning around. Her voice was hard.

"What?"

"The shadow you've been talking to, he is the dire shadow. He wants you to be his protégé." Claine stroked the spines of her books as she slowly worked her way around the room.

"How do you know that?" The Commander's words played back through her mind. *You are the first guardian I have approached who does not know what it feels like to love someone who is truly detestable.* But Claine did know. Even Keddeth had called Ardon an irredeemable asshole. "He approached you."

"Yes, Rina. He approached me, but I had the strength to turn away. If what you say is true, he approached Syrana and she too turned away. But you did not. You listened, you followed, you accepted."

"But I didn't mean it. I'd never poison the Community's feast with ichor. That's why I'm here trying to get your help." Why wouldn't Claine look at her? Couldn't she hold still for one second instead of slowly circling the room? Why wouldn't she engage with her more than simply condemning her?

"It's too late." Her voice was infuriatingly calm. "You listened to a shadow and now what he said will come true. He will destroy the Community whether by your hand or not. This isn't the death of a five-year-old, Rina. This is the death of everyone. I failed."

"You failed?" Rina twisted in her chair to look at Claine who now stood with her back to Rina, one hand resting on Rina's gambeson.

"I knew he would target you." There was a tightness in her voice as she lightly petted Rina's stuff as if she were petting a young Rina's head. "You've always been brilliant and rebellious. When you decided to listen to shadows, I knew the only way to save not only you but everyone was to make sure you either blocked out shadows entirely or never left the dome. When you told me you didn't listen to shadows, I thought Eryn had succeeded in a way I never could, but the whole time it was a lie. I knew that first time you listened to shadows, when Jemmy died, that I should have arranged an accident, but I thought I could save you."

The shink of Claine's sword leaving its scabbard brought Rina to her feet instinctively. Claine turned, revealing the tears streaming down her cheeks. "Only two things in my life have ever scared me. Ardon's death and you falling into the hands of the dire shadow. I thought if I kept you close enough, if I could break you down enough, I could prevent it. Keep your friends close and your enemies closer." She gave a tearful scoff. "But when your enemy is a six-year-old girl who just wants you to be proud of her? I fell in love with you. I want you to know that, Rina. I love you, and everything I did was in an attempt to save you. But you have left me no choice."

She advanced on Rina, her form making her intentions very clear. "You're going to kill me," Rina said unnecessarily. She was defenseless. All she could do was beg or bargain for her life. Except that Keddeth had said it correctly. When Claine decided something, there was no changing her mind, no matter what new evidence she was provided.

"If he loses his protégé, the dire shadow may hold out for another. He has infinite time, after all." She matched Rina step for step as Rina tried to put Claine's desk between the two of them.

"Or you can help us stop him. Let me fix this. Maybe it's not too late." But Claine wasn't listening. She kicked Rina's chair, slamming it into Rina's legs. Rina fell in a jumble of chair legs and her own legs.

Rina thrashed out, reaching for anything. This couldn't be the end. She had to save the Community. She'd listened to a shadow, but she'd heard plenty of things that didn't happen. She couldn't let this one come true.

She wrapped her hand around a side table leg and pulled. An oil lamp fell to the floor and shattered, sending glass everywhere. Claine kicked the table from Rina's hand and brought the tip of her blade to Rina's chest. Rina could feel the sharp point slowly piercing her skin. "I'm sorry, Rina. May the Goddess hold you and keep you."

Rina looked up into Claine's stoic, tear-stained face and knew there was nothing more she could say. Claine shifted her weight preparing for the killing blow.

A twang caught both of them by surprise. Claine yowled in pain and surprise. They both looked down from Claine's sword to her thigh, where an arrow was buried in her leg.

"Stand down," Eryn said from the doorway. A second arrow was nocked and drawn.

"Eryn, you don't understand. Rina has been listening to shadows. She is going to cause the destruction of the Community. This is the only way." Claine did not move her blade, though given how close she'd come to the alternative, Rina considered it a good thing.

"I know," Eryn said, then corrected herself, "I know she listens to shadows. She told me everything. We're going to stop the Commander together."

"It's too late for that," Claine said. "This is the future you and Syrana were foreseen to prevent, but the dire shadow interfered."

"What if it's not?" The thought hadn't occurred to Rina before Claine had said it so blatantly in the other direction. "What if the foresight wasn't about you and Syrana? What if your foresight is about us reversing the degradation of the Community? What if undoing what has been done to guardians is the change you bring to the Community?"

"It's not," Claine said, driving the point of her sword deeper into Rina's skin as if to slowly kill her before Eryn could notice. "That kind of instability would destroy the Community as surely as the dire shadow will."

"You know what was done to guardians?" Eryn said.

"Of course she knows," Rina said. In the tower she'd thought about how Claine would support the sacrifices even knowing the full consequences. "This is how you fulfill your foresight, Eryn."

Claine shifted her weight again. "She's right, it's not too late to fulfill your foresight by stopping her. You have to pick. Rina or the Community?"

Rina hissed as the blade sank minutely into her chest.

Claine groaned as Eryn shot a second arrow into her other thigh.

"The next one goes into your eye," Eryn said, another arrow already drawn and aimed.

"Why?" Claine did not remove her blade.

"Because I love her and she's right. It doesn't matter whether my foresight was about helping her or stopping her or had nothing to do with it. Because this is the change the Community needs. Put down your blade and help us. The only way we stop him is together. We can't do this without you, but we'll try if we have to."

Rina wished she could embrace that moment, but the blade poised above her heart made the moment distinctly less romantic. Instead, she turned her attention to Claine. "All I'm asking for is one last chance to fix everything."

Claine shifted her weight one last time and removed her blade. "If you don't, we all die. You understand that?"

Rina nodded and accepted Claine's offered hand to pull her to her feet. "We need to get you to the healers." She pointed to the arrows sticking out of Claine's legs.

Claine gave a huff as if the damage were a mere nuisance. "I'll go to the healers while you get Holden," she said to Eryn. "Tell him nothing, just get him to follow you. That shouldn't be hard for his protégé to achieve. Rina, I understand you have a head priest you are anxious to return to."

Rina didn't feel great about leaving Claine to her own devices, but what else could she do? Syrana and the head priest were waiting, and soon the head hero as well.

"How did you know I needed you?" Rina asked as she walked hand in hand with Eryn toward the haven.

"Syrana must have foreseen it after you left." There was relief in Eryn's smile as she pulled the sleeve of her gambeson tightly. Scratched into the fabric in thin, shallow cuts were the barely legible words, "SAVE RINA."

"She told me I had to go get Claine. She saw a future in which Claine helped us. But we wouldn't have had that future without you. Thank you for saving my life and for saying what you did."

Eryn gave her hand a squeeze and there were tears in her voice, despite the smile on her face. "I think we're long past having to thank each other for saving the other's life. Plus, everything I said was long overdue. I'm sorry that was the first time I said that I love you in front of someone else. For a moment there, I really thought Claine was going to choose to kill you, even if it meant dying. I really thought I was going to lose you."

Rina pulled Eryn into a tight embrace. "You can't get rid of me that easily. I'll meet you at the dome."

Rina spent several awkward minutes being grilled by the head priest on what she had read in the tower and what the Commander had told her. She had a strong sense that the priest was mainly trying to get her to trap herself in a lie or give information contrary to what Eryn had provided. It was a relief when Eryn and the head hero showed up, followed shortly by a limping Claine.

Syrana's energy changed as Claine stepped through the dome as if Claine's presence was enough to drive away some of her turmoil. Rina tried to tell herself that anyone would feel more grounded in the presence of their mother figure, but it still hurt to feel Syrana react to Claine in a way she hadn't to Rina. Even before Claine arrived, Syrana drifted ever closer to Eryn and farther from Rina whenever they stood still. She was like a small child; Claine was her mother figure and Eryn was her shiny object. Which left Rina as nothing more than her translator.

She did feel somewhat vindicated when it took significant concerted effort from Syrana, Rina, and Claine in order for Claine to actually hear Syrana. Even when she had been sufficiently persuaded it was Syrana and assured the head priest and hero, she still rebuffed Syrana's attempts at contact. Syrana had never been one to ask to be comforted, and Claine was never very good at providing it.

"How does this help us?" The head hero spoke at Rina, not to her. "If you're to be believed, we have a week and a half to figure out how to stop a megalomaniac who is immortal and untouchable. Does this shadow know how we can destroy her, let alone him?"

Next to Rina, Eryn shifted uncomfortably, as if his response was neither surprising nor something she wanted to be associated with. The head priest and Claine looked to Rina and Syrana respectively with an expression that said they wouldn't have asked so callously but wanted to know the answer nonetheless.

I don't know, Syrana said. *It's not like I actually want to be here. I didn't even know I was. I'm not like him. I don't feel powerful. I feel trapped.*

"Well, if you don't want to be here, what's keeping you here? Why are you trapped?" Rina asked. When Syrana shrugged, Rina directed the question at the group.

"According to you, it's the ichor inside her," the head hero said. "But how she has ichor in her blood when she doesn't have blood seems awfully suspect."

"The Commander—" Eryn said.

"Dire shadow," Claine corrected her.

"Um, the dire shadow said that you needed a moment of heightened emotion to bind the person to a commitment or a person. That's why not every person who touches ichor becomes a shadow."

Rina nodded. "He said auras move on when their hero dies because they don't feel like they have failed their obligation to their hero or the Community. So, it's more than just having ichor, it's about the combination of ichor, love, and failure."

"So what? She needs to feel hate and success?" The head hero sounded like he thought that answer was as ridiculous as anything else they'd thrown at him.

"Perhaps," said the head priest, "she needs to feel that her obligation is complete."

Rina watched Syrana drift closer to Eryn and Claine, and an idea sparked in her mind. "I think you have to release her. Both of you. She's trapped here by her love for you and her obligation to you. Her last act was to try to tell you to warn Claine about the Commander—" Rina said.

"Dire shadow," Claine corrected her.

"But she didn't finish. You were hurt and Claine wasn't warned. Instead, I became your guardian and walked right into the Comm... dire shadow's grasp." Rina felt Syrana's sense of loss grow, and tears prickled at her eyes as if Syrana were trying to force Rina to cry on her behalf.

"How do I release her?" Eryn asked and the whole group waited in silence.

This is my mistake to fix, Rina thought, but why am I the only one really trying? Eryn was trying too, but everyone else was acting as though trying to help was tantamount to accepting blame for the systemic issues that had created this problem in the first place.

"Your elegy. Eryn, tell her what you said in your elegy," Rina said.

Eryn was silent for a moment before beginning. "I said I was sorry that I didn't save you, and for pretending I was okay instead of grieving. I said I was proud to be your hero and that we would have done amazing things together. Thank you, Syrana, for being a wonderful guardian and for all the ways you gave to the Community. I'll serve the Community in your name. May the Goddess hold you and keep you."

Rina felt Syrana's energy change again, and the tears gathering at the corners of her eyes shifted from tears of loss to those of being deeply touched. "Claine."

"What?"

Rina felt on the verge of snapping. It didn't help that Claine had just tried to kill her or that she was riding someone else's emotional highs and lows. "I need you to engage. This isn't about me or the dire shadow or being right. Syrana needs you. Can you do this for her?"

"Keddeth should do it. He'd be better at it. He'd want to do it."

The wave of rejection felt as palpable to Rina as if she were the one being rejected. She supposed in many ways she was. "No. It has to be you. As the head guardian and as the person whose approval she sought, it has to come from you. She knows Keddeth loves her. She doesn't know whether you think she has done enough, whether she herself is enough." Rina knew she was talking about herself, but it didn't mean the words were any less true for Syrana.

Claine took a deep breath and closed her eyes. They all waited in silence for nearly a minute, while Rina wondered if they were being given a very childish silent treatment.

"Helping raise you was one of the greatest joys of my life," Claine said. "You always pushed to achieve that extra feat. Even when you did something perfectly, you wanted to know how you could do it better. You were a role model to everyone around you and inspired an entire cohort to serve the Community by being their best selves. Whenever I felt like a failure, I would look at you and remember that I'd done something right. You have served the Community and should be in the arms of the Goddess. May the Goddess hold you and keep you."

Syrana surged forward, embracing Claine before she had a chance to try to react. For a moment, Claine seemed stuck between surprise and revulsion. But as Syrana's emotions washed over her and Rina, Claine softened, wrapped her arms around Syrana, and hugged her back.

Tears streamed down Rina's face in a cacophony of emotions,

her own shame and anger warring with Syrana's joy and relief. She felt Eryn's hand slip into her own. She whispered at Rina's ear while everyone else watched what to them would be Claine tearing up as she leaned into an empty patch of air. "You have served the Community so much, Rina. You are a joy in my life. *You* are something right."

As Claine released Syrana, the head priest cocked her head to the side. "The ichor is still inside her, but it's just sitting there. It's not flowing. It's just there."

"You can move ichor," Rina said, remembering her creating ripples in the ichor fountain. "Can you remove it? Can you pull it out now that it isn't bound to anything?"

The head priest bit her lower lip and squinted her pupil-less eyes. "I can try." The group waited in another baited minute of silence. Rina wondered if council meetings were this drawn out, with each person waiting on someone else to make a decision. "Yes. I think I can."

"Ready?" Rina asked Syrana.

Yes, I'm more than ready for this to end. Thank you, Rina. You always saved me when I was alive. It's no wonder you saved me in death as well. I'm sorry I didn't build you up in life the way you deserved, the way she does. I love you and I'm glad that she loves you more.

"Thank you. I love you too. May the Goddess hold you and keep you."

The head priest raised her right hand and began to move her fingers and wrist in a slow, twisting pattern. "Come on," she said, her brow furrowed in concentration. There was the sound of an exhale and then Syrana was gone. She didn't dissipate, she simply ceased to exist.

Eryn and the head hero both stared at the ground beneath where Syrana had been. "It really was the ichor," the head hero said, going over to investigate the ground where Syrana's ichor had presumably been left behind. He looked over at Claine. "She's gone, I assume?" He poked at the spot before turning to the rest of the group. "So, we say nice things to this dire shadow, pull the ichor out, and poof?"

Rina and Claine both shook their heads. Claine spoke before Rina could. "He's not trapped here. He chose this."

"We can take away his horde," Rina said. The thought of fighting him by himself was extremely intimidating, but she guessed his true power lay in the masses he commanded.

"We have to," Eryn said. "Think about it. There are over a thousand guardians out there lost, confused, and commanded by someone who wants to destroy the Community. We have to free them even if it doesn't stop him. It's the right thing to do."

Rina jumped in before anyone could dismiss what she thought were excellent points as being irrelevant to the current situation. "And it's the only counter to him we have so far. Maybe if he can't have the society he wants, we'll at least earn ourselves some time."

"No," the head hero said. "Eryn is right. A guardian's job is to serve the Community and their hero, but not to the point of having their soul trapped for eternity. It's their dedication to the Community that is being twisted and exploited and it is us who created and exploited that dedication in the first place. We have to fix that first, then figure out how to face him when he is alone."

Rina wasn't sure why his statement had started with a no, except to give the credit to Eryn instead of Rina, but as long as they were on the same page, she didn't much care. She also wondered how much his ability to share the blame made him more willing to accept it.

"So how do we find the shadows quickly enough?" the head hero asked.

"We go to the heart," Rina said at the same time Eryn said, "I drink some ichor." The other three stared at them.

"When I leave the dome with ichor still inside me, it attracts the shadows. That's how we found Syrana, or rather how she found us."

Rina had no intention of letting Eryn put herself in that kind of risk again. "You'd have to drink more, and your body goes a little wacky when you do that. If we can get to the heart, there will be almost a thousand shadows right there."

Eryn shook her head. She looked determined to sacrifice herself for the greater good. "It took us six grueling days to reach the heart. How are we supposed to get there as a group when no more than two of us can be within shouting distance of each other? We need all three of you to release shadows. Holden to release them from their bond to their hero, the head guardian to release them from their duty to the Community, and the head priest to remove the ichor. Plus, you'll need us to lead you to the heart."

"A fire brigade." The head priest spoke for the first time since releasing Syrana. She didn't have to see their confused looks to interpret their silence, so she added. "Centuries ago, when ichor was plentiful, priests and heroes experimented with the idea of building a tunnel of connected ichor lanterns into the Dark Lands to see what existed beyond the mountains. The number of ichor lanterns required made the journey untenable, but a fire brigade style was attempted a few times. Instead of making a continuous tunnel, the farthest back lantern could be unlit, brought to the front, and relit in a moving tunnel. It would be slower even than walking, but it could get us there with enough ichor. The levels of ichor we have stockpiled ought to be enough."

"We only have a week and a half," Eryn said.

The head hero puffed up. "We are the heads of three castes, and we are talking about the destruction of the Community. We can recruit as many people as we need. We get the fastest heroes on the lanterns—one on each. If they always unlight the moment they are the last in line and run to the front, we should be able to keep a steady pace."

"I'll bring my strongest priests. With more of us, we'll be able to unbind the ichor faster once we reach the heart."

They all looked at Claine, who looked distinctly unmoved by this plan. "I will bring a sufficient number of guardians to transport the ichor, food, and bedrolls," she said.

Rina felt the hours drag by as the priests, heroes, and guardians prepared. Each hour felt like water slipping ever faster through her fingers as she tried to grasp it. She didn't see how they were possibly going to reach the heart before the Commander's deadline. They would have to hope that the Commander would be at the Community when Stewards Day arrived and would also have to travel to the heart when Rina betrayed him. He could only see dark futures, after all. So, if they were successful, he wouldn't foresee it.

Rina tried multiple times to find a moment with Claine but found it near impossible to locate her at all. In the end, Rina returned to Eryn's side instead, helping the head priest prepare for the trip and for Stewards Day to carry on for the Community without their head priest.

CHAPTER EIGHTEEN

Auras and Shadows

If the hours of preparation had dragged, the days of walking as hero after hero ran ahead of the pack to light a lantern so they could proceed to the next threshold oozed like solid honey. Shadows provided the only distraction from the monotony of walking.

Rina felt confident that the shadows within the Community wouldn't notice her absence since their order was to report what she said, not her lack of speaking or hearing. They weren't smart enough for that, but they were smart enough to notice the tunnel and report it. In order to keep only two people outside the tunnel at any moment, including the hero running the next lantern forward, only one person could leave at a time to attract, distract, and release any shadows.

"I'll drink ichor and they'll come to us," Eryn said, offering herself up for what felt to Rina like the hundredth time.

"No," the head hero said adamantly. "You will not be able to resist the urge to run back to the Community, and if the dire shadow is waiting there as we predict, it will tip him off. We will lose."

"I can resist it. I did it more than once in order to protect Rina," Eryn said. Rina liked the sound of her name on Eryn's lips said to someone else; the head hero's look of being taken aback was a side benefit.

The head hero shook his head, clearing away his reaction as much as saying no. "You did it briefly with the intention of going back to the Community with her. You will not be able to resist for long. No active hero will be able to resist. It will have to be a retired hero, who is no longer compelled by ichor. It will have to be me."

"Ichor will damage you," the head priest said. "You will metabolize it, but not before it wreaks havoc on your body."

"I will only drink as much as is necessary to draw the shadows in. For generations, the guardians have given beyond what the Goddess intended and beyond what we even knew we were doing to them in order to try to save the Community. As head hero, it is my duty to release them and take on any burden necessary to make that happen."

For all his talk, he seemed hesitant as he raised the vial to his lips and sipped. Rina was surprised when his body underwent no perceptible change, and she might have questioned whether he'd faked the whole thing if not for the three shadows that rushed toward him the moment he left the tunnel.

Once they were close enough, Claine pulled him back into the tunnel and took his place, fighting the beings that he could not see. As she fought them, Claine spoke, saying an abbreviated and less personal version of what she had said to Syrana—they had served the Community well and now that their service was complete; it was time to go into the loving embrace of the Goddess.

From inside the tunnel, the head hero echoed his appreciation for their service to their hero and on behalf of all heroes released them from their service. As the tunnel moved forward around them, three priests pulled the ichor out of the shadows, releasing them physically into nothingness.

For hours on end, the head hero walked alongside the tunnel, sipping more ichor whenever the head priest told him his body had metabolized his previous sips. Claine, Rina, and the other guardians traded off fighting the shadows to keep them close for the unbinding. By the time the group called it a day, they had released almost fifty shadows.

Rina loved how comfortably Eryn went to sleep in her arms surrounded by other heroes and guardians. Cuddling in front of her peers and mentor was a statement.

The guardians were the first awake the next day, making breakfast and prepping for another day of caterpillar-ing into the mountains. The head hero took up his position outside the tunnel, attracting shadow after shadow and sipping ichor.

No one seemed to notice a difference until the third morning. Rina walked past the group of sleeping heroes to retrieve water and almost jumped out of her skin when she looked over at the head hero to see him staring vacantly at the tunnel ceiling. For a moment she thought he was dead until he blinked slowly and continued to stare. She kept an eye on him throughout the day, picking out subtleties she hadn't the day before. It was the rigidity of his stride as if he were consciously fighting the desire to limp or sag. It was the way his lips trembled as he sipped more ichor.

"Does the head hero seem okay to you?" Rina whispered to Eryn over dinner.

"No," Eryn said, her voice full of consternation. "His hair is graying, and his beard is thinning. Every morning he looks markedly worse, older and more worn down."

"I'm concerned."

"Me too. I'll see if I can talk to him about it tonight."

"I don't mean to sound callous. I want him to be okay for his own sake. But we also need him to make it to the heart. We need him to be able to release the shadows there more than we need him to attract shadows here."

Eryn nodded, gulped down the last of her stew, and moved off to try to get the head hero alone. Rina watched her out of the corner of her eyes arguing.

"He tried to blow me off," Eryn said as they lay down to sleep. Rina could tell she was on the verge of tears. "Holden said he's fine and that he has to be the one to do it. Even when I suggested we send a hero-guardian pair back to get another retired hero, he refused. He said…" Eryn took a deep breath and Rina could feel the strain in Eryn's body as she fought to say the next part in a quiet, even tone. "He said that this is going to kill him whether he does a little or a lot. He will not share that burden. It won't save him, it will only damn someone else. He said he'll make it to the heart and Goddess-willing back to the Community so he can release his own guardian. He said he knew what he was doing when he took that first sip and that this is the legacy he wants to leave behind. Rina, I don't want him to die. I can't just sit back and let this happen."

Rina held Eryn as she fought first to contain her tears, and when that failed, to contain the sound. "There's nothing you can do. He chose this."

"It's my fault. I was the one who suggested drinking the ichor." Eryn buried her face in Rina's shoulder, trying to keep her volume low enough to not alert anyone else to their conversation.

"It's not your fault. You were trying to sacrifice yourself. That doesn't make it your fault. If this is how he wants to go and it's how he's going to go one way or the other, maybe the way you don't sit back and let it happen is by being by his side for it. He cares a lot about you. Maybe what he needs is someone to tell him he's doing the right thing."

"But I don't want it to be the right thing."

"I know." It hurt to not be able to take Eryn's pain away. She held Eryn close, kissing the back of her head and providing what comfort and warmth she could.

As the days passed, the head hero's condition got worse. Every morning he looked to have aged another few years. He didn't appear to be sleeping. Rina never saw his eyes close. He just stared up at the tunnel with a concerning, vacant expression. The dark circles under his eyes grew darker and his effort to look fine became more apparent.

Eryn spent her days walking beside him, her inside the tunnel while he was just outside it. Eryn told Rina that he was attempting to impart on to her the sum total of his knowledge. Eryn soaked up as much as she could but admitted to Rina each night that she prayed to the Goddess not to be the next head hero. She said how selfish she felt for it, but she'd never wanted the job. The head hero had to be able to build people up and make deliberate, measured decisions. "That's just not my strength. I would be bad at it and I would hate it."

Rina was having the opposite problem. Claine expressed no interest in being near Rina, let alone a desire to atone or reconcile. Being standoffish wasn't new, but her level of being lost in her own thoughts was. She had several younger guardians around her and yet made no effort to build their capacity. So, Rina stuck by Eryn's side and watched the head hero grow more ill as the group climbed mountain after mountain.

It took them ten days to reach the base of the final peak that would look down on the heart. The head hero spent the last day coughing up blood every time he sipped more ichor. He'd stopped speaking to not agitate the sores in his mouth and he looked like a gentle breeze could knock him over.

They made camp gathered around the head priest. Based on

their best estimate of time, today was Stewards Day. It would be the Community's first Stewards Day without the head priest and the day the Commander learned Rina was not instituting his plan. Rina hoped he was there outside the Community waiting for her to serve his vision of stewardship to the Goddess. She supposed she would find out tomorrow when they crested the final hill.

The head priest said, "We do not have a feast to celebrate the day we come together to rededicate ourselves to the service of the Goddess, but we have what is truly important—hearts full of love, hands held in covenant with the people at our sides, and devotion to living out the Goddess's plan for our lives. This year, we stand on the precipice of change. In years past, we have committed to the Goddess's vision and yet we have not lived up to it. We have allowed a part of our society to live in generational subservience. But this Stewards Day, we commit to reversing what has been for eight hundred years. Tomorrow we will free those whom we have trapped and start a new path back to the Goddess for everyone. Everyone serves the Community."

"Everyone serves the Community," everyone repeated.

The head priest led the group in the recitation of the Community's covenant. There were no scrolls for them to follow along, but they didn't need it. They'd all memorized the words in their youth and proclaimed them with renewed gusto. They ended the night with stew, each person eating their fill both in celebration and in preparation for whatever the next day would hold.

Rina and her fellow guardians prepared a light breakfast the next morning. After years listening to shadows, Rina's mind kept wandering down paths of dark predictions all her own.

Everyone was quiet as the heroes raced forward with their lanterns, creeping the tunnel ever forward up the steep mountain. Rina, Eryn, Claine, the head priest, and the head hero walked in the front. The head hero remained within the tunnel this time; they did not want to attract the whole of the shadow horde before they were ready.

Rina held her breath as they crested the hill. Her sigh of relief was drowned out by the gasps of everyone around her. The guardians and priests were taking in the host of a thousand shadows within the corpse of the giant tree, while the priests and heroes reacted to the flood of ichor pumping far below them. The Commander was nowhere to be seen or felt.

"It's time," the head hero said to Claine and the head priest. He took another sip of ichor, spat blood, and stepped ahead of the tunnel.

The reaction was immediate. The horde of shadows below surged forward, streaming through the gaps in the tree's false dome. The head priest grabbed the head hero by the back of his gambeson and yanked him back into the tunnel. The horde slowed, but those at the leading edge kept drifting toward them, like a rolled ball with no one to stop it.

"We can't face that many at once," the head priest said. She looked horrified at the masses she could feel. They had yet to face more than four at a time.

The group waited until the shadows at the leading edge stopped approaching and turned back before the head hero stepped out again. It took three such bursts to draw the closest shadows in. Claine stepped out with another guardian to fight them and release them. The resulting fight quickly drew the attention of many of the closest shadows and they turned once again toward the tunnel.

The stream of shadows wasn't fast, but it drew from a pool that looked like it would never end. As quickly as the priests could pull the ichor out of shadows, the shadows were replaced by new ones. Claine and the head hero shouted their speeches of release as one repeating string of words, trying desperately to keep up. Even Rina was struggling to keep track of which shadows were new arrivals and which had been released and were actively being worked on by the priests.

After several minutes, Claine shoved the gasping, bleeding guardian who had been fighting by her side back into the tunnel. She paused her recitation long enough to shout, "Next!" before starting at the beginning again. A different guardian stepped out while the remaining guardians tended to the first guardian's wounds.

Claine fought for almost an hour before Rina grabbed her gambeson and forced her within the tunnel. She had a bleeding gash across her forehead and her gambeson had enough blood splotches to make it look like the purple was the invading color, not red. "I say when I'm done," Claine said hoarsely.

"We need you to release them. We don't need you to fight them," Rina said as a different guardian took Claine's place outside the dome. "What exactly would you have us do if you fall?"

Claine gave Rina a dark look. "I'm in charge here, Rina. Not you. Creating this problem does not give you the right to dictate it." She didn't bother with further argument. She walked to the edge of the dome and continued her speech. Rina watched the head hero change tactics, watching Claine's eyes as he had been taught to do decades before in order to target the same shadow as her.

For hours, they stood side by side, releasing shadows as quickly as they could speak. Rina could hear their voices slowly starting to break under the pressure. Claine was known to direct training guardians for hours, but never with this level of uninterrupted speed. Even more impressive, the head hero was keeping up with her when Rina knew even normal speaking hurt his raw mouth.

"This is what I want to be remembered for," he had said to Eryn before he stopped talking the day before. It was the epitome of a hero thing to say in Rina's opinion, but it made his sacrifice no less valiant.

The head hero was the first to falter. He fell to his knees, coughing up more blood. Claine summoned the guardians into the dome and the group watched the shadows pound at the tunnel like human-sized hail stones, throwing themselves against it repeatedly to no avail.

"We have released hundreds of shadows," the head priest said. "As many hundred remain."

Rina watched the head hero sink further into his collapsed state. To him, it was all shouting into the void and trusting his companions that his efforts were worth what they were doing to his body. What he had just done, he would have to do again before he was through.

Rina felt her own sense of hope and belief in their plan sink along with him. Out of the corners of her eyes, she watched the whole group deflate into melancholy. It took her a second to recognize the sensation as anything but defeat.

"Oh Goddess," she said, as the hairs on the back of her neck stood on end. "He's here." They weren't ready. His forces were too strong. They didn't have a plan. They would be trapped here until their ichor ran out and then he would kill them all before winnowing down the Community to nothing.

She looked around the circle desperately and paused on the only person in the cluster who did not look completely despondent. Claine stood tall, a look of determination carved into her face as if she had been preparing for this moment all her life.

You have betrayed me! His voice was like spikes of iron. Rina clutched her hands over her ears, trying to block out the sound, but she felt his words as much as heard them. The shadows surrounding them parted, fleeing from his emotions in a way Rina desperately wished she could.

Now you shall die! Slow! Painful! Watching everyone and everything you love shatter around you!

Rina felt tears pouring down her face. She tried to resist the feeling, rationalize it as not her own, but it was her fear and her sorrow eating her from the inside as if she'd drunk a vial of ichor. She had lost.

Come out, little Rina, betrayer, liar, insolent lesser creature. Come out and I shall make your beloved floozy's death fast. Deny me and my wrath will know no bounds.

Movement caught Rina's attention. She turned to watch Claine drop her sword and tear off her cowl. "Don't waste your time with her," Claine said, her voice strained but just as powerful. "It was never her you really wanted. She does not understand the choice you offered her. She loves her hero consciously and by choice. She was never yours."

Claine stepped outside the tunnel, arms spread wide as if in surrender. "I have sacrificed all my life for a man who did not care a drop about me. I have sacrificed all my life for a Community that wants to throw it all away. For eight hundred years, we gave everything, and now they will wash it all away as if equality is possible. As if it will not be a continuation of the same. They will take away the understanding that we are sacrificing for the Goddess, but we will gain nothing. These guardians did not deserve to spend eternity lost and confused. Syrana did not deserve it. But they do!" She thrust her arm back at the people within the tunnel. "They all deserve to wander, to suffer, and to be ruled by the very people they cast into the sewers of society. I could not support your vision to enslave the Community, guardians and non, but this is a future I can get behind. This is a shadow Community I can rule by your side. I accept your offer. Take me!"

"No!" Rina rushed toward the edge of the tunnel, but the head hero got there first, falling more than running. He passed through the tunnel wall, made it a few feet and collapsed, coughing and spasming.

Rina skidded to a halt just inside the tunnel wall. With the head hero and Claine outside the dome, she couldn't follow without risking calling the dark gods down on them and sacrificing the whole Community. "Claine. We can fix this."

"Shut up, Rina! You can't fix anything. Before we left, I poisoned the Stewards Day feast with ichor, not enough to kill, but enough to tie every soul in the Community to the Goddess. Except heroes." She spat on the ground and turned back to the Commander taking form out of the darkness. Rina had never seen him corporeal, and just the hint of his form was monstrous and gigantic. "The Community never deserved me. I thought my sacrifice meant something. It meant nothing. You gave your life to protect the tower, but it meant nothing. Now they will lose everything to create a new Community."

Rina had to do something. She couldn't just stand there trapped inside the tunnel and watch. They could still save the Community. They could pull the ichor out of everyone and institute real change. She dropped down, thrusting her arm out of the tunnel, and tried to grab the head hero's leg as he continued to cough. If she could just get him inside, she could get to Claine.

Claine pulled a bottle of ichor from the pocket of her gambeson and downed the contents. "It was my foresight to become a commander and so shall I be. Take me as your protege, Commander."

Peals of laughter emanated from the darkness coagulating in front of them. *You were always meant to be mine.*

Understanding hit Rina as she grabbed the head hero's foot. Syrana had said they needed Claine. She had foreseen a future where Claine helped them free the shadows. But Syrana was a shadow and could only see dark futures. Rina had walked foolheartedly straight into creating a shadow's future just like Claine said she would. And now everyone would suffer for her mistakes.

Rina watched in horror as the Commander solidified, as if death and doom itself had taken a physical form in front of her. She could feel his pride and vicious glee as he swooped toward Claine, claws out.

Claine's body gave a squelching sound, like a butcher sinking his knife into a carcass, before Claine's head flew back on her shoulders and she began to scream.

Around her, people clutched their ears. Rina pulled as hard as she could, yanking the head hero back into the tunnel, and watched her mentor scream as the Commander sank further and further into her body. Rina tried to clamber to her feet, but a hand held her back.

"Wait, Rina. She's becoming—" Eryn said.

"A dire shadow," Rina wailed.

"An aura."

❖

Eryn stared in amazement as glowing, golden arms reached out of Claine's body. They grabbed the air and pulled, drawing more and more of itself out of Claine's body as it dragged something in. Once it was out far enough, the glowing body of an aura doubled back, grabbing and wrestling with an invisible foe and stuffing it into Claine's body. It looked like it was trying to fit a pillow into a pillowcase that was too small. Realization struck Eryn and she desperately wished she could see the second half of the battle waging before her. Slashes cut through the aura's arms and Eryn imagined claws of pure darkness trying to maul it. But the aura reformed every time, shoving inch by inch until the aura had its hands on Claine's chest.

A voice rang out with the perfect clarity of a bell. "The vision you see for the future is not the Goddess's vision. You are foreseeing and manifesting Her greatest fear for Her people. Your soul is not here out of obligation but a twisted dedication to create a better Community than the one that betrayed you. I am here to take that away. In the name of the Goddess and Her true wishes for Her people, I cast you out. May the Goddess take you and keep you."

The aura looked over Claine's shoulder and Eryn could feel their gazes lock despite the aura's lack of discernable eyes. "Eryn, you have to kill him," the voice said as if Claine's voice were speaking directly to her soul. "Bleed the ichor out of him. Slit my throat."

Eryn moved before she had fully comprehended the aura's words. This had to be done. It was why Claine had taken off her cowl to reveal her neck for a killing blow. Part of her wondered if she would do it whether or not she could justify the act, simply because an aura had told her to do so. "Pull the ichor out," Eryn said over her shoulder as she bounded out of the tunnel.

Claine's body was rigid as Eryn swooped in behind it, drew her sword, and slit Claine's throat. Crimson and golden blood poured onto the ground aided by the priests.

From behind her, Rina screamed a long, anguished wail. The moment Claine's unmoving body collapsed, Rina burst from the tunnel. She fell to the ground, gathering Claine's body into her arms and sobbing. "You killed her. You didn't have to kill her."

Eryn's guilt and sorrow was identifiable in the jumble of emotions swirling inside her, but it was entirely eclipsed by a relief and sense of freedom that Eryn was fairly sure was coming to her directly from Claine's aura. "She's not..." Well, Eryn supposed she was in fact dead. "She's an aura."

"We could have figured something out. You didn't have to kill her." Rina was soaked with blood as she clutched Claine's body to her and rocked. "I'll never get to tell her I'm sorry or that I love her."

"She's right here." Eryn could tell nothing she said was getting through. If she could just get Rina to listen.

"Tell her, 'breathe in for four, breathe out for four. If your mind isn't calm, do it more.' Say it until she listens," Claine said.

Eryn tried to give the words the same musical quality Claine had, but compared to the voice of an aura, her recitation was mediocre at best. It took two times through before Rina paused. She looked up, her face wet with tears. "What?"

Eryn repeated the lines again.

"Claine used to sing that to me when I was little, and I'd get so angry. It was our thing."

"Claine is an aura and she's right here. She ripped herself out of her body and pushed the dire shadow into her body." Realization dawned once more. "She became a commander just like her foresight said, but a commander of auras." She looked to Claine and felt her curiosity rise.

Claine rotated in midair toward the tree dome. A collective gasp rose from the priests and guardians inside the tunnel as they watched in fascination.

"The shadows are lining up," Rina said. "They're approaching the tunnel in an orderly line. They're calm. I've never felt a shadow calm before."

Movement caught Eryn's attention just before the whole of the valley lit up with golden light. "They're not the only ones," Eryn said in awe as dozens of auras swept over the valley's peaks and toward the tunnel. An orderly line formed near the tree dome's edge where Eryn assumed the shadow line ended.

"Claine is the Commander of Auras and Shadows," Eryn and Rina said together.

Eryn could feel Claine's smile. "I've never felt this free before.

Like there's nothing else I should be doing, no one I'm letting down, no lingering feeling of failure and regret." She turned back around toward Eryn and Rina and Eryn felt her ease falter. "Hmm, shadows and auras first, then I deal with that," Claine said, clearly referring to Rina as "that."

She seemed to be speaking more to herself than Eryn, so Eryn chose not to translate her words to Rina. The idea that Rina was her only lingering feeling of failure would only be rubbing salt in the wound.

"Is Holden well enough to release their bond to their hero?" Claine asked. She didn't seem overly concerned with his health, just the task at hand.

"I am," Holden said from the ground as he pushed up into a seated position. "Can I not yell this time?"

"I will see to it," Claine said.

For hours, shadows took their turn being released. Holden's whispers got hoarser, but he valiantly pushed forward, giving each one the attention and acknowledgment they sought. Claine sounded like she could do this forever, her voice the melodic monotone of a bell.

Seven times, the head priest stepped in for Holden and Claine, releasing the original seven priest-shadows from their guilt over failing to protect the ichor and allowing their visions of the Community's decline to come to fruition.

"Can we let the heroes back in the Community release their own aura guardians?" Eryn asked as the last shadow stepped up to have its ichor removed. "I think it would be more meaningful to them to be part of the process and see the impact firsthand. It'll also help the other heroes understand and accept the changes that will be required of them." She left out the fact that Holden also looked more and more like he wouldn't survive the journey home.

"Yes," Claine said and began to drift toward home as if she expected everyone else to just pick up and follow her as easily as her cadre of auras.

Eryn pointed after Claine. "I'm going to…"

Rina nodded. Eryn loved that Rina understood without her having to finish. "I'll help pack up and get the tunnel moving again."

Eryn bounded down the mountainside after Claine. "It's going to take them several minutes to get moving."

"They'll catch up." Her calm was contagious. From the stories Rina told about the influence of shadows, Eryn would have expected the emotions exuded by auras to be happy. She wondered if this was just Claine or if the opposite of rage and loss was actually emotionlessness and calm.

"Did you actually poison the Stewards Day feast?"

Claine's laugh was like a bird's song. "Of course not."

That was a relief, even if they did have the power to remove ichor. She didn't know how to broach the next topic she needed to discuss before the rest of the group caught up, so she just said it. "Your opinion of Rina means everything to her."

"No. You mean everything to her."

"But she has me. I love her and I always will. She thinks she's lost you. It hurts her when you say things that imply or straight up say you think she's a failure or that she's your failure."

"I know," Claine said in an infuriatingly calm voice as she continued to float forward.

"But you can't just—"

Claine stopped and spun around to face Eryn. "I said I know. I didn't say it was okay." Her tone was still calm, but there was a fraying at the edges that Eryn could feel. Her mood fractured and then came back together in a way that made Eryn's stomach feel queasy. "It's hard. My memories and the present and my foresights are all jumbled up. It's hard to keep track of what I've said to her and what I haven't."

Eryn wished Claine would give any tonal or emotional cues as to whether that meant she intended to resolve things or call it good enough.

"You should return to the group and attend to their needs. It is easier to separate the past, present, and future if no one is talking to me in the present."

Eryn accepted the dismissal and spent the rest of the trip alternating between running an ichor lantern and supporting Holden to not fall behind. She spent her nights in Rina's arms wishing she had something more encouraging to tell her about Claine than "she seems to be distracted by figuring out how to be an aura."

"You know," Rina said, kissing the back of her neck in the way she always did before saying something Eryn didn't want to hear, "you can only use my mentor-mentee problems to distract you from talking to Holden for so long." The worst part was that Rina was almost always right.

The next day, serving as Holden's crutch, Eryn spoke the words she'd been holding in since leaving the Community. "I don't want to be head hero. I appreciate your stories and all your training, but I don't want to give up the Dark Lands."

Holden smiled around missing teeth. "I know. I will not ask you to take the mantle. You are too young. I wouldn't ask you to give up the Dark Lands or seeking ichor with your guardian."

"Her name is Rina and I love her," Eryn interrupted him.

Holden nodded slowly as if trying to reconcile multiple thoughts. "Or seeking ichor with Rina. All I'm asking is not to reject the idea entirely. Be open to changing your mind after you retire. The Community needs more minds like yours. You see things for how they ought to be, not just how they are or how they have always been. Tolya will be the next head hero, but all you have to do is ask and she will train you."

"Thank you," Eryn said. She still had no interest in the position, but she was willing to keep an open mind. Seeing Holden fall apart had made the idea of trying to keep exploring the Dark Lands after retirement seem distinctly less exciting even if she didn't drink ichor after her body stopped managing it.

The return trip took less than a week, going downhill and without shadows to release along the way. Eryn was surprised by the relative ease with which the rest of the Community and particularly the heroes accepted the situation laid out before them. She supposed having the head priest and hero on their side helped. Perhaps the most convincing was Holden's release of his own living guardian. He stood, white wisps of hair falling like leaves before Frost Night, leaning on Eryn's shoulder as he told his guardian that she had fulfilled her obligation to him. Henna, who would be the next head guardian, was brought to release Holden's guardian from her obligation to the Community. Holden's grip on Eryn's shoulder alternated between overwhelming and barely there and she could tell he was desperately trying to hold on to life as the priests cut his guardian's hand and pulled out the ichor. Her life depended on his ability to stay alive during those last moments. When Holden collapsed, dead, and his guardian remained, there could be no question of what the Community had done to guardians outside of the Goddess's plan.

Eryn had still anticipated some backlash. "The dire shadow was so sure people would do everything in their power to stop this change," Eryn said to Rina as Claine announced the name of each aura and their hero stepped forward to the edge of the Community's dome to release them.

"He wasn't wrong about everyone," Rina said. "The head priest needed Claine to corroborate our story, and Claine tried to kill me. The dire shadow's hero tried to burn all the scrolls in the tower. It's easy to silence a truth that lives in the dark. It's much harder to deny truth once it has been brought into the light."

Eryn watched as Oraina stepped up to the dome and released her guardian...Pietra. She knew the guardian's name, so she had no excuse to think of her as Oraina's rather than as herself. There were tears on Oraina's cheeks as she thanked Pietra for saving her life and giving everything to the Community.

"The real question I think is whether people will be so willing to change things for the rest of the living guardians. It's a lot easier to let someone go who you already thought was dead. How's golden boy going to deal with his guardian not loving him because she has a choice?"

It took Eryn a moment to figure out who Rina meant. It was a good question. Oraina really wasn't giving up something, but Henk would be, and it was going to be a rather hard hit to his ego to have yet another person not love him when they had a better choice.

"I guess that's where everyone else comes in," Eryn said. "The head priest isn't just telling heroes that they need to release their guardians to prevent shadows and restore the Goddess's vision of the castes. She's telling everyone. There are like three hundred heroes in the entire Community, junior, active, and retired, and of that only fifty-four are active. If the head priest tells five thousand people that fifty-four people have to release their guardians to be in line with the Goddess, it doesn't really matter what Henk thinks. He's outnumbered and he's wrong."

"I'm glad you thought of bringing the head priest to Syrana. You created this." Rina swept her arm toward the crowd of heroes freeing the final auras. "Whether this was your foresight or not, you saved the Community, Eryn."

Eryn let those words sink in. They were the words she'd been waiting to hear for as long as she could remember. They were the words that she'd thought she'd lost and, in the process, almost lost herself. Only a year ago, she would have done anything to be told those words. Now, they held no power.

"No, Rina. You saved the Community." Eryn nodded in acknowledgment at Claine as she floated over to their spot along the edge of the dome. The last aura had been released, and only Claine remained.

"*We* saved the Community," Rina said, circling her finger to include herself, Eryn, and Claine.

"No," Claine said dispassionately. "She saved everyone. We actively tried to stop her, but she found a way to do it anyway."

Eryn repeated the words exactly, unsure whether the last was a backhanded compliment or not. She would rather not change Claine's words to protect Rina, but she would not be a mouthpiece for Claine to belittle Rina either.

The head priest approached their group and looked to where she could feel Claine's ichor. "I have sent a priest to Ardon's home."

Claine shook her head. "No, I will stick around until Ardon's death."

When Eryn repeated Claine's words, Rina flushed with clear frustration. "He doesn't deserve that!"

Claine laughed. It started as a melodic chuckle that became open armed, bubbling peals of laughter. Eryn imagined a person who had spent their entire life in the Dark Lands might laugh like that the first time they rolled in soft, green pasture grass. "I'm not staying for him. I'm staying for her." She pointed to Rina. "I spent my whole life afraid of her. I'd like to spend the rest of Ardon's life proud of her. There are so many things in my life that I'm only now seeing clearly. It's freeing, but humbling. Rina is my greatest failure, but she succeeded despite my many failures. She did what I never could have done. You were right, Eryn. This is the change the Community needs. No, I will remain and help Henna acclimate to the role of head guardian. She will be an excellent head guardian, but she was never bound to a hero. In some ways she will be better able to cope with the change in guardians, and in some ways, she will be unaware of what this freedom and also this loss of purpose feels like."

When Eryn finished repeating Claine's words, the head priest drew her blade and looked at Rina expectantly. Rina looked befuddled. The head priest said, "You have been released. If you cut your hand, I can pull the ichor out now."

"No," Rina said abruptly, shaking off her own surprise. "I want to keep it."

"Why would you want to keep it?" The head priest looked suspicious. It was Rina who had helped free all the others.

Eryn's heart sank as the likely result occurred to her. "You're worried you won't love me anymore."

"No! The opposite. I feel different. My puppy doesn't feel like a puppy anymore. It feels more like a mature dog. It still loves you, but it's content to sit in the back of my mind like a sign on the wall that just says, 'don't forget to tell her you love her.' The way I feel about you is entirely me and it feels amazing. If I have the ichor pulled out, how I feel won't change. But if I leave it in, then one day, decades in the future when we die, we'll do that together too. We don't know what comes next, but whatever it is, I want to go into that next place holding your hand."

"Are you sure?" Eryn couldn't hold back the tears pricking at her eyes.

"I'm very sure."

"But what if...?" Eryn would do everything in her power to always be the partner Rina deserved, but even Rina had admitted to being young and inexperienced. "What if you change your mind?"

"If I really, truly change my mind, I can always have the ichor pulled out later, right?"

The head priest shrugged. "Presumably."

"That's good enough for me," Rina said. "Eryn, I don't want a life without you. I want to use the new method for finding ichor to reclaim the lowlands by your side. I want us to teach the next generation of guardians and heroes to be equal partners. I want to marry you when we retire, raise children with you, and paint our lives on the side of a house. I want a life with you."

"That's a lot of 'I want.' Are you sure you haven't been spending too much time with me?" Eryn laughed. She wanted every aspect of the life Rina had laid out. She wanted it so badly she ached.

"Not nearly enough," Rina said. Eryn pulled Rina to her, kissing her as if no one was watching.

From beside her, Claine's glow grew, and Eryn could feel Claine's joy wash over all the gathered heroes. "That life is one of many possible futures. It will not be easy, change never is. But if you can show the same dedication to yourself and others despite adversity, despite being told you are wrong or bad, the future I see for you is truly a beautiful one."

Eryn smiled and pulled Rina back to her lips. "Any future will be beautiful with you by my side."

About the Author

Jennifer Karter lives in Minnesota with her spouse, their daughter, and their two cats. When she's not working in international development, reading, or writing, Jennifer enjoys quilting, playing board games (of which she owns over three hundred), and hiking. She is a longtime avid Dungeon Master, but only ever of Dungeons & Dragons, and collects female action figures, which are frustratingly rare.

Write to her at Jennifer.j.karter@gmail.com.

Books Available From Bold Strokes Books

Appalachian Awakening by Nance Sparks. The more Amber's and Leslie's paths cross, the more this hike of a lifetime begins to look like a love of a lifetime. (978-1-63679-527-0)

Dreamer by Kris Bryant. When life seems to be too good to be true and love is within reach, Sawyer and Macey discover the truth about the town of Ladybug Junction, and the cold light of reality tests the hearts of these dreamers. (978-1-63679-378-8)

Eyes on Her by Eden Darry. When increasingly violent acts of sabotage threaten to derail the opening of her glamping business, Callie Pope is sure her ex, Jules, has something to do with it. But Jules is dead…isn't she? (978-1-63679-214-9)

Letters from Sarah by Joy Argento. A simple mistake brought them together, but Sarah must release past love to create a future with Lindsey she never dreamed possible. (978-1-63679-509-6)

Lost in the Wild by Kadyan. When their plane crash-lands, Allison and Mike face hunger, cold, a terrifying encounter with a bear, and feelings for each other neither expects. (978-1-63679-545-4)

Not Just Friends by Jordan Meadows. A tragedy leaves Jen struggling to figure out who she is and what is important to her. (978-1-63679-517-1)

Of Auras and Shadows by Jennifer Karter. Eryn and Rina's unexpected love may be exactly what the Community needs to heal the rot that comes not from the fetid Dark Lands that surround the Community but from within. (978-1-63679-541-6)

The Secret Duchess by Jane Walsh. A determined widow defies a duke and falls in love with a fashionable spinster in a fight for her rightful home. (978-1-63679-519-5)

Winter's Spell by Ursula Klein. When former college roommates reunite at a wedding in Provincetown, sparks fly, but can they find true love when evil sirens and trickster mermaids get in the way? (978-1-63679-503-4)

Coasting and Crashing by Ana Hartnett. Life comes easy to Emma Wilson until Lake Palmer shows up at Alder University and derails her every plan. (978-1-63679-511-9)

Every Beat of Her Heart by KC Richardson. Piper and Gillian have their own fears about falling in love, but will they be able to overcome those feelings once they learn each other's secrets? (978-1-63679-515-7)

Fire in the Sky by Radclyffe and Julie Cannon. Two women from different worlds have nothing in common and every reason to wish they'd never met—except for the attraction neither can deny. (978-1-63679-561-4)

Grave Consequences by Sandra Barret. A decade after necromancy became licensed and legalized, can Tamar and Maddy overcome the lingering prejudice against their kind and their growing attraction to each other to uncover a plot that threatens both their lives? (978-1-63679-467-9)

Haunted by Myth by Barbara Ann Wright. When ghost-hunter Chloe seeks an answer to the current spectral epidemic, all clues point to one very famous face: Helen of Troy, whose motives are more complicated than history suggests and whose charms few can resist. (978-1-63679-461-7)

Invisible by Anna Larner. When medical school dropout Phoebe Frink falls for the shy costume shop assistant Violet Unwin, everything about their love feels certain, but can the same be said about their future? (978-1-63679-469-3)

Like They Do in the Movies by Nan Campbell. Celebrity gossip writer Fran Underhill becomes Chelsea Cartwright's personal assistant with the aim of taking the popular actress down, but neither of them anticipates the clash of their attraction. (978-1-63679-525-6)

Limelight by Gun Brooke. Liberty Bell and Palmer Elliston loathe each other. They clash every week on the hottest new TV show, until Liberty starts to sing and the impossible happens. (978-1-63679-192-0)

Playing with Matches by Georgia Beers. To help save Cori's store and help Liz survive her ex's wedding, they strike a deal: a fake relationship, but just for one week. There's no way this will turn into the real deal. (978-1-63679-507-2)

The Memories of Marlie Rose by Morgan Lee Miller. Broadway legend Marlie Rose undergoes a procedure to erase all of her unwanted memories, but as she starts regretting her decision, she discovers that the only person who could help is the love she's trying to forget. (978-1-63679-347-4)

The Murders at Sugar Mill Farm by Ronica Black. A serial killer is on the loose in southern Louisiana, and it's up to three women to solve the case while carefully dancing around feelings for each other. (978-1-63679-455-6)

A Talent Ignited by Suzanne Lenoir. When Evelyne is abducted and Annika believes she has been abandoned, they must risk everything to find each other again. (978-1-63679-483-9)

All Things Beautiful by Alaina Erdell. Casey Norford only planned to learn to paint like her mentor, Leighton Vaughn, not sleep with her. (978-1-63679-479-2)

An Atlas to Forever by Krystina Rivers. Can Atlas, a difficult dog Ellie inherits after the death of her best friend, help the busy hopeless romantic find forever love with commitment-phobic animal behaviorist Hayden Brandt? (978-1-63679-451-8)

Bait and Witch by Clifford Mae Henderson. When Zeddi gets an unexpected inheritance from her client Mags, she discovers that Mags served as high priestess to a dwindling coven of old witches—who are positive that Mags was murdered. Zeddi owes it to her to uncover the truth. (978-1-63679-535-5)

Buried Secrets by Sheri Lewis Wohl. Tuesday and Addie, along with Tuesday's dog, Tripper, struggle to solve a twenty-five-year-old mystery while searching for love and redemption along the way. (978-1-63679-396-2)

Come Find Me in the Midnight Sun by Bailey Bridgewater. In Alaska, disappearing is the easy part. When two men go missing, state trooper Louisa Linebach must solve the case, and when she thinks she's coming close, she's wrong. (978-1-63679-566-9)